GRITS, GUNS, & GLORY

For Carlos —
Galaxy '24

JOHN G. HARTNESS

FALSTAFF

WWW.FALSTAFFBOOKS.COM

1

LOVE HURTS

The last thing I saw was the handle of my Grandpappy's sword sticking out of my belly, covered in blood that was supposed to still be inside me. The last thing I heard was my brother's voice, speaking to me for the first time in about fifteen years, mocking me as he twisted the blade. The last thing I thought was how much family reunions suck.

The next thing I knew I was laying in a hospital bed with more tubes and wires stuck to me than Wolverine in that crappy *X-Men* prequel. I stared up at the ceiling for a minute, wiggling fingers and toes and other parts that would wiggle before I turned my head to the side. Agent Amy was asleep in the chair by my bed, a strand of blonde hair creeping loose from her ponytail to brush across one cheek. I reached out to brush it back into place but was really surprised to find that somebody had tied hundred-pound weights to my hands. Or at least that's what it felt like because I couldn't move either mitt.

Amy must have heard or sensed something because her eyes snapped open, and she reached for the call button on my bed.

"Can I help you?" came the tinny voice from the little speaker thingy that doubled as a speaker for the TV and a walkie-talkie to the nurses' station.

"He's awake. You should probably come untie him now," Amy replied. I heard what she was saying but didn't quite get what she was saying until Amy looked back to me.

"Good morning, sleepyhead. The nurses kept the keys to your restraints, and I didn't think it was worth fighting over while you were still asleep."

"Where am I?" I don't really have a problem with cliches, as long as they're valid. And this one was. I had no friggin' clue where I was.

"Atlanta. I had you flown here after Jason skewered you."

"Like a damn shishkabob. Little bastard ran me through like poop through a goose."

"That's attractive, Bubba." A new voice came from the door, and I looked up to see my best friend, wingman, and technological guru Skeeter standing in the doorway, striking a pose. He woulda looked more heroic standing there all backlit and shit if he was bigger, or maybe armed. As it was, his skinny ass was the best-looking thing I'd seen in weeks. Except for Agent Amy, but she's a chick, which gives her a default boost in the good-looking department. Anyway, Skeeter stepped into the room and flipped on the lights as a cute Asian nurse pushed past him.

"Mr. . . ."

"Bubba." I cut her off with a wave of my hand. "Just Bubba will do fine, sweet-cheeks. Now, you wanna let me loose from all these cuffs and tubes and wires and shit? I gotta go rip my brother's head off and crap down his neck."

I didn't know Asian people could get that pale, but she turned white as a sheet. I think she was afraid I was gonna kill Jason right there in the hospital. Which I reckon I woulda if I'da thought for a second that he was in the hospital.

She glanced over at Agent Amy, who gave her a nod. I reckon it was supposed to reassure the little thing that I didn't want to kill *her*. It must have worked since she set to unfastening me from the bed. "Mr. Bubba, you can't rip anyone's head off for a while. As a matter of fact, I don't think you're going to be in much shape to be ripping open a bag of Doritos anytime soon. You suffered serious internal injuries, and if it were not for the work of a lot of very fine surgeons and your friends here rushing you here in a —"

"Black government helicopter that none of us knows anything about," Skeeter said with a grin. He was sitting in a straight chair by the window, grinning like a possum that had just crossed the freeway. He'd been full of conspiracy theories since we were in middle school, so finding out that the government really did have black helicopters was the best Christmas present he could have ever imagined.

"Yes, that," Nurse Whatsherface finished. "My name is Lucy, and I'm your daytime nurse. Ethel is the charge nurse and your technician is Alex. Dr. Watson will be by later to talk with you about your injuries and how long you can expect to stay here."

"Are you serious?" I asked.

"Serious about what?" Lucy had that look on her face that said she knew exactly what I was asking about but didn't want to give me the satisfaction of just answering the question.

"My doctor is named Watson?"

"Yes, sir. Dr. Watson is one of our most competent surgeons, with experience in a wide range of internal injuries. And your injuries were apparently quite extensive."

"Yeah, that's what happens when your kid brother shoves a sword through your guts. Extensive injuries."

She looked back down at her charts, doing a good job of not asking any of the obvious questions. "Yes, well, my sibling rivalries were slightly less violent. Now Agent Hall, Mr. Jones, would you please step out of the room for a few minutes while I check the dressing on his wounds?"

They left, and Nurse Lucy did a thoroughly professional job of checking my wounds, redressing the hole in my back and my front, and making sure that nothing got kinked up in my catheter line. And if you ever need to feel like the least sexually interesting human being in the world, let a nurse slap a huge bandage across your naked belly while you're pissing into a catheter bag.

"How long?" I asked, more to take my mind off what she wasn't doing than anything else.

"How long what?" she replied, not bothering to look up from the task at hand.

"How long was I out?"

"You were in surgery for about eleven hours, then there were some issues with getting you stabilized, so it says here that they went back in to patch up a couple of other small bleeders and then you were out for about three days."

"So it's been four days since that little son of a bitch gutted me?"

"Yes. If you don't mind my asking, why haven't the authorities been involved? You came in here on a government helicopter and you've said repeatedly that you know who stabbed you. So why aren't there any police around?"

I looked up at her and tried to remember the days before I knew that the things that go bump in the night are real and that the monster under your bed was usually a boggart, not a figment. Those days were way too long ago, I couldn't drag up that innocence anymore. I gave her my best lopsided grin. "Nurse Lucy, I'd love to tell you, but it was a government training exercise, and I can't say anything more."

"But you said —"

"I'm pretty sure you misheard me. Didn't you?" I smiled a little, which is usually enough to scare normal people. It worked. The little woman turned pale again and went back to work without any other questions.

When she was done, Amy and Skeeter came back in. With only one chair, Amy sat on the end of the bed and Skeeter took the seat.

"How do you feel, big man?" Skeeter asked.

"Like I got stabbed, dipshit. Thanks for asking. Where is he?"

"We don't know," Amy said.

"What happened after he stabbed me?"

"I shot his ass," Skeeter said, his voice flat.

"Did it kill him?"

"No."

"I thought you were loaded with silver shot?"

"I was. He took a load of silver double-ought buck square in the chest from twenty yards and laughed at me, Bubba. I don't know what the hell your brother has got into, but he ain't no ordinary werewolf," Skeeter said.

"How fucked up is my life that there's such a thing as an ordinary werewolf to me?" I looked up at the ceiling, but it didn't have any answers. That made me think of something, though.

"How's Uncle Joe?" I asked.

Skeeter grinned. "I wondered when you'd get around to asking about the whole reason you got gutted. He's fine, carrying enough guilt to power the whole damn Vatican over this mess, but all that your pop and Jase did to him was beat him up a little. He's seen worse in bar fights."

"I've been in some bar fights with Joe, he musta got his ass beat."

"Yeah, pretty much. But he's gonna be fine."

"Good. Now if silver didn't kill my asshole brother, how'd y'all get me here?"

"I shot him, too," Amy said. "A bunch."

"After Agent Amy emptied a clip into him, and I pumped a couple more shells his way, Jason decided you were dead, or close enough, and he hauled ass."

"With the sword," I said.

"With the sword" Skeeter confirmed.

"I liked that sword," I said.

"I think that sword might have something to do with this whole mess," Amy said. "Our scientists said there were trace elements of some very odd things in your blood."

"Wouldn't surprise me. Grandpappy always said it was special. And why did you have the DEMON lab looking at my blood?"

"Because your recovery was . . . odd, to say the least. You've recovered a lot faster than any human should be able to, and we wanted to understand the reason."

"What was it?"

"We still don't know."

"Well that's useful. There's weird shit in my blood from my Grandpappy's sword, my super-werewolf brother is out there with said sword and a desire to chop me into pepperoni, and I'm stuck here flat on my back pissing into a zip-loc bag!"

Amy looked away for a second, and I could tell that I'd crossed a line. Usually when I cross a line with a woman, bouncers get involved, but Amy was different. I actually gave a shit about her feelings. "Look, I'm sorry. I know you're trying."

She looked back at me. "Yeah, I'm doing a lot of good here yelling at the assholes in my office over the phone."

"Well, get out of here, then. I'm gonna be fine, and I'm sure you've got a lot of 'splaining to do to the bosses back in Washington."

"Yeah, there might be a few questions about my appropriating a few helicopters to rush you to the hospital, not to mention calling off an airstrike that would have dealt with our Southern werewolf problem once and for all."

"We think," Skeeter chimed in. He'd done a pretty good job of making himself invisible while Amy and I had our little moment, but now he was back, sticking his skinny neck into things. That habit got him a lot of ass-whoopings back in high school.

"What are you talking about, Skeeter? They were ready to drop enough napalm on us to make me think I was Ho Chi friggin' Minh!" I said.

"Yeah, but Jason took a whole lot of silver to the chest and didn't drop. We got no proof that fire can still kill him. We don't know anything about him anymore. Everything we know about werewolves went out the window when he didn't die from my silver buckshot, and that worries the piss outta me."

He turned to Amy. "So we need you to get your cute little behind out of hot water with your bosses so we can put the full might and power of the government and all them black helicopters behind figuring out what's in Bubba's blood and why Jason is suddenly immune to silver."

"And what will you be doing while she's handling all that?" I asked.

"I'll be getting my car out of the shop after your daddy and brother broke it all to hell, then overseeing the contractors at my house, which your family also broke all to hell, then I'm on my way to the suburbs."

"What's in the suburbs? I thought you hate homeowner's associations."

"Funny. You know how I love those Yard of the Month contests. Anyhow, Uncle Joe told me about a case of some dead Christmas carolers that I'm gonna go look into while you're laid up. Can I borrow Bertha?" Bertha was my favorite pistol, a .50 Desert Eagle that I thought I had inherited when my little brother was murdered by werewolves. A lot of my supposed family history got flushed when the aforementioned brother reappeared alive, pissed off and furry, but I still loved that gun.

"Did you suddenly gain a hundred pounds and triple your upper body strength?" I asked. Skeeter might have been a hundred-forty pounds soaking wet with his pockets full of quarters, and Bertha tipped the scales at four and a half pounds without ammo, and almost ten pounds fully loaded, so I wasn't inclined to give Skeeter a sidearm that weighed more than his real arm.

"I'll get the Ruger. There's an iPad on the table. I hooked up the 3G and patched it into my network at home, so you've got all my files here if I need you to do some research for me while I'm out shooting things." He turned to go.

"You got any straight porn on this thing?" I asked as he walked out the door. He just flipped me the bird over his shoulder. I shrugged and looked at Amy. "Alone at last?"

She smiled a little and scooted up on the bed to where I could reach her. She laid her head down on my chest and put an arm carefully across my midsection. Somehow she found a way to be there that didn't pull any stitches or tubes out of whack, and we just lay there for a minute, not talking. I was enjoying the scent of her shampoo, probably a hell of a lot more than she was enjoying the smell of four-day-old Bubba, when the door opened.

Amy sat up and moved to the chair as a little dude that I figured was my doc walked into the room. He looked to be about my age, medium height, brown hair, medium build, kinda goofy grin with what looked an awful lot like a Rush t-shirt peeking out from under his lab coat. He held out a hand to me, and I shook it. Firm grip.

7

"So, Mr. Brabham, how are we feeling this morning? I'm Dr. Watson, and I'm responsible for you still being with us today."

"Well, Doc, I feel like refried shit that got a samurai sword stuck through its belly, how are you?" I growled at him. I hate people who use "we" when they mean "you" or "me."

He chuckled nervously. When you're my size, you get used to the fact that most people are nervous around you, even when you're flat on your back and perforated in all sorts of new places. "Well, I'm fine, Mr. Brabham. Or should I call you Robert?"

"Bubba."

"Excuse me?"

"My name is Bubba, Sherlock. Now when can I get out of here?" I tried to sit up a little, but somebody picked that exact moment to shove a red-hot poker through the middle of my guts, and I laid back down in a hurry.

"I think you'll be our guest here for at least a week while we monitor your progress. Your injuries were significant, and we had quite the time getting all of the bleeding stopped. I'd hate for you to rush yourself home, tear something, and then bleed to death before you could come back. It would be quite the black mark on my record." He grinned at me.

"It wouldn't do a whole lot for my day, either, Doc, so let's try and keep that from happening," I agreed.

"All right, then. Let's do that. Now you won't be able to leave the bed for at least another day or so, but I think now that you're conscious we can do a little bit to make you more comfortable, like removing that catheter. I'll send a nurse in shortly to help with that."

"Make sure she brings me my pants."

"I think I mentioned that you won't be walking around, Bubba," he admonished. He actually *admonished* me. I'm pretty sure that was the first time I'd been admonished since grade school, but he put on his doctor voice and scolded me like a six-year-old who got caught eating paste again.

"I didn't want to walk around, Doc. I just wanted some cash to tip the nice lady. If she's gonna be handling my junk, I figure that's at least as good as a lap dance, right?" I laughed until my gut hurt again, which didn't take long. For some reason the doctor just stared at me blankly and Agent Amy was giving me that look that said I'd stepped over the line. Either that, or it was the look that said I'd run over her cat. I get those two mixed up a lot.

They left, and the nurse came in and took out my catheter. I spent a little time learning to piss in a bottle, but finally got everything figured out and took a leak that felt like Niagara Falls was rushing out of my bladder. When I finished, I felt a little deflated and thumbed my morphine drip until I passed out watching Oprah reruns.

You don't understand the true meaning of boredom until you've been bedridden in a hospital without enough drugs to make things entertaining. The next couple of days were a whirlwind of absolutely damn nothing. Amy was back in D.C. answering all kinds of uncomfortable questions while Skeeter was out in the Atlanta suburbs chasing down rampaging Christmas carolers or some such bullshit. I was left to lay flat on my back in the hospital and watch a ton of daytime television and Hallmark Hall of Fame Christmas specials. Made me long for the days of a good old-fashioned Kenny and Dolly Christmas.

After about three days, I was ready to climb every wall in the joint. Or I would have if I'd had any strength left. The doc came back in and took out the last of my stitches, remarking on how quickly I was healing. I was just happy to not have to piss in a bottle anymore, and being able to make it to the crapper on my own was a pretty major upgrade. The downside was getting all the tubes and pumps taken out of me meant that I got downgraded from the morphine pump to a couple of Vicodin every four hours. I'm a big dude, and there's enough blood in my alcohol stream most days to get me by, but it takes more than two little white pills to keep the ouchies away. So I was pretty uncomfortable, and bored, and the only thing saving me from completely going out of my skull was football on TV.

The rest of the hospital was saved from my boredom by the airing of the college football National Championship game. Some less enlightened people refer to this as the SEC Championship and have some silly idea that the BCS Championship a couple days after New Years has anything to do with determining the best team in college football. I know better.

So I was laid up in the bed watching Nick Saban's Crimson Tide whoop up on my beloved Georgia Bulldogs. I'd played in the SEC Championship game ten years ago, and it made my knee twinge remembering the hit that took me out of football forever. But I cussed at the TV just like back in the day when I would watch the games with Jase and Pop and Grandpappy, and I woulda thrown beer cans at the set like we did at the old Zenith in the living room, except all I had was ginger ale and the nurses kinda frowned on my throwing cans around the room. I learned after they started shaving parts of me that didn't need to be shaved that it was best not to misbehave around the nurses. Especially when Ethel, a 300-pounder with shoulders like a linebacker and face like a pitbull's ass, told me she'd order me an enema every six hours if I didn't stop throwing trash around my room.

The game had just finished up, and I watched Saban take a bath in Gatorade on his way to beat up on the Notre Dame Fighting Irish in that other National Championship game, when in walked a vision of absolute perfection. She wasn't just a hot nurse, she was the absolute damn stereotypical definition of hot nurses. She was about 5' 7" with dark brown hair tied up in a bun with just a few wisps of hair trying to cut loose and show you what kind of a wild woman she could be. She had a waist the size of my wrist, hips that swooped out in the kind of curves that get put on road warning signs, and boobs like perfect half cantaloupes, round and firm and high on her chest. I just wanted to thump 'em to see if they were ripe. She had kinda half-Asian features, with a complexion that you couldn't really figure out where it came from. And I didn't care. She wore an old-school nurse's uniform. No baggy scrubs and Crocs for this hottie, oh hell no. She wore a white miniskirt that stopped just high enough that I could see the tops of her lace stockings, and a top that unbuttoned enough for me to see deep into the valley of the shadow of heaven itself.

Her name tag said Eisheth, and I figured the poor bastard in the ID office was too tongue-tied to type "Elizabeth." I woulda been, too. She didn't walk so much as she *slid* around the side of the bed, letting her fingers drift along my leg and arm as she did so. I couldn't take my eyes off her, and Little Bubba was starting to show his interest, too.

"How are you today, Mr. Brabham?" she purred.

I looked up into her half-lidded eyes and somehow managed to stutter, "F-f-fine. As a matter of fact, I'm feeling much better now, thanks."

"I just bet you are. And I bet I can make you feel even better." She leaned down to kiss me on the forehead, and the world started to fade into a pinkish-grey haze. I didn't care what she was going to do to make me feel better, but I was really looking forward to it.

Then I heard the door open, the lights flipped on bright in my face, and I threw an arm up to shield me from the startling fluorescents. I moved my arm and saw Nurse Ethel looming over me, grinning like a prison guard with a truckload of new fish. "Glad to see me, Bubba?" She grinned down at my erection, and I felt Little Bubba shrink so fast you'd have thought he was a tape measure rolling back up.

"Where'd the other nurse go? The hot one?" I asked, my voice thick with sleep. Apparently sometime between hot Nurse Elizabeth kissing me on the head and heinous Nurse Ethel coming in, I'd dozed off. Damn Vicodin might be stronger than I thought.

"What hot one, beefsteak? You think you can't handle all the lovin' Ethel's got for you?" She grabbed her pendulous boobs and gave them a shake. "You're right, hillbilly, I'm more woman than you can deal with."

"That's right, I need a lot less of a woman than you. A *lot* less. So where is she?"

"Where's who?"

"Nurse Elizabeth. She was right here."

"Bubba, there ain't no Nurse Elizabeth on this floor. Only Elizabeth I know works in pediatrics."

"Well she was right here."

"Whatever. Well she ain't here now, so roll over." She started to wedge her hands underneath me, but I held on to the rails with both hands.

"You can take my temperature the boring way, lady. It'll get you the same results, I promise." She scowled, but handed me the thermometer. I put it in my mouth, grateful for the excuse not to talk for a minute while I tried to figure out how I'd fallen asleep on Nurse Hotpants. It didn't make sense to me. I've fallen asleep a lot of weird places and been blackout drunk in even more, but I've never zonked out on a sexy brunette before. Or blonde. Or redhead, for that matter.

Ethel finally finished up taking my vitals and left. I watched some more TV, but I kept looking at the door every few seconds hoping my dream girl would come back. I drifted off after an hour of fruitless door-watching and dreamed happy dreams of nurses and sponge baths.

It felt like I'd only been asleep a couple of minutes when a ruckus out in the hall jolted me awake. It sounded a lot like a bar fight, or a Lynyrd Skynyrd concert, or an average Thursday night in my life, so I figured something bad was going on. I heaved myself out of bed and groaned a little as I reached for my pants. I got mostly dressed, by which I mean I put on a pair of jeans under my hospital gown. My jeans were the ones I'd had on when I was carried in, so they were a little crusty from blood and muddy from the creek, but I still had a pair of brass knuckles in one back pocket and a Buck folding hunter in the other. I stuck my head out the door and came nose-to-nose with a burly security guy. He was almost my size, and usually I would have laughed at the thought of him securing anything against me, but I was still weak as a kitten, so when he shook his head at me and shoved my door closed, there wasn't crap I could do about it.

About a half hour later, Ethel came in and flipped on the lights. Her eyes were red and puffy and she had a look on her face like somebody'd shot her dog, or she missed out on the free breakfast buffet.

"What's wrong, Ethel?" I tried to seem like I gave a damn and wasn't just being a nosy bastard.

"I lost a patient. I can't really talk about it."

"Sorry to hear that. Was it sudden?"

"I said I can't really talk about it." She shot me a look that would have killed an ordinary man. Of course, being run through with a samurai sword probably would have killed an ordinary man, too. So I kept on going.

"I just thought it might help." I put on my best "I'm being nice but I still don't want to sleep with you" face.

It worked. "It was that nice Mr. Ross from across the hall. He came in for a routine gallbladder and just coded. It was so strange. There was nothing wrong with his heart at all."

"That is weird. Did something happen during surgery that could have caused it?"

"That's what's strange. He hadn't even had surgery yet. It was scheduled for this morning."

"And his heart just gave out?" This was sounding less and less like something I could shoot. I was pretty disappointed, to be honest. I'd hoped it would be a cool haunted hospital and I could earn a little Nurse Elizabeth lovin' by banishing whatever was haunting the joint. Now it sounded like just another victim of the cheeseburger.

"Yeah, just poof! And he's gone. Just like Joey Porter last month. Came in here perfectly healthy to get his appendix out and rolled out two days later cold as they come." Ethel whimpered and cried her way through checking my temperature and blood pressure, but I stopped paying attention. Two healthy dudes dropping dead in one hospital in one month sounded like the kinda thing I was back to being interested in.

A few minutes later, I had Ethel out the door and was on the phone to Skeeter. He picked up after a bunch of rings, a couple of straight-to-voicemails, and about seven text messages.

"Do you have any idea what time it is, Bubba?"

"No. What time is it?" I really didn't have any idea, except that it was probably pretty late. Or early. One of those.

"I don't damn know, you dumbass sasquatch! Now please tell me you did not just wake me up to ask me what time it is when you have a perfectly good clock right there on your cell phone."

I took a minute to look at the phone before I answered. "It's 4:30 in the morning. And that's not why I called. I need you to do some research. People are dying here, and I think we need to do something about it."

"Bubba," Skeeter spoke very slowly, like when you're talking to a little kid or somebody that's not too bright. He uses that tone with me a lot. "Did you notice exactly where you are?"

"Yeah, Skeeter. I'm in a hospital."

"Do you know what happens in a hospital?"

"Yeah, I know what happens in a hospital. People get operated on and sick people come here to get better."

"Do you know what is in the basement of a hospital? That's right—the morgue! Because sometimes that whole 'getting better' thing doesn't work out so good. And when that happens, people die. Bubba, you are probably laying in the home to the greatest number of fatalities in the Atlanta Metro area."

"Except for the Georgia Tech football stadium. 'Cause all their dreams died the day they joined the ACC."

"That's funny, but not relevant, Bubba. The point is, you're in a hospital. People die in hospitals. Some of them go there expressly for that reason. So the idea of people dying in a hospital does not impress me."

"Not even when they're healthy people in for routine surgeries that suddenly drop dead of heart attacks?"

"When heart attacks kill over half a million people every year, then no! Not even then. I'm hanging up now. I just spent the evening caroling with a bunch of old white Baptist people, and you know that makes me break out in hives. And tomorrow I have to go chase down some dumbass unemployed choir director that might just be playing Frankenstein all over Georgia. I told you I hooked your iPad up to my network, so do your own damn research. Hell, if I can't find out anything on my guy, I'm probably gonna be callin' you." There was a click, then nothing as Skeeter hung up on me.

I couldn't get back to sleep, so I pulled out Skeeter's iPad and started poking around on the internet. Contrary to popular belief, I had used a computer for more than surfing porn before, so it didn't take me too long to find what I was looking for. Over the past year, my hospital had a very slightly above average number of deaths, about one every week. That wasn't enough to set my Spidey-sense tingling, it was the consistency. It only made sense that some hospitals would have a clump of dead guys one week, and a lot less or even none the next. My hospital *never* had a week without at least one corpse turning up. So I took a look at those weeks that only had one dead guy in 'em, and that's when I started to get worried. Turns out that almost every week that there was only one death in the building, it was always a guy between twenty-five and forty-five. And every week for a year, without a single exception, some dude not too far off from my age checked into the hospital and didn't check out.

Then I really couldn't sleep. Finally morning came and I figured it wasn't too early to call in my other reinforcements. Plus I figured if he was still feeling guilty about me getting stabbed on his account, he wouldn't argue too much about bringing a ton of artillery into a hospital.

I was wrong.

"Bubba, there is no way I am carrying a Mossberg 500 shotgun into a hospital. They have rules specifically against carrying guns into those places, and a tactical shotgun isn't exactly inconspicuous."

"Look, Uncle Father Joe, I wouldn't ask if it wasn't important. You know that."

"No, I don't. For all I know they've got you so hopped up on Oxy that you don't know what you're saying."

"You know there ain't enough hillbilly heroin in Georgia to get me that high. I'm a big dude with a helluva metabolism. Now I'm pretty sure there's something in here killing otherwise healthy men, and I can't exactly kill it with a bedpan, now can I?"

"I don't know, Bubba. Is it a silver bedpan?"

"Father you better stick to the prayin' and leave the comedy to them that's better suited to it. Now are you gonna bring me some hardware or not?"

I heard a heavy sigh and what sounded like a muttered prayer for patience over the line. "I'll be there in an hour."

It was more like two hours, but my shopping list was pretty extensive, so I cut Uncle Father Joe some slack. Skeeter's adopted uncle, Joe, was our liaison to the Holy Roman Catholic Church, who employed me and Skeeter on a lot of our monster-hunting exploits. Not the ones involving my brother, those were strictly pro bono.

Joe knocked softly on my door and came in, looking around like the guiltiest man in Gwinnett County, not just some priest smuggling guns into a hospital.

"I'm not really comfortable with this, Bubba," he said as he set a black duffel bag on the foot of my bed.

"Me neither, Padre. I mean, we've known each other all my life and I'm still not sure I trust you in here with me in this sexy gown." I mooned Joe and he flipped me off. It was a cheap Catholic priest joke, but it broke the ice and got him to quit thinking about committing a few firearms violations just by being in the room with me.

I yanked out a pair of clean boxers, jeans, and boots and skinned out of the hospital gown. I pulled a XXXL Colt Cabana t-shirt out of the bag and grinned at Joe. "You bring me a pro wrestling t-shirt?"

"Hey, there was a sale at welovecolt dot com on size super-fatass. And with your tendency to get perforated, I decided to stock up."

"Fair enough." I went back to digging into the bag and pulled out a silver-edged kukri with a foot-long blade. I threaded it onto my belt then clipped on a holster for a nasty-looking black Beretta 9mm. It was a fine gun, a thoroughly effective firearm, but it wasn't what I was looking for.

"Where's Bertha?"

Joe didn't look at me for a minute, then he took a deep breath and set his shoulders. "I didn't bring her."

"Why not?" My voice was very low and very calm. Joe knew exactly how pissed that meant I was.

"You're in a hospital. You need to be a little more discreet. Or as discreet as possible for someone of your size. And attitude. So I thought giving you a gun that could punch through an engine block might be a bad idea. Those magazines are loaded with blessed silver hollow-points and cold iron. They're color-coded. Now I have to get back to the church. I've got a wedding to perform this afternoon."

He turned to go but stopped at the sound of my voice. "It wasn't your fault, Joe. Jase was coming after me no matter what. He just used you as an excuse. If it hadn't been you, it coulda been anybody I care about."

"But it was me. I'm supposed to be the smart one, Bubba. And I fell right into his trap, and almost got you killed."

"Almost don't count 'cept in horseshoes and hand grenades. We're here talking about it, so we're good. Right?"

"You want to find out how good, you reach back into that bag. Now try not to get dead." I could hear the grin in his voice as he walked out the door.

I did what he said and reached back into the sack, feeling my fingertips brush against a familiar soft cloth. I pulled a small bag out of the bottom of the duffel and grinned as I read the words Crown Royal across a familiar expanse of purple. Joe had really come through. Guns and booze. All I needed for a real party was a pig in a pit and maybe something to set on fire.

I didn't have crap to do the rest of the day except sleep, annoy the nurses, and plan for my evening's escapades, so that's what I did. Along with mixing a healthy dose of Crown into my Coke over the course of the afternoon, that is. The liquor burned all the way down and settled around my bellybutton in a nice, slow burn. I watched more crappy daytime TV, then some crappy primetime TV, then it was finally dark enough to go hunting. I got dressed as best I could and loaded up with the rinky-dink Beretta Joe had brought me. He had a point about Bertha's size and power, and maybe I shouldn't be running around a hospital with something that could punch through multiple walls and probably a couple of floors of a building. But she was my *gun*, and that's the kind of relationship another dude ought never mess with. It's in the Guy Code, right under the part about not crossing the streams and how to select the appropriate public urinal when faced with multiple choices.

But I loaded the Beretta up with blessed silver bullets and stuck

17

the paddle holster at the small of my back. Contrary to popular television shows, carrying a random firearm stuck in the back of your belt is a bad idea. And we won't go into why it's an even worse idea to carry one in the front of your belt. I try not to carry without a holster if I can help it, and Joe had hooked me up. I made it about five steps down the hallway when I realized I might not be quite as healed as I expected. I was winded like I'd run the stairs back at Sanford Stadium about six times, and sweat was pouring down my face. I saw an abandoned walker stashed off to one side of the hallway, so I grabbed it. I ain't proud, but I am stubborn. I was going after this thing, if there was a thing, and nothing like a hole in my gut was going to stop me.

I made a lap of my floor—nothing. I made a lap of the floor above me, which was mainly the Cardiac Unit and the Psych Ward—more nothing. I took a loop down by the nursery, stopping to make stupid faces in the window until all the little ankle-biters were crying and the charge nurse ran me off, but still found nothing. I even stuck my head in at the hospital chapel and asked the preacher down there if he'd seen anything out of the ordinary. He gave me a look that told me a 6'5", 345-pound man with a walker and a kukri at his side was definitely the most out of the ordinary thing he'd seen in a long time, but he had nothing for me either.

It took me a good hour or so to make my rounds, then I headed back to my room. I hadn't made it in the door when Nurse Elizabeth appeared at my elbow. I must have been more out of it than I thought because I never heard the squeak of nursey shoes or anything to give me a hint she was coming. She was just suddenly *there*, smelling faintly of jasmine with a hint of something underneath it. I breathed deep, but couldn't place the scent. It was a little acrid, like maybe something burnt, but I pushed it from my mind and tried to hide the artillery I was packing, both in my holster and the artillery that had suddenly become very apparent in the front of my jeans as well.

"What are you doing out of bed, Mr. Brabham?" she asked, opening the door and placing a hand in the small of my back just an inch or so above the gun. I slouched a little to keep her hand from drifting down onto the pistol and let her guide me into the room and toward the bed. I sat down on the edge of the bed and kicked off my shoes, trying to make thankful noises to the amazingly hot nurse while adjusting all my equipment to let me lay down comfortably. Some of that equipment was attached, and that was the least manageable gear, if you get my drift.

"Let me help you, Bubba." She put her hands on my shoulders and pushed me backwards. Even as weak as I was, I didn't expect that kind of strength out of her. I flopped onto my back like a bass in the bottom of a boat, and then winced and tried to roll over as the Beretta dug into my spine.

"Lay still, this'll make you feel better," Nurse Elizabeth said and put one hand on the center of my chest. I stopped moving. I didn't have a choice, I *couldn't* move. She slapped a palm down on my chest and held me flat like I was nothing more than a newborn thrashing around. I could move my arms and legs, but she had me pinned and didn't look like she was even trying.

"What the hell are you, lady?" I wheezed, even though it felt like she was cracking all my ribs at once.

"Oh come on, Bubba. Big bad monster hunter's never seen a succubus? Well don't worry, this won't hurt a bit. Unless you count killing you as hurting. But what a way to go, right?" She turned to me, and every thought of escape flew from my head. The second I breathed in her scent, all seemed right with the world, and all I wanted to do was fall asleep in her arms, surrounded by the welcoming smell of jasmine and sulfur.

Sulfur? Brimstone? Only demons smell like . . . I snapped out of her spell with a start and gave one mighty thrash, throwing her off me and onto the floor. She landed on her butt with a *thump* and I reached around behind me for my gun, simultaneously rolling onto the floor and putting the bed between us. I felt something tear in my gut as I hit the floor and my vision went white. I looked up to see Nurse Elizabeth, make that Succubus Elizabeth, coming over the bed at me. I pressed the barrel of the Beretta against her forehead and she froze.

"Bullets won't hurt me."

"These silver hollow-points have holy water in the tips."

"I just have to wait here for you to bleed out, then I'll have you for my dinner."

"I just have to squeeze the trigger and you don't have to wait for anything."

The predator vanished from her eyes and a wave of jasmine rolled over me. Suddenly she was the sweet, innocent caregiver that I was quickly falling in love with. I dropped the gun from her forehead and stared as she talked.

"You don't really want to shoot me, do you, Bubba? You just want to make me happy, and I just want to make you feel good. I like you, Bubba. I'd never do anything to hurt you."

That one brought me back to reality. "The last time a woman said that to me, it cost me a thousand bucks and two courses of penicillin to get over her." I felt warmth spreading across my belly; I'd really ripped something important loose. My vision started to do that funny tunnel thing, so I did the only thing I could think of to stay alive.

I pulled the trigger.

And missed. From three feet away with a balanced weapon, I fired at a demon and *missed*. It was one of the most embarrassing moments of my life, right up there with the afternoon I lost my virginity. Elizabeth shrieked, dodged, and flew out the door in a heartbeat. I had just enough time to realize she was gone and shove the gun under the mattress before Nurse Ethel came in like there was a hellhound on her tail. Little did she know the hell-creature had just been there, and my tail wasn't the part she was after.

"What the hell was that?" she bellowed. "What the hell happened here?"

I didn't answer, being too intent on bleeding out on the floor at her feet. She finally noticed my condition and slapped a button on the wall. A few seconds later, a bunch of other people rushed into the room, and I felt safe enough to pass out. Good thing, since I didn't have a whole lot of choice in the matter.

It was daylight when I woke up, and I was strapped to the bed. I tested my bonds, but I didn't have anywhere near my normal strength, and I can't vouch for being able to rip leather straps at my best.

"Don't strain, you'll hurt yourself," a deep voice came from the chair beside me. I looked over at a hospital security guard who looked like he took too much advantage of the cheap doughnuts and not enough of the free gym, but who was I to judge. "I'll go get the nurse."

He got up and walked to the door. "Hey," I said.

He stopped.

"Can you help me out of this mess so I can take a leak?"

"No way. Ethel said if I help you in any way, she'll cut my nuts off."

"Dude, she wouldn't do that."

"You believe that?" He gave me a flat look, and I had to admit that no, I was full of crap and she probably would cut his nuts off, and take great pleasure in doing so.

"Fair enough. Go get Ethel. I'll take my punishment."

He gave me a grin. "Your funeral."

Ethel came in, but it wasn't the same bust-my-ass-Ethel that I'd come to know and fear. This woman looked old, shaken, and haggard. I thought she might have been crying, but then decided it was a trick of the light. Everybody knows Iron Man doesn't have tear ducts.

"You okay, Ethel?" I asked.

She didn't answer me, just undid the straps holding me to the bed and handed me the plastic urinal. I scooted around under the covers and relieved myself, trying to find something funny in the situation. I drew a blank, so I just laid there and peed. I finished up and put the lid back on the plastic pisser.

Ethel reached out and took it from me, then said, "It got Miguel last night." She didn't look up at me, just went into the bathroom and emptied out my quart of pee. I heard a flush and she came back into the room.

"Who's Miguel, Ethel? And what got him?" I figured I knew the answer, but she looked like she needed to talk, and I do have some ability to be sensitive. Not much, but some.

"Miguel cleans on the graveyard shift. He's got a wife and two little girls. He was learning English and was so proud that his daughters were doing good in school. And it got him."

I asked again, my voice soft. "What got him?"

"That bitch-thing that you tried to kill. When she couldn't kill you, she went after Miguel. Well, we're going after her tonight, and this time don't miss. I'll be back at midnight." She reached around behind her back and laid my Beretta on my nightstand. Without another word, she turned and walked out the door.

With nothing better to do, I watched a little TV and tried to move around some until Ethel came back. Turns out either I hadn't torn open as much of my guts as I'd thought, or I was healing faster than normal, because I was able to walk, move my arms, and swing my gun around almost at normal human speed. My legs still felt like rubber after about five minutes, but I could function.

I pulled out the iPad Skeeter left me and dialed him up on Skype. He was wearing a Santa hat and a Grinch t-shirt, looking like the cat that had ate about sixteen canaries.

"What's up, Bubba?"

"I need a hand, Skeeter." He applauded, then laughed like that old joke had ever been funny. I didn't laugh with him.

"Fine, if you're gonna be a spoilsport about it, what you need, oh mighty beached whale?"

"What the hell has got you in such a good mood? You been drinkin' your daddy's eggnog again?"

"I might have done a bit of that, but I also solved the case down here in Hot-Lanta, all by my lonesome. Well, with a little help from Agent Amy. But we took care of the Case of the Psycho Choir Director."

"As if there was only one of those," I replied.

"Good point. But anyway, we took care of him, now what can I do for you?"

"I need to know how many men between twenty-five and fifty checked into this hospital in the past two days for minor surgery. They should be relatively healthy, but still hospitalized. Nobody with advanced cancer, AIDS, organ failure or anything serious."

"You know that information is protected by law and the hospital's privacy policy, right?"

"You know I know you can hack into anything if you think there might be pictures of hot naked men on a hard drive, right?"

"Fair point. Okay, there have been two men admitted that fit your criteria. We've got a Kyle Cornwell, in for gastric bypass surgery tomorrow morning, in room 233, and a Nick Iammatteo, knee replacement, room 784."

"Either of those private rooms?"

"784 is private, Mr. Cornwell has a roommate."

"That makes it easy, then. Let's go save Mr. Iammatteo from getting his soul humped out."

"Is that something he's going to really thank you for?"

"I dunno, but it's kinda the job. And Skeeter?"

"Yeah?"

"Good work on the choir director thing. Thanks for covering for me."

"That's what we do. Now I'm gonna go finish getting drunk. Dad's got about half a jug of eggnog left." He clicked off, and Ethel walked in the door. She looked kinda like a parody of a nurse going into battle in a shopping mall. Over her nurse uniform she wore a catcher's mask, shin guards and chest plate, straining at her prodigious bosom. Around her waist she had a belt with a hunting knife strapped to it, and she carried a metal softball bat.

"You look . . . imposing."

"Thanks. Get up, Let's go." When I looked at her eyes through the catcher's mask, she looked a lot less ridiculous. I stopped for a minute and thought about what she was doing. This crap was just another day at the office for me, but for her it went against a lifetime of teaching, going straight into *Twilight Zone* territory, and the thing we were hunting killed her friend. She was pissed, and I was pretty happy she was on my side.

I strapped on my kukri and the Beretta, and we headed up to the 7th floor. A doctor in street clothes and a lab coat got on with us at the fourth floor but remembered an urgent appointment on five once he got a good look at our outfits. Ethel and I shared a chuckle but were all business when the doors slid open on seven. I let Ethel take the lead, and I drew my Beretta, keeping the barrel pointed low and off to the side. We rounded the corner to Iammatteo's room and found the door locked.

"I got this," Ethel growled. She reared back and planted a foot just to the side of the doorknob. The door flew in with a shower of splinters, and a very startled Nurse/Succubus Elizabeth looked at us from the bed, where she was straddling a young man with short-cropped dark hair.

"I don't think that's the approved way to take a patient's temperature, Nurse Ethel."

"I don't think that's a thermometer, Bubba."

That was all the time the demon gave us for quips because she launched herself at us from the bed. I put three silver rounds tipped with holy water in her face, and Nurse Ethel brought the baseball bat around like she was Barry Bonds, connecting with the monster's head in a ridiculous-sounding *crack* of shattered cartilage and bone. The demon dropped to the floor, and I shoved Ethel out of the way.

Kukri in hand, I reached down to chop the thing's head off when she reached up and crumpled me with a punch right in the nuts. My family jewels felt they'd been mashed to diamond dust, and I went down hard. I heard a hideous chuckle from the succubus right before a dull *thump* and *oof!* told me that Ethel had teed off with that softball bat again. I scrambled almost upright, clutching my kukri with one hand and my throbbing sack with the other, and took in the scene in front of me. I'd come up inside the room, leaning on the bed for support. A quick glance told me that the patient was alive, but his breathing wasn't too steady.

Ethel blocked the doorway in her softball samurai getup, and the succubus had abandoned any semblance of human form. The monster from *Alien* was looked a lot sexier than this lizard-skinned thing with the body of a hot woman and the face of an angry spinach dip with teeth. Lots of teeth. I looked around for anything that could help, but my Beretta had slid away somewhere when I went down, probably under the bed or out into the hall where it would be of absolutely no use.

The demon stopped feinting and weaving, and I saw Ethel's eyes glaze over. Apparently Evil Nurse Elizabeth could mojo chicks, too. Ethel took a step back, about to let the thing get away, when I remembered my ace in the hole.

"Remember Miguel and his daughters!" I hollered. Ethel's eyes cleared immediately, and the succubus turned back to me, eyes glowing red in the middle of that nasty face. I slashed out with my knife, and the monster pulled back, putting its head right in the sweet spot of Ethel's swing. She connected with the bat square in the side of the monster's head, and Nurse Soulsucker went down like a bag of potatoes.

"Is it . . . dead?" Ethel asked, stepping in to look at the monster.

I jumped over the lizard-demon in the nurse's uniform and shoved her back, hard. "I doubt it. And haven't you ever seen a horror movie? You don't ever lean over the dead monster. That guarantees that it's *not* a dead monster. It's kinda like having sex in a horror movie guarantees you're going to die."

"Are you propositioning me?" Ethel smiled a little at me. "I knew that skinny little government girl wouldn't be enough for you."

"No, I am not propositioning you, I am trying to tell you how to stay alive in horrifying situations. Now if you would stop interrupting me . . . She's on her feet right behind me, isn't she?" I'd, of course, violated another rule of horror movies—never turn your back on the "dead" monster to explain things to someone else in the party because the next thing that happens is the monster stands up and kicks your ass.

But this time I'd been waiting for it. I spun around with the curved short sword in both hands and chopped clean through the succubus' neck. The heavy blade of the kukri was made for chopping through branches and limbs. And by limbs I mean arms and legs, so one skinny demon neck wasn't a real problem. The monster's head fell to the ground and rolled off under the bed, and the body dropped, spilling greenish-black ichor all over the tile. It was one of the five grossest things I'd ever seen, and I've shared bathrooms with SEC defensive linemen.

"Now it's dead," I said to Ethel, shouldering my way past her into the hall. "You can keep the Beretta, but I'm checking out of this place. Lots of weird shit going on, makes me feel too much like home."

And an hour later, I was sitting in the Pink Pony trading my hospital wristband for sympathetic hugs and half-price lap dances. All was right with the world, for a few hours at least. Skeeter had survived his first solo case, my guts were sewn back into the right place, Agent Amy was off in Washington doing her thing, the succubus was nothing but a nasty green spot on the hospital room floor, and I was drunk in a bar in Atlanta. All in all, a pretty good day.

2

UNHOLY NIGHT

A SKEETER THE MONSTER HUNTER HOLIDAY STORY

"Did I mention how much I hate Christmas carols?" I hissed into the Bluetooth earpiece. The little old lady in front of me turned around and glared at me, breaking off right in the middle of "Good King Wenceslas."

"Did I mention I don't give a flying rat's ass?" came the gravelly voice in my ear.

"Don't swear at me, you bedridden behemoth. I'm out here doing your job while you're the one laying on your back watching porn and eating Cheetos, while I'm the one out here freezing my chestnuts off listening to some fat white heifer invent new lyrics to 'O Come all Ye Faithful!'" I might have gotten a little louder than I had hoped for in that last bit because this time the aforementioned fat white heifer turned around and gave me the evil eye.

"Skeeter, shut your pie hole." Bubba's voice crackled over the airwaves. "I'm laid up here with tubes comin' out of places I didn't even know were places on account of my shithead brother sticking three feet of samurai sword through my guts, so you gotta suck it up and sing!" There was a squawk of static, a squeal, and a hum as Bubba hung up on me.

It wasn't really unexpected, his bad mood. He had almost died at the hands of his psychotic kid brother and right after killing his father for the second time, to boot. That kind of thing would leave anybody feeling a little under the weather, and Bubba wasn't the type to enjoy lying around a hospital bed for very long. As a matter of fact, his enjoyment ended about the time he realized that they wouldn't give him unlimited morphine and that all the nurses wore underpants.

Then we got the call about something terrorizing Christmas carolers all around the Atlanta suburbs. There was a group in Athens that went out a couple of weeks before Christmas, and they came back struck dumb with their hair bleached white from fright. The next weekend in Lilburn, half a dozen senior citizens from the Methodist church went out to spread a little holiday cheer, but only three came back. One of them blew his brains out with a shotgun the next morning, and the other two, a married couple in their seventies, took a bottle of Grandpa's epilepsy pills and never woke up. Uncle Father Joe got the call from the Methodist preacher and went up to take a look at things, strictly on the D.L., since the Methodists don't really admit to believing in any of the shit that we shoot on a regular basis.

Well, technically the stuff that *Bubba* shoots on a regular basis. I don't usually shoot things, unless it's on an Xbox. But with Bubba laid up in a hospital bed and Agent Amy called back to Washington to answer a bunch of unpleasant questions about werewolves and Bubba's family, I was the only one without a priest's collar that we had to send out in the field. And while Uncle Father Joe was more than willing to get his hands dirty, the couple of weeks right before Christmas were pretty busy for him, what with all the feeding the poor and Midnight Mass stuff going on.

So I ended up dispatched to Atlanta, wandering through Buckhead with a bunch of white people singing off-key Christmas carols and standing out like a banana in a smokehouse. We'd been walking up and down the sidewalks in the richest neighborhood in Georgia for three hours, and I was about ready to shoot the next person who suggested "O Holy Night."

Then I heard the scream. And all hell broke loose.

It sounded like the noise a cat makes when you run over its back legs with a lawnmower. You don't want to know how I know what that sounds like. The noise was coming from the glary little old lady, who was now staring down at the sidewalk and screaming fit to bust a hearing aid. I pushed my way to the front of the pack to see what she was hollering about and almost tripped over the body of the head caroler. He was a fat white guy (they were all white guys, blowing my idea of blending in right out of the water), and he was deader than Vanilla Ice's music career. His tongue was lolled out of his face, and it hung down over his three or four chins like a big pink slug. His eyes were rolled back in his head, and his hair had bleached completely white.

I knelt beside him and felt around his throat for a pulse. I found nothing, no matter how many chins I dug through. I pressed a finger to the Bluetooth and clicked open my comm line. "Bubba, you there? We got another one."

"Put on your glasses, Skeeter. I can't see shit here without 'em."

I pulled on the pair of bulky glasses and plugged them into the Bluetooth. The world went away, replaced by glowing green and red globs as my vision switched into the infrared spectrum.

"That's better. Look around so I can see if there's anything warm or cold around you," Bubba said in my ear.

"It's the eighteenth of December, dumbass. Everything around me is cold," I whispered, scanning the surroundings for heat sources. The carolers bloomed orange and red in my goggles, but everything else was a uniform green or blue. I glanced back at the dead guy, but couldn't tell him from the sidewalk.

"Something's screwy here, Bubba. This guy looks cold."

"I thought you said everything was cold," Bubba replied.

"Everything *is* cold, asshole, but he just dropped dead in the middle of 'Joy to the World,' so he should be a lot warmer than the ground. But he's not. What causes that?"

"I got no idea, Skeeter. And why were y'all singing Three Dog Night songs?"

"Not *that* 'Joy to the World,' you idiot. The other one. But anyhow, what sucks all the life out of somebody fast enough to make the body go ice-cold in seconds?" I asked. I kept my head on a swivel, but nothing looked out of place. I took the goggles off. The carolers were crying, and several of them had phones pressed to their ears.

"I need a distraction, Bubba. The cops are on the way and I'd rather not be the one gay black man hovering over the body of a dead cracker in Georgia."

"I think Atlanta's got a black mayor, Skeeter. It's been a long time since they lynched anybody down there."

"Well I'd rather they not get a hankering to bring tradition back right now, so would you please send a fake dispatch call reporting a bomb at Lenox Mall so I can get the hell out of here?" I heard him typing, then heard tires squeal and the siren rapidly start to head away from me.

I leaned over the body and took another look at the dead guy. A little old woman leaned over next to me and *tsk-tsk*ed at the corpse. "Such a shame," she murmured, shaking her head.

"Were you friends with him?" I asked.

"Couldn't stand the S.O.B., bless his heart," she said without looking at me. There was no malice in her voice, just that old-money Southern disdain that can't be taught, but comes naturally to bitchy old women who sip moonshine out of ornate flasks and look down on anyone who's never served on the board of deacons of the local Baptist church.

"Why didn't you like him?" I asked carefully. I didn't look at her either. I figured everything would go more smoothly if neither of us noticed that she was talking to a black man in public. Much less a gay black man. Not to mention standing over a dead white guy's body talking to a gay black man. In public.

"He was an asshole, but he couldn't help it. Bless his heart, his mama died when he wasn't nothing but a little feller and his daddy didn't have no more sense than God gave a goose. But he had a lovely tenor, so we let him come a'caroling with us every year."

"Oh shut the hell up, Bernice." The new voice came from another old white woman, this one with lavender hair instead of snow-white like the first one. That was the only way I could tell them apart. White people all look alike, you know.

I turned to the new old woman. "Ma'am?"

"Ignore my bitchy sister," the new woman said. "She's been pissed off at Franklin ever since he ditched her for the substitute mail carrier over in Roswell. He was the heart and soul of this choir. Now we don't have a tenor. We might as well go back to the home now." The new sister seemed genuinely upset at the fact that someone had died not ten minutes ago, or at least upset that she was going to have to stop the caroling for the night.

"Well, maybe it's all for the best," the first old woman, who I now knew to be Bernice, said. She was working at that "old wise woman" tone, but she was trying a little too hard and still sounded bitchy.

"What do you mean?" I asked the question she was dying for somebody to ask. I hated to give her the satisfaction, but I needed to find out all I could about the dead guy if I was going to find out what killed him. And maybe stop it from killing anyone else before Christmas.

"Well, he was pretty depressed after getting booted out of the Singing Christmas Tree, and he'd been talking about suicide. Maybe he just willed himself to die."

"Bernice, you are the biggest bitch in the free world," her sister said.

"Mary Alice Everhart, you shut your filthy mouth," Bernice said, putting on an affronted look so fast I knew she had it in her back pocket for emergencies. Some old women carried Kleenex; Bernice carried offended looks.

"I will not shut up, Bernice. Jacob was just fine about not directing the Singing Christmas Tree this year, especially when the director they hired gave him a solo. He wasn't depressed, he wasn't upset, he was happy. You just can't stand to think about anybody being happy without your approval, that's what your problem is."

Bernice stared at her sister with her mouth hanging open for a long moment, then snapped it shut and turned away with a *hmmmph*. I took a couple pictures of the dead guy with the camera in my glasses, then turned and started walking up the sidewalk.

"Hey, where you going? We got to talk to the police!" Mary Alice yelled after me.

I just waved at her over my shoulder and called out "Can't stay. Too many parking tickets at The Vortex." I kept walking, retracing our route until I got back to my Mini parked at the Methodist church. I got into the car and flipped down the sun visor. I pressed a little button and a blue LED lit up, signaling that I had a good sync with my glasses. The glasses transmitted all the photos I'd taken of the body to the car's computer and to my servers back home, as well as to Bubba's iPad. I scrolled through the pictures on the touchscreen in the car, but I got nothing new out of them.

"Bubba, you see anything good in those pictures?" I spoke to the air, but the Bluetooth link was still active.

"Nah, nothing. You didn't even get a good down-blouse of the GILF with the purple hair."

"You're terrifying and a little disgusting, Bubba."

"Thanks. But there's nothing here to see. There's no reason that dude should be dead. I mean, he was old, but that don't mean nothing. There's lots of old farts still running around out there."

"I bow once again to the breadth and depth of your uselessness. I am continually amazed."

"Thanks."

"Sarcasm is lost on you, isn't it, Bubba?"

"Yep."

"Are you near a computer?"

"Yeah, Skeeter, I'm near a computer. They've got about seventeen of the damn things hooked up and monitoring every drop of anything that goes into me or comes out of me. And I got this iPad you gave me, too."

"Well hop on the internet and see what you can come up with on Singing Christmas Trees in Georgia."

"I don't need the internet for that one. Let's start with they suck, there's a lot of gay-ass music, and they suck. What more do you need to know?"

"I need to know if there was a Singing Christmas Tree in each of the towns where we've had deaths." I sat back in the car and listened to the tap-tap of the detachable keyboard I'd given Bubba along with his iPad. Something about an ex-defensive lineman's hands and a touchscreen seemed like a bad idea to me.

More seconds than I thought it could ever take to Google "Singing Christmas Tree" passed, and then finally Bubba's voice came back on the line.

"I got it!" He sounded like a kid at Christmas.

"It took that long?" I asked.

"No, I had the information in like ten seconds, but I kept you waiting forever because I figured that's what I was supposed to do. Since I never get anything useful out of you until about fifteen seconds after somebody's started shooting at me, I thought dragging things out was part of my new job description."

"I hate you sometimes, you know that, right?"

"Yeah, but what would you do for fun without me?" I could hear the big dumb bastard grinning and couldn't help but smile myself.

"What do we know?" I asked.

"There was a Singing Christmas Tree production within two nights of every murder, including the one tonight. The Lilburn Singing Christmas Tree was last night, and it's scheduled to be in Atlanta next weekend. That finishes out the tour."

"Do you have anything on the director?"

"The what?"

I smacked myself in the forehead, then did it again as I heard Bubba chuckle over the Bluetooth.

"I know what a director is, Skeeter. Remember, I took that theatre appreciation class in college."

"Yeah, but I didn't know you actually went to the class."

"Twice, but it was enough to know what a director is. The director of the tour is Alexander Gregory Morehouse IV, and he looks like a real piece of work. I just sent the link to your car."

"Thanks." I clicked off and swung the touchscreen over. When we fixed my car after Bubba's dad trashed it, I installed a jazzed-up Mac and a movable touchscreen that I could operate from either the driver's or passenger's seat. I will admit to playing Angry Birds Star Wars edition while stuck in traffic, but only a couple of times.

I clicked on the link that Bubba sent and delved into the world of Alexander Gregory Morehouse IV, affectionately called A.G. by those closest to him. A.G. had been a world-class choir director at one point, but the advent of auto tune and the success of the TV show *Glee* drove up the budgets on his productions past any reasonable point, and he was relegated to directing community theatre Singing Christmas Trees to make ends meet. He had a modicum of success until his wife suffered a tragic accident while decorating the set for their Christmas Eve production last year. Apparently she lost her footing while putting the finishing touches on the top level of the tree and the imported Bolivian scaffolding toppled to the stage from a height of thirty feet or so. Mrs. Morehouse tried to break her fall by hanging from the Star of Bethlehem, but the rigging failed and she came crashing through the roof of the nativity scene, impaling herself and the Betsy Wetsy doll they were using for the Baby Jesus on the fallen star. From that point on, "Away in a Manger" was removed from the set list of any production A.G. was involved with.

I typed a few other commands into the computer, and a map of Georgia flashed onto the screen. A blue line with yellow dots sprang to life showing the performance towns and dates of A.G.'s tour, then I overlaid a red line with green dots to show the string of mysterious deaths. The blinking circles on the screen told the story—A.G. had been in every town with a strange death within 24 hours of the incident. Looked like I needed to go see a man about a tenor.

Alexander Gregory Morehouse IV lived in an architectural cliché. I pulled my Mini up to the front of the single most Gothic building I'd ever seen on American soil. The place was huge, with a gray stone facade looming over the surrounding suburban homes. The house stood at least four stories high, a stark contrast to the plain ranch homes that surrounded it. I couldn't figure out for the life of me why someone hadn't just hung a neon sign out by the mailbox that said, "Evil Genius Inside." There were even gargoyles, of all ridiculous things!

"I'd feel a whole lot better about this if I had Bertha," I muttered into my Bluetooth.

"Skeeter, Bertha is a fifty-caliber hand cannon that weighs more than your head. There is no way on God's green earth that I am letting you carry her into battle with the forces of evil. There's no guarantee that either one of you would make it back in good working order," Bubba's voice growled in my ear.

"Yeah, and I just bet I know which one you're more worried about," I grumbled back.

"Skeeter, you are my best friend in the whole world, but Bertha is my gun. And the bond between a man and his firearm is something sacred. Do not pretend to understand that bond, and do not presume to supplant it." His voice had a reverent tone to it, like he was discussing something holy. I let it drop, having a pretty good idea who Bubba would shed more tears over, me or Bertha. I took out my Ruger P95 from the glove box, checked that there was a round in the chamber, and slid it into a holster at the small of my back. I strapped a Judge revolver in an ankle holster around my right ankle, and slid a butterfly knife into my back pocket.

"Where did you get all that hardware? And what the hell do you think you're going to do with that knife? Anybody gets close enough to your skinny ass to cut with a knife, they've already killed you," Bubba said.

"Ain't you the one always saying a fella can't ever be too well-armed or too well-hung?"

"Well, I reckon now you got one out of two, little buddy," Bubba shot back. I pressed the mute button on my earpiece and got out of the car. I climbed the twenty-seven steps to the eighteen-foot oak front doors and grabbed the knocker, which of course looked like Marley's face from *A Christmas Carol*. I expected the damn thing to talk to me when I grabbed the ring, but it kept mercifully silent. The door did swing open without being touched, which did nothing at all for my blood pressure, but I didn't scream and manfully strode into the foyer.

Okay, maybe I yelped a little and jumped back about eight feet, then slunk in through the open door like Gollum following Frodo, but I went in. And my jaw dropped at what I found in there.

Instead of the stereotypical gloomy, cobweb-laden grand entryway I was expecting, I walked into something out of a friggin' Martha Stewart Christmas special. There were as many lights blazing in that house as in some whole trailer parks I'd visited, unless you count bug zappers as lights, which I don't. They don't give off enough illumination, especially after they've been frying June bugs for a few hours. But anyway, this place was lit up like the proverbial Christmas tree.

And that's not even to talk about the non-proverbial Christmas tree that was standing in front of me, stretching all the way up until the star brushed the top of what had to be an eighteen-foot ceiling. And every decoration on there was top-notch. I saw stuff from Tiffany, the Disney store, and Sarabella, and you know none of that stuff comes cheap. But right in the middle, just a little bit below eye level on me, was what looked like a homemade ornament. It was just a plain white ball, and in black Sharpie someone had written "A&N," with "1995" under it. Nothing else, just a white ball with a pair of letters and a year on it, but it was the only personal touch on a tree that was otherwise yanked straight out of a magazine.

I pushed the button on my earpiece. "Hey Bubba, you got a location on this Morehouse feller yet? I'm thinking there's more to this than meets the eye."

"Heh heh, like a Transformer?" my redneck sidekick chuckled in my ear.

"No jackass, like the inside of this place doesn't match the outside. I don't know what's going on, but something doesn't feel right."

"Doesn't feel right like the bad guy's standing behind you and about to whack you on the head not right, or doesn't feel right like your underwear's bunching up and you're starting to chafe not right?" The sad part is I knew exactly what he meant.

"More like the bad guy's standing behind me—" A blinding pain shot through my head, and I staggered forward into a huge pile of presents. As the empty cardboard boxes collapsed under me, all I could think was "shit."

I woke up tied to a chair staring across a big room with a vaulted ceiling. At the far end of the room, must have been fifty or sixty feet away, was a skinny little dude in a tuxedo. And for me to call somebody skinny, he was downright emaciated. He was standing on a little box behind a podium waving one of those little sticks a conductor uses. He had an old-style boom box on the floor next to him, and there were a bunch of glowing forms floating in front of him.

He noticed I was awake almost instantly, probably because I groaned and started cussing as soon as I woke up. "Ah, Mr. Skeeter, I presume? Or at least I assume that's a name because it's what the rather profane man on the other end of this device was yelling after I rendered you unconscious." My captor held up the shattered pieces of my Bluetooth headset. Good thing he didn't know about the video link built into my glasses. Unlike Bubba's, my glasses are prescription and I'm blind as a bat without them. If he'd smashed my glasses, I wouldn't have had any chance to ever get out of here.

Not that I had a whole lot of chance as it was. I was tied tight to the chair with zip ties, those plastic ties that you get at Home Depot for bundling wires together behind your computer desk. Well, I was trussed up with those things like a Christmas turkey, and I didn't get the feeling that this guy was breaking out the cranberry sauce anytime soon.

"What are you doing?" I asked. Bubba always seemed to have good luck when he got the bad guy to do the whole evil exposition thing, so I decided to try it.

It worked. Maybe Bubba's right and every bad guy has a "monologue" button that's just waiting to be flipped. "I am Alexander Gregory Morehouse IV, but you may call me The Maestro." He paused there for dramatic effect, but when no organ chords hit, he went on.

"I am building the finest choir in the world, and I have need of many voices." He gestured out over the glowing shapes in front of him, and they broke out in song. Not like "America, the Beautiful" song, but more like a low keening, kind of an *aaaaahhhh-ah-ahhhh-aaaaaaah* kind of song. It was creepy. A.G. waved his hand again, and the choir stopped.

"I have harnessed the power of the Afterlife to bring these loveliest of voices together, and tonight we will bring back to me the greatest soprano I have ever heard, the truest, purest, more beautiful voice I have ever listened to—"

"Edith Piaf?" I asked.

"No, you idiot. I shall resurrect a truly spectacular voice, the kind of voice that generations will weep to, the one, the only—"

"Billie Holiday?"

"No! Shut up, you fool! I am bringing back to the stage my dearest, sweetest songbird, my—"

"Barbra Streisand?" I guessed again.

"She's not even dead, moron."

"I know, but I'm a gay man. You say female singer, my DNA screams 'Babs!' I can't help it, I was born this way. Ask GaGa."

"I don't know what you're talking about." The very confused little bad guy had completely lost his train of thought now.

"Which part, the gay thing or the Babs thing? I would think a choir director of all clichés might understand about being gay."

"I'm not gay!"

"Don't lie to me, I saw your Christmas tree. No straight man owns that much vintage lace garland." I watched his face turn about eighteen shades of purple and knew I'd hit a nerve. It was tough growing up skinny, short, and gay in the south. But it would have been just as hard growing up skinny, short, a music nerd, and straight. Because at least when everybody assumed I was gay, they were right. This poor bastard had to put up with all the teasing and got none of the inherent fashion sense. I knew he was really straight the second I laid eyes on him. It's all in the shoes. His were 100% off-the-shelf Wal-Mart. Total straight boy. But he was getting wound up, which either meant he was going to kill me, in which case this had been a terrible idea, or he was going to do something stupid and give me a chance to break free, in which case I was a genius.

He pulled a pistol from his pocket, sliding the meter pretty solidly toward the "terrible idea" end of the spectrum, and pressed it to my forehead. "You are a fool!"

"No argument there." I might have squeaked a little when I said it, but I maintained control of my bladder, which is a good thing. It's hard to intimidate bad guys when you smell like pee. I looked past the scrawny dork pressing a gun to my head and took a good look at the shapes that were milling about. One of them looked familiar, and when it turned to face me, I knew why—it was the old fart from the caroling group. Yeah, the one I hadn't managed to save.

"Say that again." A.G. relaxed the pressure of the gun barrel against my head a little.

"Say what?" I squeaked again. I couldn't help it. My voice has always gone up when I get scared, and I've spent a lot of my life scared.

"That! Do that again! Hit the high C!"

"I have no idea what you're talking about, jerkoff!" I said, but really I squeaked about half of it.

"That's perfect!" the nutbar shouted, and whirled to the choir. "He's got the note! Now all I have to do is capture it, and she'll be returned to me!" He was really excited about something all of a sudden. I didn't know or care until he whirled back to me with a grin on his face and a weird contraption in his hand. It looked kinda like a crystal ball, only covered in facets, like a D20, but more like a D100,000. There was a light glowing from within the crystal, a flickering, dancing light. I watched it flutter, and jump, and felt my eyes starting to close—

And then the asshole had to start talking and snap me out of it. "She'll come back to me. All I need is the perfect soprano—"

"What are you talking about, fool? I might be a little light in my loafers, but I ain't no soprano. Not the Tony kind or the singin' kind," I said, turning my eyes firmly away from the crystal. I could almost hear it murmuring to me, and I didn't want it pulling any Frodo and the Ring crap on me, so I refused to look at the thing again.

"My Nicole will come back to me once I get the perfect choir assembled. All I need is a soprano, but all those old bitches caroling were altos and mezzos. But your little falsetto is perfect, so all I have to do is harvest it and—"

"Harvest?" I squeaked, then cringed at the pleased look on his face. I was going to have to get a more manly voice.

"Your soul, of course. I need to harvest your soul to add your voice to the choir." He gestured over his shoulder, and I followed his movement with my eyes. Unfortunately, he also brought the damn crystal up and snared me again. *How does Bubba always get out of this crap? Oh yeah, he shoots everything.* Well that wasn't going to work since I was tied to the chair, and I couldn't talk my way out of the mess for a couple of reasons. One, my captor was batshit crazy, and two, my captor was batshit crazy. I felt myself slipping again, losing hold on myself, tried to close my eyes but it didn't help, and then the world started to go dark, my vision tunneled in until there was nothing but the dancing light, the flickering, ghostly light, and then—

BAM!

A.G. screamed, the crystal exploded, and I flipped over backward in my chair. The cheap kitchen chair shattered beneath me and I wriggled free. Okay, really I just rolled over and said "ow" a lot until my vision cleared, then looked around for the source of the noise. Agent Amy stood in the doorway, her pistol drawn and aimed at A.G.

"I'd really rather not shoot you, Mr. Morehouse, so please put your hands up," she said calmly.

"You already shot me, you meddling bitch!" That marked the first time I'd ever heard anyone use the word "meddling" outside a *Scooby-Doo* episode.

"Yeah, but that was the wrist. This one will go in your head. Now put your hands up," Amy replied.

A.G. didn't raise his hands. Instead, he turned around to the ghost choir and screamed "GET THEM!" Pointing at me and Amy, of course.

The choir didn't move.

A.G. repeated the command, flourish and all.

Nothing.

"Um, hate to be the one to break it to you, A.G., but they don't seem to be wanting to do too much getting of us," I pointed out, getting to my feet and trying to get the last pieces of chair off my wrists. Those zip ties were on there good.

A.G. let out a scream and ran at me. I raised a chair-tethered arm and conked him on the forehead with the piece of wood I couldn't quite rid myself of, and he went down like a sack of uncooked spaghetti. Trust me, the image works. He looked nothing like a sack of potatoes and a lot more like a handful of raw spaghetti. He sprawled on the floor, then curled up in a little ball, weeping.

Agent Amy came over to stand next to me. "Nice shot, Skeeter. You laid him out. And made him cry."

"I don't think that's me. I think that's something else," I said.

"She's gone. Forever," A.G. wailed. I knelt down beside him and put a hand on his shoulder.

"Yeah, she's gone, A.G. It's awful, and it was too soon, but she's gone. And even if you'd managed to build your choir, she wouldn't have been back. Not like you knew her."

"I just wanted to hear her voice again. One more time. Christmas was her favorite holiday." He curled up and started to cry again.

I got up and walked over to the boom box. The ghostly choir was still there, just floating. "What are y'all still doing here?" I asked.

They said what ghosts usually say, which is nothing.

I looked at the boom box, and the CD in the top was homemade. Written on it in Sharpie was "Atlanta, SCT, 2009." I pushed the play button, and a beautiful melody of strings came forth. The choir turned to the CD player, and a host of ethereal voices picked up on "Silent Night." A.G. stopped wailing long enough to listen, and it was a good thing because they really did have lovely voices, if a little breathy.

Silent night, holy night,
  All is calm, all is bright.
  Round yon virgin mother and child.

Holy infant so tender and mild,
Sleep in heavenly peace.
Sleep in heavenly peace.

When the ghosts started to sing the second verse, a soft white light filled the room and a new voice joined in. It was a woman's voice, the most beautiful soprano I'd ever heard, and in her voice I heard all the happiness of Christmas growing up. I heard the laughter of me and Bubba when he got his first shotgun. I heard the laughing arguments about religion and eating fish on Friday between my dad and Uncle Father Joe. And I heard my mom, singing "O Come All Ye Faithful" as she basted a turkey, a voice I hadn't heard in years that still brought tears to my eyes. I looked over at Agent Amy and saw tears streaming down her face and knew that she heard it too. A.G. stood up, and with a dignity far beyond the insanity he showed just minutes before, stepped up to the podium and picked up his baton.

Silent night holy night
  Shepherds quake at the sight,
  Glories stream from heaven afar,
  Heavenly hosts sing alleluia;
  Christ the Savior, is born
  Christ the Savior, is born.

Silent night holy night
  Son of God, love's pure light
  Radiant beams from thy holy face,
  With the dawn of redeeming grace,
  Jesus, Lord, at thy birth.
  Jesus, Lord, at thy birth.

When the last notes died away, a glowing shape separated itself from the choir and drifted over to A.G. It wrapped the crazy little conductor in its light for a long moment, then flared so bright we had to look away. When the spots cleared from my vision, A.G. was lying at the base of his podium, eyes closed, with a peaceful smile on his face.

I walked over to his body, felt for a pulse, and found exactly the nothing I expected to find. "Well, he got to hear her one last time."

"Don't know if he's going where she is, after everything he did," Amy replied.

"That's not our department. Uncle Joe's in the afterlife business. We just deal with 'em while they're here. And he's pretty dealt with," I said.

"I agree. Time to get the hell out of here and get some eggnog." Amy turned and headed for the door.

"Right behind you. But, uh . . . Amy?" I asked.

She stopped and turned around. "Yeah, Skeeter?"

"Could you cut me loose from these chair pieces? It's awful hard to walk dragging half a kitchen chair behind me."

She laughed, and we headed out into the winter night.

3

DEAD MAN'S HAND

"I'm fine," I said into the Bluetooth earpiece. I swear sometimes I think Skeeter shoulda just implanted the damn thing in my head while I was in the hospital. I make it a point never to suggest that where he can hear me, though. Little bastard's liable to try.

"You are not fine, Bubba," Skeeter's nasal twang echoed through my head. "You ain't been out of the hospital but a couple weeks, and you almost died two or three times while you was in there. You need to rest."

"I almost died because there was a succubus in the hospital trying to kill me. Last I checked, there weren't no succubusses in Greenville, South Carolina. But there is a helluva titty bar right off the interstate, so if we can wrap this up quick, I can get a couple lap dances in before last call."

"Succubi."

"Nah, I don't pay for the VIP room, Skeeter. You know that."

"The plural of succubus is succubi, you overfed moron. And we don't know what we're hunting in Greenville yet, so don't make no plans for any kind of adult entertainment before we know what we're up against."

"What did Uncle Joe tell you?" I pulled my truck off onto the

44

bypass that headed into downtown. If I had to stay in South Carolina, not my favorite place by a long stretch, I was at least going to take advantage of the "Heavenly Bed" at the Westin Poinsett in downtown Greenville. A little high-tone for my usual tastes, but the place had the best beds anywhere along I-85, and one of the best bartenders, too.

Skeeter was technically supposed to be on this job, but I mighta jumped in the truck the second we got notification of the case and been five miles down the road before he plugged his computer back in. My stitches had been out for three weeks, and I'd gotten back to working out a week ago, so I figured I was fit enough to handle anything Skeeter could take care of. That was the sad state of my physical well being—I was comparing my strength to a hundred-fifty pound homosexual computer nerd. I needed to shoot something, *now.*

I heard Skeeter tapping on a keyboard. I pictured him sitting in his renovated nerd-cave, surrounded by high-speed internet whatchamacallits and flashing hooziwhatsis. In my head, he looked like a skinny black male Oracle before DC screwed everything up and took Barbara Gordon out of her wheelchair. In real life, he probably looked more like a skinny black dude with bad hair, a scraggly chin-beard, and a t-shirt that says, "It's Okay to be Takei!"

After a couple minutes of tapping, Skeeter came back to me. "Uncle Father Joe thinks it might be a leprechaun."

"A what?"

"A leprechaun. You know, little Irish dudes with pots of gold and bad horror movies with the guy from *Willow* in 'em?"

"Yeah, I know what a leprechaun is, Skeeter. I just don't know what one's doing in Greenville, SC. And I don't know why we care. Leprechauns ain't usually any trouble to nobody."

"Yeah, unless you get too close to its gold."

"What happens then?" I cut off a two-seater Beamer in traffic and grinned a little as I heard the tinny *beep* behind me. *Beep all you want, asshat. I've been shot, skewered, chewed on and almost screwed to death. And that was just since Thanksgiving.*

"Didn't you watch the movies?"

"Nah, soon as I heard Jennifer Aniston didn't get naked, I stopped caring."

"Bubba, you're incorrigible."

"Can't be true, Skeeter. I don't even know what that means. So what does a leprechaun do when you get too close to its gold?"

"It kills you, and anyone around you. And it generally becomes really dangerous to be in the same zip code as the leprechaun."

"Of course. That's why I'm driving right into the same zip code as the leprechaun."

"That's why the Church keeps paying your ammo and liquor bills. I've sent the address of the hotel to your truck's GPS. Take it easy tonight and we'll get after this thing in the morning. No sense in over-doing it on your first day back on the job. And Bubba?"

"Yeah, Skeeter?"

"Be careful. I'm tired of buying you flowers and stuffed animals at hospital gift shops." There was a little *click* in my ear and Skeeter disconnected. I drove into downtown and valeted the truck at the Westin, then walked down to a nearby Irish pub to start looking for a leprechaun. I figured if there was anyplace in Greenville to find one, that would be the place.

～

The pub was just like any chain Irish pub in a middle-sized American town. A bunch of Guinness mirrors, a few pool tables, a couple of dartboards, and a twenty-something bartender with enough cleavage to stop a man's heart. I settled onto a dark wooden barstool and ordered a Harp.

"Where you in from, fella?" the wench asked with a bad enough fake brogue that I snorted beer through my mustache.

"Probably about as close to Ireland as you are, sweetheart. I just drove up from Georgia."

"Oh, Atlanta, then?" Her accent didn't get any better the second time around, but fortunately for me she stopped trying after that. "I'm Carline. Welcome to Connely's." She stuck out her hand.

I shook it and introduced myself. "Bubba. Pleased to meet ya. Say, maybe you can help me?" I gave her my best "unassuming harmless guy" face, but since I'm the size of an average door and look like an extra off *Sons of Anarchy*, I don't really have an innocent look.

"I dunno, mister. Who are you looking for, and what's he wanted for?"

"What do you mean?" The whole "wanted for" thing had me honestly confused, and that don't happen nearly as often as Skeeter lets on.

"Well, take a look at yourself in a mirror sometime. If I've ever seen a bounty hunter, you're it. So what is it? Skipped bail? Unpaid child support? Cheating husband run off with the savings account?" Her eyes were bright and her blonde ponytail was almost quivering with excitement.

I thought about it for a minute, then figured that since leprechaun are mystical creatures, they probably don't feel the same way we do about wedlock and taking care of your responsibilities, so I went for the most obvious choice. It also happened to be the choice most likely to irritate a young American woman.

"Yep, you got it. He skipped out on child support. For three kids. His mom used her life savings to pay me to chase his ass down and bring him back to face justice. I'm just trying to make sure little Ben, Ralphie, and Monique get to eat."

"Bastard. Why are all you guys such assholes?"

"Hey, I'm the good guy!" I protested, putting on the best innocent look I could muster. It still sucked. "I'm the one trying to track down the asshole, remember?"

"For money. It's not like you're doing this crap out of the goodness of your heart."

"Well, that's true, but I've got people of my own to support." I didn't bother to tell her that the people I supported were mostly single moms who danced on poles. It just didn't seem germane to the discussion.

"All right, fair enough. Who're you looking for?" She whisked away my empty pint glass and brought me another Harp. I figured if she brought me another refill without my asking, that was grounds for marriage.

"He's a little Irish fella, pretty grumpy. Probably bitching about money somebody stole from him."

"This little Irishman got a name?"

I was stuck. Sure, I knew leprechauns *had* names, but most of 'em are in Gaelic, which ain't one of my two languages. I'm fluent in redneck and pretty decent in English. And I had no idea what *this* leprechaun was going by, and from what I was hearing from Skeeter, it sounded like nobody who heard it lived long enough to repeat it.

"Well . . . I don't really know his name," I admitted. *I have got to get my crap together. I've been rusty ever since Jase skewered me.* Admittedly, having your kid brother/werewolf shove three feet of steel through your guts was guaranteed to put anybody off their game, in my business, that was good way to end up dead.

"Well if you don't know his name, how you expect to find him? You just gonna go through every bar in Greenville that serves Guinness and harass every short guy with red hair 'til yours shows up?"

"That was kinda Plan A." I finished off my second Harp, but a third wasn't coming on its heels. I reckoned the engagement was off.

"Well, I hope your Plan B works better, but you better work it somewhere else. Gimme ten bucks for the beers and get the hell outta here, mister. I don't know what part of your story's crap and what part's truth, but I ain't gonna have you in here botherin' my customers on no out-of-town bounty hunter bullshit."

"You don't sound so Irish anymore, honey."

"Why are you still here?"

I dropped a twenty on the bar and headed out to the street.

I turned left and walked uphill back towards the hotel, tapping on my Bluetooth earpiece as I went. "That didn't go so well."

"Yeah, I noticed," Skeeter replied.

"How? I didn't even turn on the ear-thingy?"

"I hacked the bar's security cameras when I tracked you there. And don't ask how I tracked you there, I ain't tellin'."

"Fine, Skeeter, be that way. You got anything from Uncle Father

Joe?" Skeeter's Uncle was a Catholic priest and our liaison with the church. I never knew "liaison" meant "dude that pays for strippers and beer," but that's what Joe amounted to most days.

"Joe says you should still be down here in bed and I should be on this case, but that's beside the point."

"That it is," I agreed.

"He also says there was a reported sighting of something unusual in Falls Park a couple nights ago. Nobody died, but a couple of kids from the art school were smokin' a little wacky weed around midnight and said they saw a monster. They got away, but it might be worth checking out."

"Yeah, I figure in a town where I'm chasing a monster, I oughta check out any reported monster sightings. They taught me that in Monster Huntin' 101."

"Don't be a smartass, Bubba. Nobody likes a smartass." He clicked off before I could make some remark about bein' better than a dumbass, and I chuckled a little under my breath as I turned left at the top of the hill and headed to Falls Park. The walk was only a couple of blocks, but I was drenched in sweat by the time I got there. Take late spring in the Upstate, add me being out of shape and the fact that when I'm in shape I'm way north of 300 pounds, and you get one sweaty redneck. It got so bad Bertha even felt heavy, and her holster was custom-built to distribute weight across my shoulders. A Desert Eagle is a hefty pistol, but when I'm in top shape, I don't even notice she's there.

I sat on a bench at the entrance to the park, catching my breath and looking out at the bridge that spans the falls. I mighta dropped out of the one engineering class I ever took at UGA, but even I know that a curved suspension bridge is something impressive. The sound of the falls beneath me soothed me, and I might have drifted off for a second or two.

Until a jab in my ribs rudely awakened me. "Ow," I said, not opening my eyes.

"Get up, shithead, you can't sleep here."

"I was just resting my eyes, Officer. I wasn't hurting anybody. I'm a guest in your fine city. See?" I held up my room key. Unfortunately, when I reached into my back pocket to get the key, my over-shirt gapped open and Deputy Dawg got a glimpse of Bertha under my arm. My night took a turn for the spectacularly crappy when I heard the pistol cock.

"Get up slowly, put your hands on top of your head, and turn around." I opened my eyes, and sure enough, there was a fat cop with about eight chins, greasy black hair, and a uniform shirt stretched way past the tensile strength of cotton pointing a Glock 19 at my head.

"I have a concealed carry permit. Can I get my wallet and show it to you?"

"You can do what I say or I can put a bullet in you!" His hands were shaking like a dandelion in a hurricane, so I put my hands on top of my head.

He fumbled at his belt for a radio, snatched it up to his mouth and said, "This is Unit 219 requesting backup at Falls Park. I have a suspect in the Shredder killings in custody."

I sighed, thinking about the time about to be wasted, then what he said registered. "Hey, dingleberry! I didn't kill nobody!" *Nobody here, and nobody human in a long time. And I had a good reason for all of them, so we won't talk about that.*

"Did you just call an officer of the law a dingleberry, you raving jackass?" He stepped closer and pressed the gun into my face, hard. I closed one eye, but kept the other one trained on his trigger finger. I was pretty interested in how much force he was putting out right then.

His radio squawked and Deputy Dingleberry's eyes flicked away from me for a second. That was all I needed. The second his finger went slack on the trigger, I stepped to the side and wrapped my left hand around his right, gun and all. With my right I laid an uppercut onto Dingleberry's jaw that shut his mouth with a loud *thwack*. His eyes rolled back into his head, and he slumped to the ground. I steered him toward the bench, so he didn't hurt himself, and took advantage of the moment to relieve him of his sidearm, taser, and radio. I used his handcuffs to fasten him to the bench, then put his uniform hat down over his eyes so it looked like he was just sleeping.

"Sorry about that, Deputy . . .Ventimeglia," I read off his badge. "But I've got work to do and being hauled in as a murder suspect would just slow me down."

"And what exactly do you think going to jail for assaulting a police officer is going to do to your 'work'?" A woman's voice came from behind me. She sounded like a well-armed woman that wasn't used to hearing the word "no." In other words, she sounded *hot*.

I turned around and was right. She was a woman. Not spectacularly hot, but not bad. Probably just middle-of-the-road hot, except for the gun she was pointing at me. Leave me alone. Well-armed women are a turn-on.

"You must be Deputy Ventimeglia's partner." I put my hands back on top of my head, thumbing on the Bluetooth transmitter in my ear while I did so.

"Officer Ventimeglia, and yes, I am his partner. Officer Silva. I see you know the position."

"It may come as a surprise to you, Officer Silva, but I have irritated a police officer or two in my time. "

"Somehow I'll keep my surprise to myself. Now what did you do to Russell? He's an idiot, and little bit of a blowhard, but he's not a bad cop."

"He saw the gun under my arm and flipped out. I've got a permit, but he wouldn't let me show him."

"Okay, using one hand, very slowly, remove the weapon from the holster and place it on the ground." I did as I was told. "Are you carrying anything else?"

"I have a backup piece in an ankle holster."

"Put it beside the cannon."

I reached down and pulled my Judge revolver from its home on my left ankle and deposited it next to Bertha, then stood back up slowly.

"Anything else?"

I shook my head. This was not the time to be splitting hairs over the Ka-Bar strapped to my other ankle, or the push dagger tucked behind my belt buckle, not to mention the silver brass knuckles I had in one back pocket.

"All right, then. Very slowly take out your concealed carry permit and pass it over here."

Once again, I did what I was told. I don't usually attack cops, but her partner jammed his gun into my face, and frankly I didn't trust him not to shoot me by accident. Officer Silva was calm, collected, and ten feet away. Too close for her to miss shooting my giant ass, but too far away for me to bum-rush her.

She looked over my permit, then said, "This is from Georgia. We're in South Carolina."

"South Carolina and Georgia have a reciprocal agreement for concealed-carry."

"No, they don't. We have reciprocity with a bunch of states, but Georgia ain't one of them. So unless you're military or a federal agent, you've got a couple of big problems." *Crap.* Usually I can bluff them with the reciprocity thing, because most folks assume Georgia and South Carolina would have one, being neighbors and all. And full of rednecks. Not so much.

"Okay, but don't shoot me while I pull out my other ID." I reached into my back pocket and took out a small badge holder that Agent Amy had bestowed upon me on her last visit. After the run-in with my brother and her appropriation of a few black helicopter-types to save me from bleeding to death, she'd gotten me duly deputized in DEMON, the Department of Extradimensional, Mystical and Occult Nuisances. I gave Officer Silva my badge and waited for the standard response.

"What kind of crap is this? I've never heard of any government agency called DEMON. Who the hell do you think you're dealing with, Mister?" Yep, that was exactly the response I was used to.

"Call the number."

"What number?"

"There a number on the other side of the wallet. Call it. They'll explain more than you want to hear, and you'll give me my crap back."

She handled her tech way better than her partner, who was starting to come around by that point. She pulled out a cell phone, dialed one-handed, and never left me uncovered for a second. This chick was a total pro. She gave her name and rank into the phone, told the folks on the other end what had gone down, and then her eyes got big. She listened to the voice on the other end of the phone for a couple more seconds, nodded a few times, then lowered her weapon and put her phone away.

She was ghost-white when she walked over to my guns, picked them up, and handed them back to me. "Mister, I don't know who or what you are, but those people knew shit about me that my husband don't know, and they said to give you back your gear and send you on about your business, so here you go. I apologize for any inconvenience." She backed away, then remembered her partner and got him unfastened from the bench and led him away.

"Thank you, Officer Silva, and your country thanks you," I said to her back. I heard Skeeter snicker in my earpiece, then he and I both cracked up. I laughed so hard I had to sit down on the bench again to catch my breath.

"What the holy hell did you do the that poor woman, Skeeter?"

"Don't you mean Director Robinson?" Skeeter affected a much deeper, less rednecky and significantly less gay tone.

"Of course, Director. Sorry about that."

"Officer Silva has a few indiscretions in her past that she thinks are safely walled off in her private blog, but what she doesn't know if that even if you make something private on a blog, it's still living on the internet. And if it's on the 'net..."

"You can find it, I know. What did she do?"

"Nothing major. A little weed, coke once or twice, but that was all back in college. Nobody would care, but sleeping with the watch commander in her rookie year on the force . . ."

"That might be the kind of thing someone should never, ever write down."

"Ya think?" Skeeter agreed. "When I mentioned a few things that the government would never want to make public about her, she agreed that those things should remain private, and decided that your rather minor indiscretions weren't worth her career."

"So you blackmailed her?" I tried to sound disapproving, but it was damned effective.

"You beat up her partner, and I don't see you crying any tears over it."

"True enough." I had to give him that one. "Now what?"

"Now we continue what you were supposed to be doing before you stopped for naptime—check out the park."

I did as Skeeter instructed for once and made my way into the park. I started on the bridge, which was a truly impressive bit of construction. It was a huge suspension footbridge, curving out over the waterfalls to make a nice viewing platform. It was still too cold out for anyone to be playing in the water, but I could see the place turning into a happening hangout once summer rolled around. My nap and my subsequent disagreement with the local constabulary had taken me through dusk all the way into full night, so my vision was pretty limited, and I couldn't hear anything out of the ordinary over the noise of the falls. Until I neared the other end of the bridge, that is. Then I heard a scratching sound that was bore absolutely no resemblance to the sounds of teenagers making out under a bridge at night. Unless those teenagers weighed a quarter ton and had claws strong enough to chip stone.

"Skeeter, you hear that?" I whispered into the air. Sometimes I think my job has made me crazy. Other times I'm completely sure of it.

"Yeah, sounds like something big under the bridge."

"I think I'm gonna go check it out."

"Why?"

"What do you mean, why?" I froze with one leg already over the railing. Skeeter has said some weird crap to me over the years, but that one word hung me up more than anything that had ever come out of his mouth. And that's saying something.

"I mean that you are chasing a leprechaun. And whatever is under that bridge is big. Like pick you up and beat you to death with yourself big. So it ain't a leprechaun. So why are you going to mess with it?"

"They don't call me Bubba the Monster Conversationalist. I hunt monsters. Then I shoot them. Sometimes for a change of pace I stab them, or maybe even just beat 'em to death. But hunting monsters is what I do. So if you'll excuse me, I'm gonna go do it." I clicked off the Bluetooth, then swung my other leg over the rail and jumped the few feet to the bank where the bridge ended.

I couldn't see crap under there, but I heard a surprised grunt. It sounded like it was about ten feet away, and I drew Bertha and pointed her in the general direction of the noise. The grunt turned into a growl, then a full-blown roar, and something huge and kinda slimy exploded out of the darkness, catching me right below my floating ribs. The air went out of me and whatever it was slammed me into the bank like a deflated tackling dummy. I got kind of a glimpse of a big slimy back and big naked ass, then the critter backed up off me, and I got as good a look at it as I could in the sparse streetlights. It woulda been about nine feet tall if it stood straight up, but it slouched to a much more manageable seven and a half feet. It had a mop of long stringy hair hanging over a face that looked like ten miles of bad road. A bulbous nose stuck out between a pair of beady eyes, and the lower jaw jutted forward to show off fangs the length of my thumb. It had long arms covered in ropy muscle and dripping with river muck. It was buck naked and absently scratched its balls as it looked at me, tilting its head one way or another like it was trying to figure out where to start eating.

I pushed the button on my Bluetooth and Skeeter picked right up. "Did you come to your senses and now you called to apologize, or . . ."

"It's a rock troll. Can I kill it?"

"Can you get away?"

"I don't think so. I can't really see and it's between me and the bridge, so I'm on his turf."

"You know you're an idiot, right? Don't you remember what happened the last time you messed with a troll?"

"Yeah, I got dropped through the roof of my truck. Not one of my favorite memories. Now how do I kill it?"

"Fire."

"I'm standing on a waterfall, Skeeter."

"This is gonna be a problem. I'll call you back. Try to stay alive 'til then." He clicked off and I looked back at the troll.

"Nice troll . . ." I put on my best smile, and the nasty bastard just ran at me again. I put three rounds from Bertha in his upper chest, and that at least slowed him down so he more fell on me than tackled through me the second time, but five hundred pounds of troll hurts like hell no matter how it hits you. And that ain't even saying nothing about the smell.

I reversed my grip on Bertha and brought all ten pounds of Israeli firearm down on the base of the troll's skull, getting a satisfying *crack* in response. It slumped down and I managed to roll it off me onto the rocks. I emptied the rest of my clip into the back of the troll's head, then gave it one more good kick for good measure. Then I cracked my back a couple of times to try and get everything back in the right place and turned back to the bridge. I limped the ten yards or so to the railing and pulled myself up.

Skeeter rang in just as I was about to throw my leg back over the rail. "Don't worry about it, Skeeter. I took care of it. Turns out no matter how tough you are, a few rounds from a fifty-caliber pistol in the back of your head is gonna ruin your day. I don't think I'm gonna have any more trouble out of that troll."

"That's good. How big was she?"

"What do you mean, she? This was a boy."

"Are you sure?" Skeeter sounded nervous for some reason.

"The damn thing was almost ten feet tall and scratching its baseball-sized nuts, Skeeter. I'm pretty sure it was a dude! Why?"

"'Cause the females are the big ones. And they're protective of their mates."

"Oh shit."

"I think you better . . ."

I never heard what Skeeter thought I'd better do because that's when a giant troll hand came down and palmed my head like Larry Bird palming a basketball. That thing picked me up by the head and flung me a good thirty yards into the middle of the river, which was colder than my first girlfriend's black little heart. I hit the water and all the air went out of my lungs in a rush, only to be replaced by about half a gallon of freezing river water. Even in late March, the river was still running pretty chilly, and I knew I had to get out of the water and get warmed up if I was going to survive. Only problem was I had a twenty-foot troll-ess stomping after me, a lungful of water, and at least two broken ribs from when I finally hit bottom.

I managed somehow to get out of the deepest part of the water, which wasn't anywhere near deep enough to blunt my impact on the rocks, and puke up a whole bunch of water and what felt like about three goldfish. There might have been a crawdaddy in there, too, but that coulda been breakfast. I heard the troll splashing toward me, and as big as it was, it only needed two big steps to cross the distance. Its huge hand wrapped around my legs this time, and I was hauled twenty feet straight up to hang upside down in front of a troll's face.

If I thought the boy troll was ugly, it didn't have anything on the female. Her head was the size of a boulder and had about the same color. Her whole body looked like nothing more than a huge pile of river rock, which I guess was how something the size of a small apartment building had stayed hidden in the middle of downtown Greenville for all this time. She stared at me with one basketball-sized eye, and her face split into an ugly, but very toothy, grin.

"Yum," she growled, and the stench that floated out of her mouth was worse than my farts after a week in Tijuana living on refried beans and tequila. I reached behind my back, pulled my Judge revolver out of the waistband of my pants, and emptied five .410 shotgun shells worth of silver buckshot into her right eyeball. I didn't know if it would kill her, but it sure as hell made her drop me.

Which wasn't my best move, seeing as how I was twenty feet above a shallow river full of huge rocks. Or, for all I knew, full of other female trolls, but I tried not to think about that or I'd never go fishing again. If I can't tell a rock from a man-eating two-story monster, it might be time to hang up my guns.

All that rushed through my head as I fell to the water, except I didn't land in the water. The troll-ette had flung me ahead of her a little ways when I shot her in the eye, and a little ways in her scale was about ten feet in the real world. Which was just far enough for me to crash into the railing of the bridge, flip over backwards onto the relative stability of said bridge, and land facedown on the concrete walkway.

I lay there cataloguing everything that hurt, and when I ran out of places that *didn't* hurt, which was a much shorter list, I got up and pulled myself to my feet with the railing. I kept low to the rail, hoping that I'd be indistinguishable from the white metal in my flannel and blue jeans. I know, sometimes my idea of camouflage leaves a lot to be desired. I looked over into the river, fully expecting to see either a dead troll-babe sprawled in the water, or the face of a live and angry troll-babe staring at me from not nearly far enough away. The last thing I expected to see was what I saw.

Nothing.

There was absolutely nothing down there, at least not that I could see. I even dug a keychain flashlight out of one soaked pocket and beat on it until it spit a weak beam of light down onto the rocks. Still a whole lot of nothing. I reckoned I'd killed them and they disintegrated, or I'd hurt them bad enough that they ran off to heal. Either way, it looked like I had enough time to make my getaway, so I leaned on the handrail and limped my dripping frozen carcass back across the bridge and hailed a bicycle cab to take me back to the Westin.

He looked at me a little funny when I told him I need a ride for two blocks, but I glared at him and waved two twenties in his general direction. "Not the stupidest thing I've ever done, mister. Let me tell you about the time me and two buddies raced around a block down here each carrying a load of drunken card players. That was even weirder than you."

I only halfway listened to him, paying more attention to getting my guns secured and hidden away and confirming that I hadn't broken any bones. I probably drifted off a little, too, since the next thing I knew he was shaking my shoulder and getting a face full of Bertha for his troubles.

"Hey man, chill! I was just trying to wake you up. Keep the fare, man. Hell, keep the bike!" He backed up a few steps, then turned and ran like hell. Or like somebody who'd just woken up a hillbilly the size of a brown bear and gotten a gun pointed at him in thanks. I dropped the twenties on the seat and went inside. A few minutes later, I was up the elevator and facedown in the softest beds in the Upstate.

"I think they just figured you were more trouble than you're worth, an assessment I often share," Skeeter said in my ear the next morning. I was alone in the hotel dining room eating the last remnants of the breakfast buffet and talking to thin air. Anybody that hadn't run for the hills as soon as I got in went scrambling the second I pressed the button in my ear and started talking about trolls. I gotta give the hotel staff credit, though. They never batted an eye. One bartender told me they got a lot of entertainment types through, so that kinda thickened their skin.

"Really? I was pretty sure I killed the boy-troll," I said around a mouthful of grits. If I've gotta give South Carolina credit for something, I'll give 'em credit for good grits. Everywhere I eat in South Carolina, the grits have just the right amount of pepper and butter, and just a hint of bacon. Perfect.

"If you'd killed her mate, she never would have let you live. She woulda just ripped you in half the first time she laid a hand on you. No, it sounds like they just wanted you away from their lair for some reason . . . holy shit."

"Holy shit what?" I mumbled, still shoveling grits down my throat as fast as I could. I figured it was gonna be one of those carbo-loading kinda days. Not that every day isn't a carbo-loading day, but it gave me an excuse for more grits.

"I think she was nesting. I think you stumbled on either a pregnant troll or one that had just given birth and was still protecting her young. Did she look pregnant?"

"Hell, Skeeter, I don't know what a pregnant troll looks like! She looked like a cross between a skyscraper and a walking Zen rock garden!"

"Well, you don't have to get huffy with me. I ain't the one picked a fight with a momma troll."

"Skeeter," I said in my best "be calm so you don't cuss out your best friend in front of the entire kitchen staff of the hotel" voice. "Do we know anything new about the L-E-P-R-E-. . . the thing we're after?" My attempt to spell out leprechaun ended in miserable failure when I realized I couldn't spell "leprechaun."

"There was another attack last night. And underground poker game just outside of town. I'll send the address to your phone."

"Okay, I'll head out there as soon as I finish breakfast."

"You mean you ain't finished? Damn, Bubba, even hobbits only eat two breakfasts. Save something for lunch." I flipped off the air and pressed the button to hang up the phone, then headed back upstairs to shower and get dressed to face the day. Somewhere in Greenville, SC, there was an Irish mythical creature killing people and raiding poker games. I needed to find it and kill it. And maybe stick around for more grits tomorrow morning.

I pulled up to the doublewide trailer at the end of a dirt road. I winced a little at the cloud of rocks and dust I kicked up, hating what it was doing to the finish on my new F-250. I'd finally replaced my old truck, and I was kinda babying this one, at least until something threw me through the roof of this one. I stepped out into the cloud of dust and opened the back door. I pulled on a blazer to cover my shoulder holster and smoothed my hair down, making sure nothing had escaped my ponytail. I didn't have a whole lot of chance of pulling this off, but I figured I oughta be able to BS my way past a couple of bumpkin deputies.

"What the greasy green hell are you doing here?"

As long as the bumpkin deputies weren't bumpkin deputies I'd already met, which of course, the first officer on the scene was.

"Officer Silva." I nodded at the lady cop from the night before and felt the grits in my gut sour just a bit.

"Mister, I don't know who the hell you think you are, but this is a crime scene, so you better get your fat ass back in that truck and get the hell out of here."

"I think we covered the question of my identity pretty well last night, didn't we?" I put on my best "affronted douchebag cop" face, which is pretty well informed, given the number of douchebag cops that I've affronted in my time.

"Yeah, except for one problem. There ain't no government agency called DEMON, and the number I called is registered to a William James MacIntyre Kwame Jones III in Georgia. And that don't sound like no 'Director Robinson' to me." She had her sidearm out, but it wasn't pointed at me. Yet.

"Yeah, well, there might have been a couple of inaccuracies in my explanation to you yesterday, but trust me that what is going on here is something you do not want to be messin' with. Now why don't you just pretend that everything I told you yesterday was true and take your doughnut-humping partner somewhere safe for a couple hours. I oughta be able to get this wrapped up without too much trouble as long as I don't have a lot of interference from well-meaning but hapless amateurs."

Her eyes went wide, then her brows drew together in a scowl as I realized I'd gone too far. I used to be better at handling the local cops than that, but I had a family member try to gut me recently, and that screwed with my social graces a little.

"I don't think so. I think I'm going to arrest you for assaulting an officer, for impersonating an officer of the law, and for impeding a murder investigation. Then I'm going to get you in my jail and figure out exactly who you are, what your deal is, and what all else I can charge your ass with. How does that sound, asshole?"

I heard the chuckle behind me, and that was the only hint I had that her partner was back there. That and the smell of cheap hair gel and Italian dressing. I turned around and Deputy Fatass had a shotgun leveled at my gut. I put my hands up and turned back to Officer Silva.

"Look, Officer. I'm sorry, I've had a rough couple of weeks and I shouldn't have been so rude. Can we talk about this?"

"No. Cuff him, Russell. Then let's see what happened in here." Deputy Lardo slipped a pair of plastic zip cuffs on my wrists and pulled them a lot tighter than he really needed to. I guess that was his version of payback for me knocking him out last night. Didn't matter, they weren't staying on a second longer than I wanted them to. I let them lead me over to their squad car and settled into the back seat to wait.

I didn't have to wait long. They went in, or at least Officer Silva went in. Her fat-ass partner made it as far as the threshold before he spun around to puke in the bushes. Silva got into the house, was out of sight for about a minute and a half, then came rushing out to deposit her breakfast in the bushes on the other side of the door. Those azaleas were having a bad day. I decided that sitting on my hands, literally, wasn't getting me any closer to catching the leprechaun, so I flexed my shoulders and pulled against the plastic cuffs. I felt a little give, took a deep breath and really *strained*. The cuffs made a thin squeak in protest, then the plastic lock gave with a *crack*, and I was free. I flexed my hands to get the blood flowing back into them, then rolled over onto one side. I jammed my shoulders against the seat, reached over my head with my arms, and kicked the window out of the back door. It took a couple of good shots, but even after my run-in with the trolls the night before, the county budget wouldn't buy anything strong enough to hold me. I squeezed my enormous frame through the hole and pulled my legs out after me. It wasn't the prettiest dismount, but I was free.

I walked over to where the cops were wiping puke off their lips and stepped up behind Officer Silva. "You know, a real partner would have held your hair back while you puked."

She whirled around, drawing her sidearm in a blur, but I was expecting exactly that move. I slapped the pistol out of her hand and stepped sideways to draw the taser off her partner's belt. I jammed the cartridge into his fat gut and pulled the trigger, dropping him to the dirt in a twitching pile of sweat. I felt a little bad about him landing in the vomit, but not much.

I turned back to Officer Silva and tossed the spent taser at her. She instinctively reached up to bat the device out of the air, which gave me enough time to grab her right wrist in one hand and take her own taser away from her. I gave her a little push and twist, and she stumbled backward to land on her ass in the grass. At least she missed the puddle of puke.

"Now behave," I growled at her. She froze and I peeked over at her partner. He was still laying there twitching, so I turned back to the more reasonable one. Although admittedly I hadn't given Officer Ventimeglia much chance to be reasonable, knocking him out both times we'd met.

"I'm going to go inside now and have a look around. If I'm lucky, there's something in there to tell me where to find the little bastard that made all the mess. Then I can find it, kill it, and be far enough from here by sunset that you can forget you ever met me. Does that sound like a good plan to you?"

"I - I've never seen anything like it. Maybe in a horror movie. But that stuff ain't real. Is it?" Officer Silva looked up at me with big eyes, but I didn't have the heart to lie to her.

"Officer, just about every monster story you've ever heard of is real. And for a lot of people, the only thing between the big bad and them, is me. Welcome to my world, I'm sorry you had to find out about it. Now I'm going to go do my job." I nodded to her, and she stayed sitting there in the grass while I went into the house.

The smell of blood isn't usually a big deal, but when there's enough blood spilled in a small enough space, the acrid scent just gets into everything. It overpowers every other scent in the room, getting into the nooks and crannies of your sense of smell like a bad song gets stuck in your head. Well, there had been enough blood shed in that doublewide to make the air take on a pinkish tinge. The carpet squelched when I stepped into the living room, and I looked down to see nothing but red liquid pooling up around my boots. There was blood everywhere, making puddles in the carpet and splashed on every wall. There were even long swaths of blood painted across the ceiling. It looked like a slaughterhouse, only not as sanitary.

The living room was dominated by four poker tables, two of them overturned to make rough shields. It didn't look like they'd helped. I counted enough arms to make about eight people, but I only saw four heads. One bald guy, one fortyish looking guy with red hair turning to gray, one dude with perfect hair even after decapitation, and one dark-haired dude with expensive sunglasses on. I helped myself to the Gucci shades, figuring he didn't need 'em anymore. One guy looked like he'd put up a helluva fight before finally bleeding out. He was bald, looked to be in his early forties, and had the compact build of somebody who lifts a lot of weight several times a week. His Pokerstars.com t-shirt was stretched tight across his biceps, and his knuckles were bloody, so I figured he'd gotten a couple of shots in before the leprechaun gutted him.

"I hope you gave almost as good as you got, pal." I reached down and closed his eyes.

"Well, ain't that sweet o' ya?" a voice said from behind me in a thick Irish brogue. I stood up and turned around slowly, every muscle coiled like a spring, ready to dive somewhere out of the way of claws, fangs, or whatever leprechauns used to kill people.

What I saw rocked me back on the heels of my size sixteen boots. It was a leprechaun all right, a little short dude with red hair and a green suit sitting cross-legged in the middle of one of the poker tables. He was cleaning his fingernails with a wicked curved knife, and as he grinned at me, I saw a glint of gold tooth.

"Why'd you kill these men?" I didn't really care. I just needed time to think about how to draw Bertha before the little bugger opened my windpipe.

"They stole me gold, of course. They stole me gold, and I was bound to get it back. I got it all back." I recognized that fevered look in his eyes, but from where?

"Stole your . . ." My jaw dropped. It really did. I've fought undead creatures all over the South, chased my werewolf father and brother through half a dozen states, been beat up by vampires, zombies, lycanthropes and all other manner of nasty, but this took the cake.

"You lost your gold in a poker game, didn't you?"

"They stole it! They cheated me, and nobody cheats the little people and lives!" He started brandishing that curved knife through the air and I took a step back. He was *fast*, like Jet Li on meth fast, and that knife was sharp. There was no way I was gonna take the little dude in a fair fight, not even at my best. And I was long from my best. He kept flailing around with the knife, and I kept backing up. Eventually my butt bumped into a side table, and I was fresh out of room to move.

That's when I remembered where I'd seen that look before. It was on Grandpappy's face the one time we took him to Tunica to check out the casinos. He was a helluva monster hunter, but a god-awful craps player, and he ran through about six grand before we got him away from the table. And that didn't end pretty, either. I had to throw the old man over my shoulders and carry his ass out of the casino. For some reason we weren't invited back. Remembering Grandpappy reminded me that when he got the fever to gamble into him, nothing could get through. Nothing but calling his ass out, that is.

"You know, I bet they didn't. I bet you're just a crap poker player and can't admit it. It's okay, most of the terrible gamblers I know can't admit it. Of course most of them don't end up gutting the people they lose to, either. So I guess you're a crap poker player *and* a sore loser. And that's just no good."

"Well, what are you going to do about it, fatty?" Now that was just uncalled for. I might have put on a few pounds in my recent convalescence, but nothing that I'd describe as fat. I was still a lean, mean 350 pounds of redneck love machine, and I didn't need any Irish midget telling me different.

I took a deep breath and pushed down my anger at the leprechaun denigrating my physical appearance. "Well, I'm gonna have to kill you. But in the interests of fairness, why don't we try a little game of chance first?"

His eyes lit up as I reached around behind me and picked up a deck of cards from the side table. I know a degenerate gambler when I see one, and this beastie had all the signs. If I could get that knife out of his hand long enough, I might have a chance.

"What kind of game are ye proposin'?" The leprechaun jumped off the table and into a chair, standing in the seat with both hands on the table. I pushed the corpse of a gray-haired guy in motorcycle leathers out of the chair opposite and sat down. There was a little *sploosh* as I sat in a puddle of blood, but I tried not to think about it.

"I think we could play one hand of seven-card stud. You win, you get one free shot at me with that little nut-cutter of yours. I win, I get to hit you in the face as hard as I can."

"That sounds like a win-win for me. I get to beat you at cards, and then I get to gut you like an overweight fish! I'm in!" I was really getting tired of fat jokes from the guy whose head stopped at my belt buckle, but I didn't want to appear insensitive and make a short joke in response. Instead I just shuffled the cards and held them out to him to cut.

"First two down," I said as I flipped cards out to the leprechaun, then me, then him, then me.

"Third street showin'," I said as I tossed a card face up to the leprechaun, then one to me. He got the ace of diamonds to my four of clubs.

"Not lookin' so good for you, is it hillbilly?" The leprechaun grinned.

"How do you know I don't have rolled-up fours?" I asked, peeking at my hole cards. I didn't have rolled-up fours, but I did have queens in the hole, which was a pretty good hand.

"I know ye're not rolled up because I've got a four in the hole to go with me other ace, boyo." He flipped over his hole cards to show me the four of spades and the ace of spades.

"Well, I'm glad I'm not betting my queens into your aces, then." I grinned as I flipped my hole cards and dealt fourth street face up. I picked up a ten of diamonds to the leprechaun's eight of hearts.

66

"I'm still leading, sonny-boy. Tell you what, if I win, I'll give you two steps to get to the door before I gut ye."

"The song says gimme *three* steps, asshole," I muttered as I flipped over fifth street. I picked up another ten to give me two pair, but the damn leprechaun got the eight of diamonds.

"Aces up beats queens up, sonny-Jim, and the luck of the Irish beats everything." He leaned back in his chair and laughed until tears streamed down his face. His laugh cut off like a switch when I dealt him a Jack of spades on sixth street and dropped the pretty little queen of hearts on my board to fill me up, queens full of tens.

"What was that you were saying, ginger?" I grinned across the table at him.

"Deal the card, you cheating bastard," he grumbled, and I knew the men in this trailer hadn't cheated him. Just like none of his other victims cheated him. This little bastard was just another shitty card player and sore loser. There's nothing I hate in life more than a sore loser. I set the deck on the table and pulled the top card off, flicking it facedown across the table to him through the air instead of sliding it along the felt like the others.

"Last card's down and dirty, you sorry bastard," I muttered as I sent the little square of cardboard flying through the air.

He snatched that final card out of mid-air, looked at it, and grinned fit to beat the band. He turned his grin to me, and his eyes went big. I pulled the trigger, and Bertha barked, putting a fifty-caliber slug of cold iron right between the leprechaun's eyes. His little body flipped over backwards, slammed into the wall of the trailer, and slid to the ground, leaving a snail trail of blood down the wall.

His card fluttered to the table face down. I flipped it over, revealing the ace of clubs. "Aces full of eights. I hear there's a name for that hand." I stood up and walked out into the afternoon sunlight, right past the two cops standing by the front door as I got in my truck and headed out of Greenville. It wasn't until a couple miles later that I remembered my jeans were still covered in wet blood, and I'd just ruined the upholstery in my new truck. I really hate South Carolina.

4

SHE'S GOT LEGS

"I hate I-40," I said to the air as my tires sang out at about 85 miles per hour. I was making good time since I got out of Memphis, but the bad taste of that long-ass highway tends to linger with a body.

"I know, Bubba, but there ain't a whole lot of ways to get from North Georgia to Forrest City, Arkansas, that don't involve I-40," Skeeter, my technology expert and the world's worst wingman, said into my Bluetooth earpiece.

"That don't help," I grumbled, reaching for the radio. Mojo Nixon was screeching on my satellite radio, and I needed a little relief. I turned the radio down and focused on Skeeter again. "What's the job this time?"

"Don't you read your email? I explained all that when I gave you the destination."

"I only read the ones that promise to make my pecker bigger or give me a million dollars. Crap from you I know I don't have to read— I can just ask you about it later."

"You're a huge pain in my ass, Bubba."

"Yeah, what are best friends for, anyway? So what's the gig?"

"Men are disappearing out of the greater Memphis area, mostly around the St. Francis National Forest."

"You sure they aren't just going on the lam after a bad run in Tunica?"

"We have seven men, all vanished from within fifteen miles of the edge of the forest in the last month. Only three of them had been to Tunica within a month of their disappearance, and two of those three had actually won money. So no, they aren't dodging a casino debt."

"All right, then ditching a girlfriend or wife?" Money and women were the reasons I'd beat a hasty retreat from more than one small Southern town. Usually both of them together.

"Only four were married, one was gay, and none seemed to be particularly unhappy in their relationships. And other bright ideas?" I hate it when Skeeter gets snide. Snide is my shtick, and he needs to leave it alone.

"Nope, I'm not the idea guy, Skeeter. I'm the shoot things until they don't move guy. What about you, any brilliant ideas?"

There was a pause at the other end of the line. "Actually, no. There haven't been any signs of struggle, or any signs of anything, really. These guys just wander off into the woods and are never heard of again. Or at least they haven't been heard of for a couple of weeks, at this point."

"I guess I'll check it out. Got any real leads for me?"

"Yeah, turn off at the next exit and head into the park. The last guy just disappeared a couple days ago, and Amy was able to get the locals to keep the campsite secured for you." Amy Hall is an agent for DEMON, the federal Department of ExtraDimensional, Mystical and Occult Nuisances. She's part of a super-secret government agency that does pretty much the same thing I do, just with a bigger budget. And black helicopters. No matter how often I ask Uncle Father Joe, our liaison to Rome, the Vatican keeps refusing to buy me a black helicopter.

"So I gotta be official?"

"Kinda. They're park rangers, so you don't need a real shirt or anything like that. Just flash your badge and you oughta be okay."

By this point I was pulling into the St. Francis National Forest. I parked my F-250 in the gravel lot at the front of the ranger station and got out. My beat-up old Wolverine boots clumped on the wooden porch, and I banged on screen door.

"Anybody home?" I yelled.

No answer. I walked around to the back of the ranger station, peeking through windows and banging on doors. The only thing I found was a very confused squirrel scampering over a woodpile. I pressed the Bluetooth earpiece, calling Skeeter.

"There's nobody here, Skeeter. Was the ranger a guy? Maybe we need to add him to the list of missing dudes."

"Maybe we do, 'cause Jerome Davis is the ranger you're looking for. He's supposed to take you to the last known whereabouts of one Aaron Kennedy, a climber last seen in the park Friday morning."

"Well ain't nobody here, so I'm going on in." I opened the screen door and stepped into the abandoned ranger station. The place was small but neat and clean, with all the maps and logs in their place. I picked up a clipboard from the lone desk in the room. Titled "Climbers," it had a list of names in small, tight handwriting. There was a check mark by each name except for the last one, Aaron Kennedy.

"Looks like our ranger went off looking for Mr. Kennedy on his own, Skeeter. I don't see any signs of a struggle, and there's an empty spot in the gun rack."

"How can you tell it's not just an empty spot?"

"The dust in the floor of the case has an oval spot in it, like the butt of a gun usually rests there. And nobody leaves an empty spot one from the left in a gun rack, Skeeter. Even you're redneck enough to know that."

"I'm redneck enough to never have seen a gun rack that wasn't full." He had a point. Skeeter's daddy owned more guns than even my family, and we were better armed than some third-world countries.

"Well lemme look around and see if I can find out where Ranger Jerry might have gone off to, then we'll try to figure out what's been stealing men in the Arkansas woods." I sat at the desk and looked through the stacks of papers arranged neatly on the blotter. Nothing. I flipped through the stack of pink message slips by the phone. More nothing. I looked over the blotter for notes. Even more nothing. I was just about to give up and start randomly wandering through the woods, always a good way for me to find trouble, when I remembered the list. I grabbed the clipboard and looked at it, then smacked myself in the forehead with it.

"What?" Skeeter said in my ear.

"The clipboard."

"What about it?"

"It lists their planned climbs. It tells me right where to look for this Kennedy fella. . ."

"And by extension, Ranger Jerry."

"Yup. Sometimes I think I'm a real dumbass."

" . . ."

"Shut up."

"I didn't say nothing!" Skeeter protested.

"I heard you thinking," I said and pushed the button to sever the connection. I grabbed the top page of the clipboard and a topographical map that Ranger Jerry had lying around, and then went back to the truck to gear up. I grabbed Bertha, my Desert Eagle, in her shoulder rig, slid my Taurus Judge revolver into a paddle holster at the small of my back, and threaded a Ka-Bar through my belt loops. My backpack had a couple bottles of water, a handheld GPS and some camping supplies, just in case. I didn't bother with a tent or anything that heavy since I wasn't planning on being gone more than a couple hours. I used the map to figure out GPS coordinates for Ranger Jerry's most likely destination, plugged them into the handheld unit, and headed off into the woods, machete in one hand and MP3 player in the other. Nothing like a little Alabama Shakes to help guide a brother through the deep dark woods, I always say.

It took an hour or so of hard hiking to get to the right GPS coordinates. The trail, if a deserted deer path could be called that, opened up to a clearing at the base of a three-story rock incline. It looked like a pretty simple climb, as long as you weren't a thirty-something 350-pound redneck weighted down with thirty pounds of guns and gear. In other words, it looked damned impossible to me. But the bright purple rope running down the face of the rock told me that somebody thought it looked like a good idea, and recently.

But it wasn't the cliff that stood out most of all. That honor went to the small cottage nestled up against the base of the cliff, complete with chimney and delicate white smoke wafting up into the afternoon sun. I pressed the Bluetooth button but got nothing. I pulled out my cell phone and saw the blinking "No Service" icon.

"Shit. Well, I guess I can find a bunch of lost hikers without Skeeter's help." I hoped I could, anyway. I'd never tell him this, but Skeeter's pretty important to my hunting. Not only does he look up how to kill whatever I find, but just having his voice in my ear keeps me kinda calm. Like having somebody to bicker with keeps me centered. If I believed in therapy, I'd probably talk to somebody about that. But since I don't, I just drink.

The only sign of a climber was the rope dangling from the rock face, and there was nothing to indicate that Ranger Jerry had been by here at all, so I did exactly what everybody in their right mind screams at the TV for people not to do in horror movies—I walked up to the front door of the mysterious cottage that appeared where it had no business being and knocked.

The door swung open silently at my touch, not even an eerie creak to warn me of what was about to happen. But that was probably because the little old lady that opened the door seemed to keep a neat house.

She looked up at me from just inside the door and said, "I wondered if you were ever going to have the guts to come knock. What took you so long?"

She was a little old lady in all ways. Skinny, stooped over, maybe five and a half feet tall if she stood up straight, with white hair pulled into a bun on top of her head. She smiled up at me from underneath bright blue eyes, and I got the distinct impression that this lady didn't miss anything that happened in her woods. No matter how weird it was that she was in the woods to begin with.

"Sorry, ma'am. I was a little confused. I didn't think anybody lived out here, it being a national park and all."

"Oh, dearie me, we don't pay much attention to nations out here. My sisters and I have lived in these woods for years and years. Now what brings a strapping young lad like yourself to my doorstep, and here in my old age no less." She sounded disappointed, like she wanted me to go away and come back later.

"May I come in? I'm looking for a few friends of mine and was hoping that you might have seen them."

"Of course, of course, please come in." She stepped back and I followed her into the cottage. It was a small, open room with a tiny kitchen, a table set for three, and a living room with three chairs. A doorway opened up off the back of the room, leading to bedrooms, I supposed.

"Do your sisters live here with you?" I asked, waving at the place settings.

"Oh no, but we do like to gather for dinner from time to time. I usually do the cooking. Grissy does most of the hunting because she's the youngest. The animals just seem to flock to her for some reason." She glanced away when she said that last bit, like it offended her somehow. I decided I didn't want to get into family politics, especially not a fight over which sister was prettier. There was no way that ended well for me.

I followed her into the living room and sat down on one of the chairs. Fortunately for me, antique furniture like her house was filled with was built to last and to support big men. The chair creaked a little and maybe even whimpered as I sat down, but it held me and was pretty comfortable to boot.

"Ma'am . . ." I started, but she held up a hand.

"Call me Esme, darling. It's been so long since a man called me that."

"Well . . . Esme, I'm looking for some people, and since a couple of

73

them were last headed in this direction, I was hoping you could help me."

"Well, of course, dear. I suppose you're looking for that boy with all the climbing equipment and the nice park ranger, aren't you?"

"Yeah, I mean, yes, ma'am. That's two of the folks I'm looking for. Do you know where they went?" If I could wrap this up before dinner, I could get out of these woods and get something real to eat, not just the granola bars I had in my pack.

"Well, they were both here. The climbing fellow a couple of days ago, and the ranger just this morning. The climbing man played around on the rocks behind the house for a while, but then he fell and hurt his arm. My middle sister Minerva is a wonderful healer, so I took him to her house so she could help him out. I suppose he decided to visit with her for a while until his arm was all better. That's what I told the ranger when he came by this morning. He took off for Minerva's house without even finishing his tea." She motioned to a cup sitting next to the chair I was in. Sure enough, it was three-quarters full of what looked like tea.

"Can you show me on this map where your sister's house is? I really need to find these people." I unfolded my topo map and dug a Sharpie out of my backpack. Esme looked at the map for just a second before taking the marker and putting a small circle down. I plugged the GPS coordinates into my handheld and figured it was a little more than another hour to get there. My watch told me it was about two o'clock, so if I wanted steak for dinner, I was gonna have to get a move on.

"Thank you so much for your help, Esme. I really appreciate it." I stood up to leave, but she grabbed my wrist. Her grip was strong for somebody so apparently frail.

"Please come back by and visit me sometime. It gets very lonely here in the woods, all alone." She pressed herself into my side in a distinctly non-old lady fashion, and I felt myself blush a little. I danced backwards a little and got out of the cottage before Granny Esme decided to really throw herself at me. I mean, I love the ladies, and I'd dipped my toe in some older rivers from time to time, if you know what I mean, but I draw the line at fooling around with women who remember V-J Day.

Once I was back outside, I followed the GPS southwest past the house and was soon back into the deep woods. I kept trying the Bluetooth, but even though it felt like I was traveling higher and higher, there was no signal. I guess there are still a few places that cell phone companies haven't invaded yet. And, of course, I end up in all of them sooner or later.

I trekked deep into the woods, so deep that I could barely see the sky. My sense of time went all wonky, and I couldn't tell if I'd been walking for one hour or three. All I was sure of was that my feet were sore, my water bottle was empty, and if I didn't find this woman's house pretty soon, I was going to need to find a stream or some other source of fresh water. Just when I was starting to think thirst was a serious problem, I stepped out into a clearing, almost identical to the last one.

Just like her sister's place, this cottage sat in a cleared patch of woods, with a nice little picket fence and a neat little chimney blowing a thin plume of white smoke up into the late afternoon sky. There was no cliff behind this cottage, just more woods, but otherwise it was almost indistinguishable from the first one. I stepped through the gate and up to the front door, raising my hand to knock.

The door opened before I touched it, swinging in to reveal a beautiful fifty-ish woman dressed to kill in slinky black pants and a clingy black shirt that wrapped around her midsection and fastened in the center of some truly impressive tracts of land with a sparkling pendant. The brooch, not that my eye was drawn to that area at all, was a Celtic knot work that looked familiar somehow. Then I remembered that her sister wore a necklace of the same design. I supposed it was a family thing.

"Hello," she said with a raised eyebrow and a smile. "I'm Minerva, and you must be Robert. Esme told me you were coming." Her dark eyes shone with anticipation, and her red lips turned up to mine invitingly. I stepped forward, into the cabin . . .

And shook myself back to my senses. "Sorry to barge in like that, ma'am. Could I trouble you for some water? My bottles ran out a while back, and I think thirst has made me forget my manners. I'm really sorry about that."

Something flashed across her face faster than I could track, but it was gone before I could even swear it existed and was replaced by a sweet smile.

"Of course, dear. Let me hold your . . . sack and I'll refill your supplies." I handed over my backpack and watched as she walked over to the sink. I took in a deep breath as I checked out her ass. For an older chick, she was smokin'! Her butt cheeks looked like a pair of kittens playing in a pillowcase.

I snapped out of my contemplation of her rear to see her looking at me, a little smirk on her face. Busted. I realized she was waiting on me to answer, and I had no idea what the question was.

"I'm sorry, what did you say? I guess I was out there a little longer than I thought. Do you mind if I sit down?" I stepped over to her couch and took a seat. The cottage was almost identical to Esme's on the inside too—a little sitting area, a kitchen, a dining area, and a hallway leading off into the back. I noticed one thing conspicuous by its absence, though.

"Y'all don't have TVs?" I asked.

Minerva paused halfway across the living room and looked at me like a startled rabbit. "Um . . . no, we . . . um . . . never have enjoyed television the way some people do."

"Huh." I shrugged, reaching out for the water glass and knocking back half of the tumbler in one gulp. "Well, can't say as I blame you. There's never anything on except smut and bad news. You're probably better off reading a book." I looked around, but there were no bookshelves, either. Or board games, or computers, or anything a person might amuse themselves with. These women kept some strange households.

"Yes, well, the library is in the back of the house. That's where I spend much of my time. There, and the bedroom." Her voice was like smooth velvet, and before I noticed, she was on the couch with me, pressed tight against me. "Is there anything else I could get for you? Anything?"

I looked down into those dark pools and felt myself slipping away, just comfortable to sit there on the couch with her and leave the lost men to their own devices. But then I remembered Skeeter, and Agent Amy, and that steak I wanted for dinner, and my focus went sharp again.

"Yes ma'am, there is. I'm looking for some hikers that vanished near here, and a park ranger that went missing this morning. I visited your sister because her cottage is near the last known destination of one of the hikers, but she didn't seem to know anything. She told me I should talk to you because you might have some idea where these men have vanished to."

That shadow flickered across her face again, almost too fast to see but not quite, then she answered me. "Well, there was a man by here this morning, looking for another man he said was missing. I told him I hadn't had the company of a gentleman caller in some time and that he should talk to Grissy."

"Who's Grissy?" I asked.

"Grissy is our youngest sister. She lives a little further into the wood." Just what I needed, another hour of hacking through honeysuckle and dodging deer poop. My steak was fading into dream territory with every minute.

"I thought Esme said she brought the climber here. She said he was hurt and you were nursing him back to health."

"Well I was, but he got better and went to visit Grissy for a few days."

"I thought he just went missing two days ago?"

"Well, I don't know anything about that, young man. I just know that he was hurt, and the moment I got him all healed up right as rain, he ran off with my little sister." Her dark eyes flashed, and I got the feeling this wasn't the first time a guy she was interested in made a play for the younger sis.

"So you told this to Ranger Jerry?"

"I did indeed, and just like all the others, he ran off to little Grissy's house." Bitter, party of one, your table is now available. I decided it was time for me to get out of there before this chick started boiling bunnies and swinging cutlery around. I stood up from the couch and reached for my bag.

"Thanks for the water, but now it looks like I need to go see your sister and get this mess all cleared up."

She just sat there on the couch, looking up at me like an abandoned puppy. An abandoned puppy with huge knockers spilling out of her shirt, but a puppy just the same.

"Do you have to leave? Aren't you sure you wouldn't rather stay here? With me?" At that last bit, she stretched out one long leg and ran her bare toes up the inside of my leg. As her foot approached the promised land, I stepped back out of reach. Her foot dropped to the floor, and she gave me a pout before standing and going to open the door.

"Well, you have fun with little Grissy, but remember how to get to my house when you want to talk to a real woman."

"Yeah . . . That reminds me. I don't have any idea where your sister lives. Could you mark it on this map for me?" I held out the map and a Sharpie, and she took them both in a huff. She stomped over to the little table, marked an "X" on the map, and stomped back.

"Here. Now get out."

I did just that, and kept one hand on my knife as I backed away from the cabin. No way was I letting that one out of my sight. I thought to myself as I left the clearing that maybe it was a good thing these chicks lived deep in the woods. I heard the sound of something big and probably hungry rustling around in the woods nearby, but that didn't worry me nearly as much as the thought that Minerva might be following me.

The map took me over a couple of rivers and through a helluva lotta woods, but Grandmother's house was nowhere to be found. Okay, it was more like a couple of little streams that I managed to hop over without even getting my boots wet, but there were plenty of woods. Another hour or so of clumping through the woods brought me to one more clearing, marked just where Minerva said it was on the map. And once again, there was a tidy little cabin in the center of it.

The cabin looked a lot like the other two, your basic log cabin, but with a nice picket fence around it and a little flower garden out front. There was a big overturned pot by the front door of this one, though, and I couldn't for the life of me figure out what it was for. It looked like a giant stewpot, a good five feet deep and six feet around, but it was made out of porcelain instead of cast iron. On the ground next to it was a porcelain stirrer, but it was thicker than anything I'd ever seen before. In my stew experience, you just needed a cast iron pot about four feet around and three feet deep, and growing up we always stirred ours with a busted oar from somebody's jon boat, but this rig was a lot fancier.

The rest of the cabin could have come out of a fairy tale, it looked so stereotypical. There were even window boxes full of flowers. A thin tendril of smoke wafted up into the air from the brick chimney, and the scent of cooking spices filled the air. I stepped into the clearing and walked up to the front door, a little entranced by the delicious smells. I raised my hand to knock, but the door opened before I had the chance to bring my meaty fist down on it.

A blast of good food smells wafted out and floated around my head, taking me back to some of the best meals I've ever had. Mama's fried chicken and gravy danced on my tongue, while memories of my college girlfriend Brittany's spaghetti sauce tingled feelings a little lower. I even thought I smelled Waffle House chili in there for a second. Don't judge me, you ain't lived until you've been knee-walking drunk at three-thirty in the morning in Birmingham, Alabama, eating Waffle House chili at the bar with one hand while you hold your buddy's head out of his grits with the other hand.

I blinked a couple of times to cut through the food smells and the memories and looked down at the woman who stood in the doorway. I had to catch my breath all over again when I saw her.

"Y-you must be Grissy," I managed to stammer while I drank in every inch of her. And they were some good-looking inches, too. She had long, dark hair cascading down over her shoulders, exotic part

Asian-part Latina-part American-all hottie features that made Angelina Jolie look boring, with big brown eyes, dimples in her cheeks and a smile that melted my heart and stiffened a couple of other things.

She had a slender neck, smooth skin and long, long legs in a short, short skirt. She was barefoot, and her toes were painted a crimson to match her fingernails. She had on a men's tank top tied up to show a flat belly with a silver ring in her bellybutton and exposing enough cleavage to make me want to dive in there and explore for a day or so. In short, she was hot.

"Yes, I'm Grissy. What brings a big, strong man like you all the way out here?" She reached up and stroked my shoulder as she asked the question, and when the words came across her lips, I had no idea what the answer could be.

"I - I - I'm just taking a hike, I guess," I said after a minute of staring into those pools of blue. I might have diverted my gaze a little further south once or twice, too, but it was in a purely respectful way. And I didn't drool. Or if I did, my beard caught most of it.

"Wow, you must be thirsty. Why don't you come in, have a drink of water, and sit down for a minute. After all, it's soooo hot out there." She turned and walked into the cabin with me in tow. I followed her like a bulldog chasing a convertible, not having any idea what I was going to do with it when I caught it. She motioned to the couch and I sat. She didn't so much sit next to me as she oozed in beside me, pressing all her curves up to every inch of the side of my body. All thoughts of water went right out of my head. Come to think of it, pretty much every thought went right out of my head. I just sat there, enjoying the feel of all that soft womanliness pressed up against me.

"Now," she continued, trailing a fingertip down the line of buttons on my shirt, "what brings a big, strong man like you out to my cabin deep in these woods?"

Somehow I focused my thoughts enough to answer her question. "I'm looking for some people. Several men have gone missing in these woods lately, and when I spoke to your sisters, they thought maybe you might have seen them." I pulled a couple of pictures out of my back pocket and showed them to her.

She glanced down at the pictures for about an eighth of a second, then turned her dazzling smile back to me. "Never seen them before. Now, why don't we get better acquainted before dinner?"

I was all set to call her out on not even looking at the pictures, but then she had to go and mention dinner. Now let's review—I arrived on her doorstep after traipsing through the woods all damn day, chatting with her oldest sister, practically being molested by her middle sister, and now this most delectable thing had to go and mention food with me sitting in the middle of an olfactory orgasm zone. Well, my stomach did what it does when somebody mentions food—it grumbled out a little "hello" to the room just to remind us all that it was there. She heard my stomach growl—hell, people three states away probably heard my stomach growl—and giggled. Like she thought my barbaric manners were cute.

I've been called a lot of things by a lot of women, and a lot more by their fathers, husbands, brothers, boyfriends, and priests. But I'm seldom what anybody thinks is cute. And it's even more rare that I get giggled at. So I didn't really know what to do with the situation. So I sat there like a jackass with a giggling sex kitten laughing on his chest, with all the appropriate jiggly bits of her doing what jiggly bits of women do when they laugh. So yeah, I didn't mind being giggled at so much.

After a few seconds of confusing frivolity, she looked up at me and said, "Sounds like somebody's hungry. Would you like to join me for dinner?" And she batted her eyelashes. She batted. Her. Damn. Eyelashes. It was about as cute as a bucketful of kittens. And I was hungry.

"Of course. I'd hate to leave you out here all alone to eat by yourself. Besides, it smells delicious. What are you having?"

"Oh, don't worry about that. I won't be alone. As a matter of fact, my sisters should be along in just a few minutes. We always take our meals together." I wondered about this since old lady Esme didn't look like she could walk across her living room without breaking a hip, much less meander through the woods for two hours to get here. But then I caught another whiff of whatever was in the oven, and I didn't care so much about Esme. I did make sure that Bertha was still in her holster, though. Minerva scared me a little.

"Do you have anywhere I can wash up?" I asked. "I've been tromping through these woods for hours and I'd hate to sit down at your table all grimy."

"Of course. Right through there." She pointed down the hallway that led, I assumed, into the rest of the house. I heaved my bulk up off her couch and walked down the hall. The door to the right was open a little bit, so I peeked inside. Nope, that ain't it. I pulled the door to her bedroom shut, but not before I took in the huge canopy bed in the center of the room and thought about all sorts of gymnastics that a guy my size could put a woman her size into in a bed that size. I turned to the opposite door and tried the knob, but it was locked.

The door at the end of the short hall opened into a small bathroom with an old-fashioned claw tub and a cute little pedestal sink. I closed the door, took a long-needed leak, and set about making myself some level of presentable. My hair looked like a bigger rat's nest than normal, so I took my ponytail down and ran my fingers through the mop, trying to tame it a little bit. I had no luck, so I opened the medicine cabinet in hopes of finding an old boyfriend's comb or something that I could use. I wasn't snooping, really. Much.

No comb, just a bunch of old glass bottles with paper labels on them. I grabbed one down but couldn't read it. The script was spidery and faded, but also written in some kind of Latin or Greek or hell, if I was being honest, it coulda been Korean for all I knew what it was saying. I put the bottle back and went back to washing my hands and face. I reached over to the side of the sink for a towel, and with all my usual bull-in-china-shop grace, knocked it to the floor. I knelt down to pick up the towel and saw something gold and shiny behind the toilet. Never one to leave something shiny behind, I reached down and pulled out a cheap gold star with the name "Davis" on it below the symbol of the National Parks Service. My brow knit, I slid the badge into a pocket, and clambered to my feet.

Or at least I started to clamber to my feet because just about the time I got to kneeling position, the door opened behind me. I turned to see Grissy standing there, looking pissed and holding a black iron skillet. In my experience, that's always been a bad combination.

"You just had to get all snoopy, didn't you? Couldn't just leave well enough alone, could you?" I didn't bother trying to answer because she swung the skillet at my head like Babe Ruth in Yankees Stadium. I dove under the swing and scrabbled forward, trying to get out of the bathroom and somewhere that I could defend myself without having to shoot the really hot girl with the really big pistol. I ran into Grissy's legs, and instead of bowling her over like I would expect a 350-pound dude to do to a hundred-or-so pound woman, it was like I'd run into iron bars. I looked up in surprise and saw nothing but skillet rushing down at my face. The world exploded into stars, and that was the last thing I remember.

I woke up butt-naked and hanging by my wrists from a pair of handcuffs. The handcuffs were suspended from the ceiling by a chain that went up to a thick wooden beam, but I couldn't see how it fastened up there. The cuffs had just enough slack in them to let me stand on tiptoes, but I couldn't get much relief from the pressure on my shoulders. As my vision cleared, I realized that unlike every other time I'd woken up naked swinging by handcuffs in my life, this time wasn't a dream. And there were no Playmates anywhere. I was a little disappointed, then downright disconsolate when I looked around enough to see that I was hanging naked in a room with two other guys.

"Ranger Jerry, I suppose?" I asked the one hanging closest to me.

"Yeah, how'd you know?" He observed the talking at urinals section of The Guy Code and looked only at my face.

"I'm Bubba. I been looking for you. And I reckon the rest of these guys, too."

"Yeah, they're all here. I don't know what she's going to do to us . . ."

"But it probably won't be near as much fun as what I had planned, Jerry old pal." I grinned, and he chuckled. I heard a weak laugh from behind me and spun around to look at the other guy. He was hanging the same way I was and looked a lot worse off than me. I recognized him as Aaron Kennedy from the pictures Skeeter'd sent me, and figured that I'd found some of the folks I was supposed to rescue, now I just had to get on with the rescuing.

Suddenly the floor lurched and I lost my footing, putting all my weight on my wrists and shoulder sockets. I tried to reach up to the chain to take some of the strain off my wrists, but couldn't get twisted right, so I just hung there in agony as the floor rocked back and forth, like we were suddenly on a boat in the middle of a storm.

"What the hell is that?" I asked Jerry.

"I don't know. I just got here this morning," he said.

Aaron didn't have anything useful to add, and after a few minutes, the ride stopped and I managed to get my feet under me. My shoulders gave a sigh of relief, and I took another look around the room. In one corner was a big sturdy table, with enough knives and saws hanging over it to make a dozen Ginsu knife commercials. Dark brown stains covered the surface of the wood, and my stomach did a little flip-flop.

"Hey, Jerry. Did she say anything to you about coming to dinner?"

"Yeah, she did. She mentioned dinner just before she drugged my tea."

"What about you, Aaron?" I raised my voice. He answered in the affirmative. That sinking feeling in my gut came back, stronger than ever. We'd been invited to dinner, but not as guests. We were the entrees.

I looked up at the cuffs and the chain again, mentally measuring the strength of the average set of police-issue handcuffs against my own sense of self-preservation. I figured most days it was about fifty-fifty. I jumped as much as I could off my tiptoes and grabbed the chain, then started to pull myself up hand over hand.

"This might be uncomfortable, Jerry," I told the ranger as I started to swing my feet back and forth. The more I swung, the closer I came to Jerry. He started to pull back from the giant naked redneck swinging at him from handcuffs, but I wrapped my legs around his torso, using his body to take some of the strain off my arms for a second.

"Don't get any ideas, pal. I'm really not interested. But I gotta get us out of here before she decides who she wants to be the appetizer. I managed to wriggle around until my ankles were on Jerry's shoulders, and pulled myself up until I could at least see the end of the chain. I heard a choir of angels singing in my head when I saw the tiny shackle holding the chain wrapped around the beam. Obviously Grissy hadn't expected anybody to be crazy enough to get to the beam, so she just used a normal screw-pin shackle to hold the chain together. If I could get my hands up there, I could unscrew the pin and be free.

But that meant that I had to get my big ass up there, and even pulling myself up the chain and getting my feet onto Jerry's shoulders, I was still a good four feet under the beam.

"Crap. This is gonna suck," I muttered under my breath.

"Well it ain't exactly peaches and cream from here," Jerry muttered right back, keeping his eyes squeezed shut against the sight of my dangly bits hanging right in front of his nose.

I pulled myself up a little more on the chain, then reached up with one foot as far as I could without losing my grip or my footing. Imagine a Sasquatch doing one of those aerialist acts with the bands of silk, only bare-ass naked, and you get a little idea of how bizarre that whole thing must have looked. I got my foot high enough to loop one big toe over the edge of the beam, then I pulled the other foot up. I managed to get my whole right foot hooked over the beam, then pulled my left over and locked my ankles together.

I let out a huge sigh and relaxed my grip, swinging upside-down from my crossed ankles and almost bumping into Jerry's face. He jerked back, a look of horror on his face.

"Don't worry," I said, grinning at him. "I don't kiss on the first date." I took a deep breath and swung up to the beam using my abs and the chain to pull myself up. I got my left hand on the beam and set to unscrewing the shackle pin with my right. A few seconds later, I dropped down from the beam to land on both feet in front of Jerry. I was still cuffed and still had six feet of chain hanging from the cuffs, but I wasn't dangling in midair anymore.

And of course that's when the door opened and Grissy walked in holding a cleaver and a carving knife that could have doubled as a short sword.

"You are a very naughty entree," she said, with a grin spreading over her face that said, "I am batshit, paste-eating, carve my initials in your butt cheeks crazy." She walked toward me, her pace slow and deliberate, her path cutting off any chance of escape, weapons flicking out side to side like she knew exactly how to use those toys to carve up a whole side of redneck du jour. I backed away, always keeping one hanging dude between me and Grissy, until my butt hit the table.

"Nowhere to go, Bubba. What are you going to do now? There's nowhere to run, no place to hide, no way out. What do you do?"

"Like Rowdy Roddy said, I chew bubble gum and kick ass. Only I ain't got no bubble gum." I butchered the quote, but I spun around and grabbed a couple knives of my own and charged Grissy with a lot more bravado than most folks expect from a naked dude.

The key to a knife fight isn't in not getting cut. It's in understanding that you're gonna get cut. You just try not to get anything cut off that you care too much about, and you try to cut more bits off the other guy than they cut off you. I had a serious reach advantage over Grissy, but she was a lot faster than me, and she didn't have her hands cuffed together.

She dodged my first charge without any real effort, but she got a little too close to one of the dangling men, who put a knee in the small of her back for her troubles. She winced and turned to him, then remembered that she was fighting me and spun back around. I was almost on her then, and she ducked aside again. Again she danced too close to one of her captives and got a kick in the side as a reminder. We kept dancing that way for a long minute or two, me charging, her dodging, the other guys kicking. It was starting to wear on Grissy when suddenly her eyes gleamed with an evil idea and she ducked behind the nearest hanging dude and threw the cleaver at me.

I knocked it to the ground with my chain, not willing to let it fly past and maybe kill somebody, then I froze as I saw her plan. She was using the hanging guy as a shield, hiding behind him so I couldn't get at her, and she had her hand wrapped around his pride and joy with the edge of her knife pressed against it.

"One more step and I geld this stallion." She giggled at her clever-ness, and the guy whimpered. Aaron Kennedy, missing climber, was about to be missing a piton unless I thought fast. Too bad for him thinking fast ain't what they hire me for.

"Go ahead," I said and took one step closer.

"I mean it!" Grissy screeched.

"Dude, stop!" Aaron Kennedy was looking very concerned, and I didn't really blame him.

"I don't care, lady. Cut it off. You want to chop us all up and serve us in a stew, so go ahead and start with the shrimp cocktail." Some-times I amaze myself with my wit.

"What? What kind of hero are you?" She looked baffled. I get that look from women a lot. Especially when they're looking at me naked.

"I'm no hero, lady. I'm a hunter. I'm here to find out what happened to these dudes and kill whatever was making it happen. I found out there's a psycho hosebeast out in the woods that wants to chop dudes up into Hamburger Helper, so now it's time for Part 2— the killing part. Now you do what you gotta do to Aaron there, but I'm gonna rip your head off regardless."

She looked at me for a long time, like she was trying to see if I was serious. I was, by the way. I'm sure Aaron Kennedy is a nice dude, but I didn't really care if he got to keep his pecker or not. I was hired to kill the bad guy, or girl in this case, and I was gonna do that no matter what happened to him. After a minute that probably felt like a year to the guy with a butcher knife on his junk, she burst into tears and fell to her knees. The knife clattered to the floor and Aaron let out a huge breath.

"But I don't WANT to get old!" she wailed, pounding on the floor with her fists. I looked around, but none of the dudes hanging like sides of beef had anything to contribute. I stepped forward, picked up the knife, and snatched Grissy up by the hair and dragged her over to the table. I threw her face-up on the table and pressed my knife to her throat.

"What the hell are you squalling about?"

"I have to eat the stew to stay young. It's the flesh of men that keeps the change from happening."

"I repeat—what the hell are you talking about?" She curled up in a little ball on the table, sobbing uncontrollably. I wasn't getting anything useful out of her until she got her crap together, so I frisked her. For the keys, not just for fun. The keys were in her pocket, so I unlocked my cuffs and used them to chain her to the table. Then I let the other guys loose and sent Ranger Jerry off to look for our clothes.

He made it almost to the door when he froze. "Uh, Bubba? We've got company."

I turned to the door and there stood Esme and Minerva. Grissy's older and way, way older sister, and they looked pretty irritated.

"Hey y'all. How's it going? I hope you weren't expecting dude stew for dinner 'cause there's been a little change in the menu." I motioned to Grissy, tied to the table, and the roomful of naked men.

"That's how she was doing it," Esme said, as if I'd unlocked some great secret.

"Of course, how could we be so stupid?" Minerva replied.

I was confused, but that's pretty much my normal state around women, so I waved Ranger Jerry on to go find clothes. "I'm not gonna have to fight y'all too, am I? 'Cause I really feel like I've hit my quota on beating up crazy women for the day."

"No, Bubba, you won't have to fight us. Why don't you come into the den and we'll explain everything." Minerva turned and walked away, Esme following. I shrugged and started after her. Then I paused and handed the knife to Aaron.

"If she tries anything, stab her. A lot." He grinned a little and stood over Grissy with the knife. I decided that she really didn't want to move right then.

Minerva and Esme were on the couch when I made it back into the den. Ranger Jerry came out of the bedroom dressed in his uniform and carrying a pile of clothes. I held up a finger to the ladies in a "just a sec" gesture and retrieved my pants from Jerry. I pulled on my jeans and t-shirt, then strapped on Bertha and sat down in a chair facing the sisters.

"Would you mind telling me exactly what the hell is going on here?" I asked.

"Where to begin?" Minerva asked.

"Try the beginning, dear," Esme chimed in.

Minerva glared at her, then went on. "Have you ever heard of the Baba Yaga, Bubba?"

"Yeah, I think so. Flies around in a mortar and pestle, house with chicken legs, that Baba Yaga?"

"That's the one," Minerva replied. "Except there isn't just one of us. We are all the Baba Yaga."

"Wait, like you're all three the Baba Yaga? Like, all of you?" Then it hit me. Shit. The Crone, the Mother, and the Maiden. The Furies. Double shit. I just chained one of the Furies to a butcher's table and left her with a bunch of pissed-off naked dudes. This might be bad.

"Are you sure I'm not going to have to fight you two now? I did just beat up your sister, after all."

"Not only are you not going to have to fight us, you have done us a great service. Griselda has held the form of the Maiden for longer than is natural, using her manflesh stew to prevent the rotation from taking place," Minerva explained calmly.

"It's my turn to be young and beautiful, and that bitch has held on too long!" Esme spat.

"So what, y'all take turns being . . ." I wasn't even sure what I was trying to say, so I shut up and waved at Minerva.

"Yes, exactly. We alternate which aspect we represent. We change with the solstice, the holy days."

"But the summer solstice was like a month ago." Then it all fell into place. "And she's been making dinner for y'all ever since, making some excuse as to why you weren't changing. And I bet it was stew every time."

"Once it was meatloaf," Esme said. I felt like puking, but I kept it together.

"So you've been eating the men that went missing in the forest, and that's what has kept you from changing into your other forms." I stood up and loosened Bertha in her holster.

"Where are you going?" Minerva asked.

"I'm going to shoot your sister in the face."

"You can't do that."

"Would you like to watch? Because I'm pretty sure I not only can, but I'm going to. You see, that's how the whole monster hunter thing works. I find monsters, I shoot monsters. Crazy witch-hotties that eat dudes definitely qualify as monsters. So I'm going to go shoot the crazy witch-hottie."

"It won't matter. It won't kill her. We're immortal."

"Let's test that theory. I've got white phosphorous rounds for the fire-haters, blessed rounds dipped in holy water for the demonic, cold iron rounds for the Fae, silver rounds for the lycanthropic, and hollow points for every damn thing else. I bet I can find something that she doesn't like."

"I never said she'd like it, I just said it wouldn't kill her. She'd just heal, and then she'd hunt you down forever. And with the flying mortar and the house, there's nowhere she can't go."

That created a problem. I thought for a minute, then offered Minerva a deal. She and Esme talked about it for a long time, then finally agreed. They packed up their crazy-ass sister and toted her off into the woods, her shrieking the whole time about revenge.

Ranger Jerry and I went outside, turn the mortar over and set it up to be the enormous stewpot I'd originally mistaken it for, and used the furniture from the cabin to build a roaring fire. Then we did the only thing you can do to disable a magical walking house on giant chicken legs. We cooked the legs into chicken stew. Let me tell you, magical-house chicken legs really do taste like chicken.

5

H O W L

I was already pissed off when the phone rang, so I went ahead and answered it. "What?" I growled into the little speaker. I knew it was Skeeter on account of his face showing up on the screen and also on account of him being the only human being brave enough to call me on a Saturday afternoon in September. It was the first game of the season, and my Georgia Bulldogs had just finished losing, and worse than that, losing to the Clemson Tigers. It's one thing to lose a football game, that's bad enough, but to lose to a team from the *ACC*, that just didn't feel natural.

"Bubba, you gotta get over here right now!" Skeeter's voice was higher than usual, which was not only a little frightening, it was also just barely on the edge of human hearing. I was pretty sure if he got any more excited, any dogs within a hundred yards were gonna start going nuts.

"What's wrong, Skeeter? Your internet go out in the middle of *Edward Penishands* again? You know how the story ends, just reset the router and watch something else for a minute."

"This ain't no joke, Bubba! I'm in the panic room. Get over here and bring Bertha!"

I sobered up instantly. Of course I was going to take Bertha, I didn't take a piss without my .50 Desert Eagle slung under my arm, but for Skeeter to hole up in his panic room meant some serious shit was going down. I switched off the TV and reached for my boots.

"I'm on the way. Are you in the basement, or all the way in the closet?" I slammed my feet into my steel-toed boots and headed for the door. I stopped just before I hit the porch and grabbed my heavy-duty jacket, the one with plates of body armor sewn into the lining. I'm a big dude, but the last time Skeeter had gone into his panic room, I ended up with three feet of steel poking through my gut. If a twenty-pound leather and ceramic plate jacket could keep that from happening again, it was worth breaking a sweat.

"I'm downstairs. It ain't got through the front door yet, so I don't see any need to get into the safe room. And don't call it a closet, that's offensive." Skeeter gets touchy about any kind of closet references. I don't understand it, but I didn't grow up the only gay kid in three counties, either.

I was at my truck by the time he quit bitching at me. "What is 'it' exactly, Skeeter? You never bothered to tell me what I'm coming to rescue your ass from."

"It's a Bigfoot, Bubba. There's a goddamn butt-naked Sasquatch on my front porch knocking on the door and hollerin' for you. Now would you please get your ass over here before it decides to stop being polite and rips my door off the hinges?"

I froze behind the wheel of the truck. I'd run into a Bigfoot about a year ago, and he solid whooped my ass. But once he got done beating my head in, he turned out to be a pretty reasonable dude. If it was the same monster, there was a chance we could avoid bloodshed. If not, there wasn't a whole lot of doubt that blood was gonna spill. I was just worried it was all gonna be mine.

I got to Skeeter's house about ten minutes later, and sure enough, there was, as Skeeter so delicately put it, a butt-naked Sasquatch sitting on the rocking chair on Skeeter's front porch. I got out of the truck and started toward the house slowly, one hand on Bertha and the other pointing at the Bigfoot. The monster stood up when I approached, holding up both hands like he was harmless. As harmless as an eight-foot tall hairy half-man covered in brown fur and swinging his kielbasa all over a front porch could look anyway.

"Don't move, or I'll shoot your big hairy ass."

"I don't think you will, Bubba. You tried that before, and it didn't go so well." So it was the same Bigfoot. That relaxed me a little bit, then another thought hit me and I stopped.

"What are you doing here? When I last saw you, we had an agreement about me killing my old man and you staying hidden in the woods. I thought that sounded like a pretty good idea for everybody."

"Except it didn't work out that way, did it? You didn't get the job done, and now I need your help."

My Bluetooth chirped and I pushed the button. "Come on out, Skeeter. This dude ain't gonna kill you. He just wanted to get my attention. Now he's done it, but I ain't sure he knows what to do with it."

Bigfoot sat back down on the rocking chair and said, "Oh, I know what to do with you, and your little friend. But I hate repeating myself, so why don't we wait for the last member of our little party to show up?"

"Huh?" It might not have been the most eloquent thing to ever come out of my mouth, but it was honest. "What in the hell are you talking about? I ain't called nobody else."

"I did." Skeeter opened his front door and stepped out, a Mossberg shotgun that probably weighed half what he did held on the Bigfoot. "I buzzed Amy the same time I called you. I didn't talk to her. I just sent a distress signal."

"What, you didn't think I could handle this hairy prick?" I asked, a little insulted.

"You couldn't last time," Bigfoot said calmly from the chair. I looked back at Skeeter, a little annoyed that my best friend didn't think I could take out one Sasquatch without help.

"It wasn't that, Bubba. I just thought you might not answer, it being Saturday and all." He had a point. It was football season, and if Georgia had won, I probably woulda been too drunk to find the phone, much less fight a Bigfoot.

I didn't have to defend my honor and the bro-code sanctity of coming to the aid of a friend in need because just then a black Suburban roared to a stop beside my blue F-250 and Amy Hall vaulted to the ground. She was in all black tactical gear with her long blonde hair pulled back in a tight ponytail, a Glock in one hand and a SOG knife in the other. She looked like something out of *La Femme Nikita*, and the sight of her in full ass-kicking gear made my jeans a little tight in the crotch all of a sudden.

"Where is it? I got here as fast as I could." She was halfway to the porch before she realized that we were all standing around in a fairly civilized fashion. That slowed her up a bit, and then she saw Bigfoot sitting on the porch like somebody's hairy third cousin who showed up for the family reunion, ate all the white meat fried chicken, and then sat around like a king even though nobody really remembered what side of the family he was on or how exactly he was kin. Just for an example.

Bigfoot stood up, not quite straight because of the porch roof, and nodded to Agent Amy. "Agent Hall, good of you to join us. May we go inside? I'm sure you'd all be more comfortable." He made a grand gesture with one arm, and we all filed inside like it was an every Saturday kinda thing, being escorted into Skeeter's living room by a Sasquatch with excellent manners.

I did what I always do when I first get to Skeeter's house, ever since we were teenagers—I went to the fridge. Except nowadays I get a beer instead of a Coke. I grabbed a Bud for me, a Mike's Hard Lemonade for Skeeter, a Stella for Amy, and then stopped. I realized I had no idea what kind of beer a Bigfoot drank. Or even if he drank beer. I immediately discarded that last bit because he seemed pretty civilized, so of course he drank beer. Then I remembered that I first met him in Virginia, so I grabbed another Bud and went back into the den. Agent Amy was sitting on the couch, her Glock on the table beside her in easy reach. Skeeter was in his favorite chair, a striped thing with a footstool that he called an ottoman. He got it at Ikea in Atlanta or some other froofy store and spent a small fortune getting it reupholstered after my pop and his werewolf pack tore up all his crap and peed all over everything last fall. Bigfoot was sitting in my usual spot in the rocker/recliner, so I passed out beers and sat down next to Amy, careful to keep enough space between my side and her elbow so I could get to Bertha in a hurry if I needed to.

We sat there sipping beer and staring at each other for a good half a minute before I finally spoke up. "Well? What do you want?" I asked.

Bigfoot had the good grace to at least pretend to be a little embarrassed. "You wouldn't believe that I just came to visit?"

"Across two states and a couple hundred miles? On foot? Nah, somehow I don't buy it. You said something about needing my help. So spill it." I leaned back and knocked off the rest of my beer in one long pull.

Bigfoot matched me swallow for swallow and then passed me the empty. "You might want to go get another round. This is going to take a while."

∼

BIGFOOT'S STORY

First of all, call me Ishmael. Get it? I didn't expect you to, but I had to hope. Anyway, my name is Brar'kan, and I'm the *sheeran* of all the Eastern Sasquatch. That's similar to a crown prince in human terms, but it's a little more complicated than that. My father is the leader of the gathered tribes, and provided I prove myself worthy, I will lead the tribes when he dies. But my role is also that of the protector, the guardian of our youth and our women. We are a nomadic people, and our lives have become very difficult since the arrival of the white man on our shores. We can no longer range freely through the forests, hunting at our leisure, and moving on when an area becomes short of game and food. Now we must hide deep in the woods and mountains, and we cannot roam as far afield as we once did.

But we survive. We are few, and there are fewer of us born each generation. Once thousands of us roamed this land in peace with the animals and the brown men, but now maybe a hundred remain scattered from what you call South America all the way up to the tip of Canada, which we call The White Land.

When last we met, I told you of The Messiah, who you called your father. Many of my tribe wished to follow him and rise up against the humans. My father and I did not want this, and there was much dissension in the tribe. They even cast me out and stripped me of my rank for my belief. But when I returned to them with news of the Monster Hunter who would kill The Messiah, my father was able to sway the mind of the tribe, and I was restored to my place as *sheeran*. We heard no more from The Messiah, and we assumed that you had kept your word. We moved on from that place to the swamplands near what you call Mobile, far from the mountains and far from The Messiah. We settled in and were happy.

But all were not pleased with these events. One in particular, the Sasquatch who had taken my place as *sheeran,* was angry at my father's decision, and at my return. His name is Clag'tin, and he is a mighty warrior, almost as mighty as I. He left our tribe to seek out The Messiah and join his cause. I paid him little heed because Bubba the Monster Hunter was going to kill The Messiah, so Clag'tin's quest was in vain. I expected him to return weeks later, his tail tucked between his legs.

No, we don't really have tails, stop looking. I'm allowed to use metaphor. Unlike some in this room, I know what the word means.

Clag'tin did indeed return to our tribe some weeks later, but he did not return in shame. He returned at the vanguard of a host of wolves and bears and trolls, with a huge werewolf walking beside him. This werewolf carried a sword and spoke with the tongue of a man, and he ordered my tribe to bend knee before him and swear loyalty. My father, a proud Sasquatch of one hundred twenty summers, snarled that he would die before he bent his knee before a dog.

And he did. The Messiah lashed out with his sword faster than my eye could follow and struck my father's head from his shoulders. He murdered our clan leader without the blink of an eye, and my people, instead of tearing this monster limb from limb, knelt before their new master.

I did not kneel. What I did was much worse. I saw the look in Clag'tin's eye as he scanned the gathered people and knew that he looked for me. I knew that I would not be given the chance to kneel, so I ran. I turned my back on my people, on my tribe, and I ran. I ran for three days through woods and fields before I found a monster that knew of you. After that I ran for a week or more before I found you here. And now I sit here before you, a coward seeking help he does not deserve from a man sworn to destroy his kind. I deserve nothing but death, but my tribe deserves freedom. Will you help me save them?

I stood up, walked across Skeeter's living room and looked out the picture window. Skeeter had a helluva view, I had to give him that. The Smoky Mountains spilled out in front of that big window like a postcard, and I stood there for a long time processing what Bigfoot had just told me. After a minute, I saw Agent Amy standing next to me in my reflection, and I reached out to take her hand in my gigantic mitt.

I turned back to Bigfoot, finished off my beer, and gave him a long, level look. "What ain't you telling me?"

"I have told you everything of importance."

"Bullshit." I walked into the kitchen and grabbed another beer. When I walked back into the room, Bigfoot was on his feet and Amy had her Glock pointed at his nose.

"Put that down," I said, pushing the barrel of the pistol down. She holstered her sidearm, and I stepped up to the monster. He towered over me, but right then I knew it didn't matter which one of us was bigger, or which one of us was tougher, or smarter, or braver. All that mattered was that he thought I had a snowball's chance in hell of

kicking my brother's ass and taking his tribe back. I didn't, but that
was beside the point. First I needed to know one thing.

"Boy or girl?" I asked, looking up into his big brown eyes.

There was a little bit of water there, making my reflection waver
in his pupils. *Crap. I hate it when I'm right.*

"A daughter. He has my mate and daughter. Please help me save
them." The eight foot tall monster sat down in Skeeter's recliner so
hard I was pretty sure we were taking another trip to the La-Z-Boy
store if any of us were alive next week.

"Quit boo-hooin' and start drinkin'. We leave after tomorrow's
Mass. Might as well get drunk tonight." I killed one more beer and
then moved on to getting seriously shit-faced.

"Why tomorrow?" Brar'kan asked. I was gonna have to get that boy
a nickname pretty soon. Names with apostrophes in 'em belong on
Stargate, not my best friend's living room.

"Because that's when Uncle Father Joe will be off work, and if
we're huntin' the Messiah of yours—"

"Who happens to be your asshole kid brother," Skeeter cut in.

"Who happens to be my asshole kid brother—" I agreed. "It
wouldn't hurt to have some higher firepower on our side to go along
with all the guns and silver bullets in the back of Amy's Suburban."

"How did you know I brought a truckload of ammo?" she asked.

"I heard it spill when you slid in sideways like Dale Earnhardt on
his way to a fistfight. Trust me, I've dumped enough ammo out in the
back of a truck to know what it sounds like, even from outside. And
you got a helluva mess to clean up, young lady." I grinned at her. "But
all that hardware might come in handy. Jason's a tough bastard."

"I remember." There was no answering grin on her face, and I
knew she was remembering the last time we fought my kid brother.
She'd airlifted me to a hospital in a black helicopter that belongs to a
government agency that doesn't exist, and I almost died in her arms.
Then I almost died again in the arms of a succubus masquerading as a
nurse, but that's a whole different thing.

"This time'll be different. I promise."

"How?" she asked.

"This time I'm not going to let him stab me."

"Good idea." She waved an empty beer bottle at me and raised an eyebrow. I was halfway to the kitchen before I realized that she had me jumpin' even before she said "frog." I thought about that for a second, decided I didn't mind the least little bit, and got an armload of beer out of the fridge.

~

I didn't make it to Sunday school the next morning, but Amy, Skeeter and I were sitting on the front row of the Catholic Church when Uncle Father Joe walked down the aisle for Mass. His eyes widened when he saw us, and he gave me a little nod. After Mass, we stayed right where we were until Joe finished greeting his parishioners and came back in. Joe was Skeeter's uncle, the priest of the local Catholic Church, and our liaison to the Church leadership in the US. Usually we took assignments from Joe for what to hunt down and kill. This was a little bit of role reversal, and I could tell from the worry line between Joe's eyebrows that he didn't like it. There was a touch of gray in his hair that hadn't been there six months ago, but I reckon being kidnapped by a psychotic werewolf would do that to a body.

"What's going on?" he asked, stripping out of his robe. I covered Amy's eyes and she elbowed me in the ribs. She was right; Joe was fully dressed under his robes, down to a paddle holster on his right hip with what looked like a 1911 in it.

"You expecting trouble at the offering plate, Padre?" I asked, giving an eyeball to the sidearm.

"There's been an incident or two in town over the past year or so," Joe said. "There's a twelve-gauge behind the pulpit loaded with silver shot and all the ushers are packing revolvers with silver loads and stakes, just in case your brother expands his flock to include vampires."

"I thought vampires couldn't come onto holy ground," I said. I wasn't sure whether I was more disturbed or relieved at the fact that

Joe had turned the church into an armed compound, but I let the Waco jokes alone.

"I thought werewolves couldn't fight in their half-transformed state, but it seems that where Jason is concerned, all bets are off. I figured better safe than sorry." He had a point, but if Jase added vamps to his little army of furballs, I was gonna have serious trouble. Weres are bad, but they at least act like people or animals, depending on what shape they're in. Vamps are mean, nasty, fast, and smart. They think like humans, only humans out of a Jack Ketchum novel, and that's some seriously scary shit right there.

"Now what's going on?" Joe asked.

"Better to just show you," I said. I walked over to the side door of the church and pushed it open. Brar'kan ducked through the door into the church, and I heard Joe breathe in sharply behind me.

"It's cool," I said. "This is Bart. He's a Bigfoot—"

"Sasquatch. And my name is Brar'kan," he corrected me.

"It's hard to pronounce. So you're Bart. Or Barry. Think of it like a nickname." I turned back to look at Joe. "Barry here needs help. Jason killed his pop, the clan leader, and took over his clan. Barry wants 'em back. Especially his wife and kid."

Joe's eyes were big. "There's more than one Bigfoot?"

"Sasquatch," Barry corrected, a little more gently this time in deference to the collar.

"Sasquatch," Joe repeated. "There's more than one of you? And you travel in clans? And you breed?"

"Of course we breed. You don't think we'd mate with *humans* do you? You have practically no hair. That would be disgusting, all that flesh sliding around and slapping together. How sweaty." Barry shuddered a little at the thought.

"Some of us like all that flesh sliding around, pal. But that's not the point," I added quickly as Amy shot me a look that said *keep your mouth shut you jackass, we're in a church*. "The point is that we gotta go after Jason and get Barry's wife and kid back. Since it's kinda my fault that this all happened in the first place."

"How do you figure it's your fault, Bubba? I mean, I'm cool to blame you for just about everything bad and stupid that's ever happened in my life, but even I can't put this one off on you," Skeeter said.

"It's my fault because I promised Barry I'd kill Jason and I didn't get the job done. So now it's time to finish what I started. I can't do it alone, so I need y'all to help me."

That hung in the air of the church mixing with the incense and smell of cheap red wine until Joe nodded. "Let's go. My bike is behind the church. I'll meet you around front."

He pulled his Harley around front, and I noticed that he had made a couple of modifications to the bike since the last time I'd seen it. Most notably the Mossberg shotgun in a sling beside the gas tank and a windscreen with a cutout to shoot through. I didn't say a word, since my truck had a few after-market accessories that Homeland Security wouldn't be too thrilled with, and we won't even talk about what was under the back seat. Barry slid into the passenger seat and Amy hopped in behind me while Skeeter headed home. He'd finally learned how to shoot without too much fear of him shooting off his own toes, but I still didn't want to be in the same zip code as him and a firearm. He was much more use to use at home on the computer, running technical interference with the local constabulary and researching whatever we were getting ourselves into.

I pushed a button next to the map lights in my truck's roof and a little blue light came on. "Come in, Skeeter, this is Big Papi."

"Who the hell ever called you Big Papi?" Skeeter's shrill voice came through the Bluetooth connection loud and clear, maybe a little clearer than I wanted.

"I figured I needed a handle, so we could know who was who on the comm link," I said. I thought Big Papi sounded cool, personally.

"I think I'll probably know you if you says it's Bubba, jackass." I heard Joe snicker and realized that Skeeter had patched him in so we could all talk.

Joe's new full-face helmet cut most of the wind noise out so we all heard him crystal clear. "Bubba, where are we headed?"

"Mobile," Barry said.

I looked over at him. "Mobile? I like a good poker game as much as the next guy, but seriously, your tribe is hanging out in the gambling capital of the Southeast?"

"Drunken gamblers are terrible witnesses. Most of the sightings in the area are quickly dismissed and that makes it a good place to raise our young. They get the experience of avoiding humanity without heavier consequences. And we like to fish," Barry said, fidgeting a little in his seat. "Do I have to wear these things? They bind a little." He pulled at the cotton on his leg.

"Yes, you have to wear the shorts. I'm pretty open-minded, but I don't want some butt-naked dude sitting on my upholstery." I had to cut up a perfectly good pair of sweatpants to make shorts for the gigantic Sasquatch, but then got a good giggle out of him walking around in bright red sweats with "Go Dawgs" written down the legs. It seemed ironic, somehow.

It took about seven hours to get from Joe's church to the outskirts of Mobile, Alabama. We pulled off on a little dirt road just outside of Blakely Park, a little town east of Mobile that looked like a cross between Mayberry and *Duck Dynasty*. We got out of the truck and Joe pulled up behind us and put down his kickstand.

"What now, big guy?" I asked. Once everybody was out of the truck, I flipped up the back seats to give access to the custom gun cabinets I had built into the truck. Bertha was in her normal spot under my left arm, but I figured this was going to be a more up-close and personal kind of fight, so I tucked my Judge revolver into the back of my belt and loaded up on my dirtiest fighting tricks. A pair of brass knuckles went into each pocket of my cargo pants, and I strapped a pair of kukri knives onto my belt. Another couple of Gerber Guardian Backup double-edged tactical daggers went into sheaths on my lower legs and my new Benchmade tactical tomahawk slipped into a sling over one shoulder. I tucked a couple of other knives, spikes, and surprises in pockets and slipped my jacket on top of all of it. I was about fifty pounds heavier when it was all said and done, but I was armed to the teeth and reinforced at all the joints and soft spots from the neck down, so I figured I could go toe-to-toe with a badass bigfoot if I couldn't talk my way out of this mess. And if Barry was any judge of character among his own species, there was no way in hell I was talking my way out of this scrap.

"You look like Darth Vader and Bane's love child," Joe said.

"Yeah, well you look like a storm trooper, so I guess we're even. Joe still had his helmet on, but had swapped out his tinted face shield for a clear one. His riding leathers would protect him from most claw strikes, and he had his Mossberg on his back and Colt 1911 on his hip. He was a badass Man of God, all right. Amy pulled her hair back into a long ponytail and yanked a black balaclava down over her face and hair, leaving only her eyes exposed. I knew she was wearing a lot of Kevlar and toting a pair of Sig Sauer 9mm pistols loaded with silver hollowpoints, not to mention any nasty surprises she had tucked away under that tac vest. A H&K MP5 with a suppressor was her preferred short-range gun, and I'd seen her put in work on the range, so I wasn't worried about her ability to hit anything she wanted to put holes in. I was more worried about whether or not we could live long enough to get a shot off.

"What's the plan, Barry? You want a gun or something? I got a couple spares."

He looked into the back seat of the truck and shook his head at the arsenal there. "I don't use weapons. None of our people do. It's a matter of pride."

"It'll be a matter of dead if that asshole we're hunting has changed his mind about that. But whatever you say. Now where are we going?" I made one last gear check, slipped one more magazine for Bertha into my back pocket, and locked the truck. I've never been in the situation where I've regretted carrying too much ammunition, but I've damn sure experienced the opposite once or twice.

"Our last camp was a few miles north of here. We should go on foot so as to avoid arousing notice." Barry turned and headed up a trail so narrow as to barely deserve the name, and I was wishing I was the one wearing a motorcycle helmet in a few seconds as the branches started to lash me across the face.

"Whoever said this was the way to avoid attention has obviously never traipsed through the woods with Bubba," Amy said from behind me, and I heard Skeeter snicker in my ear.

"You got us on GPS, Skeeter?" I asked.

"Better than that, I got video through Joe's helmet cam. You want to duck now." I did and missed a branch that was just high enough to be out of my eye line but low enough to piss me off.

"Thanks, Skeeter."

"That's what you keep me around for, bro," he said in my ear. We walked the rest of the way in silence, giving me way too much time to think about the mess we were walking into. My baby brother had somehow developed dreams of megalomania, got himself turned into a werewolf, built a whole half-assed religion around killing me, and come pretty damned close to achieving his personal nirvana the last time we tangled. I didn't know if I could take him if he was here, but I owed it to Barry and his people to try. They were in a mess because I didn't get the job done the first time, and damned if I was going to let that happen again.

"Penny for 'em," Amy said, sliding up next to me at a wider spot in the trail.

"You don't want to know." I kept my voice low both to keep from attracting predators and because I didn't need Barry hearing my doubts.

"This isn't your fault, Bubba."

"You want to explain exactly how that could be, darlin'? 'Cause way I see it, if I'd stuck a sword through my brother's guts a couple months ago instead of the other way around, Barry's daddy would still be alive, he'd still be sheriff or whatever his word for it is, and his woman and kids wouldn't be in trouble. Then we could be out on a lake getting drunk and pretending to give a shit about fishing instead of traipsing through the woods in Lower Goddamn Alabama hunting Bigfoot and the mother-lovin' Wolfman."

"Okay, maybe it is all your fault. Maybe you should have just smothered your little brother in his crib like all those self-righteous assholes who talk about traveling through time and killing Hitler when he was a baby. Bubba, shit happens for a reason. I'm not smart enough or holy enough to pretend to know what that reason is, but there's a reason for it. And if you had killed Jason, then some other monster would have come along and given Barry's asshole friend Clag'tin an excuse to kill his father and steal his tribe. And then we'd be down here hunting that asshole instead of Jason. But we'd still be here. Because this is what we do. Shit gets fucked up, and we fix it. Now get your head on straight before you get yourself killed." She reached up and grabbed me by the collar and I couldn't tell by the fierce look on her face whether she was going to beat my ass or kiss me, but she pulled the bottom of that ski mask down and laid the hottest damn kiss on me that I'd ever felt by a human being. Shit, it was hotter than the last time I got dry-humped by a succubus, and that's not something I say every day.

She let me go and I stood up straight, looking down at her with my eyes crossed a little. I shook myself like a dog getting out of a creek on a July afternoon and squared up my shoulders. I looked around at Barry and Joe, who were leaning against a tree watching our little exchange, and said, "What are you assholes looking at? Let's go kick some furry ass. I got shit to attend to with this woman."

Joe grinned, Barry let out a low growl, and I heard Skeeter sniff in my headset. "That's just about the sweetest thing I've ever heard you say, Bubba."

"Fuck off, Skeeter."

We tromped through the woods for another hour or so before we came to a clearing with a camper and a little Hyundai SUV parked in it. There was a dirt road coming in from the north that must have been how the campers got in, but there were no signs of anything moving when we crossed the tree line.

"Don't move," Barry said, holding up a fist at right angles to his arm.

"You know we ain't in the army, right? The 'don't move' is fine; we don't need the G.I. Joe arm signals. What's up?" I said, stopping right behind him.

"I smell something."

"Yeah, sorry about that. I meant to warn you when we stopped for gas and I got them barbecue pork rinds. I love 'em, but they don't always sit so good, if you know what I mean."

"I'm not talking about your flatulence, Bubba, which is spectacular, by the way, and makes me very glad that I usually travel by running outdoors instead of riding in enclosed vehicles with you. There's something dead here."

"I said I was sorry."

"No, in the camper."

"Oh. Shit."

"Yes, shit." I liked that about Barry. Even though we weren't the same species, we were still able to communicate in that way that guy can, with one curse word taking up a whole sentence or two.

"What's up?" Amy asked.

"Barry smells dead things, and it's probably the people that drove that camper in here," I said. That whole "communicate with one curse word" thing doesn't work with women. Something about all that estrogen makes them want shit explained.

"Why do you think that? Couldn't it be an animal or something like that?" she asked.

"It could, but it ain't real likely. You see, out in the woods, dead things get eaten by things that eat dead things. They don't just hang out and rot. So if something's just hanging out and rotting, there's a good reason for it. And that reason is usually that it's either hidden away somewhere that scavengers can't get to it, or it's too dangerous to go near the kill. Both of those things point to there being one or more dead people in that camper, and probably killed by Jason or our band of bitchy Bigfeet. Bigfoots. What's the plural of Bigfoot?"

"Sasquatch is the plural of sasquatch. And we really hate the term Bigfoot," Barry said.

"Yeah, and I hate people getting eaten in the woods when all they wanted was a little fresh air for their nookie." I stepped out into the clearing and started looking around. The SUV looked pretty intact, so they hadn't tried to leave. The camper was set up, the sides extended and the front feet down and locked. There was no fire pit built, but there were a couple of chairs and a cooler set out in a half-circle around a cleared spot of dirt where a fire was obviously going to go. I opened the lid of the cooler and stuck my hand inside, coming out with a Coors light can.

"Bubba! You are not stealing dead people's beer! That's too far, even for you," Amy shouted, stalking towards me from the trees.

"You're right, I wouldn't drink Coors from a live city slicker, much less steal a dead one's shitty beer. But this was recent."

"How can you tell?" Joe asked. He glanced my way but was keeping a close eye on our perimeter, shotgun at the ready.

"Mountains are still blue. Can's still really cold, and this ain't a very good cooler. So this wasn't here more than last night at the most. Amy, watch my back. I'm going inside."

Campers are a tight fit for me on my best day. I'm 6' 5" and tip the scales at 350 buck naked. Loaded for bear like I was, I pretty much had to crouch and walk sideways to get into the camper. That didn't leave me a whole lot of room to turn around and puke when I saw what was left of the campers. They were ripped open from throat to groin and their insides turned to outsides. The stench in the camper was enough to knock a buzzard off a shitwagon at a hundred paces, but I toughed it out, breathed through my shirt and tried to see any kind of evidence that might have been left behind. There were a few tufts of hair caught on a cabinet and the glint of something caught in one of the wounds. I pulled out my Leatherman and used the needle-nosed pliers to yank the piece of whatever out of the man's collarbone. I could tell it was stuck in his collarbone because he was laid open all the way up to it.

I stomped out of the camper and back over to the cooler. I flung the lid open and grabbed a beer out of it, pressing the cold aluminum to the little bump on the back of my skull until I was pretty sure I wasn't going to puke. I turned around and sat on the lid of the cooler. The plastic whimpered a little, but held under my weight.

"Bad?" Amy asked.

"As bad as anything I've ever seen," I replied.

"Goblins in the mines bad?" she asked, and I could almost hear her smile. God bless her, she was trying to get my mind off what I'd just seen.

"Drunk rakshasa puking on my shoes bad," I shot back. I held out the Leatherman for her to take a look at.

"What's this?" she asked. Joe and Barry had come over by this point, so I spoke up for everyone to hear.

"Werewolf claw, I'm pretty sure. Jason was here, along with something big. Probably your people, Barry. But it was the wolf that did that in there." I shuddered a little at the memory of what I'd seen.

"How many . . ." Joe started.

"Victims?"

He nodded.

"Two. A man and a woman. They were apparently up here for some together time, and that didn't end well for them."

"How do you know that's why they were here?" Joe asked.

I laughed for a second, then choked it off as the visuals came rushing back. "They were naked, Joe. They were naked, and they were together, and this monster ripped them apart. They just wanted to get away for a little while, and my goddamn brother . . . sorry for the G-D."

"Don't sweat it. I think it's pretty appropriate in reference to Jason." Joe turned and walked back over to the camper. He stopped at the door, but I watched as he pulled out his rosary and a small Bible from one of his back pockets and started waving his hands around.

"What is he doing?" Barry asked.

"I think he's giving them Last Rites," I said, a little confused. "Isn't it a little late for that?" I asked louder.

Joe didn't turn around until he was finished with whatever he was doing. Then he looked at me and said, "It's never too late to ask for the Father's grace and blessing upon his children. But those poor people don't need His help anymore. We, on the other hand, could use every advantage we can get. So I asked for a favor."

"What did He say?" I asked.

"All prayers are answered, Bubba." Joe gave me one of his inscrutable priestly smiles and closed the door to the camper.

"Yeah, too bad most of the time that answer's no," Skeeter said in my ear, perfectly echoing what was running through my head.

After the scene at the campsite, it was pretty easy to track the wolf. Bloody paw prints led off into the woods to the north, so that's the direction we took. The blood trail faded pretty quickly, but a werewolf and a bunch of Sasquatch moving through the woods leave a trail even Skeeter could follow, so it didn't stretch our woodcraft to find the furballs in question about two miles from where the campers had been slaughtered.

I waved Amy and Joe to fan out to the sides as Barry and I crouched at the tree line. There was a big cave mouth with a pair of Sasquatch standing guard, and a little trickle of smoke crept out of the cave and trailed off into the sky, letting us know that there were more folks inside.

"Does your tribe have some kind of tradition of honorable challenge and combat?" I whispered to Barry.

"Yes, why?"

"Because I really want to beat the shit out of something, and that seems like my best bet," I replied, stepping into the clearing. The Sasquatch to the right of the cave bellowed something that sounded like Chewbacca's mating call and ran inside. The one on the left looked at his buddy in surprise and then ran straight at me.

I had about fifty yards between me and the guard, so I had plenty of time to draw Bertha and put a round in his knee. I didn't warn him, didn't bother giving him a chance to surrender, I just shot the big hairy sonofabitch in the leg and chuckled a little as he rolled ass over teakettle to a stop right in front of me. He lay screaming in the dirt about ten feet away, making more racket than a two-peckered rooster in a henhouse, so I stepped up to him and pointed Bertha at his nose.

109

"Shut up," I said.

"It hurts!" he wailed.

I was very aware of the fact that it was male, since nobody was making him wear cutoff sweatpants, so I lowered my aim to something he might value more than his nose and repeated myself. "Shut. Up."

He shut his mouth so fast I think he bit off a piece of his tongue but was too scared to whine about it.

"Now we're just going to sit right here and wait until your boss comes out of that cave, then I'm going to kick his ass, kill my kid brother, and go home. If everything works out right, we'll be home in time to go to the grocery store before Monday Night Football. Worst case, I run a little late and have to do with what beer's in the fridge. Sound good?" He just lay there bleeding. I couldn't tell if he wasn't a football fan or thought his boss was going to kill me.

It was about another half a minute before the biggest damn Bigfoot I'd ever seen came storming out of that cave, carrying what I thought was a club the size of a small pine tree, until I realized that it *was* a small pine tree. He swung that thing like he was the real Big Papi and I was a little round ball, and would have taken my head off if I wasn't quicker than the average bear. Or human, for that matter. I ducked, rolled, and came up with Bertha leveled at the face of what I could only assume was Clag'tin.

"I reckon you're the HBIC?"

"What?" He growled.

"Head Bigfoot In Charge? Are you Clag'tin?" I asked. Monsters, they have no sense of humor.

"I am Clag'tin. What are you? You smell like human, but you move strong, like Sasquatch."

"I reckon that's a compliment. I'm Bubba. I shoot monsters. You're next on the list. Wanna run away now and save me a couple bucks in ammo? There's a recession, you know."

"I know you. You are human that pitiful Brar'kan battled. He bested you, and he is weak. I will kill you and feed your kidneys to my children."

"I ain't done with my kidneys yet, bub, so why don't we talk about this for a minute, then I'll beat your head in."

"No talk, just fight." He threw his sapling to one side and stepped towards me, arms out to crush me in a giant bear hug. Or Bigfoot hug, if we're gonna be all specific about it.

"I claim challenge," I said, never moving. He stopped so fast you woulda thought he was in a cartoon and just got hit with Daffy Duck's Freeze Ray. His eyes went wide, then he laughed, right in my face. And there are not very many things more disgusting than Sasquatch breath, lemme tell you. Watching goblins fornicate will do it, and pretty much any episode of a reality show featuring a Kardashian, but that's about it.

"You claim challenge? You challenge Clag'tin for leadership of my tribe? In combat?" He kept laughing, so it took a lot longer to get that out than it should have, but finally he wiped his eyes and said, "I accept!"

Clag'tin turned to the cave mouth and bellowed, "Challenge has been brought! Clag'tin must kill the human Bub'ba to remain *Sheeran-kor*!" He laughed again and pointed to me as a dozen or so Sasquatch came out of the cave and made a big circle around us.

Barry came out of the trees and walked over to me, shaking his head sadly. "Do you have any idea what you have done?"

"Yeah, I've challenged this asshole for the right to be the chief. Now I shoot him a couple of times, he falls down, and I give you the badge. Then I go home." I was feeling pretty good about myself and my plan. I'd even thought past the first punching part, which was kind of a new thing for me.

"Bubba," Skeeter said from my ear. "You are the most impressive example of human stupidity I have ever seen outside the Darwin Awards."

"What's wrong with my plan?" I asked Barry and Skeeter.

"You issued the challenge to Clag'tin?" Barry asked.

"Yeah, you saw me. You were standing right over yonder when I did it," I said.

"Then he gets to choose the weapons."

"So what? I'm pretty good with all kinds of weapons. As long as he doesn't pick eight-foot saplings, I think I'm okay."

Clag'tin laughed again, and I was really starting to dislike that sound. "Then Clag'tin choose unarmed combat! We fight barehanded, human! We fight barehanded to the death! Now come, let my coward cousin Brar'kan watch as I rip you limb from limb."

I looked from Barry to where Clag'tin stood butt-naked in a circle of his people, literally salivating at the idea of getting his hands on me. "Well," I said, "I didn't see that one coming."

"So much of your life can be encapsulated in that sentence, Bubba." Skeeter's voice came through far too loud and clear for the moment. "Now what are you going to do?"

"Well, I ain't gonna strip naked and wrestle a Sasquatch, that's for damn sure." But I did shrug out of my jacket, shoulder holster, and kukri sheaths. Then I peeled off my t-shirt and added the rest of my daggers and brass knuckles to the growing pile of weapons lying useless in the dirt beside my feet. When I was bare to the waist, I stepped forward into the circle of bigfeet (bigfoots?) and rolled my head from side to side. My neck made some scary popping noises left over from college football, and I looked across the bare patch of dirt at Clag'tin.

He was huge. I mean, "sasquatch" kinda implies a big mother, but this dude was big even for a Bigfoot. It was like Chewbacca mated with the Ultimate Warrior and out came something that was half Tasmanian Devil and half grizzly bear. And all pissed off.

"We fight without clothes, stupid man," my furry opponent yelled across the ring.

"Unless you got a mouse in your pocket, I don't see no 'we' over there. Cause I'm keeping my damn britches and shoes on. You might be used to running bare-assed through the woods, but I ain't giving you another advantage just because I was brought up civilized."

"To use the loosest possible definition of civilization," Skeeter muttered. I snatched the Bluetooth out of my ear and tossed it back to land next to my shirt. I didn't need the distraction of Skeeter's commentary while I was trying to keep from getting absolutely friggin' destroyed.

Clag'tin must have decided that enough talking was definitely enough 'cause he lowered his head and charged me. He was like something out of the legends, and not the ones about unicorns and butterflies, either. I sidestepped him pretty easily and gave him a swift kick in the upper thigh as he ran past. He let out a yelp and turned on me a whole lot faster than I expected, and I barely ducked under his big looping left paw. I dodged to the left as his other fist came swinging up past my ear in an uppercut that would have broken my jaw if it had landed, and I found myself on one knee right in front of his waist.

It wasn't my proudest moment in a fight, but I've always said if you can't win clean, then fight dirty. So I lashed out with my right fist and nailed the Sasquatch right in his ginormous balls. I hit him as hard as I could right in the jewels, and I think I felt one squish under my fist. All the breath went out of Clag'tin, and he dropped to both knees in a huge puff of dust. I stood up, teed off on his head like Adam Vinateri in the fourth quarter, and kicked the nasty bastard in the jaw as hard as I could.

I heard a *snap* as Clag'tin's jaw broke, and he actually flew all the way back to his feet before collapsing flat on his back, looking up at the stars cross-eyed. I turned and mugged for the crowd for a few long seconds, holding my hands above my head and jumping up and down until I caught sight of Barry gesticulating wildly in the back of the crowd of Sasquatch. After a second or two, I got over being proud of telling him apart from the other Bigfoots and stopped celebrating.

"What's the matter, Barry? You act like . . . he ain't out, is he?" Barry shook his head right about the same time a sledgehammer hit me between the shoulder blades. I splayed out face-first in the dirt and then immediately tried to cover up as more boulders started bouncing off my back, ribs, and shoulders. I rolled over, trying to keep my face covered, and realized that all those huge rocks were Clag'tin's fists, and all I'd done by breaking his jaw was made him mad. He straddled me in a full mount, moving right towards a picture-perfect ground and pound except there was no ref to save my ass if he knocked me out, there was no padded ring, we weren't getting paid, there were no TV cameras, and he was four-hundred pound naked Sasquatch straddling my waist. There were so many things wrong with my situation that I couldn't even begin to list them all.

After about ten seconds of getting the ever-loving shit pounded out of me, I decided to play dead. It wasn't much of a ploy, since I could barely hold my arms up and more, I was pretty sure at least three ribs were broken, and it felt like I had another concussion. Clag'tin saw my guard drop a little and took the bait. He sat up on his knees a little to get better leverage and reared back for a killing blow right between my eyes.

That's when I did something I never thought I'd do in all my days. I grabbed Clag'tin's shlong. And pulled. I yanked on that Sasquatch wiener like it was the last lifeline on the Titanic. I pulled that ding-a-ling like I was Quasimodo ringing every damn bell in Notre Dame. I tweaked that twanger like I was in a tug-of-war against Hulk Hogan, Andre the Giant, and half a dozen elephants. It was the most uncomfortable thing I'd ever felt, and I've been stabbed, burned, beat by a troll, and kissed by Mary Sue Jenkins under the bleachers at a middle school football game. His woolybat was thick and rubbery, like all those nature shows say boa constrictors feel, but with more hair on it. And when I latched on to that johnson and pulled with every ounce of my remaining strength, Clag'tin's eyes bugged out like a wolf in a Tex Avery cartoon. He tried to stand up and back away from me, but I was latched on like a lamprey and all he did by standing was to pull me to my feet, and there's no way having three hundred and fifty pounds of bleeding redneck dangling from your wangdoodle feels good.

"Let go of me!" Clag'tin screamed, and his breath of a million dead things and no Crest almost made my beard fall out. But I gave his gherkin a quick jerk upward, and he slammed his mouth shut and stood up on tippytoes trying to relieve some of the tension. I scrambled to my feet, never letting go of his hairy hammer.

"Now let's talk about this," I said, trying very hard to only look in his eyes and ignore what was in my hand. "We've got two options here. One is you surrender and declare me the *Sheeran-kor* (I was probably proud of myself out of all proportion for remembering what the hell the Bigfoot word for "Bossman" was) or we go with Option Number Two."

"What is Option Number Two?" Clag'tin asked, although the words were muffled on account of his broken jaw and the fact that his voice was pitched a full two octaves higher than normal thanks to me yanking his eleventh finger sideways anytime he looked at me wrong.

"I don't think you'd like Option Number Two. Option Number Two is I yank your little shaggy savage here right off by the roots and turn it into a walking stick like they do bull's peckers at that big-ass flea market in South Carolina. Then I leave you to bleed to death dickless and disgraced in Lower Damn Alabamastan. And nobody wants to die in the shithole suburbs of Mobile, Alabama."

Clag'tin moved in close to me, and I tightened my grip on his abominable snowmanhood. He winced but knelt in front of me. At least he tried to kneel, but I was still holding his one-eyed wrinkle-beast, so that put a little hitch in his giddy up. Anyhow, he knelt down as best he could and mumbled something.

"What? I couldn't hear you," I said. I dropped his pecker and knelt down, hoping it wasn't all a ruse just get me to drop his dingus so he could kill me.

"I surrender," he muttered again. His voice back to its normal range and only marred by his broken jaw. "Clag'tin surrender. Bub'ba is new *Sheeran-kor*." I raised my hands in victory, and Barry came over to give me a huge bear hug, lifting me clean off my feet in his enthusiasm. I usually would have made some smart-assed and half-homophobic joke about gay monsters, but since I was the one with more than a handful of brown bushy behemoth not two minutes before, I let it go. This time.

I walked back over to my clothes with Barry and waved him down so I could whisper in his ear. "Challenge me," I said.

"What?" he asked, whispering back.

"Challenge me. I don't want to run your tribe, and your pop's dead, so you gotta do it. But to do it, you gotta kick my ass."

"No way, I saw what you did to Clag'tin's Little Foot, no way do I want to fight you!"

"I had to win that one, he wanted to kill me. I don't want to be your chief, so you'll win this one. And you won't kill me, I promise."

"And you won't rip my dick off?"

"I promise not to go anywhere near your sascrotch. I have had more than my fill of yeti penis for one day," I said, pulling on my t-shirt and putting my Bluetooth back in my ear.

"Boy did I come in at the wrong point in that conversation!" Skeeter's voice echoed through my ear, and I laughed 'til I almost puked.

"I challenge Bub'ba for right of *Sheeran-kor!*" Barry bellowed. I jumped a little, since I was right next to him, and Skeeter squeaked in my ear in surprise.

"Bubba, are you gonna fight another Bigfoot? Because if you are, can we get a videotape this time? I'm pretty sure that TV show with Bob Saget woulda paid us ten grand for a tape of your last ass-whoopin'."

"Shut up, Skeeter. I know I'm gonna lose this time."

"So what else is new? You lost last time, remember?"

I ignored him. So far, everything was going right according to plan. Admittedly, the plan never involved me performing an impromptu trouser snake handling in the backwoods of Alabama, but shit happens. "As you issued the challenge, I set the weapons and terms of our duel. We fight barehanded to first blood!"

The crowd didn't like this very much, since the last match had been to the death and it's bad booking to set up the card so your matches don't escalate, but since I wasn't writing Wrestlemania, I didn't much give a damn. I looked over at Barry, and he was staring at me wide-eyed, with a huge grin on his hairy face.

I stepped forward and put my hands up in a low guard, easy enough for a critter of Barry's size to reach over and pop me in the nose. Which is exactly what he did. He tossed a big, looping right hand that caught me right on the tip of my shnozz. My poor nose got broke so many times in college it's a miracle I can breathe today.

Between football and football parties, seemed there was always some-body wanting to smash my sniffer flat, and most of them succeeded. Of course, I'd already stole their beer or their woman to get them that pissed off, so I had my fun, too.

But the problem with a nose that's been broke more times than the speed limit—it's hard to get it to bleed. So he nailed me pretty good, and I heard the familiar *snap* that told me I was gonna have to set it again or allergy season was just gonna get worse. But there was no blood. I ran my fist across my nose three or four times, and nothing. Finally, I lowered my head and charged Barry, wrapping my arms around his waist and uselessly pummeling his body and sides.

"What are you doing?" he asked me. Barry just kinda stood there while I whaled on him, having not had the benefit of Sunday after-noon WCW broadcasts throughout his childhood to teach him how to sell a punch.

"Hit me in the mouth," I muttered.

"What? I couldn't hear you." Barry bent down to get a better listen to me, and I looked up just as his giant hairy forehead came crashing down on my lips. So I wasn't sure if he head butted my face, or if I just kissed his forehead real aggressively, but either way, he split my upper lip and blood starting dripping down into my beard. Mission friggin' accomplished.

I backed up, waving him off and spitting blood onto the ground. I wanted to make sure everyone around could see the blood, see the evidence that Barry had drawn first blood. "He wins!" I yelled, wincing a little at my busted lip.

Barry raised his hands to the sky and bellowed like a cross between a horny rhinoceros (do not ask how I know what that sounds like) and an orgasmic hellhound (and you really don't want to know how I know what that sounds like). A female Sasquatch and a little girl Sasquatch ran out from the back of crowd and hugged Barry like he was Rocky at the end of the first movie. Or the second one. Whatever movie where he won the fight, I don't remember which it was. There was some general rejoicing around the camp, and Clag'tin got to his feet and stomped over to Barry. I cleared my throat, and the former

Sheeran-kor froze in his tracks, his hands instinctively going to cover his fine furry friend. When he saw that I wasn't going to start anything, he relaxed and extended a hand to Barry.

Barry looked at the hand for a second, obviously weighing the choice of peace in the tribe versus shaking the hand of dude that just had his junk in his mitts. Being much more diplomatic than me, Barry shook his hand. Clag'tin then took Barry's hand and raised it high over both their heads. The cheering of the crowd swelled to a fever pitch, and I finished getting dressed again.

I pressed the button on my Bluetooth and said, "Win another one for the good guys. Come on down and meet me back at the truck." I looked up on the ridge over the cave mouth and saw Uncle Father Joe stand up, fold the bipod down on his Remington 700, and turn to head down the trail. I turned to where Amy should have been doing the same thing and saw nothing.

"Amy?" I called into the headset.

Nothing.

"Joe, you got eyes on Amy?" I asked.

"Negative. I haven't seen her since she settled into her blind. Why?"

"She didn't respond to my call," I said. "Skeeter, what does her GPS show?"

"She's still close, unless she's left her phone somewhere. I'm accurate to about twenty meters, and it looks like she's right on top of you. But her dot ain't moved in half an hour or so."

"I'm on my way," Joe said, and I saw him start to move to Amy's sniper nest. It's not that I didn't have faith in my ability to beat Clag'tin, I just thought that a pair of snipers might be good insurance. Looked like my snipers needed insurance more than I did.

"Her pack is here, and so is her rifle," Joe said. I looked up and he stepped to the edge of the overhang with a black backpack and another Remington in his hands.

"Are you looking for this?" A voice came from behind me, and I knew that I wasn't going to like whatever I saw when I turned around. I hate it when I'm right.

I turned around and standing there with Amy's neck in one giant paw was the biggest bitch werewolf I'd ever seen. I recognized her instantly as Jason's right-hand woman, or wolf, or bitch, or whatever. She was seven feet of bad news, and she had my girlfriend by the neck. I took one step and she lifted Amy off her feet. I froze and the she-wolf grinned at me, her tongue lolling out to one side in that way a dog'll do when their human does something particularly stupid or amusing.

"Come closer and I kill her like you killed your father, pup."

"Let her go and I'll show you what that feels like, bitch."

She dropped Amy to her side and stepped forward. "Your brother sends me with a message. You must bow or destroy all you love. Just like you murdered your father, you'll kill everyone you care about if you oppose him. He is the Messiah, and he has come to deliver us from the darkness to dominion over you pitiful humans.

"Never." Barry's voice was strong and clear. "We will stand with Bubba and we will never allow this murderer you call Messiah to prevail."

"It matters not what you wish, *Sheeran-kor*, half your tribe is already dead," The wolf replied with an evil glint in her eyes.

"What do you mean?" Barry's head turned from side to side, looking from one Sasquatch to another, but several refused to meet their new leader's eye. I took that as a bad sign.

"Skeeter, do you have any idea what's going on?" I asked under my voice.

"Not a clue."

"I have the shot," Joe's whisper came into my ear, reminding me that I had a sniper on the ridge.

"Green light," I said.

"Green light," Joe repeated, but the wolf must have heard us, because she snatched Amy off the ground and held her up as a shield before Joe got off a shot.

The wolf-woman grinned at me again, and all I could do was stand there. "Maybe I shouldn't snap her neck. Maybe I should gut her, like my mate did to you. Where did the sword go in?" She traced her claws down the front of Amy's tactical vest and I knew the Kevlar would stop a bullet but wouldn't do crap against claws or a knife.

"Why don't you fight somebody your own size, hairball?" I said, stepping forward. I held my hands out to my sides, palms up. "I'm still empty-handed, why don't you try me. My candy-assed brother couldn't put me down. Maybe you can. Maybe then you get to play Messiah instead of just being his errand-bitch." Her eyes tightened at the corners and I knew I hit a nerve.

I did what I do when I find a sore spot—I poked at it some more. "Sucks, doesn't it? He's off who-knows-where, doing who-knows-what with God only knows who, while you're here spreading the good word. Like a good puppy."

"I spread much, much more than just my word here, fool. Why don't I take a little nibble out of your mate here and she can see just how much more." She leaned in and licked the side of Amy's neck. I like a little girl-on-girl as much as any other red-blooded hillbilly, but it loses a lot of its luster when one of the girls has more body hair than me.

"Oh shit balls, Bubba," Skeeter's whisper came into my ear like he was standing next to me. "You gotta get the hell out of there before sunset."

"Why?" I tried to mutter without moving my mouth, but the wolf's ear's pricked up and I knew she heard me.

"She turned the Sasquatch. She spread the lycanthropy virus to the tribe. And tonight is the first night of the full moon. They'll be completely out of control. You have . . ." I could almost hear the math happening right through my earpiece. "Two and a half hours to be very, very far away from those bigfeet. Bigfoots. Whatever the shit you call 'em, you gotta be gone before they turn."

"As strong as they are normally, I don't wanna think what a were-bigfoot could do. But there's still the little problem of the werewolf holding my girlfriend by the neck."

"Yeah, that's a thing. Sorry, buddy. I got nothing." I looked up at Joe, who shook his head slightly. So I did the only thing I could think of. I drew Bertha from her holster, set her on the ground, stepped forward, and knelt down a few feet in front of the big wolf.

"What are you doing?" she demanded, giving Amy a shake for punctuation.

"I'm doing just like you asked. I'm surrendering. You wanted me to kneel. I'm kneeling. You wanted me to lay down my arms, there's my gun. Now let my girl go." I didn't look up, counting on Joe to yell if she came at me. I don't know what I thought I'd do about it. I was six feet away from a half-shifted werewolf that could turn my guts into jump ropes in about three seconds. I just knelt there, keeping my eyes closed in an effort to make my ears a hair sharper. I had the beginnings of a plan tickling around in the back of my head, but just as usual when I started trying to make plans, it all went straight to crap.

"What is this stench of dog?" I heard Barry say behind me, and my heart fell a little further towards the bottoms of my Doc Martens. Yeah, I still wear Docs. Some things never go out of style, and ass-kicking boots are on the list.

"Be ready, Joe," I whispered into my Bluetooth.

"Standing by." His reply came in as more breath than sound, and I knew he was in his zen shooter place. I just needed to give him an inch to put a bullet in and we could solve part of this problem. But Barry had brought a whole new set of problems to the table.

"What's wrong, coward? Does your mate smell different? Better, maybe? More . . . alive?"

"You turned my mate?" I heard Barry's voice and knew that we were about to have an eight-foot hairy problem. Then I heard Clag'tin and a few other Sasquatch around the circle start to growl and realized I had a whole forest full of eight-foot hairy problems.

"Skeeter, I don't think they're keeping to that whole sundown timetable," I muttered.

"Well, I don't think magical creatures are an exact friggin' science, Bubba. Just blow something up and get the hell outta there!" Skeeter's voice was shrill, the fear seeping into every word. I knew the feeling. This was about to get bloody.

Barry let out a bellow like a cross between a lion challenging for territory and Marlon Brando screaming for Stella. I heard the wolf let out a little chuckle and then looked up in time to see her toss Amy to the ground, us mere humans forgotten in the thrill of her new fight. I aimed to make that a mistake she wouldn't live to regret. My right hand yanked a small cylinder off my belt and I flung it upwards at the wolf's face at the same time that I shoved off hard with my right foot and threw myself sideways.

I yelled "flash-bang!" at the top of my lungs, buried my face in the dirt, and clapped both hands over my ears as the grenade exploded in a spectacular cacophony of sound and light right in front of the she-wolf's face. My ears rang through my hands, and the world was full of sparkles even with my eyes averted, so it was no surprise to see the wolf-bitch on her knees holding her head when I got myself together enough to roll over and come up on one knee. I'd thrown myself near enough to Bertha to grab the Desert Eagle and train it on the wolf, but she was too busy writhing in pain and clawing at her eyes to pose an immediate threat.

Unfortunately, the explosion had scared the crap out of the Sasquatch, too, and the ones that had started to turn had the process jump-started by the adrenaline. So now instead of facing one psychotic werewolf that wanted my liver for lunch, I was facing seven brand-new super-sized werewolves who just wanted lunch. And weren't going to be too particular what they ate, including me, Amy, Barry or their fellow bigfeet.

Amy got to her feet and pulled a machete from a sheath across her back. A bigfoot-wolf stalked her in four-footed form, but it got no further and six feet from her when its head exploded in a red mist.

"One down," Joe's voice came from my headset. I'd forgotten about my air support in the explosion, but his voice had never sounded so good.

"Nice shot, Joe. A few more like that and I might even come to Sunday service," I said.

"Just keep them tied up down there and I can end this quick. Silver or no silver, even werewolves can't function without a brain stem."

"Somehow Bubba manages, though," Skeeter's voice came through the ringing in my ears. "You wanna warn a fellow next time? You almost blew all my audio equipment with that thing."

"Quit your bitchin', worst thing that could happen is you'd have to watch porn with the sound off," I grumbled.

"But then I'd miss all the dialogue. How would I follow the story-line?" he protested.

"You're like that one dude in America that actually reads *Playboy* for the articles. Now shut up, I gotta go kill a dog." I struggled to my feet, my balance still a little off from the flash-bang, holstered Bertha, and pulled the pair of silver kukri from my back. I headed toward the she-wolf, but stopped when I saw her and Barry going at it hammer and tongs. I'd fought Barry once, but his heart wasn't in it, and he only kinda whooped my ass. But this time he was *pissed*, and he laid into that wolf-chick with everything he had and then some. Punches, claws, and kicks flew almost vampire-fast, and I knew I didn't have anything to add to that fight.

Besides, I had a damn nine-foot tall half-shifted were-sasquatch in my face. Clag'tin had apparently been first in line to the lycanthropy buffet, and he figured out pretty quick how to stop his shift while he was still bipedal and unfortunately, able to communicate.

"Now we see who is alpha, human." I hate it when monsters use "human" like it's some kind of insult. I'm no more ashamed of being human than I am ashamed of being a redneck. It's just who I am. I'm a little insulted by being called fat, but not much 'cause that one's pretty much true, too. I just don't like being reminded of it all the time.

"I would come up with some snappy comeback, but truth is I'm just tired of your ass. Joe, green light." I waited for the shot, but nothing happened. "Green light!" I said a little louder, and maybe a little more panicked.

"A little busy up here, Bubba."

I looked up to the ridge. "Shit."

"That's a pretty accurate assessment, I'd say," Joe replied over the comm link. One of the were-squatches was circling the bottom of a tree that held one very nervous Catholic priest-slash-sniper. Joe fired off an occasional round from his .45 down of the dogfoot, but his aim sucked through branches and one-handed while clinging to a tree, so he didn't do much more than keep the beast occupied.

"I'll get up there as quick as I can," I promised, hoping that I'd be in one piece when I made it there. I turned back to Clag'tin just soon enough to duck his first punch, a looping roundhouse that would have probably crushed my skull if it had landed. But it didn't, and I dug a long slash along his ribs with one kukri as I spun out of the way.

This was not my usual fight. This time I was the little guy, trying to stay out of the way long enough to land a killing blow. I was more used to being the big dude swinging haymakers, but I tried to adapt real fast. Clag'tin came back with an uppercut that I was supposed to stick my face right into because that's where my face woulda gone if I'd ducked and spun left, opposite his punch. Instead I ducked and spun right, away from the uppercut and scored his rights with my left, backhanded. I continued my spin all the way down to one knee and flashed both kukri up and across in big diagonals, aiming for the femoral arteries in the Sasquatch's legs. He skittered back and I pressed the offensive, coming off my knee in a hard upward slice across his gut. He sucked his gut in and swung both clawed hands at my face, but I ducked forward instead of drawing back. This put my right-handed kukri in a perfect spot to slice his left quad right off the kneecap. So I did. The silver bit deep and the big muscle of his tree-trunk thigh parted like butter. I was inside his guard then, and the only thing left to do was finish it. I straightened up, my right shoulder bulling his arms up and outward, and buried my left-handed kukri in his belly. I cut up along his torso and across with one blade, punched the other in a throat-opening strike across his throat, and the big monster collapsed in a pile of blood and entrails, bleeding out into the dirt in a matter of seconds.

I heard a snarl behind me and turned, adrenaline still pushing me at top speed, to catch another wolfsquatch darting in for my hamstring. *They learn wolf behavior pretty damn quick*, I thought, but it didn't matter. I caught it on the side of the neck with one kukri and almost decapitated the beast. It dropped to the red-soaked mud and didn't move again.

I looked around the clearing until I found Amy, her back to a big oak tree and two wolves stalking her. She kept them at bay with her machete and reflexes, leaving bloody noses and muzzles whenever one got too close, but I could see the machete starting to droop in her hand and knew the next two or three seconds were all we had. I dropped one kukri and drew Bertha, putting a .50 round in the back of one weresquatch's head from thirty feet. It blew up like a watermelon at a Gallagher show, and when the other wolf-foot turned to see what made the mess, I put one in its ear with similar results.

"Thanks," Amy said, pulling her MP5 around and aiming it at my head. I dove for the turf and she sent a three-round burst right where I'd been standing. A huge weight crashed down onto my back, and I scrambled to get back to my feet before whatever it was ate my spleen. I shouldn't have worried. I shoved the dead weresquatch off me and saw the tight grouping of three rounds in its face. Amy didn't play. Three 9mm hollow points with silver nitrate in the tips made a mess out of the front of the wolf-foot's face, and I didn't want to think about what they did to the back of its head.

I crossed the clearing to where Amy stood, her Remington braced against a leaning tree. She put her eye to the scope, let out a slow breath, and squeezed the trigger. The wolf at the base of Joe's tree jumped slightly, then fell over and didn't move again. The crack of the rifle cut through the sounds of the struggle like even Bertha's bark hadn't managed to do, and everything in the clearing turned to stare at us for just a second.

A second that turned out to be too long for Barry. His attention wavered from the she-wolf for just an eye blink, but it was all she needed. They were in close combat, and Barry was a lover, not a fighter. She ripped his throat out with one swipe of her claws, and his eyes went wide for a second in surprise and pain. Then they went blank, and he toppled over backwards. Dead in seconds. No music, no slow-motion long shots, no wire fights. Just a surprised look on his face and then his blood fountaining down his fur.

I froze. It had been a long time since I watched somebody I liked get killed in front of me, and it wasn't something I planned on ever seeing again. And I *liked* Barry. He was a little pretentious for a monster who ran around with his oversized wiener in the breeze all the time, but all in all, he was pretty cool dude. And in the span of three heartbeats, that bitch killed my friend. I let out a holler that froze everything in the clearing again, and I charged her.

But she had other plans and charged us at the same time. I drew up and pulled my kukri, wanting this to be personal, but she just lowered a shoulder and knocked me sideways. I've been hit by a few pickup trucks in my day, the product of some stupid high school pranks a whole lot of Budweiser, but that wolf at a dead run knocked me flat on my ass. I rolled to my feet pretty quick and spun around to give chase, but she was almost on Amy at that point. Amy had dropped her Remington and was just standing there, arms out like she expected to judo her way through this scrap. At that point I truly expected to bury two friends that afternoon.

I forgot how much smarter Amy is than me.

When she got to about six feet away, the big wolf-woman dove at Amy, claws out in front of her face ready for disembowelment. Amy threw herself onto her back and covered her face as the she-wolf went at her hammer and tongs. She shredded Amy's Kevlar vest in seconds, and I expected to get covered in a splash of gore as the wolf ripped her guts out into the dirt. Instead, I saw the wolf rear back and scream in frustration, revealing a layer of metal under Amy's tactical vest.

"Yeah, chain mail's a real bitch, ain't it, bitch?" Amy said. Then she reached for the sling around her shoulder and emptied a thirty-round clip from her MP5 into the wolf. Red blood stitched across the monster's torso and up her face, and the beast fell off Amy backwards and scurried back the way she came. Bad news for her was that put her heading right for me, and my silver-edged kukri left a deep cut across one shoulder and sent the wolf spinning back in the opposite direction. I sliced through a hamstring and heard a satisfying howl of pain. The wolf went to one knee, and I tossed the kukri in my left hand to Amy. We were under some trees near the edge of the clearing, so Joe had no shot and we had to do things the old-fashioned way. We worked hard at staying out of reach of those razor-sharp claws as we ducked in for one long bleeding cut after another. It took several strikes and almost a full minute of fighting, but we finally got her laid out on her back in the middle of the clearing.

She looked up at the sky as I stood over her, a strange smile across her lips. "Go ahead, Monster Hunter. Kill me like you kill everything you care about."

"I might kill everything I care about eventually, but I'm killing your furry ass today." I pulled the tactical tomahawk from my back, raised it high, and brought it down on her throat, severing the head with one clean stroke. I didn't use a silver blade, but like Joe said, if you ain't got a brain stem, you ain't getting better from that. She shifted back to human form as she died, and I stood up, staggering back in shock as I recognized Megan Wyatt, a third cousin of mine and Jason's that we went to high school with. She'd always followed Jason around like a puppy dog, talking about how cute he was and how smart, basically blowing sunshine up his ass. I guess he remembered her, and when he turned, he came home to recruit. I looked at her long dark hair and remembered the shy girl she'd been in school. One more thing my asshole brother had to answer for.

"Joe, what's the situation? Are we clear?" I said into the Bluetooth.

"Seems to be good. There's one wolf still active, but she's not attacking. I have the shot if you make the call," came the answer.

I looked around, and saw the wolf he was talking about. She was pacing back and forth at Barry's body, licking his face and whimpering. I realized with a shock that this was his mate, the whole reason we'd come back here in the first place. Now Barry was dead, and she was turned into a werewolf, and there were a whole lot more dead Sasquatch than there were live ones left in the tribe, and it all felt a little useless. I walked over to where Barry laid, his blood making the dirt under his body a thick reddish-brown mud, and sat down on a big rock next to him. The wolf looked up at me, her eyes brimming, and she sat on the other side of Barry's body, waiting.

I just sat there. I didn't say anything for a long time, just sat there looking at the dead "monster" wearing my cutoff sweatpants and laying in a forest with his life's blood spilled out around him. I cleaned my kukri and put them away, then cleaned my tomahawk and put it away. I put a fresh clip in Bertha and re-holstered her, then checked all my pockets and pouches to make sure I was ready for any surprises. Amy came over and sat on the ground by my rock, her back pressed up against my hip, just calmly reminding me of her presence. Joe made his way down from the ridge and leaned his rifle against a tree. He sat on a fallen log a few feet away.

After a while the rest of the tribe came out and either sat on rocks, or the ground, and we sat. Barry's little girl-squatch came out and knelt beside her father's body and cried a little, but not much. Her mom butted her head up against her, and the girl threw one arm around the wolf's neck and wept quietly into her fur. It all felt too familiar, too human somehow. Then I figured it out—it felt just like a human funeral.

I cleared my throat. It was dry after all the fighting and all the dust and the yelling and cussing that goes along with such a thing, so I pulled a flask out of one of the side pockets of my pants and took a slash of some of Lynchburg, Tennessee's greatest export as the warm caress of Gentleman Jack soothed my throat. I passed the flask to Joe and started to speak.

"I didn't know Brar'kan very well, or for very long, but I know he was a good man." I paused there and looked around. I didn't want to offend anybody by calling Barry a man, but nobody seemed to mind. "He and I threw down a few months ago, and he whooped my ass good. I couldn't outfight him on his worst day, and he knew it. But he didn't kill me when he could have, because he didn't need to. He knew that there were times to fight, and times to kill, and times to talk, and times to walk away. And unlike way too many people nowadays, he had a good sense of when those times were.

"He had honor, something that way too many people nowadays can't even spell, much less possess. And for all I made fun of him for being a butt-naked savage, he was more honorable than most humans I've met in my life.

"And he loved y'all." I knelt down and put a hand on the girl's shoulder. She pulled her face out of her mama's fur and stared at me, her eyes huge and red-rimmed. "If there's anything I would want you to remember about your daddy, little girl, it's that he loved you enough to leave you when he knew he'd die if he stayed, and he loved you enough to come back when he thought he could win." I stood up, and looked around at the gathered tribe.

"That's the hardest thing for a man to do, walk away from a fight that he can't win. We ain't wired for that. We're wired to bash our heads against the wall until something crumbles, be it the wall, or our skull. But Brar'kan was smarter than that. He was better than that. He knew he couldn't fight Clag'tin and . . . " I took a deep breath before I could say the name. "Megan alone. But he knew that with me," I gestured to my team sitting around me, "with *us*, that together we had a chance. So he came to get help, leaving the people he loved most in this world in danger so he could get help to get them out of that trouble. I don't know if I'm brave enough to do that. I hope I am, if it comes to that.

"So that's the kind of man Brar'kan was. He was your *Sheeran-kar*, but he was my friend. And I'll miss him. I'm sorry for your loss." I turned to sit back down, but the wolf pawed my leg.

I looked back and the little girl was standing, her hand on her mama's back, fingers buried deep in the fur on her neck. She looked up at me and said, in that kind of gravelly voice most Sasquatch have, "Thank you, Bub'ba. Thank you for bringing my daddy back. Thank you for bringing his honor with him. Thank you for freeing us from the wolf. You will always be friend of this tribe." She reached up a hand and I shook it, surprised at how solemn and mature the little girl was. Of course, for all I knew Sasquatch age like elves and she could be a hundred and twelve.

I turned to one side, reached down and helped Amy up. Joe stepped forward and knelt by the wolf and little girl, murmuring those comforting kinds of words that priests just naturally have in those moments when shit is at its ugliest. He stood up, nodded to me, and we made our way back into the woods. There was the normal patting of shoulders and shaking of hands like at the end of a funeral, but none of the moonshine-fueled banjo picking that often followed.

129

As we reached the spot where we'd left my truck, it had gone full dark and we were walking by flashlight. But when we stepped up to the truck, the moon came into a break in the trees and its full light shone down bright enough on us to put our flashlights away. And as we got all the gear loaded up and I reached down to crank the truck, I heard the mournful howl of a single wolf echo across the forest.

6

DOUBLE TROUBLE

Somebody with a better sense of the ironic would comment on the fact that I was enjoying the company of two identical twin sisters when the call from Uncle Father Joe came in. I don't have a good sense of the ironic, so I checked my caller ID, saw that it was work, dropped my cell phone in my beer pitcher, and returned to the gyrations being performed in my immediate vicinity by two proponents of elective plastic surgery known locally as Bambi and Barbi, the Boom-Boom Twins. The establishment where I was abusing my liver, my wallet and my moral standing didn't have a name, it was just a nondescript building on a frontage road off Highway 74 in North Carolina. Nondescript, that is, except for the eight-foot high, twenty-foot wide blinking neon sign that bellowed "TOPLESS" in redder than Satan's drawers red to all who passed. I wondered about the local sign ordinances, then remembered that just as I'd turned into the parking lot, I passed the "Welcome to Charlotte" sign, putting this establishment well into unincorporated territory and thus less likely to have pesky visits from the sign police. I also figured that meant there weren't too many visits from the health inspector, either, so I decided to forego the seafood buffet.

I make it a policy never to eat the buffet at strip clubs. I'm always afraid I'll get too splattered in grease and sauce, and that could lead to an irreparable lap dance injury. And since I've experienced one or two reparable lap dance injuries in my time, I don't ever want to get one of the irreparable kind. So Barbi, or maybe it was Bambi, had just unwrapped a pair of the finest triple-Ds money could (and did) buy when my backup phone rang. I fished it out of my pocket and pressed my thumb up to the screen. It scanned my fingerprint and gave me access to the phone.

Living in the future is pretty cool, but the first couple of times I tried that trick, I did it with clean hands, so my phone never recognized me. Eventually I learned to only use the fingerprint recognition software when my hands were covered in blood, beer, or gun oil. The machine's never had a problem believing it was me as long as I kept to that plan.

I pressed the phone up to my ear and said, "Is the world ending? And by that I mean is the world going to end at any point in the next three songs?"

Skeeter's nasal, high-pitched voice came back in my ear, sounding like a cross between a Jewish mother and a dentist's drill. "No, but as soon as your time on the jukebox is up, you better call Joe. He's got a case. And keep your hands off them girls, you're old enough to be their daddy!" Skeeter hung up on me before I could protest.

I dropped the phone on the table, this time next to the beer, and did some quick math in my head. Once I satisfied myself that I was not early bloomer enough to have a child dancing at a topless bar, I leaned back and enjoyed the three-songs-for-one special I'd negotiated. I love me some afternoon shift girls at the strip club.

I blinked and batted at the sun, but it stayed hanging right there. I dug out a pair of sunglasses blacker than my high school football coach's soul and slipped them on. I got behind the wheel of my Ford F-250 and mashed a few buttons on my phone. "Call Joe," I said.

"I do not recognize that command." My phone recently developed this bad habit of talking back to me instead of doing what I told it to. I blamed Skeeter, since that's pretty much exactly how he behaves, too.

"Call Joe," I repeated, as clearly as I could, being from North Georgia and all.

"I'm sorry, there is no one by that name in your contacts list," the cultured mechanical voice came back at me.

"Goddammit you ignorant hunk of plastic, call Joe before I throw you out the friggin' window and scatter your circuits all over the highway!" I screamed at the phone.

"Calling Joe. Please hold." I hate technology.

"Hey, Bubba. Did you get my message on your other line?" Uncle Father Joe came on the line, all pleasant business and good cheer. He's Skeeter's adopted uncle, but he's also a Catholic priest, so I usually call him Uncle Father Joe. Unless I hate the assignment he's giving me, in which case I call him a whole bunch of other things. Joe is my handler. I'm the Southeastern Regional Monster Hunter for the Holy Roman Catholic Church. Technically, I'm an independent contractor, so I have to buy my own health insurance, but Joe assures me that since I'm at least tangentially employed by the Church, I get a couple of free venal sins between confessions that I don't have to worry about.

I'm pretty sure that two hours in the Champagne Room with the Boom-Boom Twins had exhausted my supply of grace.

I didn't remember a message from Joe, then it came back to me—the beer phone. "No, Joe, I'm sorry. That phone died on me and I had to switch to my backup. That's why I'm calling on this number."

"You threw it in the beer again, didn't you?"

"This ain't confession time, I ain't gotta tell you. Now what's the deal?" I was hoping that by changing the subject we could avoid any discussion of my afternoon's activities. Uncle Father Joe was my confessor, but sometimes I spread my confessions around. I do a lot of killin', and lot of random sinning' on the side, and that's a bunch for one priest to handle. I like Joe, and I don't want to overload his circuits. Plus my girlfriend works for a secret government agency, and she likes to tap my cell phone. She doesn't specifically object to me going to titty bars, but some things are just better left alone.

"We've got a shapeshifter robbing banks all through Alabama. We think it's headed for Georgia, and if it gets to Atlanta before we catch it, we'll never find it," Joe said.

"Yeah, that makes sense," I said. "If that thing gets into a big city, it can just keep changing faces and robbing a different bank every day. I'm in North Carolina, so I'm a good four hours away. Can I even get to wherever this thing is before it gets to Atlanta?"

"Probably, if you don't stop for any detours, particularly in the Greenville area." I knit my brow for a second, wondering exactly how a priest knew about my favorite titty bar in the I-85 corridor. "I see your receipts before they go to Rome, Bubba. And I do not approve Platinum Plus as a travel expense."

"I don't know why not. I'm traveling when I go there," I protested as I cranked the truck and pulled back onto the highway. I headed toward I-485 and pointed the big blue machine south.

"Bubba, if you can't understand why the Catholic Church objects to paying your bar tab and topless clubs, then perhaps it's time you went back through Sunday school."

"Anything but that, Father. I can't handle them nuns. They kicked my ass."

"Probably with good reason. Amy is flying in now. Please pick her up at the Greenville-Spartanburg Airport."

"There's an airport in Greenville?"

"Yes, and indoor plumbing, too, Bubba. She'll be landing about the time you pass through, if you leave now."

"I'm rolling." I hit the on-ramp the same time I hung up with Father Joe, and headed south into trouble. Again.

Agent Amy Hall stepped out of the front doors of the airport with a backpack and a small rolling suitcase. I was standing by the truck parked under a No Parking sign at the end of the sidewalk waiting for her. An airport security guard was taking a little nap in the bed of the truck after a conversation about my ability to stay there and wait for my almost-girlfriend. She walked up to me, gave me a little hug and a quick kiss on the lips, then handed me the handle of the suitcase.

I opened the door for her and took the backpack. "Where's the rest?"

"The rest of what?"

"The rest of your luggage?"

"Bubba, we're only going after one doppelganger. I packed light."

"I understand that, but I'm afraid I'm going to have to ask you to take your shirt off."

"What! Why would I take my shirt off in the airport parking lot?"

"I need proof that you're really a woman if you're gonna claim to be traveling with nothing but a couple of carry-ons. Besides, I want to check out your boobs." I tossed her bags in the back seat of the truck and leaned in the window. "So, how about it?"

"Sorry, Bubba, today is not the day you get to second base with a federal agent in the parking lot of an airport."

"Well, shit," I said as I walked around and slid in behind the wheel. "But you can't blame a guy for trying."

"You're insane." She laughed and tossed her blonde hair in a way that made me remember how much I missed her just about every second we weren't together. I put the truck in gear and pushed a few buttons on the big LCD panel that took up half the dashboard and reminded me every time I drove anywhere that my truck is smarter than me.

Skeeter's face popped up on the dash a few seconds later. "Hey y'all. I wasn't expecting you to call for at least an hour or two."

"We ain't got time for all that, as I've been so painfully reminded," I grumbled.

"Hello, Skeeter," Amy replied, all business. "What's the situation?"

"Well, our boy, or girl, or I reckon it can be whatever it wants to be, hit another bank in Birmingham this morning, so we're pretty sure it's made it to Atlanta by now, if that's where it was going in the first place," Skeeter said.

"So now what? There's too many banks in Atlanta to cover, and we don't know what the thing looks like now even if we were gonna try.

Do we just go to Atlanta and ride around waiting for this thing to rob another bank?" Amy looked grumpy. I reckon flying a puddle-jumper from DC to South Carolina on a wild doppelganger chase will do that to a body.

"Y'all ought go to the first robbery site and see what you can figure out from there. If this critter started robbing banks last week in Shreveport, there's gotta be some reason it's headed for Atlanta," Skeeter replied.

"And some reason it just started robbing banks now after all this time. I mean, it's an adult, right?" I asked.

"Yeah, it is. We call that a trigger event, Bubba, and you're right, maybe there's something in Shreveport to tell us what started this whole mess," Skeeter said.

"Who you calling 'we,' redneck? You and every other shut-in that watches every *Criminal Minds* marathon they run on A&E?" I said. I swear Skeeter even blushed a little bit, which was impressive since he's blacker than the ace of spades.

"But that's a good idea," Amy interjected, probably so she didn't have to listen to us bitch at each other the whole drive. "If we can figure out what the end game is, we can get there first and maybe keep this mess from escalating."

"All right, we got a plan. Now what can you tell us about the robberies before we get there, Skeeter? How do we know it's a shapeshifter?" I asked.

"Does it use a gun? Has anyone been injured? What do we know?" Amy added.

"Here's the deal—there have been five robberies counting the one this morning in Birmingham, one every day since last Thursday," Skeeter said.

"That's pretty damn fast," I said. "Sounds like something is pushing our boy to get a pile of money fast."

"And whatever it is looks to be in Atlanta," Skeeter continued. "Every robbery starts the same way, and this is how we know it's a shapeshifter. Elvis Presley walks into a bank with a shotgun and fires a round into the nearest security camera. Then he cleans out the teller drawers and runs outside, but not before disarming any guards and herding everyone into the vault. He then leaves them on the floor of the open vault and hauls ass."

I cleared my throat. Skeeter looked at me on the monitor, one eyebrow up in that disapproving way that only gay men have of saying, "Go ahead you stupid straight man, ask your stupid question that's a waste of my time, but I'll answer it anyway because you're so fashion-deprived as to be almost dangerous." Skeeter might have given me that look a time or two.

"So how do we know it's a shapeshifter and not really just Elvis knocking over a bunch of banks? I mean, Priscilla got all his money when he 'died,' so maybe he's broke," I asked.

"Bubba—" Skeeter started, but Amy interrupted him.

"Two reasons. First, it's young, skinny Elvis on these videos, not fat Elvis. And second, we've verified Elvis' whereabouts for the times of the robberies, and he was nowhere near Alabama."

Skeeter sat there on the video, his mouth hanging open. I nodded. "Okay, that makes sense. So it's a shapeshifter, and he, for lack of a more specific gender definition, hasn't hurt anybody yet. I reckon we can work with that."

"Wait a second," Skeeter said. "You mean Elvis is —"

Amy held up a hand to cut him off. "This isn't a secure line, Skeeter. We can't discuss that over the airwaves." His mouth closed with a *click* I could hear over the video link, but his eyes kept darting back and forth like a Cylon on crystal meth.

"All right, so we know it ain't Elvis, we know it's a shapeshifter, and we know the party started in Shreveport, and we know that there's three South Carolina Highway Patrol cars on my ass for the last three miles and they're starting to look pissed. So I'm gonna keep rolling while you two figure out the deal with the local po-po. Sound good?" I grinned at Amy, flipped Skeeter the bird, and switched the center console over to Outlaw Country. I swear, XM radio and Mojo Nixon are the only good things about having a truck smarter than most of my third-grade class.

∼

A my did her thing with the "I'm from the government, I'm here to help," and the state troopers suddenly found themselves called to something way more interesting than a big-ass truck rolling down I-85 at about 95. It took us a good twelve hours to get from the Greenville-Spartanburg airport to the outskirts of Shreveport, where the first bank robbery took place. We woulda made it a lot faster, except Atlanta happened. There's a rule of travel in the South—if you're going to Hell, you're gonna change planes in Atlanta. And no matter what time you drive through Atlanta, it's rush hour and there's a wreck on I-285. We didn't have to change planes, but after two hours to get around the city that Coke built, I damn sure wished I could fly.

We pulled into a Courtyard parking lot about 1:30 AM local time, which meant I had half an hour to get checked in and find a convenience store before they stopped selling beer at two. I told Amy where I was going and she mumbled something about a shower and seeing me in the morning as she closed the door to her room. I had tried to convince her that there was only one room left and all it had was one bed, but since there were three cars in the parking lot, she wasn't buying it. I didn't mind too much, since either Uncle Joe or Uncle Sam was picking up the tab. I Froggered my way across six lanes of traffic to get to a 7-11, bought myself a twelve-pack of Bud Light in hopes of watching my girlish figure, and headed back to my room.

I stopped cold when I saw a figure standing next to my truck. He was tall, not as tall as me but over six foot, and thin. He'd been skinny when he was a kid, but age and turning into a goddamn werewolf had put some pounds on him. His hair was long and pulled back into a ponytail, but where I wore a beard that I thought made me look distinguished and Skeeter said made me look like a Duck Dynasty reject, he was clean-shaven. He had my sword slung across his back, with the hilt poking out over his right shoulder for an easy draw. A pair of matched .45 pistols hung on his hips, and I felt pretty damned unarmed with only my Judge revolver in a paddle holster at the back of my belt and a couple pair of brass knuckles in my back jeans pockets.

"Jason," I said as I got close enough to be heard without yelling over the roar of traffic.

"Bobby." There were only a handful of people who ever called me Bobby and lived. My mama, Granny, Pop, and Jason were about it. Even Grandpappy always called me Bubba. Or Shithead, but that was when he was feeling generous.

"We gonna fight?" I asked. I was pretty tired from twelve hours on the road, and I was at a serious disadvantage weapons-wise, but if my psycho little brother wanted to throw down, I was ready—any place, any time.

"Not unless you got your heart set on it. And it didn't go so well for you last time, so I thought we might be able to talk instead. Give me a beer?" He reached over to his left and dropped the tailgate on my truck. I came around the side and sat next to him, putting the twelve-pack between us. Most days I wanted to kill him, and I figured that was what it would come to eventually, but he was still my brother, and if there was a chance to talk him out of trying to take over the world and setting himself up as the second coming of Jesus Christ for Monsters, I decided to take it. I handed him a beer, and he drained it, pitching the empty can into the bed of the truck like we used to back in high school. I handed him another and sucked one flat myself.

I popped the top on my second as he pitched his into the bed and grabbed a third. "Go easy, there Speed Racer, I didn't buy but twelve."

"We can get more, jackass," he replied.

"Store closes in ten minutes, peckerwood." We fell back into the relaxed profanity brothers have in the South.

"Bubba, I'm a friggin' super villain, you think I give a shit if the store's open or not? Now drink up!" He laughed and sucked the sides flat on another can.

I grabbed his wrist as he reached for his fourth beer. "Yeah, well, Lex Luthor, I don't want to try running across that highway half-drunk, and if anybody gets to kill you tonight, it's me, so slow down. You ain't got nothin' to prove."

"I've always got somethin' to prove." He said it low, but I heard it, and knew it to be true. Jason had always been compared to me, and always came up short. Not as tall, not as strong, not as athletic—all that made for a rough time when he was just a couple years younger than me and all the teachers and coaches always remembered what I'd done. But he'd been smarter, craftier, and with a head for numbers like nobody'd ever seen. Too bad that don't count for shit in the backwoods of North Georgia.

We sat there for a while, just drinking beer and looking at the stars. After the last beer was tossed over my shoulder into the bed of the truck, Jason took a deep breath. I held mine, knowing that the time had come for whatever had brought him here. We were about to get into some serious shit, either talking or fighting, and I didn't know which one.

"You killed Megan." It wasn't a question.

"I ended her, yeah. But you killed Megan when you turned her, you son of a bitch."

He laughed, a dry little bark of a laugh. "No pun intended, right? I'm not gonna fight you tonight, Bubba, but Megan is one you're going to pay for."

"You got a lot more than her on your list to answer for, Jason. But she was our blood. She wasn't close kin, but she was kin. And that's one you'll answer for."

"Kin? You ignorant redneck, she was more than kin, she was my mate! She was my other half! She was my life you fucking giant idiot, and you killed her! You took her away just like you took everything else from me!" He was crying, and yelling, and starting to shift. I saw his shoulders start to bulk up and hair start to come out on his arms and face. He started to grow, and I knew it was about to be on.

"Jason, chill. We said we weren't going to do this tonight."

"I changed my mind."

"Look, I'm sorry about Megan. I didn't know. I didn't know she was your . . . woman, or wife, or mate, or whatever you want to call her. I'm sorry for that. I know how bad that hurts." I looked him straight in the eyes and let him remember. I let him remember a blonde girl, a bloody shoe, and the day he took the woman I loved away from me. He stood there, halfway between panting and sobbing, just staring into my eyes for a long minute or two, then he let out his breath in a long, raggedy exhale.

"You got a flask in that truck?" he asked after he sat back down on the tailgate.

I reached down into my sock and pulled one out. "Nope. I never leave it in the truck." I passed it to him, and he knocked off about half of it in one long pull. Damn werewolf metabolisms. If I did that, I'd be dead. Nonetheless, I tried my best when he handed the flask back to me. No way was I gonna sit on my tailgate and be shown up by my little brother.

"What happened, Jason? How did you get this far down the road?"

"What, you mean the whole Messiah thing?"

"Yeah, dumbass, I mean the whole Messiah thing. I want to know how my little brother went from monster hunter to monster Messiah."

"I wanted to be the Alpha. I found a pack, and I wanted to be the Alpha. But I couldn't beat the Alpha they had, so I had to come up with a good reason to cheat and kill him when he wasn't looking. They bought it and made me Alpha. Then another pack moved in, and I killed their Alpha and took their pack, and they started to believe it. And after a while other monsters started talking about this Messiah of wolves, and they started coming for me 'cause they didn't want nobody to be over them. But by then I had like half a dozen packs following me, so I killed everything that came at me. Then the monsters started following me and asking when we were taking out the humans, and one thing led to another, and now we're at war."

"So you didn't want any of this?" I shook my head, trying to make it all make sense.

"I wanted the first pack. I wanted to be in charge. I wanted to never be told what to do again. And the only way that was going to happen was for me to kill anything that got in front of me. You don't get it, Bubba! You've never been the second-string. You've never had anybody tell you what to do. You've always done what you wanted and got what you wanted, and now it's my turn! Finally, it's gonna be Jason's turn, and anybody that don't like it can burn!" He jumped off the tailgate, flung his empty beer can into the air, drew Grandpappy's sword, and sliced it into three pieces before it hit the ground.

Then he turned to me, sword in hand and nostrils flaring. "This was a mistake. I shoulda known you wouldn't understand anything about it. You've always been the favorite, the golden boy. I just thought I could get you to see my side of things for once. I guess I was wrong."

"Yeah, you're wrong if you think I'm gonna understand how you got from feeling like Mommy didn't love you enough to killing entire bands of peaceful creatures." I stood up, slowly, but I figured I needed to be on my feet if he was gonna start doing anything serious with that sword.

"What, your precious Sasquatch? Those peaceful creatures deserved it! They killed three of my wolves for moving through their territory, and then wouldn't kneel to me as their rightful ruler. So yeah, I killed a bunch of 'em and turned a bunch more. And now the ones that are left know that if they mess with me, they're gonna get hurt." His eyes were dancing around like a meth cook at a cop convention, and the tip of Grandpappy's sword wavered in the moonlight.

"Jason, chill out, man. We can work this out. We can step it all down and get things back to where they used to be —"

"Don't you understand, Bubba, I don't want things like they used to be. I like it like this. I like being the boss, the one everybody's scared of. I don't want to go back. And now that you killed Megan, there ain't no going back for neither one of us." He stepped back, giving himself plenty of room to swing his sword.

I took a couple of steps sideways, making sure I had room to duck and hopefully get out of the way before he shoved three feet of steel through my guts again. "So that's it, little brother? We gonna do this now after all?"

"I guess we are. I wanted you to leave me alone, hoped once you understood what started this whole mess, you'd back off a little, but I guess you're still fighting Pop's fight, trying to be the damn good guy."

"Don't talk about Pop to me."

"Why not? You killed him." He grinned at me, and I saw red for a second before I realized the little bastard was baiting me.

"Just like Megan, dumbass. I ended him, but you killed him when you turned him. I did what we do—kill things that go bump in the night. Now I reckon it's your turn." I reached back and slid my hands into my brass knuckles. It wasn't much, but maybe the metal would give me a tiny edge. I made a mental note to get some of those things made in silver. With spikes. And maybe a flamethrower built in. Or hell, just to get a flame-thrower.

Jason growled, crouched and leveled Grandpappy's sword at me, then yelped and grabbed the back of his thigh. He spun around, looking up at the front of the hotel. Four stories up, a sliding glass door was open, and I saw the cylindrical barrel of a rifle with a flash suppressor poking out from the curtains. A tiny red dot lit up above the suppressor, and then a glowing red dot appeared on the ground in front of Jason. I watched with a smile as Amy walked that laser dot across the asphalt and settled it right on Jason's crotch.

"I'd think about running, little brother. That's a highly trained federal agent holding a Remington 700 with a laser sight loaded with silver-tipped full metal jacket rounds aimed right at your balls. I don't think you'd be much of an Alpha if she turned you into a little bitch, now would you?"

Jason snarled back at me, some mindless growl from deep in his throat, then blurred into wolf form and hauled ass off into the night. I looked up at the hotel, gave Amy a thumbs-up, and grabbed what was left of my twelve-pack. I made it to the door of my room before Skeeter called me, but just as I pressed the receive button on my Bluetooth, Amy's door opened. She stepped out into the hall wearing a tattered University of Michigan t-shirt and a pair of shorts that were short enough to have fit her about right in kindergarten.

"I'll tell you all about it in the morning, Skeeter," I said, then pushed the disconnect button and carried my beer into my favorite government agent's room. She looked good enough that I didn't even mention the goddamn Michigan shirt, just made a mental note to buy her some sleepwear from a college with a decent football team.

~

"How do you think he found you?" Amy asked as I set down a plate swimming with maple syrup. I had about fourteen pancakes stacked high on that plate, with a generous dollop of butter between every one and enough maple syrup to bankroll all Vermont's highway repairs for three years poured over the whole mess. It was my third plate of the morning, and the manager of the Shoney's in Shreveport was seriously reconsidering his All You Can Eat Breakfast Bar. I figured I had maybe one more plate before I got cut off. It wouldn't be the first time a waitress at an all you can eat restaurant had informed me that I had already eaten all I could eat, and all three small countries could eat besides, and I should get the hell out of her establishment. But before that happened, I was gonna eat me some dam flapjacks.

"I don't know. I don't think he's tracking the truck somehow. It's new since the last time we ran into him. He could be tapping Skeeter's phone, but that don't seem like his style."

"Not to mention a goddamn technological impossibility," came the chirpy and indignant voice in my ear. "And how the hell are you gonna eat all them pancakes? You gone be big as the side of a barn you keep that up."

"It takes a lot of fuel to run this big machine, Skeeter, so you just piss off about my eating habits." I might have been feeling a little sensitive since I found out Duluth Trading Company pants weren't available in my waist size. Those were my favorite pants, and now I was gonna have to find a new place to buy pants or lose weight. This was a funeral meal for my belly, kinda.

"None of that makes sense, though," I continued. "I think he was tracking me somehow, but it probably wasn't real high-tech."

"Magic?" Amy asked. She was sipping on coffee. She had eaten a bagel with light cream cheese, a couple of scrambled eggs and some bacon. Her entire meal all fit on one plate. I don't understand skinny people.

"What kind of magic? I mean, Jason's a werewolf, but he ain't a magician, far as I know," I said around a mouthful of syrupy goodness.

"Could the sword have something to do with it?" Skeeter asked in my ear. I froze, then almost choked on my pancakes as a bunch of things clicked together all at once. The weird test results in the hospital. Me healing from what should have been a fatal wound faster than anybody had a right to. Me feeling stronger when I fought the Sasquatch. Jason finding me without scent or technology.

"That's gotta be it," I said. "Somehow when he stabbed me with that sword, it bonded with me, and now Jason can feel my presence." That was kinda creepy. I didn't like my little brother that much before he swore to kill me, but thinking that he could track me across thousands of miles on account of a magic sword made me downright uncomfortable.

I changed the subject. "Where's our first stop today?" I'd let Skeeter and Amy plan all the detectivin' while I drove yesterday, figuring that my contribution to this part of things would be to drive around and beat up anything that needed punching.

"We're going to the First Bank of Louisiana, Shreveport. It's about three miles away, and it's where the first robbery took place. Hopefully someone there can give us some clues," Amy said.

"Are we talking to the FBI or the local police?" I figured not, since neither organization was really cut out to hunt down a shapeshifter, but I wasn't sure how far Amy's governmental cooperation programming had gone.

Not that far, it turned out. "Nah, they're not really suited to this kind of thing. They'll keep pursuing it from the mundane angle, and we'll come at it as though the crimes were committed by a shapeshifter."

"But we know they were, right?" I asked.

"We don't know anything until we catch the guy. Until then we just think this is the deal," Amy replied.

"But f we catch up to skinny Elvis robbing a bank somewhere, we know it's our guy."

"Right."

"Because Elvis' whereabouts are well-documented."

"Right."

"And you're not going to tell me anything else."

"Right."

"Dammit."

"Right."

"Sometimes I think you're an obnoxious bitch."

"Sometimes you're right, but it happens a lot less often than you think it does." Amy smiled at me, slid out of our booth and headed for the door. I dropped a five on the table and headed to the counter to pay.

The waitress that rang us up looked at me kinda funny when I walked up to the register, then said, "This is covered, sir."

I cocked my head to one side. "What do you mean?"

"I mean somebody already paid for your breakfast." She pointed over at an empty table. "He was sitting right over there. Young guy, thin, tall, longish hair." I looked at Amy. There was only one person it could have been—Jason. But we'd both scouted the restaurant when we first got there, and it was clean. What the hell was going on? Was Jason developing new abilities?

I thanked the confused lady, tossed another five on the counter for the waitress, and followed Amy out the door. I pressed TALK on my Bluetooth. "Skeeter, you there?"

"Yeah, Bubba. I just talked to you two minutes ago. What's up?"

"Jason was in the restaurant."

"Did you kill him?"

"No, we didn't even see him."

"How did you miss him? He's a six foot tall psychotic werewolf."

"I don't know. That's what I need you to figure out. I need you to get into the computer system at the restaurant and scan their security footage, then tell me if Jason was really in there or not."

There was a long pause on the line. "Bubba, let me get this straight.

You want me to assume that a Shoney's on the side of I-20 in Shreve-port, Louisiana not only has security camera, but has a networked security camera system that I can hack into and get an image of your psycho brother off the hard drive?"

"I reckon that's what I mean. I just want you to do some of your computer bullshit and get me a picture of who paid my tab at the breakfast bar so I know if Jason can disguise himself from me or not."

"All right, then. I'll get right on it. You want me to part the Red Sea when I'm done?"

I hate it when he gets all pissy and sarcastic. I knew it wouldn't be as hard as all that because I'd seen the cameras all over the restaurant while we were there, and the monitor and hard drive for the security system were sitting right behind the counter where the manager could watch the busboys scarfing tips and the waitresses taking extra smoke breaks and re-serving used desserts. But since he was being all pissy, I wasn't going to tell Skeeter about all that. Just let him figure it out on his own. So I decided the best way to fight his sarcasm was with feigned ignorance. "Nope, the Red Sea's fine, as far as I can tell. But if it needs parting, Skeeter, I'm sure you're the dude to part it."

He didn't even say goodbye, just grumbled something I couldn't understand into my headset and clicked off. I grinned at Amy, said, "Skeeter's on it," and we headed to the bank.

People naturally get a little nervous when I walk into a bank. I'm six-five, weigh about three-fifty, and look like the "mean guy" off a *Sons of Anarchy* rerun. So it didn't surprise me when the guard immediately wandered over to see what was going on when Amy and I walked into the First National Bank a little bit after ten in the morning and asked to speak to the manager. It did surprise me when he went ahead and drew his sidearm.

"Calm down, there, Junior. I ain't gonna hurt nobody. I don't think." I glared at him and he holstered his weapon. Of course, maybe Amy flashing her badge at him helped, too. We waited for about ten minutes before the fat little bank manager came out of his office and offered me his sweaty hand. I shook the dead-fish hand and let Amy do the talking.

"Mr. Drum, we need to look at the footage from the robbery last week," Amy said.

"Well, the FBI took all that."

"They left you a copy on your hard drives. That will be fine."

Mr. Drum looked a little disappointed that she knew about that. Maybe he was planning to leak it to TMZ for a pile of money. Joke was on him, everybody quit paying for Elvis sightings years ago.

We walked back into the office, and I sat down in the guest chair. Amy didn't bother; she just went around behind Drum's desk and sat down. She clicked a few keys on his computer, then slid the keyboard to the side where Drum stood looking flustered. "Password, please," she said.

Drum leaned over and typed a few characters, then hit "Enter."

He straightened up and Amy gave him a big smile. "Thank you, Mr. Drum. That will be all for now. I'm sure you have plenty of work to do. We'll let you know when we leave."

The little fat man looked a little affronted and opened his mouth to say something. I cleared my throat, and he looked over to where I was overflowing his side chair. He thought better about protesting and left us to it. Amy pressed some more keys, and I flipped through a brochure on mortgage rates. I didn't know anything about mortgages —my house and property had been in my family for hundreds of years —so I was lucky in that regard.

"That's interesting," she said after a few minutes. I started awake, having nodded off after perusing the pamphlets on Drum's desk.

"What you got?" I got up and moved around behind the desk. I took the chair with me, which made for a tight fit, but with a little shoving, I made it work.

"This guy is on the video three times in the week leading up to the robbery. He had one meeting with a loan officer, then two meetings with Mr. Drum. Take a look at the second one."

The video didn't have any sound, but it was pretty easy to see what was going on. The guy in the video was an average working-class-looking dude, like the guy you'd expect to see working in a machine shop or replacing a transmission. Medium size, with brown hair to his collar and a couple days' worth of stubble. He had permanent hat hair and wore the same pair of khakis in all three meetings, probably the only pair he owned. Same tie, too, but different dress shirts. In other words, he was my people. His meeting with the loan officer took about half an hour by the time stamp on the video, but we watched it in fast forward.

"Looks like he comes in to get a loan and doesn't get the answer he wants," I said.

"Yeah, I've seen that look a lot," Amy replied.

I cocked an eyebrow at her. "My dad wasn't the best with money. I sat out in the bank lobby and watched him plead with loan officers a lot. It usually looked pretty much like this." She gestured at the video where the guy was walking out of the loan officer's glass cubicle with his head down.

The next day was a repeat of the process, except this time he met with Drum. That meeting only took about five minutes and mostly consisted of Drum looking at papers and shaking his head. I couldn't tell if he was faking sadness or really gave a shit, but given the dead-fish handshake, I knew what my money was on.

"So he came back the next day and got the same answer," I said.

"Looks that way. But now we have a real lead."

"Yeah, I figure Drum will remember this guy."

"Especially after this." Amy rolled the video forward to just two days before the robbery. Same guy, same khakis, same necktie. Same Drum, but this time the result was a little different. After two minutes of Drum sitting there shaking his head, our guy got up and slammed his fists down onto the desk, then started yelling and tossing shit around. He didn't pitch the computer monitor, but he cleared Drum's desk otherwise. Security got there in a few seconds and hauled the guy out. I watched on the monitor as he was bodily taken out of the bank and dumped on the sidewalk outside. The image that stayed with me was his face, the tears pouring down his cheeks as he thrashed and screamed.

I pushed the "Page All" button on the phone and said, "Send Mr. Drum to his office, please."

Drum appeared at the door to his office and said, "You called for me, agents?"

"I'm the agent," Amy replied. "Mr. Marbury is merely assisting in my investigation. What can you tell us about this man?" She pointed to the image frozen on the screen. It was a shot of the man's face as he was dragged from the building.

Drum entered the room like a small man in a big job, all self-important swagger and high opinions of himself. He stepped around his desk and sat as Amy vacated his chair. "Mr. McCalla? He's been a customer of the bank for years but recently fell on some hard times. His farm hasn't produced like it did in years past, and he is several months in arrears on his note." He gave Amy one of those sideways smiles, like he wanted to tell her everything but his hands were tied, the kind of look that said he didn't really want to tell us shit and would use every little rule to keep from being helpful.

"This looks like he came in looking to borrow more," I said.

"I can't really discuss personal banking matters—" His voice cut off as I stood. I walked over to his office door and closed it, then turned the knob to lock it.

I turned back to face the sweaty little turd. Something about him irritated me the second I met him, and every word that came out of his mouth cemented my low opinion of him. "Look, you officious little prick. If McCalla is our dude, then he has been robbing about a bank a day since he left here, and if we are going to have any chance of catching his ass, we need to do it in the next forty-eight hours, before he either gets enough money to buy an island, or just decides to fade away into the ether. So far he hasn't hurt anybody, but robbing banks is serious business, and if somebody gets killed because you're dicking us around, I will take it very personally."

"I don't think you'd enjoy that, Mr. Drum," Amy said.

"I might enjoy it a whole lot, though," I replied. "So what's the deal,

Drum? Why did McCalla want the money? What was he so upset about that he trashed your office and might have started robbing banks all along I-20?"

Drum looked paler than ever as I leaned over his desk at him. "Talk," I said through gritted teeth.

"It's his son."

"Shit," I said. "I hate it when there are kids. What about his son?"

"His son has a rare form of leukemia, and the treatments are very expensive. His son was scheduled to start a new experimental treatment in Atlanta this week, but his insurance refused to cover it. His son is very ill and is probably going to die. Even with the treatment, they were only hoping to prolong his life for five to seven years."

"Shit," I said again. "How old is the kid now?"

"Seven." Drum looked down at his desk, finding something very interesting in the surface of the wood. I didn't blame him. I wouldn't have wanted to look me in the eye, either.

"So you're telling me that this man came to you with a story about a seven-year-old boy, who would likely die without a stem cell transplant, and even though this man has been a customer of this bank for years, and even though he had collateral to back up the loan in the form of his house and farm, you refused to lend him the money. Is that what you're telling me?"

Drum sputtered for a few seconds before he took deep breath, stood up, and looked me in the eye. "Yes, that's what I'm telling you. I'll say it to you just like I said it to Mr. McCalla. I wish I could help, but I can't. There are rules that must be followed and after all of the economic mess we're finally dragging ourselves out of, those rules are more ironclad than ever. I cannot lend money to a man who already owes more than he can possibly ever earn, and I cannot use a farm as security against a loan for more money than the farm will ever sell for. If that makes me the villain, so be it."

"I don't know that it makes you a villain, Mr. Drum," Amy said. "I understand that you were just doing your job. But can you tell me anything about Mr. McCalla's state of mind when he left your office the last time?"

"He was distraught. And I felt horrible for him, I still do. Nobody wants to see a child suffer. But I am not the final authority. Even if I tried to write a loan to Mr. McCalla, it wouldn't make it through our underwriting department. My hands were tied."

"What about insurance?" I asked.

"Apparently they were denying the procedure because it is experimental. Mr. McCalla had the necessary paperwork completed by his doctor, but the insurance company refused to pay for it. He needed somewhere in the neighborhood of thirty thousand dollars or the hospital would not perform the operation."

"Between banks, insurance companies, and hospitals, we're getting all my favorite things wrapped up in one case," I grumbled.

"Yeah, can we go back to being chased by werewolves and getting in fistfights with Bigfoot?" Skeeter said in my ear.

"I forgot you were there," I whispered.

"I wasn't, but you were gone so long there had to be something interesting going on, so I switched on the speaker from here."

"You can do that?"

"Yeah, fool. You think I'm going to depend on your technologically illiterate ass to keep me wired into the world? Hell, no." Skeeter laughed, then went on. "But I been all up in this mofo's computer since you started talking to him. He ain't lyin'. McCalla is six months behind on his mortgage, got medical bills piled up to his nut sack, and hasn't worked in almost a year on account of taking care of his sick kid."

"That's fucked," I said under my breath.

"You ain't just whistling' Dixie, sugartits. And please don't whistle, you're tone deaf. Here's something interesting, though."

"What is it Skeeter?"

Amy's head whipped around to me.

"Looks like McCalla's kid Andrew was checked into Grady Memorial this morning, and he's scheduled to have a stem cell transplant at four o'clock." I repeated this to Amy, who nodded and started heading for the door.

"What does that mean?" Drum asked. "Did his insurance company give in?"

"I think it means he found a private carrier to deal with his medical bills," I said. "Sorry for being up your ass, Drum. It just sucks."

"It does, Mr. Marbury. It sucks a lot. There are people I want to help, and the rules won't let me. And there are people that don't need any help at all, and those are the people with big-ass lawyers that manipulate every loophole and screw the little guy. I'm just glad Andy is going to get his treatment."

I shook his hand. It was still damp, but there was a little more firmness to it this time. "I'm glad of that, too, Mr. Drum. Now I reckon we're gonna go make sure nobody dies to make that little boy better."

We got into the truck, and I pushed the button to send Skeeter's face to the screen in the dash and his voice through the speaker system. If you ever want the definition of irritating, run the voice of an African-American homosexual tech nerd from North Georgia through car speakers. It sounds kind like somebody's torturing a cat, except with an occasional "bless his heart" thrown in there. I've never known a cat that would bless anyone's heart.

"Plot me the best route to Grady, Skeeter," I said as Amy clicked her seatbelt. I looked over and gave a long look at the way the seatbelt cut in between her boobs and made them look bigger. I offered up a silent thanks to the god of shoulder restraints before Amy caught me looking and slapped my shoulder.

"Pay attention, we've got a monster to catch."

"Yeah, yeah," I mumbled.

"What's wrong?" Amy asked. Skeeter looked up from whatever he was doing and stared out from the screen at me.

"Is this dude really worth catching? I mean, yeah, he robbed some banks. Let's face it, it's not like he hurt anybody. Banks are all full of assholes, and they're insured by the federal government, which is full of even more assholes."

"Watch it, pal," Amy said, but there was no heat in her voice.

"Present company excluded, or whatever I'm supposed to say so you don't think I'm calling you an asshole. But you know I'm right. This dude just wanted to get his kid an operation, and he couldn't pay for it. So he did what any father would do—he started kicking ass until he got his kid taken care of. I don't want to hunt this dude down, I kinda want to give him a medal," I said. I still hadn't put the truck in gear. I still wasn't sure if I was going to.

"If we catch him and put him away, he'll go to jail. If some redneck cop catches him, he's liable to get shot. And then where would his kid be?" Skeeter's image said.

"Even if we apprehend him, he may not spend any time in prison. DEMON may decide that he has value as an operative and offer him a field position. So we might be doing him a favor," Amy said.

"Yeah, we're from the government, we're here to help," I muttered.

"For once, that might be true. But how will we find him? He can look like anyone?" Amy asked.

"He'll be the one that won't leave that little boy's side for anything," I said. "Skeeter, how long to Grady?"

"Nine hours with no stops."

"So ten and half accounting for Amy's bladder," I said, putting the truck in gear and pulling out of the parking lot. "That means McCalla's boy ought be long since done with surgery and recovery before we show up to put his daddy away."

"That's good, right?" Skeeter asked.

"Not most days. Once the kid is safe, McCalla is free to use his powers as hard and fast as he wants to protect him, protect himself, or just get out of Dodge. But I think no matter what, he's gonna feel a lot better about putting up a fight than he did this morning. And that ain't good for nobody."

I t was closer to eleven hours with a couple of pit stops, one refueling stop, and a decent lunch, so it was almost nine at night when we rolled into downtown Atlanta. Which is about the end of rush hour in that godforsaken town, so traffic was only moderately miserable. Parking my F-250 was worse, but I finally just took up three spots in the hospital parking garage and gave up. A man can only circle a friggin' parking deck so many times before he starts to get dizzy.

I opened the back door of the truck and flipped up the bench seat. I opened the top drawer and put Bertha into her slot in the foam, then stripped off my shoulder holster and laid it in the top of the weapons chest.

"What are you doing?" Amy asked from the other side of the truck. She had her back door open and the passenger side weapons compartment open, but she was adding magazines to her shoulder holster, not taking it off.

"This dude isn't a monster. He's a dad scared he's gonna lose his kid. I ain't gonna shoot him." I didn't go in empty, though. I popped open the bottom drawer and pulled out an asp baton, a pair of custom silver-plated knuckle-dusters, and a small can of pepper spray. I figured that was all the less-lethal stuff I needed, plus it would be a little much to walk through the halls of a hospital toting a Mossberg 500, even if it was loaded with beanbag rounds.

We entered the hospital, Amy's badge on a chain around her neck and her sidearm in full display, me just looking like a walking wall with a bad attitude. Which I suppose I kinda was. We followed the signs to reception, then asked for Andrew McCalla's room. At first the nice lady didn't want to give me the number, what with me looking like I eat babies for breakfast and all, but a glance at Amy's badge changed her mind. We took the elevator to the fifth floor, the soothing music a sharp contrast to the Rob Zombie soundtrack playing in my head.

"Last time I was in a hospital was to visit you," Amy said quietly. She looked up at me, and her eyes were full. "Don't you die on me, Bubba."

"Don't worry. It's not on my list. And if I recall, I managed to not die last time, despite the best efforts of my brother, a chicken shit priest, and a soul-eating nurse from Hell. I think I can manage a worried father."

"That looks like Elvis."

"A worried father that looks like Elvis. Yeah, I think I can still kick Elvis's ass." Then the elevator dinged for five, the doors slid open, and we were face to face with Elvis.

Sometimes the world just throws you a curveball, like when you go to a hospital looking for a shapeshifter, and the elevator doors slide open and the King of Rock n' Roll is standing there staring at you. I'm pretty sure I said something brilliant like "Hey," then Elvis/McCalla threw a cup of coffee in my face, turned around and beat feet down the hall. I charged after him, wiping hot coffee out of my eyes and bellowing like a bull in a china shop, but McCalla was *fast*.

Of course, so was Amy. Maybe it was not having a face full of coffee and cheap hospital creamer, or maybe it was the fact that she was about a third my size, but she kept right on McCalla's tail as he burst through the double doors leading to the maternity ward. I hit those same doors a split second later, but they were already out of sight. I stood at a Y-intersection in the hall, trying to figure out right or left, when I heard a crash of metal off to my left. I barreled down the left-hand fork and caught sight of Elvis just as he turned right around a corner. *Shit, shoulda took the hall less traveled,* I thought as I gave chase. Amy was still close behind him, but she didn't seem to be gaining any, just keeping him in sight so he couldn't shift and disappear.

Amy looked back at me and hollered, "Cut him off!"

"With what? I left my sword at home!" I yelled back.

"I mean get in front of him, dumbass!"

I turned around and doubled back, trying to get back to the nurses' station so I could get in front of them, but they were dashing through the nursery, overturning empty bassinets and sending one proud papa in a rocking chair ass over teakettle. I was hot on their tails when they came through the other side of the nursery, and I swiped a cigar from a confused and deliriously happy-looking grandpa. Elvis led us a merry chase, but finally turned down a hall that didn't end in two more hallways. I swear to God and all the saints they build hospitals so nobody can ever find anything. But of course what was at the end

156

of the hallway—stairs. He flung open the door and darted down the stairs, Amy in hot pursuit.

I cooled my pursuit right the hell off. I've never liked stairs. I didn't like stairs when Jason and me were tumbling down the dozen or so steps leading to the church basement in Vacation Bible School. I didn't like stairs when coach made me run the steps in the stadium in college, and after I wrecked my knee, I pretty much gave up on the damn things. So five or more flights of hospital stairwell at a dead run was not gonna happen.

I took a gamble and headed back to the elevator at a brisk walk. No point in running if I wasn't gonna catch the guy, right? I got in and pushed the button marked "B." If I was gonna lead somebody on a chase down a flight of stairs, I'd keep going down stairs until I was out of options, then head back into the halls. I got off the elevator in the basement and ran to the end of the hall. Sure enough, the stairwell door banged open about the time I got there and Elvis barreled right out in my direction.

I got down in my best quarterback-crushing stance and waited for him. Agent Amy yelled, "Be careful, he's got a—"

But whatever she was trying to tell me he had got lost in the explosion of light, sound, and pain that erupted from my every pore when he ran into me, and I wrapped my arms around his scrawny ass, intent on driving him back into the stairwell, or through the brick wall, whichever was easier.

Instead, I hit him in a leap, right across the middle, and wrapped my arms around his chest. Then every nerve ending in my body exploded, like little tiny nerve ending-sized grenades were going off, with strobe lights attached to them. I twitched, and jiggled, and wiggled, and spasmed, and finally fell down flat on my face right about the time his taser ran out of charge. I lay on the floor, my face very lightly touching cold tiles and the smell of burnt hair wafting out from under my shirt.

Unfortunately for Elvis, or McCalla, I landed right on him as the momentum from my tackle left me in a rush. And since he weighed about one-eighty soaking wet with combat boots on, he wasn't going anywhere. Judging from the wheezing noises I heard coming from underneath me, he wasn't breathing any too well, either. I lay there for a second, then checked every orifice for sympathy. Didn't find a drop, so I decided I didn't give a flying shit how he felt, and I just lay there for a few more seconds while I frantically tried to gain mental control of my bladder functions.

"That hurt, asshole," I mumbled as I came completely back to my senses.

"Lying under you doesn't feel great, either, you giant buffoon. How have you ever had sex without killing someone?"

"I use a swing and flexible women. Now if I get up offa you, you gonna try to run?"

"He's not going to run," Amy said from somewhere over me. "And what was that about a swing?"

"It's need to know, Agent. And you don't need to know until we're done with this case," I said as I got up from the floor, shaking each limb to make sure it was responding to my orders.

Elvis stood up, his face melting into the image of the man we'd last seen on video thrashing a bank manager's office in Shreveport. Wayne McCalla was an average-looking fella. Maybe a little shorter than normal, but I'm a bad judge of that, being halfway to giant myself. He was bald, wore glasses, and was clean-shaven. Not the kind of guy who stood out too much in a crowd, just a normal-looking dude, with the power to turn himself into anything he wanted and a string of successful bank robberies under his belt.

"I suppose you're here to take me away in a black helicopter for government scientists to study so you can use my DNA to make some type of self-camouflaging super-soldier. Well, it doesn't work like that. I can become any human I want, but I can't shape shift into any thing I like, and I'm not a chameleon. I can't blend in with my surroundings. There's no way to militarize what I am, so you should just let me go on about my business," he said, directing all that at me.

"I don't know why you aren't talking to the one with the badge, bro. I mean, haven't you ever seen a movie? If ever there's been a guy built to play the role of big dumb muscle, it's me. I don't negotiate. I hit what she tells me to hit, I shoot what she tells me to shoot." I pulled a gurney over and sat down on it, turning it sideways across the hall to cut off his route to the elevator in the process.

He turned to Amy. "Well, now that you know—"

"Shut up." She held up a hand. "Even if I was inclined to ignore the half dozen bank robberies you've piled up in the last week, which I'm not, you'd still be of great interest to my organization." I noticed she wasn't mentioning DEMON out loud. I thought it might be partly because it's a stupid acronym, but it might be partly because she wasn't convinced she was taking him in. I was kinda hoping it was the second. My Bluetooth beeped and I tapped my ear.

"I just hacked the hospital's computer. His kid came through the transplant, but it's going to be a long recovery, and they aren't sure if it will get rid of the cancer," Skeeter's voice came in my ear. I reached down with a foot and pushed the gurney a little ways down the hall so I could talk without them hearing me. I still wasn't very steady on my feet after the tasing, but I didn't want McCalla to think he could push past me, so I put some distance between us, hoping he wouldn't see my legs twitch.

"Who was the donor, Skeeter?" I asked.

"I don't know, lemme check." I heard keys clicking in the background. "This is weird, it says that Andrew's stem cells came from his twin brother, which is the closest match other than getting your own cells back."

"What's weird about that?" I asked.

"McCalla only has the one kid. Andrew is an only child."

"Well, apparently not, because—holy shit." Skeeter stopped in midsentence.

As soon as he said it, I understood what he meant. "Holy shit is right. I didn't know you could even do that." I turned back to McCalla and said, "When did you figure out how to do it?"

"Do what?" He asked.

"Copy your kid's DNA."

"I don't know what you're talking about. And I want a lawyer."

"You aren't under arrest. Yet," Amy said. She turned to me. "What are you talking about, Bubba?"

"He turned himself into his son's twin brother and copied him down to the DNA so he'd be a perfect match for the transplant," I said. Skeeter let out a low whistle in my ear.

Amy pulled a rolling stool over and sat down. "This happens so rarely as to be amazing, but I'm the one behind here. Please explain to me what my large friend is babbling about."

McCalla looked around for a seat, then sat cross-legged on the floor. "I'm a shapeshifter. I guess you figured that out already."

"Nah, we thought you just looked like Elvis," I cracked.

McCalla glared at me, then went on. Some people just don't appreciate humor when they meet it in real life. "A year and a few months ago, my son was diagnosed with leukemia. We went through a couple rounds of chemo, but it wasn't working. The doctors recommended a stem cell transplant, and we did all the paperwork to run it through the insurance company."

"And that's when it all went to shit," I chimed in.

"Yeah, that's when it all went to shit," McCalla agreed. "I did everything they asked for. I got letters from the doctor, from the head of Oncology, from two or three other doctors agreeing with the course of treatment, the whole damn thing. But they said no."

"The insurance company?" Amy asked.

"Yes, the damn insurance company!" McCalla yelled. "Those bastards weren't interested in helping Andrew get better. All they wanted to do was save a dollar! So I figured I'd have to get the money somehow. I ain't been working in a few months, on account of taking care of my boy, so there wasn't anybody who'd loan me anything. My house is mortgaged to the hilt, I don't own my car, and all my credit cards are maxed out. I didn't know what else to do."

"So you started robbing banks," I said. I tried not to sound judgmental, or accusing in any way, 'cause frankly, I don't know that I woulda done any different in his place.

"Yeah, I started robbing banks. I read up on the FDIC insurance, so I knew the people with money in there wouldn't be losing anything, just the federal government. And fuck them. No offense, ma'am." He blushed a little as he apologized to Amy.

"Don't sweat it. I feel the same way a lot of the time," Amy replied.

"So I robbed some banks. I never took much; I just wanted to get enough for Andrew's surgery, and maybe a little to help get me out of the hole for once. But I wasn't trying to get rich; I was just trying to get by. And help my kid."

"And then you got here, and you copied Andrew's form down to the DNA to make for a better match," I said.

"Yeah," he answered. "I knew the best match comes from taking your stem cells out and putting them back in after the chemo has killed the marrow and the cancer cells, but Andrew's cancer was spread too far and they were worried that he'd just get cancer cells injected right back into his marrow. So they couldn't use his cells."

"So you turned yourself into his twin," I said.

"It's the next best thing—same DNA."

"I didn't know you could do that," Amy said.

"I didn't either. It's amazing what you can do sometimes when you're out of options."

"Speaking of out of options, I might have an option for your situation." I said. I looked over at Amy with an eyebrow raised.

Amy shrugged at me. "I don't know, Bubba. He did rob half a dozen banks. And that is a federal offense. As a federal agent, I don't know if I can let that slide."

"And he is a shapeshifter, and DEMON was created to keep dangerous creatures like that off the street," I agreed.

"But maybe . . . " Amy started, then shook her head. "Nah, they'd never go for it. And how could we trust him?"

"I'm pretty sure they would," Skeeter said in my ear. "Go for it, that is. That is, if you're thinking what I think you're thinking."

"He never hurt anybody in any of the robberies. He didn't even try to fight us when we cornered him," Amy added.

"Except for that whole stun gun thing," I grumbled. I figured I'd forgive him when I could wiggle all my toes again.

"Oh, get over yourself," Skeeter said. "We're working on something here."

"I know, I just don't want us to be too quick in forgetting who tased who around here," I muttered.

"Whom," Skeeter replied.

"What?" Our conversation was starting to feel like an Abbot and Costello routine.

"Who tased *whom*," was Skeeter's reply.

"This son of a bitch tased me! Pay attention, Skeeter! Now, Mr. McCalla, do you want the job or not?" I asked.

It was finally somebody else's turn to look confused. "What?" McCalla asked. "I thought y'all were here to arrest me."

"We were," Amy answered. "But as we've been talking, it seems that my agency could use someone with your abilities. So we are prepared to make all of this—" she waved her hand in the air like half a dozen federal offenses and tasering my nuts off was just so much little BS, "— disappear in exchange for you coming to work for us."

"Work for you doing what?" McCalla asked.

"Helping protect people from monsters. You have a gift, Mr. McCalla, and that means that you also have a responsibility to those who don't have such gifts. People like us help people like them." She waved her hand again, encompassing the whole hospital in her gesture. "You intended to steal, but it was to help your son. And you worked very hard not to hurt anyone. So I don't see any reason why you need to be hurt for that."

"I wouldn't go to jail?"

"Nope."

"I wouldn't have to give back the money?"

"What money?"

"I'd have insurance? Real insurance, not the BS plan that almost killed my boy?"

"Trust me, with the kind of shit we get into, there's serious health insurance." I chimed in on that one, even though the Church paid for my health coverage.

"And you're sure I wouldn't go to jail?" he asked.

"Could one really hold you if you wanted out bad enough?" Amy asked him right back.

He grinned a little sheepish grin and said, "Probably not."

So McCalla joined DEMON, and there was much rejoicing. Really, there was a lot of yelling, and threats of gunplay, and there might have been a couple of broken telephones, but in the end, Skeeter found some pictures of an Assistant Regional Director in a compromising position with a succubus, and everything turned out okay. Except for the Assistant Regional Director, who found himself transferred to the Lichtenstein field office of DEMON to watch over one particularly dangerous but completely inert artifact that hadn't manifested any abilities at all since 1907, when it glowed purple for fourteen seconds and all men within six miles got an infestation of ear mites in their genitalia.

Don't ask me, I don't do the international shit. I got enough problems without the words "mite" and "genitalia" being used anywhere around me.

ELF OFF THE SHELF

"I hate Christmas," I grumbled from my recliner.

"Nobody hates Christmas, Bubba. There are people who don't believe in the story of Jesus, and there are people who believe Christmas has become too commercialized and wish it could be something simpler, but nobody really hates Christmas," Agent Amy Hall said from her spot on the couch.

"Nope, he's not joking, sweet cheeks, he hates Christmas. Has for as long as I've know him, and that's longer than either of us care to admit," Skeeter said as he wove his way through the chairs, discarded shoes, and TV trays scattered across the living room. He passed me another beer, handed a mug of steaming spiced cider to Amy, and sat on the other end of the couch, his legs crossed with his feet under him and basically curled himself around a giant-sized cup of eggnog.

"Why in the world do you hate Christmas?" Amy asked, muting the TV. I could have kissed her for that. We were in the middle of Skeeter's annual Christmas DVD marathon, and if I saw another *Glee* holiday special, I was gonna shoot the television. I mean, I like a good cover song as much as the next guy, but there were not near enough guitar solos on this show for my tastes. I was afraid that if somebody didn't save me, I was going to go out and buy a Taylor Swift record.

"I don't like much of anything about it, Amy. I don't like shopping, so that sucks. I don't like most people, and about everywhere I go is so damned crowded you can't move, so that sucks. I don't like Christmas music, so that starts sucking in *October*, and my only living family is a psychotic werewolf who wants to cut off pieces of me and use them to decorate his tree, so *that* sucks. Oh, and I hate tinsel." I waved my hand around the living room, which looked just like it did every other month out of the year, except there was a skinny fake tree with white lights and a green blanket under it standing in one corner of the room. I wouldn't have even done that, but Skeeter nagged me for three weeks until I finally went down to Big Lots and bought the cheapest tree they had that didn't look like it came off a Charlie Brown cartoon.

There were plenty of presents under the pitiful little twig, though. I might hate Christmas, but I like presents. I like giving them, and I like getting them. I'd already shaken mine until it sounded like I broke one, and I knew Skeeter had run a portable X-Ray machine over his. That's why I always used lead-lined aluminum foil when I wrapped his presents. That and it made it funnier when he inevitably dropped one on his foot.

"Well, I get what you mean about Jason, but the rest of it sounds like just a great big pile of humbug to me. I love Christmas, and I don't have any more family than you. Less, in fact, and mine have all been gone for as long as I can remember." She looked down into her cider, then took a long drink. "That's really good, Skeeter, what did you put in there?"

"I put in a little splash of Captain Morgan Dark to give it some kick. How do you like it?"

"It's good, makes me warm all the way down to my toes." She looked over at me with her hair falling down over one eye and gave me a little smile. "Can I crash here on the couch tonight? I probably shouldn't drive."

I smiled back at her. "Nope."

She sat up a little straighter and frowned. "No?"

I grinned at her. "Nope, the way Skeeter pours Knob Creek into his eggnog, he'll be out on the couch before these goofballs get around to singing 'Silent Night.' You'll just have to find someplace else here to crash."

Agent Amy unfolded herself from the couch and walked slowly over to my recliner, then curled up in my lap like a Siamese cat, all slinky purr and bad intentions. "Well, where might I find a place to sleep?"

"I think I can come up with something," I replied, then leaned down and kissed her. I went for a short kiss, the little "I like you but there are people in the room" kiss that we usually trotted out for polite company. Either there was a lot of rum in that cider, or she decided Skeeter was family, because she slid her arm around behind my head and held me tight, kissing me like she knew what she wanted.

I kissed her back, reaching around behind her back to pull her close, then froze as I heard running footsteps on my porch. I stood up, knocking over a TV tray and tossing Amy onto the couch. I put myself between the front door and Amy and Skeeter, hearing the click of Skeeter opening the hidden gun safe in the back of the couch. Bertha was hanging in her holster on the back of a dining room chair, but that was a good ten feet away. I'd have to make do with what I had on me. I drew my Judge revolver from the back of my jeans and flipped open my pocketknife left-handed.

"Got you covered," Amy said from behind me, and I knew she either had her Smith & Wesson .40 or her Glock backing me up.

The door burst open, and Uncle Father Joe ran in, immediately throwing up his hands at the sight of the small army he was facing. "Don't shoot!" he shouted.

We all lowered our weapons, and I said, "Damn, Joe, you scared the crap out of us. What's going on?"

"Scared the crap out of you? I run in here and think I've stumbled into a war zone. What's with all the firepower?"

I looked around. I had a pistol and my pocketknife, a Buck 110 folder. Agent Amy was still in a perfect isosceles stance with a Smith & Wesson M&P40 pointed at the floor, and Skeeter had my trusty

Mossberg 12-gauge slung over his shoulder. Seemed like an ordinary Saturday night to me, but my definition of normal might be a little skewed.

"There have been a few break-ins in the neighborhood, Padre. You might remember one of them, involved my brother?" I prodded.

"I remember. It's why I don't go anywhere without this—" Joe lifted his pants leg to reveal a Ruger LCP strapped to his right leg. "But I still didn't expect y'all to draw down on me."

"Sorry, we had the TV on so we couldn't see you on the monitors," Skeeter explained. "Bubba rigged the remote so it doesn't flip over when the motion sensors trip anymore."

"Too many interruptions when I'm watching football," I grumbled.

"So Saturday afternoon in the fall is the time to mount a surprise attack on the Bubba compound. I'll keep that in mind," Joe remarked. "Is that cider? It smells great. I'll help myself, it's cold out there."

Joe walked over to the stove and ladled out a coffee cup full of Skeeter's spiked cider. I didn't say nothing. I figured I'd let him figure it out on his own. He took a big sip and smiled. "Perfect."

Joe looked at me, then at Skeeter, and said, "What? The rum? It makes it warm you up all the way down to the toes. What are y'all looking at? I'm Catholic, not Baptist. We invented Irish coffee."

"I just figured y'all couldn't . . ." I couldn't figure out exactly how to say it, so I shut up.

"We can't have sex, Bubba, if the Lord wanted to take drinking away from us too, nobody would *ever* enter the priesthood!" Joe laughed and knocked back the last of his cider. "Now, gear up, but keep everything concealable. We've got a problem downtown."

"Yeah, they call it a parade, Padre. It happens every year." I finished off my beer in one long pull, then started back toward the kitchen for a replacement.

"There's an elf tearing through the town square, Bubba. It's wreaking havoc with the celebrations, and I'm afraid somebody's going to get hurt if it isn't stopped."

"An elf?" I asked.

"An elf," Joe confirmed.

"Like little Keebler elf?" Amy asked.

"More like a really pissed off Legolas, with a bastard sword and a bad attitude," Joe corrected.

"I always wondered why they called it that," Amy mused as she turned and started poking around in the gifts under the Christmas tree.

"They call it that because it's a bastardized long sword, with a handle just a little . . ." My voice trailed off as I got distracted by the view of Agent Amy down on her knees, buried up to her shoulders in presents. The view from my angle was truly spectacular, and I turned to Joe.

"Padre, this had better be a real serious crisis downtown because that is a seriously fine-looking woman, and I am now going to wreak some serious havoc of my own with whatever is taking her off my lap this afternoon."

"I understand, Bubba. I'm celibate, not dead," Joe replied.

"You're gonna have to pray about that later," Skeeter said, heading for the door.

"Where you going?" I asked the little tech wizard.

"I'm going home where I can monitor things, research things, make smarts comments over comm to y'all while you try not to get yourselves killed." He didn't even break stride as he walked out the front door, down the porch steps and out to his little Blue Volkswagen Beetle. He kicked up gravel all across the yard as he hauled ass home.

I turned back to Agent Amy, a little disappointed that she was on her feet. The view from the front was impressive, too, but my eyes dropped to the package in her hand. "What's this?" I asked.

"It was going to be your Christmas present, but I think we might end up needing it tonight. She handed me a box wrapped in red snowman gift-wrap. I set it on the table beside my recliner and went over to the tree.

"What are you doing?" Amy asked me.

"We do have a crazy elf running loose that we need to stop, remember?" Joe said. "I'm as much a proponent of togetherness and exchanging gifts as the next guy, but can we prioritize?"

"I am prioritized, and from the weight of that box, so is Amy. Here you go, doll. Merry Christmas." I pulled a big box out from under the tree and handed it to Amy.

"You might want to sit down first?" I said, not quite fast enough to keep her from collapsing under the weight of the box. Sometimes I forget that normal people can't just hold a hundred pounds of high explosive ordinance without being prepared for it.

Amy tore through the blue and gold menorah wrapping paper in seconds, making a blizzard of paper and ribbon all over the floor. She let out a little squeal when she saw the U.S. ARMY stencil on the green metal box, but she got a confused look on her face when she opened up a crate of 40mm grenades.

"Um, Bubba?" She looked up at me, holding one of the grenades. "These are amazing, but there's something—"

"I know." I cut her off by holding out a long package in matching paper. This one wasn't wrapped nearly as well, and its shape was pretty distinctive, so there wasn't a whole lot of surprise when she tore off the paper and saw a Heckler & Koch HK69A1 grenade launcher, complete with shoulder strap and bandolier for grenades.

She jumped up and gave me one of those full-body hugs that women can do if they're small enough, where they jump on you and wrap arms and legs all around you. She kissed me all over my big fuzzy beard, and we would have progressed to more serious kissing if Joe hadn't been tapping his foot and making sure we didn't forget that we had a can of whoop-ass to go open on Captain Keebler.

"There's a bunch of different grenades in there—frags, smoke, flash-bangs, flares—whatever you need," I said, putting her down. Amy immediately started loading a selection of grenades into her bandolier.

"Well yours is a little more designed for close work, since you've got Bertha for anything at a distance. And you've got this bad habit of punching things meaner than you, so I went old-school." I opened the box to find out that she wasn't joking about going old school. She had a pair of ceastus made for me. I could tell they were custom because they fit; nothing store-bought ever fits when you're six and a half feet tall and over three-fifty.

These were basically juiced up mechanic's gloves with the finger-tips cut off past the first knuckle. There were steel bands running along the long bones of the hand, with screw holes for different types of studs and enough padding backing the metal strips that I could punch through solid steel and not hurt my hands. I looked through the box and selected a set of screw-in knuckle-dusters, thinking I'd start out with the less-lethal option and upgrade to spikes if I needed to. This basically just gave me a set of flexible brass knuckles screwed into my reinforced gloves, adding weight and strength to my punch without taking away the use of my fingers for my gun or knife.

"They're beautiful. I'll treasure them and get them bloody right away," I said, slipping the gloves on my hands and clapping them together. "Let's go downtown and beat some elf ass."

The elf was easy enough to find. He was the seven-foot tall male model in plate armor swinging a sword through the Christmas floats and generally making a spectacle of himself. We pulled my F-250 as close as we could, which was still several blocks away 'cause of traffic and the pieces of floats, which were basically now overturned flatbed trailers with a bunch of wrecked paper máché.

"Our first task is to get him out of the public view. If we can contain this quickly, we can get a story spread of an escaped mental patient," Amy said. She was in full Secret Agent of DEMON mode now, in all black tactical gear with a flak jacket, ballistic helmet, shooter's glasses with infrared coating to let her track heat signatures, black combat boots, hard rubber knee and shin guards, elbow pads, black shooter gloves and her hair pulled back in a tight ponytail. Her Glock was on one hip, a collapsible baton on the other, a Taser in a Velcro holster at her waist, and an MP-5 slung across her chest.

I looked like Grizzly Adams just stepped out of a mosh pit, in blue jeans, old Doc Martens, a Dimebag Darrell Lives! T-shirt, a CM Punk hoodie over that to hide Bertha, my Desert Eagle pistol in a shoulder holster. My Judge revolver was at the small of my back, and a silvered kukri hung off my belt. I was wearing my new ceastus on my hands and a black University of Georgia baseball cap on my head. Father Joe was wearing the same thing he always wore—black dress shirt, black jeans, black harness boots, priest's collar and a motorcycle jacket. He might have been a priest, but he was a pretty badass priest. He had a Colt 1911 on his hip and a crucifix around his neck. I wasn't sure which one was going to get more work tonight.

People were running every which way but toward the elf, which made our approach not only difficult, but pretty obvious. It's hard to hide in the masses when you're the only salmon swimming upstream. The elf turned to face us when we were still fifty feet away.

"Who dares approach Rec'teer, Prince of Flowers?" he bellowed, bringing his sword around into a guard position.

"I'm Bubba, Guardian of, um, these rednecks!" I hollered back, trying to give as much challenge as he did. I think I fell short by a few miles.

"Do you come to challenge me, Bub-ba?" the elf said with a sneer. He was a pretty bastard, I had to give him that much. He had long blond hair flowing in the light breeze, gold plate and chain mail with a white tabard, and features that looked like they'd been chiseled out of marble. There was an otherworldly grace that would have given away his supernatural nature even if he hadn't been sporting three-inch pointy tips on the tops of his ears. He had tuners that made Spock look human, for crying out loud.

"That depends, Keebler. Can I get you to put the sword down and stop crapping all over the Christmas parade any other way?" I drew my kukri 'cause I assumed the answer was gonna be no. The answer is always no, by the way. It don't matter what I'm asking, the damn critters I hunt are always disagreeable.

"I know not of this Christ-mass you speak of, but these humans are defiling the holy Solstice. They must perish for their insolence!" He turned and sliced the roof off a Subaru parked beside him. The super-sized can opener he was swinging didn't even hiccup as it cut through steel and glass. I was starting to really miss Great-Grandpap-py's sword, and reminded myself not for the first time to beat Jason's ass for stealing it from me. That was in addition to the ass whooping he was going to get for stabbing me with it.

"Hold on here, Legolas, let's put a kibosh on the perishing for a second." I stepped forward, hoping I could get the elf to talking and give Amy and Skeeter enough time to come up with a plan. I had a Plan B, but it was "hit the elf in the fist with your face until his arms get tired," so I wasn't in a real hurry to put that one into motion.

Rec'teer didn't seem very interested in parlaying, as he flicked out that big sword toward my head almost faster than I could see. I got my kukri up in the nick of time, and a shower of sparks flew off our blades. He bore down on me as our blades slid off each other, and followed up his sword slash with a backhanded shot to my face that left me spitting blood. I staggered back a couple of steps, then dropped to one knee as he went for another big swing with the sword. I exploded up off my knee and planted my shoulder right in his gut under the ribs. In football, that gets you under the pads and you can fold a quarterback up like origami. In armor, it works about the same way. I came in under the breastplate and picked the elf up off the ground as I charged. I carried him about ten feet, just enough room to get up a good head of steam, then I rammed him into a parked Subur-ban. His head cracked the window and his ass left a pair of dents in the rear door, but he was still relatively un-squished.

I went back down to my knees as the elf laid a double axe-handle blow between my shoulder blades. He slid out of my grasp, and I figured I was about to get introduced to the edge of that big stupid sword when I heard a *uuhhh* from above me. I felt something like pop rocks pouring down on me, and looked up to see what looked like an elf with a sparkler erupting in his chest.

I spun away just as the flare went off, blowing the elf six feet back and setting his big blond ass on fire. I looked around, and Agent Amy was standing back by her Suburban, her new grenade launcher aimed at the sword-wielding psycho. I gave her a grin and a thumbs-up, and got a big grin back, then saw her grin fade and her eyes go wide. *That's never good*, I thought, and turned to see what kind of terrible thing was coming my way now.

At least it was the same terrible thing and not something new to deal with, that was the bright side. The less than bright side was there was a seven-foot-tall elf stomping back in my direction with a sword the length of my legs and no more damage than a couple scorch marks on his armor. I decided that it was time to screw fighting fair and drew Bertha. I came up to one knee and sighted on the chain mail piece right between his plated shoulder pads and squeezed off seven fifty-caliber rounds. Rec'teer stopped in his tracks and jerked like he was getting hit by a sledgehammer, which was probably what it felt like.

Unfortunately for me, sledgehammers don't do shit to elves. All seven rounds hit him square in the center mass, and all seven rounds fell to the ground a couple feet to either side of him, all their energy spent trying to punch through his chain mail. I holstered Bertha and drew my Judge, spinning the cylinder until a .410 shotgun shell was next to fire. I pulled the trigger and sent a shell full of silvered bird-shot into the elf's face from eight feet away. Then I did it again for good measure.

Silver works wonders on a lot of supernatural creatures. Elves are not on the list. He wiped the shot away like it was dirt I'd thrown in his face and knocked the gun out of my hand with an easy slap.

He laid his sword against the side of my neck and said in a low voice, "Do not move, mortal. I would rather not kill you while your woman watches."

"I'd rather you not kill me no matter who's looking, Elrond," I growled right back in his face and popped him on the point of his jaw with a sharp uppercut. His head snapped back and he staggered back a step or two. I felt a little better seeing that he could be hurt, then my vision exploded into stars and everything went black.

"Bubba? Bubba? Bubba, are you all right? Are you awake?" I heard Amy's voice, but it was like it was coming down a tunnel from a long way away. I tried to say something to her, make her know I heard her, but it was no good, I couldn't make my mouth work. I concentrated on making my eyes work, instead. If I could open my eyes I could make her understand that *OHHHH SHHHIIIIITTTT thathurtslikeasonofabitchmotherofgodthathurtsholyshitbiscuitsBatmanthat'spainful.*

"Ow," I managed to speak after a few seconds of moving my mouth and nothing coming out.

"Oh thank God you're alive! I was really afraid I might have killed you for a minute," Amy said. She was kneeling next to me, one tear rolling down her cheek. I wanted to reach up and brush it away, but I didn't have my fine motor control back yet. In fact, I was doing pretty good managing monosyllables and keeping my bladder in check.

"Bubba? Thank goodness you weren't hurt," Joe said. I didn't bother to mention that he has a stupid definition of "not hurt." I tried to reach out but could only move a couple fingers. Joe and Amy got the idea, though, and they heaved me into a sitting position with my back to the Suburban.

"Elf?" I asked. I still wasn't sure I could say anything longer without puking, and I wasn't sure that I could puke without drowning.

"He ran off after Amy shot him with another grenade." Grenade. That made sense. If I was standing next to the elf when a grenade hit him. . . Nope, still didn't work. I couldn't figure out why I wasn't dead. This time.

"It was a concussion grenade, Bubba. And I shot it over the two of you to land right behind the elf. It blew him off his feet, but I guess you were a little too close and I might have blown you up a little bit. Sorry about that."

"Happens," I croaked, and reached out my arm to Joe. "Help me up." He looked like he wanted to argue, but since I'd managed a full sentence, I guess he thought I was okay, or at least better.

I leaned on Joe and the hood of the Suburban for a long minute trying to get the ground to stop doing cartwheels. It finally stabilized, and I looked at Amy. "Which way did he go?"

"He headed off that way." She pointed off down Main Street.

"Did he look like he had a plan or was he just running away?" I asked. My head was starting to clear, and a high-pitched noise was starting to ring in my ear. After a couple more seconds, things calmed down enough for me to recognize Skeeter's voice.

"Hey Skeeter, you can quit yellin'. I ain't dead."

"I know you ain't dead, jackass. I monitor your heart rate when you're in the field. You probably have a concussion, though."

"Yeah, my vision's a little fuzzy. I probably shouldn't be the sniper on this gig. Why don't I leave that to somebody who can see and I just hit things real hard?" I asked.

"You mean like every other time?" Skeeter shot back. "Fine. But you might want to move your ass on over to the church."

"Why, Midnight Mass ain't for a couple of weeks—oh shit."

"Oh shit is right. Your dance partner is at the church doors and he looks like he's fixing' to tear some shit up."

I turned to Joe and Amy. "He's at the church. Amy, you drive." I tossed her the keys to my truck and started toward it. I stopped by the passenger door and looked back at Amy, who hadn't moved. "You comin'?" I asked.

"You're letting me drive your truck?" she asked. She turned around but still hadn't moved.

"Yeah, I got a concussion and probably shouldn't drive."

"But I'm your girlfriend, and you're letting me drive your truck. In Georgia isn't that common-law marriage?"

"Only if we're cousins. Now please get your cute ass in here and drive us to church. And don't get any weird ideas about us both being in a church and that "M" word coming out your mouth. I love you, but we ain't nowhere near ready for that conversation."

Amy took about three steps and then came to a dead stop again. "You . . . love me?" She looked up at me, and I heard Skeeter suck in a breath over the comm.

"Don't fuck this up, Bubba," he whispered in my ear.

Don't fuck this up, Bubba, I thought at the same time.

"Of course I love you. And I'll be happy to show you just how much *after* we take care of the psychotic elf currently turning Uncle Father Joe's church into tiny little holy relics."

Amy nodded, then ran to me and threw her arms around my neck. She kissed me on the lips, then whispered in my ear, "I love you, too, you big ox."

She let go of my neck and stood there looking up at me. She was grinning like the kid that really got a pony on Christmas morning, and I felt a big stupid grin come across my face too. We stared at each other until Joe slammed the back door of the truck, snapping us back to the reality of a mythical creature hell-bent on our destruction waiting a few blocks over. You know, like every Tuesday night.

I left Bertha in the truck along with the Judge. Bullets and silver shot didn't do anything to the elf, so I didn't need the extra weight. I opened the weapons case under the backseat and poked around for anything useful, but it was full of guns and knives, not really anything that I could use.

"Elves hate iron, right, Skeeter?" I asked the air.

"We don't really know, Bubba. The mythology is so jumbled between elves, fairies, and creatures of the Fae realms that we can't separate reality from one of a hundred books. Tolkien's elves had no ill effects from iron, but I've read some books where elves and fairies are interchangeable, and both are weakened by iron."

"So we don't know?" I asked.

"Unfortunately, no."

"Well that ain't exactly helpful, Skeeter."

"Sorry." And he sounded like it, too. It wasn't often Skeeter couldn't answer something, and when he couldn't, it bothered the piss out of him.

"Hey Bubba?" Skeeter asked again.

"Yeah, Skeet?"

"Where did this elf come from?"

"What?" Joe and Amy both looked at me. We'd all been so caught up in the catching, killing, or just stopping of the lanky bastard that none of us had even asked about how he got here or what he was doing.

"There ain't never been elves in Georgia, Bubba. They're a European thing. There's some out West, up outside of Portland where there's still some old-growth forests, and there's even some swamp elves down in the bayou of Louisiana, but this guy calls himself a prince, and those are old-school German or French elves. So what the hell is he doing in Georgia?"

"Skeeter, I'll put that on the list of things to ask him right after I finish kicking his ass," I said, then snugged up my ceastus and walked up the steps to Joe's church.

The elf prince was standing at the front of the church, just on the other side of the communion rail. He whirled around as I stepped through the doors and drew his sword.

"You come for more pain, human? You are either stronger or more stupid than I expected." He looked none the worse for wear for having a grenade go off right behind him. I'm sure I looked way the worse for wear since I was seeing two of him about every other time I blinked.

"I ain't sure which one myself, Keebler, but it's time we figured out how to get you sent back to elf-land and out of my town without any more property damage." I started down the aisle, and the elf grinned and hopped the communion rail to meet me.

He put his sword away, I reckon to make the fight a little fairer, but I wasn't sure that was going to help. He was bigger, faster, stronger, and made of magical elf-stuff. I was concussed, bloody and beat all to hell, but this son of a bitch was in my town, and I was determined to get rid of him one way or another. I started my charge when I was twenty feet from him, so I had a full head of steam when I laid into the elf's jaw with a haymaker that would have made Mike Tyson proud.

It didn't do shit. I hit him square in the jaw with my iron-loaded fist at a dead run, with three hundred fifty pounds of pissed-off redneck behind it, and it knocked him back all of two feet.

"A mighty blow, human. Almost worthy of an elf," he said, then laid an uppercut on me that lifted me off my feet and took out three pews when I landed.

I lay there for a second, then rolled under what was left of another pew as the elf leapt into the seats to plant both feet in my sternum. I made sure my sternum was nowhere near his feet and came up with a broken piece of pew in both hands. I laid that thick oak across the back of his head and shoulders like an old-school Mick Foley chair shot and shut my eyes tight as the pew exploded into splinters across his shoulders and armor.

That drove him to one knee, and I pressed my advantage. With Rec'teer down on one knee, I slapped him in a rear chokehold and tried my best to pop his head like a zit. His armor kept me from getting much pressure on his throat, and he stood up with me on his back like I was nothing but a big hairy backpack. I wrapped both legs around his midsection and squeezed with my arms and legs. I heard a rib pop through his chain mail, and he actually sucked in a breath like I'd hurt him.

Then he got serious about kicking my ass. He reached over his shoulder and grabbed my head in one hand like he was palming a basketball. He pulled me over and tossed me in a flip that sent me flying a good ten feet before I plowed through another four or five pews and got a faceful of splinters. I lay there for a second, then pushed myself up on all fours. That turned out to be a mistake because it left my ribs exposed to the football kick the elf unloaded into my middle. I flopped over like a flounder sucking for air, and all I could do was look up helplessly as a big armor-clad foot came crashing down at my face.

BOOM! The air was split with a huge explosion and the foot disappeared from my vision, along with the rest of the elf. *BOOM!* Another explosion, and the smell of high explosives filled the church. *Amy's here* was my thought as I tried to pull myself to a standing position. I made it to one knee and looked around before the pain in my ribs froze me in position.

Amy was standing at the back of the church, grenade launcher in hand. She would fire a round at the elf, lay him flat for a few seconds, then calmly pop the spent shell out of the launcher, load up another round, and lay into him again. This went on for three or four rounds, her shooting the shit out of the shiny elf prince, him getting back up, her shooting him again, until the last time he came up with his sword in hand. That time she fired, but with a flick of the wrist that would have won Wimbledon, he volleyed the grenade right back at Amy. The concussion grenade hit the ceiling right above her head and exploded, showering her with drywall, wood, and roofing material.

"Amy!" I yelled.

"She's fine, Bubba," Skeeter said into my ear. "She got out into the vestibule just in time. But she can't get back to you for a minute or two."

So I was on my own against the elf. Again. I stood up, using my fingers to push my broken ribs back into place. Between the pain of my ribs and the concussion, there were a lot of flashing lights going off in my head, and more than a couple of flashes coming from the inside of the church, too, from little fires and sparks that we might have caused in our scrap.

"All right, you pointy-eared son of a bitch, come get some," I said from the middle of a field of splinters. I had to use a pew to hold myself up, but I was determined to put this bastard down once and for all.

"Time to die, mortal. You and your pitiable race have defiled the holy solstice. The penalty for that blasphemy is death. And I am happy to deliver the sentence."

"Not in my house, elf." I looked past the elf to see Uncle Father Joe standing on the pulpit, the Christian flag in his hands like a quarterstaff.

The elf turned to him and laughed. "The girl was armed with magic. The male is at least overlarge for one of your ilk. What makes you think you can stand against me, little human?"

Joe reached up and stripped the flag off the pole, leaving himself with a six-foot pole with a gold cross on one end. He carefully unscrewed the cross from the pole and set in on the altar. Then he stepped down off the pulpit and walked down the aisle to the elf. They met in the center of the church, Joe a two hundred pound, six foot tall man armed with faith and a big stick against a seven foot elf in full battle armor with a sword that could cut through solid steel and a punch that could knock a rhinoceros out cold.

"What lets me stand against you, elf? God. This is His house, and I am his servant. And you will no longer defile my place of worship." Joe spun the flagpole around over his head and laid into Rec'teer like he was the star of the Sunday afternoon kung fu movies me and Skeeter grew up on.

Joe was a man possessed, almost literally. He lashed out with the flagpole again and again, and every time he landed a blow, the elf staggered backward. He blocked sword strokes with the wooden pole, and the sword bounced off like it had hit solid rock. Rec'teer went for an overhead strike, but Joe knocked the sword aside and struck back with two quick raps to the back and a spinning shot to the forehead. Another upward strike to the point of the jaw and Rec'teer's eyes crossed. One more overhead twirling strike to the temple and the elf's helmet went flying across the church to clatter against the brick wall. Rec'teer spun in place and sagged to the floor, his eyes rolling up in the back of his head.

I looked at Joe, standing in the center aisle with moonlight streaming in the stained glass windows. There seemed to be a glow around him that didn't come from the moon, but I couldn't be sure. I did know one thing—that wasn't just Joe swinging that flagpole like a damn ninja.

"What the hell was that, Joe?" I asked, limping over to the unconscious elf.

"I don't think it was anything from there, Bubba," Joe grinned at me, leaning on his staff.

"Have you been taking Jackie Chan lessons when I wasn't watching?" I asked.

"No, Bubba. That didn't come from me. I can't do those things. I've never had a karate lesson in my life, you know that."

"Then what was it?"

"What do you think it was? We deal with the worst things the supernatural world has to offer on a daily basis. Why is it so hard to believe that the good things in the legends are real, too?" He gave me one of *those* looks, the kind you only get from a priest or a mother.

"I don't know, Joe. It's easy to believe all the bad stuff is out there because I see it. I fight it, I kill it. But if all the good stuff is there, too, then . . . I don't know. I guess what I'm saying is if all the angels and good stuff is real, why do we still have to fight so damn hard? Why doesn't He just send us a bunch of angels down to clean up the mess?" Out of the corner of my eye, I saw Amy come into the sanctuary through the side door, then stop cold as she saw the unconscious elf.

"Maybe it's our mess, Bubba. And He only lends a hand when we need it, not necessarily when we want it." Joe held out his own hand, and I took it. He pulled me up, and then into a hug, and I felt *something* run through me. It was warm, and for a second in his hug I smelled my dad's aftershave, and my mother's gravy, and the privet hedges at Sanford Stadium, and Amy's perfume. I hugged him back, maybe a little harder than I intended, but he didn't whimper much. After a few seconds, I pulled away and watched as the last of the glow around Joe faded. That's when I noticed my ribs didn't hurt anymore. And my vision was clear. And all my bruises were gone.

"Joe, what the hell?" I asked, then shut up as Joe's eyes widened.

"You're healed," he murmured.

"Yeah, it sure feels like it."

"Your face, your nose is fixed, your eye isn't bloody." He reached up to poke at my jaw, where there had been a mother of a bruise blossoming from the elf's punches. It didn't hurt. Whatever had possessed Joe had healed me before it went away. *Cool.*

"Are you two finished having your moment?" Amy asked, stepping into the aisle. "Because I think we'd better find some way of tying this big bastard up until we figure out how to get him back to wherever he came from."

"And whenever he came from," Skeeter's voice came over the comm. We all looked at each other, and shrugged in turn.

"What do you mean, Skeeter?" Amy said. It was good having a girl around when the obvious question needed asking and our guy code wouldn't let us ask. It also gave me somebody who could read a map or in a pinch, ask for directions, both serious violations of the guy code.

"I've been researching that armor, and a couple things he said, and I'm convinced that he's not French or German."

"That's good," I said. "I don't like the French. Buncha cheese-eating surrender monkeys if you ask me."

"We didn't," Skeeter went on. "But the reason he ain't French is because he's English."

"Whatever. French, English, German. It's all a big bunch of 'yonder' to me," I said. "All I care about is how he got here and how we get him back."

"Well, that's the thing. If he was a contemporary elf, we could just send him home. But since I think he was pulled through about a thousand years of time as well as space, it's going to take more magic than just Uncle Joe's holy beat stick to fix this part."

"I prefer 'blessed beat stick,' I think," said Joe.

"Why do you think he's that old, Skeeter?" Amy asked.

"It started with something he said early on, about being a prince of flowers. Turns out that is the royal family of English elvendom, except that line died out after the Battle of Hastings."

"Like 1066 Battle of Hastings?" I asked.

"You were awake in World History?" Skeeter asked.

"I sat right behind Mary Lynn Dogget, and she had an ass that wouldn't quit and a tendency to wear low-rise jeans before they were cool. I did a lot of whale-tail watching in that class. Every once in a while something got my attention. Like wars and shit."

"Well, there were a couple of things going on at Hastings that they didn't mention in our history classes. Like the war between the House of the Sun and the House of Flowers, two rival branches of elven monarchy. Looks like our boy Rec'teer was in line for the throne if the House of Flowers was successful, but if the House of the Sun won the battle, he was screwed."

"Who won?" I asked.

"The House of Flowers was aligned with William's army," Skeeter said.

"Yeah, I didn't pay *that* much attention in history class. Who won?" I asked.

"They call him William the Conqueror for a reason, jackass. Our friend is destined to sit on the elvish throne if we send him home," Amy said.

"Well I'm all in favor of that. The sending him home bit. I don't really give a sweet damn what happens to him then. So we need to find some way to tie up the little prince here, and then we need to figure out what brought him here, and how to send him back."

"Binding him is easy," Skeeter said. "Silver-plated handcuffs will do. Now that the moon is up, his ties to the sun are weakened and the silver will sap his strength. It didn't work in daytime, but it'll hold him now. At least if I've been reading about the right elves, it will."

"I'll double up just in case," I said. I pulled a pair of silver-plated cuffs from my belt and clapped them around the elf's wrists. He was starting to come around as I rolled him over, so I borrowed Amy's cuffs and helped him onto a pew and sat him up.

I moved around in front of the groggy elf and slapped him a little. He jerked awake and strained against the cuffs. He couldn't budge, so I figured we were okay.

"Look here, shining boy. We figured out a few things while you were getting your beauty rest. You don't belong here, and we don't know how you got here. But we're gonna go figure that out, and figure out how to send you back there. Now you just sit tight until we get back, and try not to break anything else. Especially no more people."

The elf just glared at me, saying nothing. That might have had something to do with the bandana I'd shoved into his mouth and tied in place with part of Joe's communion tablecloth, but I just took the win.

I stood up and looked at Joe and Amy. Joe still had his Blessed Beat Stick, and Amy looked like a SWAT commander's wet dream. "All right kids, let's go find out who's been summoning elves, and I don't mean the cute kind that make Fudge Stripes."

"Mmm...Fudge Stripes," Skeeter said in his best Homer Simpson voice.

"Shut up, Skeeter," I said.

"I love me some Fudge Stripes, Bubba."

"Focus, dammit. We gotta figure out how to get this elf back to his shelf so we can move on with the Christmas imbibing. I lost my buzz hours ago, and I can't start drinkin' for distance until this mess is dealt with," I said.

"Well, let me work a little magic . . . Yeah . . . That's good . . . Okay I have a couple ideas," Skeeter said after about a minute of us listening to clicking keys and otherwise standing around scratching our butts.

"Well, let's hear it, Skeeter," I demanded.

"I ran some facial recognition from the parade to try and figure out who from the town wasn't at the parade, so I cross-referenced with the DMV records of everybody who lives within thirty miles."

"You have access to the DMV records?" Amy asked.

"I don't exactly, but DEMON does. And since I'm working for DEMON now . . ."

"Occasionally, as a contractor," Amy corrected.

"Well, I might not have bothered to mention all that when I talked to the dude at the DMV's IT department. I mighta just said I was with DEMON, and if he didn't know what that stood for then he obviously wasn't a high enough pay grade *to* know, so he should just give me access and get out of my way."

I snorted. "You told him to know his role and shut his mouth."

"Pretty much. There were eighty-seven people in the area who weren't at the parade. I eliminated some people as obviously not our elf-summoners—"

"Who did you eliminate right off the bat?" Joe asked.

"And what made you so sure they weren't our guys?" I asked.

"Well, the first four I eliminated was us, because I was pretty sure I'd remember if any of y'all had summoned an elf in Bubba's living room. Then I eliminated Jason, who still comes up in the database because his license is still valid, but we know couldn't summon a sneeze in January. Then I took out anyone under thirteen and over eighty."

"How many did that leave you with?" I asked.

"Forty-six. I cut out the people who lived out of town, and that cut the number to nineteen. Then I eyeballed that list and cut out the people who were actually *in* the parade, and not just in the crowd. That left me with seven names. Three of them stood out." Skeeter sounded awfully proud of himself, and I didn't blame him. He'd narrowed down almost a hundred suspects to three in just minutes.

"Let me guess," I said. "One of them is Jennifer Oakes, and at least one of the others is her boyfriend, Ryan Norris. That Knudsen kid that follows Ryan around like a puppy dog is my guess for the third one, but it might be a brother for all I know."

"How did you know that?" Skeeter sounded like I'd just told him Tom Cruise was really straight and there wasn't a Santa Claus.

"I noticed when we were fighting Legolas that the doors to that hippy store Jennifer's mama runs were open. Everything else on the side streets was shut up tight so people could watch the parade, but this joint was open, but still looked deserted. So I thought there might be a connection."

"Damn, Bubba, that's some good detective work," Skeeter said.

"I keep tellin' y'all I'm more than just a pretty face," I said.

"Thank God, because if you had to get by on your looks—" Amy said.

"We'd all starve!" Skeeter finished, and the two of them broke up laughing.

I stood there for a minute listening to my girlfriend and best friend laugh their asses off at my expense, not really minding a bit. But after a minute I said, "Now that you got that out of your system, can we go talk to the Oakes girl and her little band of elf-summoners?"

Joe zipped up his leather jacket against the outside cold and said, "I think that's a great idea. Let's go find out where our friend came from and see about sending him home." I motioned for Amy to go ahead of me and we walked out of the church through one of the remaining side doors and hopped in my truck.

The door to Golden Oakes was still standing wide open when I pulled my F-250 up in front of it. I strapped on Bertha, but figured I wouldn't have a whole lot of need for her in intimidating a trio of high school kids. Amy and Joe followed me into the store, which smelled of incense, herbs, and musty books. I pulled a flashlight from my jeans pocket and clicked it on, flashing the beam around the inside of the room. I blinked a couple times as the shop exploded in light, then turned to see Joe standing by the door, his finger on the light switch.

"I thought it might seem less suspicious to just turn the lights on. After all, we're not here to rob the place or hurt anybody, we just want to ask a few questions." He pitched his voice louder than normal, I reckoned to make sure anybody hiding in the shop heard us.

"I don't see nobody," I said, then immediately got proven wrong as a muffled *thump* came from the back of the store.

We made our way through racks of books on yoga and the healing power of crystals, shelves displaying all sorts of herbs, powders, and substances to cure everything from erectile dysfunction to planter's warts.

I picked up a jar and shook it. "I never knew there was such an epidemic of planter's warts in our part of the world. I mean, look at this, Amy, there's three different drugs for it just on this shelf."

"Can you focus?" Amy said. "It sounds like there's somebody trapped back here."

"Well, I'll just bring this along. If they've got a planter's wart, I'll be ready."

"Put it back, Bubba," Skeeter said in my ear. "And it's a *plantar* wart, not a planter's wart."

"You ruin all my fun," I grumbled at him, but I put the jar down on a shelf and kept working my way back to the source of the noise. We eventually found a door behind a rack of shelving that had toppled half over, obscuring it from the front of the store. I straightened the shelf in a clatter of bottles and other falling glassware. The door flew open and a skinny girl with long strawberry blonde hair ran into my chest and bounced off, landing on her butt in a puddle of broken glass and scented lamp oil.

"Be careful," I said. "Don't cut your ass. Here, lemme help you up." I reached down and hauled her to her feet. She tried to run past me again, and I grabbed the back of her String Cheese Incident t-shirt as she shot past me, pulling her back in front of me and shoving her back into what looked like the shop's storeroom.

"Let me go! I've got to save him!" She ran at me again, this time pounding on my chest with her little fists. It was kinda cute, if a little annoying. I mean, she was probably twenty, but she was a *little* chick, maybe five-six and a hundred fifty pounds soaking wet. In addition to the long hair and the required jam band t-shirt, she had on Birkenstocks and jeans with daisy patches on the legs. She looked a lot like a refugee from a *Woodstock* remake—like Hollywood's idea of a hippy more than a real one.

I just stood there for a minute until she stopped hitting me. I looked down and said, "Tired yet?"

She nodded, and I pointed back into the storeroom. "Then get your ass back in there and let's have a little conversation." I followed her into the back room, which was almost the size of the shop's front. It was set up for classes or meetings, with a big open space and a couple dozen chairs in rows at the front of the room. Sitting in the floor was a dirty-looking kid that I recognized from catching him hunting on my land a time or two.

"Well, Skeeter, we found Ryan and Jennifer, but I don't see that Knudsen boy here anywhere. What's his name?" I asked the air.

"Tommy," Skeeter said. "Satellite imagery only shows me five heat signatures in the building, so he's not back there with y'all."

Amy and I looked at each other, then she pressed her comm into life. "Skeeter, did you say . . . satellite imagery?"

"Yeah, I might have borrowed a satellite or two to keep tabs on y'all."

"Did you tell them that it was DEMON business?" Amy asked.

"I didn't tell them nothing. It's a Chinese satellite. I didn't figure anybody we cared about would mind if I stole it for a little while, and the Chinese wouldn't admit it anyway."

Amy looked up at me and I shrugged. "He's got a point. So, Skeeter, you're saying that there ain't nobody back here but us, Jennifer and Ryan?"

"And Ryan doesn't look so good," Joe said. He was kneeling next to the boy, who was sitting cross-legged on the floor at the edge of a circle. I looked over the circle for a second and immediately recognized it for what it was—a summoning circle. Ryan was rocking back and forth like an autistic kid that had withdrawn completely. Only problem was, I'd seen Ryan just a few days ago, and he wasn't autistic. He was a normal, engaged twenty-something dude, thinking about hunting deer and Jennifer.

"Yeah, Skeet, something went seriously wrong in here," I said.

"Jennifer?" Amy asked. "I need you to tell me what happened here. Did you kids try to perform a spell? Did something go wrong?"

Jennifer looked from Amy to Joe, then over at Ryan on the floor, then at me, then back at Amy and said, "No, we didn't do anything like that. I don't know what's going on, but we didn't do anything to cause it."

"Really?" Amy said. "Because your boyfriend is almost catatonic, his best friend is missing, there's a summoning circle on the floor of your mother's shop, and there's a mysterious elf tied up in the sanctuary of the Catholic Church. But you don't know anything about any of that?"

"Nope, nothing." Jennifer crossed her arms and leaned against the wall nearest the door. "Can I go now?"

"Nope," I mimicked, drawing Bertha. I put the gun to the back of Ryan's head and looked at Joe. "You should probably move, Padre. It's hell washing brains out of leather. I know from experience." Joe stood up and stared at me, mouth hanging open for a long second, then nodded and stepped back.

"You're right, Bubba. Without enough information about what came through this circle, we can only assume that Ryan is possessed. Just give me a moment to administer Last Rites before you put him down." Joe pulled out his rosary and started mumbling over the boy. I had no idea if he was talking real last rites or if he was just saying "watermelon" over and over again in Latin, but whatever he was doing, it worked.

"Wait!" Jennifer cried and put herself between my gun and her boyfriend's head. Good thing for her I wasn't rolling cocked and locked like normal. I'd never chambered a round in Bertha, just pulled the hammer back and counted on Jennifer not knowing the difference.

"You got something to say, young lady?" I deepened my voice and looked down at Jennifer, doing my best looming bad adult imperson-ation. It gets easier the older I get.

"We didn't want to actually summon anything bad. We just wanted to bring a nature spirit to show those idiots out there what winter solstice celebrations used to be like, back when the pagans ruled and stuff!"

"So you tried to summon a 'nature spirit' on the winter solstice, just because you thought it would be cool?" I asked. Jesus, these kids were even stupider than I thought. They were lucky they hadn't called up a whole damn Wild Hunt instead of just one grumpy elf.

"Where's the book?" I asked.

"What book?" Jennifer wouldn't look me in the eye, so I moved one step past mildly disapproving looming adult into straight up pissed off Bubba the Monster Hunter. I grabbed the girl by her t-shirt and yanked her over to me. I didn't trust the thin cotton not to shred if I pulled on it too hard, so I reached down and grabbed her by the belt buckle and picked her straight up until we were eye to eye.

"Little girl, you have fucked up so royally you don't even have words for it. The 'nature spirit' you summoned turned out to be a goddamn warrior elf from the eleventh century, who was impres-sively pissed off at being yanked out of his time and dropped into ours. He's thrashed half a dozen parade floats, smashed about eigh-teen windows, turned at least four cars into scrap metal, completely demolished the inside of St. Peter's, and put your boyfriend into a coma! And that's on the first friggin' day of Christmas, cupcake! Now if you aren't going to help us find out how to send Tinkerbell back to the rest of the Lost Boys, then I don't have any more time to screw around with you. So tell me where the goddam spell book is pronto or I'm going to turn this shop into a pile of bricks and patchouli and find it my damn self."

I dropped Jennifer onto her feet, and she sagged to one knee, never taking her eyes off me. I'd holstered Bertha, but I stood there, clenching and unclenching my fists like they'd really like to be wrapped around her skinny neck. It was an easy act to put on because it wasn't an act. I was pretty pissed at these kids, who had endangered my whole town with almost everybody in the world I cared about, just by being stupid.

Jennifer stood up and walked over to a bookshelf and pulled a thin brown volume off it. She handed it to me, open to a spell about three-quarters of the way through the book, and went over to sit beside Ryan. She took one of his hands between hers and patted it as he rocked back and forth. I looked down at the spell, then handed it to Amy.

"What am I supposed to do with this?" she asked.

"I dunno. I shoot things. Sometimes I punch things. In rare but highly enjoyable situations, I blow shit up. I do not, under any circumstances, cast spells. No matter how good the intentions. And I don't speak Latin."

"You barely speak English, Bubba," Amy replied.

"Give it to me," Joe said, stepping over to Amy. She handed over the book and he read it over quickly, his finger tracing the lines of the spell.

"I can cast this. I think I can even devise a reversal given a little time. The two of you go get our displaced elf and bring him back here, along with some holy water. By the time you return, I'll have this sorted out."

"You okay to do this, Joe? I don't want you un-holying yourself or something by casting some kind of spell," I asked.

"It should be fine, Bubba. It's no different than an exorcism, really.

I'm just casting the unwelcome spirit out of our time instead of casting a demon out of a body."

"You sure about that?" I asked.

"Not at all, but I'm the best opportunity we have," he said. So Amy and I went out to go get the king-sized Keebler and hopefully send him back where he came from.

Joe had transformed the storeroom completely by the time we got back. He had candles lit at the cardinal points of the circle, incense burning all over the place, and the fluorescent overhead lights off. He was kneeling in a corner of the room when I walked in with the elf over my shoulder. I deposited him on the floor in a clatter of plate mail and profanity, then gave him a little kick.

"Get up, asshat," I said.

The elf glared at me. "I told you I was perfectly capable of walking, oaf. Now you dare to defile my person with your touch? Once I am free of these bonds I shall UMMMFFF!" I put a quick end to his bitching by shoving a bandana in his mouth. It might have been the same rag I had in my back pocket that I checked my oil with earlier in the day, or it might have been the one I was using for a snotrag,

"Sorry about the interruption, Joe, but your asshole is here," I said.

Joe stood up and walked around until he was in front of the elf. "I am going to remove your gag, and then we're going to discuss removing your bonds. But if you are rude or threatening, I will gag you again. I am trying to help you, not harm you, do you understand?"

The elf just glared at him for a few seconds, then nodded. Joe took my bandana out of the elf's mouth and handed it back to me with two fingers.

"That's gross, Bubba," he said. Yup, it was my snotrag. Oops.

Joe turned his attention back to the elf. "Now, I believe you said your name was Rec'teer, and you are a Prince of Flowers?"

I might have snorted just a little but kept every single joke about gay knights and *Game of Thrones* to myself. Skeeter, however, heard me snort and completely cracked up over comm. Joe gave me an irritated look and tapped his ear, shutting off his comm.

The elf spat once onto the floor, and I grinned again. "Yes, I am Rec'teer, Prince of the House of Flowers. And who are you, wizard?"

"I am Father Joseph Jones. I am the pastor here. The priest, or holy man, as you would call me."

"I know what a pastor is, human. I have lived through many generations of your invasion into my world, do not think to educate me in your barbaric ways." He spat on the ground again, but this time when he turned his head, I met his nose with my fist. I wasn't wearing my ceastus, but he got the point.

"Be nice, dickhead. Father Joe is trying to send you home. And he's going to be a lot more gentle about it than I will." I tapped the handle of my kukri for emphasis.

"Fine, priest. What do you plan to do? I am obviously far from my home, and I wish to return," Rec'teer said.

"And we wish to return you. I think that the spell these children cast was intended to summon a harmless nature spirit. A dryad perhaps, or a nymph —"

"Ha!" The laugh exploded out of the elf. "Then they are truly fortunate their spell failed. Have you seen the havoc a nymph can wreak on a gathering of humans if left unchecked? They are spirits of nature, indeed, but their natures are intensely sexual. One nymph could have quickly had every male of breeding age in her thrall, battling for her affections and killing each other for the honor of mating with her. The cost in lives would have been extreme. I merely destroyed some effrontery to the spirit of the solstice."

"You wrecked a Christmas parade, asshole," I grumbled. "Kids love a parade."

"Fat men throwing candy from the back of a wagon? Young women dressed like trollops dancing like harlots atop moving carriages? These are the things you use to celebrate this holy time? You celebrate the turning of seasons and rebirth of the world with these stupid trappings? They all deserved to be destroyed! The solstice is a holy time, a time of hope, a time of reflection, a time of promise. Not a time for frivolity and mayhem. I did your village a favor. Now they can focus on the import of the season without the distractions of your silly fat men and their candy. But my work here is done, send me home."

"Can I just punch him a couple more times before you send him packing?" I asked.

Joe shook his head. "Step into the circle, please." Rec'teer stepped into the circle. He turned around and held out his hands.

Amy looked at me, then at Joe, then back at the elf. "You promise no more fighting?"

"I promise to fight only in defense of my person or an innocent," he replied.

"Good enough for me," Amy said, then unfastened the handcuffs and stepped back out of the circle.

Joe looked up at the elf. "This should send you back directly to where you were taken from, but I'm not a mage. I've never done this before, so all I can say is good luck."

I put a hand on his shoulder. "This morning you woulda said you've never kicked an elf's ass with a flagpole in the middle of the church. But you handled that one. You got this." I gave him a pat on the back and stepped back. "But just in case." I drew Bertha and took up a diagonal position behind Joe facing the circle. Anything nasty coming through that circle was going to get a fifty caliber welcome wagon.

Joe muttered a bunch of stuff in Latin, and the circle started to glow. He read from a sheet of notebook paper, and as he kept reading, the glow got brighter and brighter, until he finished with a bellowed "AMEN!" and the circled flashed super-bright for an instant, making me throw up an arm in front of my eyes.

When the flash subsided and the spots in front of my eyes shrank to something I could see around, the elf in the circle had been replaced by a skinny white kid with glasses sitting cross-legged on the storeroom floor. He was about Skeeter's size, but whiter than the damn Easter Bunny, with bright red hair and about forty-seven tattoos all over his chest and arms. We could all see this because he was wearing a leather loincloth and nothing else.

"Holy shit! I'm back! Thank God!" He jumped up and ran out of the circle as soon as he saw where he was, then turned around and scrubbed out part of the circle on the floor with one foot and knocked over one of the candles, ruining the thing for spell casting.

"Oh thank you, thank you, thank you!" The skinny little bugger kept running around hugging people and thanking folks until he got to me. I put a hand on his shoulder and stopped him before he could get too close.

"Alex Knudsen, I presume?" I asked. "Just stand still for a second, junior. We've got some questions."

"Starting with where are your clothes, A?" I turned to the corner and saw Jennifer staring at the kid. I'd forgotten she was there, honestly. She'd just been sitting in the floor holding on to her shell-shocked boyfriend through the whole banishment, but now she was on her feet, and Ryan was standing beside her, his eyes clear. The two kids ran across the room and hugged their friend, and I made for the door.

Amy caught me before I made it out of the room. "Where are you going?" she asked.

"We're done. I'm going back to my place to get drunk and watch *Rudolph the Red-Nosed Reindeer*. Wanna come?"

"Don't you want to know what happened?"

"I already know what happened. The albino got switched for the elf, and while he was there, the elves mistook him for some kind of magical being. He probably used something like his cell phone to convince them of his power, and he got laid for his troubles. A lot. Now he's back, Ryan's head is unpacked because his best friend isn't dead, and it isn't his fault, and Jennifer is going to pretend to be sorry, promise never to do it again, and in five years, we're going to have to have another meeting with her about her witchy activities, only this time it'll be a hell of a lot more serious. In an effort to keep that from happening, Joe's going to confiscate the spell book and I'm going to talk to her mother. We'll see if it helps. She'll break up with Ryan because he was too chickenshit to go into the circle, which was why Alex was in there in the first place, and she'll go out with Alex for a little while. But he's seen things in the world now, and he's nailed hot

194

elf chicks, so she won't be able to keep him. He'll be fine, and his after-noon of godhood will give him something he's always been missing—confidence. Ryan will be fine, and after a few months will convince himself that this was just too much stolen eggnog at his Aunt Genevieve's Christmas party. And the elf is home. So now it's time to get drunk, and call this one a win. At least for today."

"How can you know all that? You don't know what's going to happen to these kids, and there's no way you know what happened to Alex back there," Amy said.

"Don't bet against human nature, Amy. Everything I said makes sense, and that's how shit usually plays out, whether we like it or not. And as for Alex, well, the symbols on his fake tattoos might be in Elvish, but the language is pretty damn close to pixie, and I might have had some familiarity with pixie mating rituals at some point in my early twenties." I didn't quite meet her eyes with that last bit.

"Oh really? Pixie mating rituals, huh? And how exactly are those different from human mating rituals?" she asked, a smile starting to curl around the corners of her mouth.

"Well, for one thing, there's a lot more water involved, typically."

"Hmmm. Didn't you just have a new hot tub installed this fall?" Amy asked, putting her arms around my neck and bringing her face very close to mine.

"You know, I did do that. You think you might want to go investigate these pixie rituals?" I asked.

"It is my duty as a DEMON agent to familiarize myself with all sorts of extra-natural beings that might interact with humans."

"Well, if it's in the name of duty, how could I refuse?" I asked. "Joe, you got this?" I didn't wait for an answer as I picked Amy up around her waist and headed for the door. Joe didn't answer. He was in full-on Priest Mode, lecturing the kids about the dangers of screwing around with magic and magical beings, property damage, the kind of community service they'd be doing until everything in town was repaired, and to turn over every scrap of spell book they had in their possession, blah, blah, blah. The kids were trying to look contrite, but they'd touched the magic now, and come through it alive, and their eyes couldn't be closed again. I just hoped they could handle whatever they dragged up next.

Then I looked down at Amy, glanced back at Joe and thought about Skeeter, and I figured even if they couldn't handle the next mess, we'd be there to take care of them.

I reached up to my ear and said, "Merry Christmas, Skeeter."

"Merry Christmas, y'all," he said, just as I pressed the comm button to turn it off and carried Amy laughing to my truck.

8

CASKET CASE

"I hate cemeteries, Skeeter," I muttered as I climbed out of my Ford F-250 and approached the back gate of the cemetery. Three and a half hours of driving through the mountains at night had left me with a crick in my back, and now it looked like I was dealing with a conscientious caretaker in a town of barely anybody in the middle of nowhere, Tennessee. Sure enough, I got to the gate and saw a bright shiny chain with a big new Master lock hanging from it.

"It's locked, Skeeter."

"Well, what do you expect, Bubba? A welcome mat?" Skeeter's high-pitched, nasally voice came through my earpiece way louder and clearer than I really wanted it to. "There's been half a dozen graves robbed all over Telford for the last couple of months, so I'm not surprised they've beefed up security."

"I didn't say there was security, Skeeter. I said it was locked."

"Well, that's about what passes for security in the middle of nowhere, East Tennessee," Skeeter replied.

I couldn't argue with him, or with the caretaker. After all, what was somebody gonna steal in a cemetery? A dead guy? Of course, that's exactly what had been stolen six other times in recent weeks, so I reckon that's where I come in.

"I still hate cemeteries."

"We've been over this before, Bubba. You hunt monsters. Monsters hang out in cemeteries. Ergo, you gotta go to a lot of cemeteries."

"I know, but I ain't gotta like it."

"You gonna cut the lock?" Skeeter asked.

"Nah, it's one of them shrouded jobs, and heavy-ass chain, too. I ain't got a pair of bolt cutters with me that'll get through that. The fence ain't real high. I'll just go over and have me a little look-see."

I walked back to the truck and strapped on some gear, just in case I found something interesting or irritable in the graveyard. I already had Bertha in her shoulder rig under my left arm with two spare magazines under my right. I added a Judge revolver to a paddle holster at the small of my back, all five chambers loaded with .410 shells packed with silver shot. On my left hip, I strapped a Cold Steel Gurkha Kukri with a blacked-out blade, a solid foot of sharp edge and bad attitude rigged for a cross-draw, and on the right, I slipped a spike-ended tomahawk, just in case I needed a little additional persuasion. I slipped the caestus on my hands that Agent Amy got me for Christmas and gripped the top of the wall. I heaved myself up the eight-foot wall, my Wolverine steel toes scrabbling for purchase on the uneven rock. It wasn't pretty, and I was real glad I didn't have an audience for it, but I got my big ass up to the top of the wall. I sat there for a minute, more to scout the situation than to catch my breath, really.

It wasn't a very big cemetery, but Telford wasn't a very big town. Nestled in the mountains of East Tennessee, it had one of each major Protestant churches, a couple of spare Baptists and probably a couple of snake-handling Pentecostals back in the hills. I looked out over a couple hundred years worth of headstones, most of them just simple rounded rectangles announcing birth dates, dates of departure, and meaningless platitudes like "beloved father" or "loving wife and mother" or some such shit. I made a couple of visual sweeps across the graveyard before I saw movement out of the corner of my eye.

"I got something, Skeeter," I whispered as I jumped down off the wall and crouched in the dewy grass behind a big headstone.

"What is it?"

"Well, it looks like two or three dudes at a grave. They're too far away for me to see if they're robbing the grave or doing something else."

"I think it's a pretty safe bet they aren't there for the dancing girls, Bubba."

"Fair enough. I'm going' radio silent 'til I see what's going on." I stayed as low as I could as I crept across the cemetery toward the other men. As I got closer, I could see that there were three of them, and they were, in fact, digging. Since I had Skeeter check the newspapers before I got here, I knew that there were no funerals scheduled for the next day, and besides, even in little mountain towns they didn't dig legit graves by hand anymore. So I knew they were probably the grave robbers I was after. This looked like the easiest case ever, and I didn't even need Amy or Skeeter's help.

And the second I thought that, I stepped on a beer bottle some jackass left lying out in the middle of the graveyard, my foot slid out from under me and my whole night went to shit in one big clatter of falling giant redneck. I flipped almost completely horizontal, landed on my ass with a huge *THUD*, and the grave robbers all froze and turned to look at me. They stayed frozen just long enough for me to get to one knee, then they all three took off running in different directions.

Shit, I thought. Running ain't what you'd call my strong suit. I'm more the stand still and beat something all to hell kind of guy. Skeeter's better at running, but his skills lie more in the "running away" department than the "running after." Amy would have probably caught all three of them without having a hair out of place, but if I wanted to catch them all, it was gonna mean shooting two of them. Since I didn't know exactly who or what they were, I thought shooting them might be a little excessive. If I had a smaller gun, maybe, but there's no "shoot to injure" with a Desert Eagle. I shoot somebody in the leg with Bertha, there ain't gonna be a lot of leg left when I'm done. So I chased after the one that ran to my right. He was a couple feet closer than the others, and that seemed like as good a reason as anything.

Problem was, he was fast. I used to be fast. I mean, fast for a three hundred pounder wearing forty pounds of football pads, which meant I was fast for twenty yards or so. I was never fast for long distances, and I did not have nearly the motivation for speed that the fellow I was chasing had. In other words, I was a lot less scared of him than he was of me, so he was keeping a pretty damn good pace. He had a few yards head start on me, and he stretched that out to half a football field or so before I gave up and turned back to the grave. I trudged back through the dark cemetery, thinking back on the last jumbo milkshake I'd had from Cook-Out and how bad an idea that felt like right at that particular moment.

"I lost 'em, Skeeter," I panted into the earpiece.

"I reckoned, what with running being a factor and all."

"What is that supposed to mean?" I snarled.

"Bubba, you are more the stand in one place and beat the shit out of everything around you guy than the run down the monsters in a prolonged chase scene guy. Besides, after running more than a couple hundred yards, what would you have done with him when you caught him?"

"Puked on him until he gave up, I reckon."

"That's nasty, Bubba."

"I am what I am, Skeet. And right now what I am is back at the grave, so lemme check out who they were digging up. I'll get back to you if I find out anything."

"Later, tater," Skeeter said, then clicked off.

I pulled a flashlight off my belt and looked around the grave. The robbers had gotten a couple feet down with just shovels, so the ground must have been pretty soft. I looked around until I found the dates on the headstone and read, "Sanford Blinn, August 14, 1967 - September 5, 2014."

I clicked on the comm again. "Skeeter, see what you can dig up on a Sanford Blinn. He died about six months ago."

"Is that whose grave they were digging in?"

"And I'm currently standing next to holding a shovel? Yeah, that's him."

"Says here he died of pancreatic cancer, left behind a wife and a twelve-year-old son, worked in the local sawmill, high school diploma, clean driving record, no arrests . . ."

"You got all that out of the obituary?" I asked.

"Bubba, I ain't even read the obit. This is all stuff I got by punching his name into DEMON's database. All them conspiracy theories about the government keeping secret files on just about everybody? Looks like they ain't just theories. I've got his phone records, credit card statements, voting records going back the last five presidential elections, way more information than I'm supposed to have."

"Anything peculiar in any of it?"

"You mean like membership in the Necromancer's Guild, purchase of a *Necronomicon* on Amazon or getting caught sacrificing bunnies in the woods behind the Boy Scout Lodge when he was thirteen?" Skeeter asked.

"I was thinking maybe something a little more subtle, but yeah, any of that would explain why he was being dug up in the middle of the night," I said.

"Nope, nothing."

"Nothing?" I asked.

"Do I stutter?" Skeeter shot back.

"Only when Ryan Philippe comes on the TV," I teased. Skeeter had an unhealthy obsession with *Cruel Intentions*. Me, I never got into it. Not enough explosions, but I did enjoy Sarah Michelle Gellar in a bathing suit. "So we got nothing on this guy?"

"Bubba, he's more ordinary than eggs for breakfast," Skeeter said. "There is absolutely nothing supernatural about Sanford Blinn."

"All right, then I reckon there ain't nothin' for me to do but fill this hole back in and let the poor man get some rest. I'm out." I clicked off the comm again and climbed out of the hole.

I had only got about four shovelfuls of dirt thrown back into the hole when a pair of headlights came over the small hill between me and the front gate of the cemetery. I turned to run but saw a pair of flashlights approaching on foot from where I'd left my truck. *Shit*, I thought.

"Freeze!" hollered the cop behind one of the flashlights. I turned toward the voice and put both my hands up, thumbing the comm back on as I did.

"We got a problem, Skeeter," I said under my breath as the cops approached. The tiny headlights belonged to a golf cart that carried a withered old dude and a fat man in a sheriff's department uniform. I reckoned the skinny old fart in brown everything and work boots was the caretaker 'cause he stood back as the fat deputy waddled toward me, one hand on his gun belt and the other twirling his nightstick. I figured it would take me about three seconds to break that nightstick over his head, disarm him and shoot the other two behind me, but my New Year's resolution had been to beat up fewer police officers, so I just kept my hands up and my mouth shut for once.

"What in the hell are you doing, son?" the fat deputy asked as he reached me. He stood about five foot eight and probably weighed about the same as I did, so he was almost five-eight in every direction. I felt like I was talking to a khaki basketball with a bad rug and too much Just for Men in his mustache.

"I'm filling in a grave, Deputy. I came along to pay my respects to my uncle Sanford and saw three men digging in his grave. They ran off before I could get to 'em, but I couldn't let Uncle Sandy be defiled like that." I heard Skeeter groan through the comm, but I thought I'd done pretty well for myself, at least as far as thinking on the fly.

"Boy, I'm not even gonna bother asking you again. I'm just gonna let you finish filling this grave back in, then I'm gonna cuff your ass and take you in for obstruction of justice. And that's for lying to me. If I find out you had anything to do with robbing these graves, I'll probably just make up some shit to make sure you go away for a long time."

"What are you saying, Deputy? Are you calling me a liar?" I bowed up a little at the round man, but he just stood there.

"First off, it's Sheriff, not Deputy. And second, Sanford Blinn was no more your uncle than I'm Will Smith. I think I might have known if the only Samoan man in the Tri-Cities had a lily-white nephew, wouldn't I?"

I didn't say anything, just filled in the rest of the grave and hoped Skeeter had a plan to get me out of this pile of shit.

I'll give the constabulary of Washington County, Tennessee, credit for one thing — they keep a clean jail with cloth pillowcases. I've been in my fair share of Southern drunk tanks, and I'll tell you that rubber mattresses are about the best that I've come to hope for. But the deputies that ushered me into the cell must have thought I was nuts when I started telling them how nice the accommodations were. I didn't bother stretching out on the cot. I knew either my head or my ankles would hang over the end, so I was sitting up leaning against the far wall when a mountain of humanity filled the door to my cell.

The giant wearing a badge actually had to stoop down to make it through the cell door, and he had to kinda go sideways to get in, his shoulders were so wide. He stomped across the room and sat on the cot against the opposite wall. I watched him warily, wondering what the hell was in the water at his mama's house, or if he was just half-ogre.

When he spoke, it wasn't the growl I expected. His voice was deep, yeah, but it was more a Paul Robeson kinda thing, all silky smooth and rich. "I'm Sheriff McGraw. Who are you and what were you doing in that cemetery?"

"I reckon you ain't gonna believe that Uncle Sanford story either?" I asked.

"Not any more than I'd think you were my long-lost twin brother." He held out a giant hand, then rubbed the dark brown skin on the back of it. "Nope, still don't rub off. Now, since I know from your wallet that you're Robert Brabham from Dalton, Georgia, we're left with the why of you being in the United Methodist Church Cemetery with a shovel at two in the morning."

I chuckled and said, "Would you believe I was filling the grave back in?"

"I might do that, but that begs the question of who started emptying it in the first place and where they were when you were filling the hole back in. Not to mention the bigger question — why was anybody digging up the assistant high school football coach in the first place?"

"I wish I could help you, Sheriff. I really do. But you see —" I snapped my jaw shut as I heard a commotion coming from the office part of the jail. "I think you're wanted up front, Sheriff."

"What are you talking about, son? I promise you, I am not in the mood for any foolishness. I've got —"

"Six grave robberies in the past month and one brand-new attempt tonight, no leads, and no real idea what the hell is going on in your sleepy little mountain town, if I can stretch the truth and call it that." I stood up and motioned toward the door. "There's a nice young lady out there with a shiny badge. She's my ride. We're from the government. We're here to help."

About the time the sheriff decided he was tired of my smart mouth and stood up to administer a little mountain justice, the deputy that found me in the graveyard ran back into the jail. "Sheriff!" He was almost quivering he was so excited. Amy must have busted out the black helicopters again.

Deputy Dawg went on. "There's a smokin' hot blonde out here from some federal agency I ain't never heard of before. She landed a black helicopter right on the courthouse lawn! I didn't even know we had those."

"*We* don't, Beaufort. The government does." Sheriff McGraw opened the cell door and motioned for me. "I suppose I could save time by taking you out with me?"

"It sure would speed things up," I agreed. "Deputy, why don't you ask my smokin' hot girlfriend and federal agent if she'll meet us in your interrogation room? Sheriff?" I extended an arm for him to take the lead. Might as well, I didn't know where the damn interrogation room was.

The deputy stared at me, then looked at the sheriff with a question on his face. The sheriff nodded, and the little deputy almost broke into a run.

"Hey, Deputy?" I called after him.

He stopped at the door and looked back at me. "Yes, sir?"

"Bring my guns and gear with you, please. And maybe a couple of beers. I think we're gonna be in there a little while." I followed the sheriff down a short hallway and into a typical interrogation room. The "perp chair" was a basic straight chair with one leg a little shorter than the other three. I didn't sit. There was no way that little thing would hold my big ass. McGraw sat in the "cop chair," which was super-sized to fit him, and I leaned against a wall. It only took a couple minutes for the deputy to materialize with Agent Amy and a duffel bag containing all my gear. I plopped the bag on the table and started strapping guns and knives into their proper places. Amy looked at the wobbly chair, then looked back at the deputy. She never said a word, just exuded disapproval all over the poor boy until he ran out again and came back with two solid chairs.

Amy sat down across from the sheriff and motioned me into the other chair. I sat, like a good boy. This was her party, and I was willing to dance to just about any tune that got me out of jail and back on the case of the grave robbers.

Amy leaned forward and unplugged the tape recorder in the center of the table. "We won't be needing this. Now, I'm sure you have some questions, and I assure you they all will be answered, but first I want to be clear that we are not here to step on your toes. We're not here to steal an arrest or make headlines. As a matter of fact, the fewer people that know we were ever here, the better."

"Especially if any of them are Tennessee fans from the early 2000s. Some of those old boys hold a grudge," I interjected. Amy shot me a "shut up" look, so I zipped my lips and leaned back in my chair.

"Well, I reckon my first question is who the hell are you people and what was this fella doing messing around in the cemetery in the middle of the night?" Sheriff McGraw asked.

"I am Special Agent Amy Hall, and I work for a very select branch of the government that deals with out-of-the-ordinary law enforcement issues. Your grave robbing popped up on our radar, and Mr. Brabham came to investigate."

"So you're Scully and he's like an oversized Mulder," The sheriff mused.

"If it helps to think of us that way, yes," Amy replied.

"I can live with that. So what are y'all here chasing?"

"That's what we don't know," Amy said. "So far, we have no evidence that there is anything supernatural about the grave robberies."

"Except that there's been a bunch of them and they just started in the past month," McGraw chimed in.

"What else has happened in the last month? Has there been a rash of suspicious deaths in the area? Anybody move into an old house that's supposed to be haunted? Anyone start a construction project on a Native American burial ground?" I asked.

"Nothing," McGraw replied. "As a matter of fact, it's been even more boring than usual. We've hardly had anybody die at all. I mean, there was the old Skinner lady who had a stroke and died in her living room a couple weeks ago, and then there was Junior Peabody who fell into the chipper down at the pulpwood mill, but other than that I don't think we've had a death in the community in six weeks."

I looked at Amy, who shrugged. "I can't think of anything significant about that, Sheriff, but it's something to keep in mind. Is there anything you can tell me about the victims of the grave robberies? Other than living here, did they have anything in common?"

McGraw stood up and stepped to the door. He opened it, and the weedy little deputy jumped about twelve feet into the air. I reckon he knew he'd been busted 'cause he scurried off and came back in about eight seconds with a stack of manila file folders. McGraw came back into the room and dropped them on the table.

"Here's the case files. They're pretty thin 'cause we ain't got shit. Pardon my language." He blushed a little and nodded at Amy.

"I work with this assclown, Sheriff. I don't think you could possibly offend me." Amy replied, pointing in my direction.

"Hey! You're also dating this assclown, so what does that say about you?" I grabbed a couple of the file folders and started flipping through them.

"It says I had a moment of weakness, Bubba," Amy said, taking a couple of files for herself. "Do you have these digitized?" she asked McGraw.

"No, just hard copies. We ain't exactly Silicon Valley out here, Agent Hall."

"That's fine. Once we've given these a look-see, I'll have you fax everything to our tech expert. He can run things through some computer simulations and do some deep background checks to make sure there aren't any connections we've missed." She fell silent as we pored through the files.

We spent the better part of two hours reading files and passing them back and forth. McGraw was right — they didn't have shit. In each case, the grave had been dug up, the lid to the vault removed, and the coffin opened. The bodies were all removed with no trace left behind, and the empty caskets and burial vaults were left standing empty. The first one had been found by a jogger on her morning run and the rest by caretakers. They were buried in seven different cemeteries, counting the digging I'd interrupted the night before, and all of the bodies were recently buried, within the last few months.

"What wants to eat dead people?" I asked, shoving a folder away from me. A couple pieces of paper flapped to the ground, and Amy picked them up.

"Well, let's see," she said. "There are fewer than you'd think. Zombies, obviously, will eat dead flesh, but they can't handle tools. Aswang are cannibalistic, but they're only native to the Philippines. Harpies have been known to snack on human flesh, but that's mostly as a punitive measure, not a consistent source of nourishment. Various types of lycanthropes will eat human flesh, but I've never heard of one going for anything months old, and I've never heard of a werewolf eating anything it didn't kill."

"So what does that leave us? Ghouls? Wendigo? Scylla?" I asked.

"Scylla's still under surveillance in Athens," Amy replied. "She's a travel agent now. I wouldn't think it was a wendigo; they tend to be solitary and very destructive. You saw three men or creatures working together, and they ran from you. A wendigo would have attacked and probably killed you."

"So ghouls? They're usually good for grave robbing," I asked.

"It's either ghouls or a fledgling vamp that can't control himself."

"Vamps got no use for dead folks. My money's on ghouls," I said.

"Now we just have to find them," Amy said, closing the file in her hands.

"Now wait a minute, y'all. Are you telling me you really believe in all this shit?" Sheriff McGraw stood up and started gathering his files, looking at Amy and me like we'd grown two heads all of a sudden.

"It didn't seem so farfetched when you were dropping *X-Files* references earlier, Sheriff. What's changed?" Amy asked.

"That was before you said with a straight face that there was a pack of ghouls robbing graves in East Tennessee. Do you know how ridiculous that sounds?"

"About like a werewolf attack in North Georgia? Or a pack of vampires masquerading as a ballet troupe in Charlotte? Or a chupacabra attack in Florida?" I said, standing up. "Well, we've had all those, Sheriff, and a lot more besides. So do you want to help us figure out who the ghouls are in your town, or do you just want to think we're crazy?"

The big man stopped fiddling around with the files and stood still for a moment, head down, hands on the table. I could almost hear the thoughts running through his head because I'd had them myself once in a while when I stood back and tried to look at my life objectively. It's a hard thing, having your worldview forcibly shifted in a matter of minutes, and the sheriff struck me as a man who wasn't accustomed to anything contradicting his opinions. Finally, he let out a long breath, squared his shoulders, and looked up at Amy and me.

"Let's catch these bastards. This would be a real good time for y'all to be wrong and it turn out to be a couple of stupid high school kids playing Frankenstein in the back yard," he said, pulling all the files into a stack.

"I wish I thought that would happen, Sheriff," Amy said.

"Well, where do we start?" McGraw asked.

"I'd reckon we look at the graves," I said. "If there are clues, that's where they'll be."

"We've gone over the graves with a crime scene team out of Johnson City, Bubba. There was nothing there," McGraw said.

"Nothing you were looking for," Amy said. We might have some different criteria."

"I reckon that could be so," McGraw replied. "Where do you want to start? With the newest grave or the newest robbery?"

"They ain't the same thing?" I asked.

"No, they go in the opposite direction, actually. The most recently deceased was the first victim of the grave robbing, and the grave you were in last night was the oldest of the lot."

"Hmmm... that could be significant. Do you have a whiteboard?" Amy asked.

"Out in the bullpen. Let's go out there. I could use some coffee, too. You need anything?" McGraw asked, opening the door.

"Is it typical police station coffee?" I asked. I've had more than my fair share of cop coffee in my life, which might say something about the number of times I've woken up in a jail cell with a hangover the size of Stone Mountain, but that's neither here nor there.

"Hell no," McGraw said. "We can't make coffee for shit. I get a deputy lives over in Jonesborough to bring in some from Dunkin Donuts every morning. There oughta be a couple cups left."

My estimation of this backwoods cop went up several notches. He was a smart hillbilly, and the coffee was *good*. We settled in around the whiteboard with the case files on an empty desk. Amy took up a post in front of the board, so I figured she was gonna do all the scribblin'. Good thing, too. My handwriting sucks.

I put my comm back in my ear and clicked it on. "Morning, Skeeter."

"How was your night in jail?" Skeeter asked.

"Uneventful, so that was good. I didn't have to break nobody or nothin'. I can't complain. They even got good coffee here."

"Cops that can make good coffee? Remind me to get arrested in

East Tennessee next time."

"They ship the coffee in, Skeet, and you ain't never been arrested anywhere."

"Well, that's true enough. Now, what are we working with?"

McGraw gave me a sideways look as I talked to the air, and I said, "Sheriff, I've got my tech expert Skeeter on the line. He'll research stuff for us as we go along. So what have we got so far?"

Amy took up a dry erase marker. "We've got nine deaths in the county in the last six months and seven disturbed graves. What was different about the other two?"

"Well, if that old boy fell in a chipper, there wasn't enough of him left to bury, so there wasn't nothing in his box for a ghoul to eat. And you said the other one was an old lady who had a stroke?" I looked at McGraw.

"Yeah, she . . . she had cats," he said, turning a little green.

"I don't get it," I said.

"She lived alone. And she had cats," McGraw said again. z

There was still something I was missing. "I still don't get it."

"She lived alone. She had a stroke. It was a while before anybody noticed she was missing. And she had cats."

I got it. I was real grossed out, but I got it. "I get it."

Amy looked a little green, too. "So seven of the deaths left significant tissue, and those are the graves that have been disturbed."

"Yeah, but how does writing that on a little whiteboard help us figure out our next step?" McGraw said.

"Well, ideally we'd stake out a funeral, but since people in this county are unfortunately healthy, we need to do a little more work than that, Sheriff." Amy sounded grumpy. It made me feel all warm and fuzzy to hear her be grumpy at somebody else for a change. She's real hot, but she can whoop ass when she needs to, and she seems to feel like she needs to a lot around me.

A passing deputy stopped in his tracks. "Why don't y'all just stake out the Wilson boy's funeral this afternoon, then?"

Amy and I both turned our gaze on the sheriff, who looked at the table and squirmed.

"Sheriff," Amy said, "would you care to enlighten us?"

"Andrew Wilson died in a car wreck Saturday night. He ain't been buried yet because of the autopsy, but they released the body yesterday. Visitation was last night, and he's supposed to be laid to rest at the Presbyterian church this afternoon at two." He hadn't looked up yet; instead, he was studying his fingernails like the cure for cancer was under there.

"And were you planning on telling us this any time before the funeral?" Amy asked. I shivered a little at the icicles dripping off her words.

"I hadn't decided yet." McGraw lifted his head and gave Amy a level stare. "Look, lady, you can be as pissed as you like, but I don't care. This was my town before you got here, and it'll be my town long after you get in your fancy-ass helicopters and fly away."

"I drove," I pointed out. Everybody ignored me. It was kinda neat 'cause nobody ever ignores the giant redneck, but in this room I was barely super-sized.

McGraw went on. "I know you see freaks and monsters behind every tree, but I see a bunch of stupid kids stealing dead bodies for who knows what purpose, and I won't have you disrupting the funeral of one of the town's most beloved young men for no good reason."

"But even if it is just a normal kid thing, wouldn't you put people at the funeral to have a look around anyway?" Amy asked. "Isn't that kind of protocol?"

"It would be protocol if this were a murder, but this kid wrecked his pickup driving home from a bonfire. He was drunk, the autopsy proved it, and now it's not a crime, it's just sad. So I'd appreciate it if you'd leave this one alone. A professional courtesy, and a personal favor."

Amy started to speak, but I held up a hand to stop her. "Who was the kid, Sheriff?" I asked.

"He was my wife's cousin. Her whole family is all messed up about it, and I'd never be able to forgive myself if anything happened to his body."

"Then let us make sure it doesn't," I said. "We'll be out of the way, in the back of the crowd. Nobody will ever know we're there. Then after the ceremony, we'll stake out the gravesite and make sure nobody does anything to your cousin's body."

"My wife's cousin," he corrected automatically, but I could tell this kid meant something to the sheriff. Probably a protégé of sorts, a big, tough kid, plays football in a small town, goes into the family business, law enforcement. Kinda like my story, except for the part where I didn't die young and my family business is a lot creepier than babysitting speed traps and wrestling drunk farm boys on Friday nights.

I stood up and walked over to the big man. I put a hand on his shoulder and he looked me in the eye. I stared into his eyes for a minute, not quite long enough for the *Brokeback Mountain* jokes to start, but almost. "We'll make sure nothing happens to him," I said.

"Fine," McGraw said. "Funeral's in three hours. You think you two can look presentable for church by then?"

"We won't have to, Sheriff," Amy replied. "Nobody will know we're there. Let's roll, Bubba. I need a shower and a change of clothes. And so do you, you smell like a mix of dirty wet dog and drunk tank."

I sniffed but couldn't smell anything out of the ordinary. "Is that bad?" I asked, following Amy to the door. I was glad to see that somebody had moved my truck to the station but less glad to see that they'd moved the seat and mirrors. I got everything fixed the way I liked it and put the truck in gear.

"Where to?" I asked.

"There's a Courtyard about three miles from here. I booked a room on the flight in," Amy said.

"Do you have a bag or something with clothes in it? 'Cause I ain't got nothing with me but what I'm wearing and another pair of underwear. I didn't expect to be going to church."

"We're not going to church. We're going to stake out the cemetery. There's a difference." Amy turned around in her seat and grabbed a bag from my backseat.

"How'd you get that in there?" I asked.

"I unlocked your truck for her," Skeeter said over the comm.

"You can do that? I don't think I like that you can do that?"

"I hacked OnStar, Bubba. I can do all sorts of shit to your truck."

"Don't even joke about that, Skeeter. So where are we going to stake out the cemetery?" I asked Amy.

"Skeeter, what did you find out?" she asked the air.

"There's a Big & Tall Men's Shop two miles from where you are. I sent the coordinates to the truck's GPS." Sure enough, the screen in the dash blinked to life and showed us a map with a blinking arrow on it.

"I thought we weren't going to the funeral?" I asked.

"*We* aren't," Amy replied. "You are. I'm going to set up on the roof of the church with a spotting scope. You're going to stand around at the back of the crowd and watch for anything suspicious."

"Like somebody picking their teeth with a femur?"

"That would do, but we might have to dig for more subtle clues." If only she knew how not-subtle this case would become.

Two and a half hours later, I gave Amy a boost and enjoyed the view as she pulled her long legs up onto the roof of the Presbyterian church. She walked the roof like a circus performer, only without the feathers, scaling the building to its highest point and pulling a spotting scope out of her backpack. Once she had that set, she unspooled part of a hundred-foot roll of paracord and lowered it to me. I took the little silver carabineer and ran it through the strap of the Remington 700 and sent the rifle up to her. She flipped out the bipod and peered through the scope.

"I'm good." I heard through my comm. "I've got a clear field of fire on most of the cemetery. There are some areas under the canopy I can't get to, but that's what you're there for," Amy said.

The funeral home had a green canvas tent over the case and three rows of folding chairs. Judging by the crowd already filling up the church parking lot, they were going to either need more chairs or a shorter graveside service. I skipped the church portion of the service and moved straight across the cemetery to the tent. Sheriff McGraw and two of his deputies were already there, looking as inconspicuous as a giant can in a small town where everybody knows him on sight. He and his deputies all wore lightweight grey and black suits, and all three of them were sweating. March in East Tennessee means only one thing is certain weather-wise, nobody knows what it's going to do. One day it could snow a foot, then hit sixty degrees the next day. This was one of those warm days, but the deputies did a good job of suffering in silence.

The sheriff not so much with the silence. "What the hell is going on here, Brabham? I thought your little girlfriend was going to be down here being all investigative and governmental, and now I see her up on the roof of the church with a friggin' sniper rifle! What are y'all thinking?"

"We were thinking that if something does go to shit," *and it always does*, I added silently, "that we want somebody on the roof with a clear view of things and the ability to leverage some high power negotiations our way."

"And she negotiates with a .30-06?" McGraw was right up in my face now, towering over me like I do to people all the time. I didn't like it very much.

"Yeah, she's pretty damn persuasive with it, too. Now let's get back and wait to see what happens at the funeral."

"What if nothing happens?"

"Then we spend tonight with your whole police force staking out every graveyard in this town. I'll be over yonder." I pointed to a monument a couple rows back. It was almost big enough to hide behind, and it would certainly mask some of my approach if anything did go down. We took up our positions, trying to blend in as best we could. One thing about the Presbyterians, they didn't waste any time on the funeralizing. We probably weren't out there thirty minutes before Amy clicked her comm twice, our signal that the service was over.

I motioned to the sheriff, who got out of his patrol car and took up a position near the gravesite. He'd had the good sense to park close, so he not only had someplace comfortable to wait, but he also looked like he belonged there with his lights flashing to slow down passing traffic. The funeral procession loaded up and rode around the half-mile loop surrounding the church and cemetery and pulled the hearse up close to the grave. The pallbearers, most of them high school boys themselves, did a good job of holding themselves together, but there was more than one tear rolling down their faces. The rest of the procession was in no better shape. A man in his early forties walked a woman up and sat her in the front row next to a couple that looked about sixty. I pegged them for grandparents, and the couple for the parents. The man had the red eyes of somebody who'd been up all night crying and drinking himself all the way back to sober, and the woman had that zoned-out look of the heavily medicated. They were surrounded by men and women who bore a family resemblance, all wearing the pain of the day on their sleeves.

There were probably a hundred teenagers there, most all getting their first grown-up look at death. A couple of girls were playing it to the hilt, weeping loud until nobody was looking at them, then checking their makeup discreetly in tiny compacts. Most of the boys just looked stunned and out of place, like they didn't know what to do with themselves, but a couple were openly crying and patting each other on the shoulders in that way that teammates will band together in tough times.

The funeral director, a skinny man of well over six feet with enough rouge on his cheeks to join RuPaul's production staff, stepped forward and passed out a couple of small packets of Kleenex to the weepier of the adults under the tent. Like I figured, only a few of the relatives sat. Most folks stood around in a big circle. I made sure I was on the side of the circle nearest the street, in case I had to cut off an escape. The funeral director stepped back to one side of the casket as the preacher ducked under the tent to deliver some final words.

"Brothers and sisters," the preacher began "it is with the heaviest of hearts that we gather here today to lay our brother Andrew to rest. We understand that while his time on earth is done, his everlasting spirit is now and forever with our Savior, Jesus Christ. And as much as we miss our Andrew here, we know that even now he goes with Jesus to prepare for our coming to Heaven to be with him again." Then he led the assembled mourners in the Lord's Prayer. I kept scanning the crowd for anything out of the ordinary, but all I could see was small-town grief and the tragic loss that people always feel when a kid dies too soon. Nobody in the crowd looked at all supernatural, they just all looked sad.

His prayer finished, the preacher stepped aside and motioned to the pallbearers. The young men stepped forward and each took off their flower, placing it amongst the spray of flowers on the casket. They stepped back, and the front row stood up. The father took a step toward the casket, but his wife laid a hand on his arm, and he turned back to her. She slumped against him as if her legs wouldn't support her own weight anymore, and he walked her back toward the waiting limos. A couple of the older relatives approached the casket, passing a hand over the wood and moving on, but nobody tried anything out of line, like taking a bite out of the corpse. All in all, it was just a very sad, very normal funeral for what looked like a popular kid.

Until it all went to hell. I could see the whole situation unfold, but I was too far away to stop any of it. A girl, maybe fourteen from the looks of her, broke away from a bigger boy that looked to be her brother and threw herself on the casket, knocking aside a couple of the cheap folding chairs, sending the flowers scattering into the open grave, and unsteadying the coffin just enough to send it teetering onto one edge, then over to crash to the ground.

As happens when large heavy boxes come crashing down on one side, the casket popped open, spilling its contents to the ground. As horrific as that would normally be, sending the retouched body of a car crash victim to the ground is one thing. It's another thing entirely when the victim has no arms or legs, and the torso and head roll over three times before coming to rest face-up in the middle of the aisle at its own funeral.

"Holy shit, what happened to his body?" somebody yelled, then the screaming started. Two of the undertakers tried to wrestle the casket back onto the platform while a man, a relative from the look of him, took off his suit jacket and threw it over the limbless torso. The father deposited his wife into a folding chair and whirled on the funeral director, grabbing the gaunt man's tie and pulling him close. I couldn't hear anything over the teenage girls' screaming, but I figured he was asking about the disposition of his son's arms and legs.

Just about the time I saw the father pull his arm back for a big roundhouse, the makeup on the funeral director registered. I looked around, trying to find the rest of the undertakers. The two wrestling the casket were wearing heavy base and eyeliner, too, as were the two limo drivers. It all clicked into place the same time the father's punch landed, knocking the funeral director's dentures out and exposing two rows of razor-sharp teeth.

"The funeral home is run by ghouls!" I said into my comm, then drew my retractable baton from my belt. The sheriff had forbidden me from bringing Bertha or the spiked caestus that Amy had given me for Christmas, and he just glared at me when I suggested my kukri, so all I had on me was my baton and a Judge revolver. I snapped the baton out to its full length and started toward the fracas, just as the grieving father's gaze locked onto the newly revealed dentistry of the funeral director.

"What the hell?" He got that far before the ghoul stepped forward and bit clean through his throat.

"That escalated quickly," I said. "Skeeter, is there anything I need to know about ghouls?"

Skeeter's voice came over the comm. "You mean like they can't be killed without silver, or fire, or anything like that?"

"Yeah, exactly like that," I grumbled.

"Nah, they're hard to kill, but nothing special. Just crush its head and you'll be okay."

"You got that, Sheriff?" I asked.

McGraw's voice came over the comm. "I got it, now let me get these people out of here."

I looked over at him, and he was gesturing frantically at his deputies to clear the crowd. The funeral director was covered in blood, and about half the crowd was frozen in place while the other half had already started hauling ass toward their cars. Unfortunately, all their cars were parked bumper to bumper in a straight line tucked in behind the limos, so they couldn't go anywhere, just get in the cars and lock the doors.

Still, that was better than under the tent where the other undertakers had tossed the casket aside and jumped on a pair of mourners, ripping out custom dentures to expose their fangs. Each ghoul was over six feet tall and scrawny, but when they buried their teeth into a man's neck, he went down under a pile of jangly arms and spurting blood. I was closer to the feeding duo than the director, so I started there. I kicked a couple of folding chairs out of the way and laid into the back of one ghoul's head with the asp. He didn't budge.

"Skeeter, I thought you said these things could be killed," I said.

"All my research says they shouldn't be that tough. You nail one good with that baton, and it oughta crack its skull wide open."

I drew back and laid a hit on the ghoul that should have sent the contents of his head across two lanes of traffic. It barely moved, just grunted a little and kept on eating, ripping flesh from the heavyset mourner and swallowing like a tiger on a zebra's ass. I tossed the asp aside and drew my Judge revolver. I pressed the barrel of the gun to the back of the ghoul's head and pulled the trigger.

"That did the trick," I said into the comm.

"I think a .45 long from a distance of three inches oughta take care of about anything," McGraw said.

"I only wish," I replied, repeating the process on the second ghoul. The monsters fell off the dead funeral-goer, and I turned my attention to the funeral director. Much to my disappointment, he wasn't facedown in a two-legged happy meal. He stared at me for a couple of seconds, then sprinted for the nearest limo. I hauled ass after him, but he had a head start and a lot of motivation, namely the giant man chasing him with a gun. He dove into the limo and gestured wildly for the ghoul standing by the front of the car to put down the teenager he was chewing on and drive.

After a couple seconds, the other ghoul got in the car and peeled out of the cemetery driveway. Well, as much as you can peel out of anything with dozens of people crowded around your car and a shit-load of other vehicles in your way. So the car hadn't reached much in the way of speed when they turned right onto the street in front of the graveyard, and I jumped onto the hood at a dead run.

For the record, there are a lot of things about jumping onto a moving vehicle that differ from TV and the movies. For one thing, jumping onto a car and landing flat on your belly *hurts*. It also puts your nutsack right at the front of the hood, which might have resulted in my having a silver Lincoln hood ornament embedded in my taint at fifteen miles per hour. That might not sound too bad, but please take a moment to reflect on the words *embedded in my taint* before you judge me. Then there's the problem of inertia and a freshly waxed limousine. Sir Isaac Newton said that a redneck in motion tends to stay in motion, so when I hit the gleaming surface of the polished hood of the limo, everything about me wanted to keep sliding right off the other side. I managed to stop this by grabbing onto the windshield wipers and holding on for dear life. Literally.

I watched my pistol clatter to the street as I clutched the wiper, thinking the entire time that I was proud of American engineering that could build windshield wipers robust enough to hold me onto the hood of a car. I was also thinking *fuck, there went my gun*, and *my balls really hurt*. The ghoul floored the accelerator, and I slid a few inches up the windshield, just enough to dislodge the wedged hood ornament.

A crack rang out, and I felt the car buck underneath me. "Amy, are you shooting at the car while I'm laying on the hood?" I asked. I was pretty calm, I thought, given the situation.

"Yeah, keep your head down."

I ducked my head down and buried my chin into my sternum.

Another crack from overhead and the windshield spiderwebbed underneath me. The car swerved back and forth wildly across the lines before running up onto the sidewalk and slamming into a parked green Tacoma. Momentum did what momentum does, and I slid off the front of the car with enough force to snap the hood orna-ment right off with my testicles. I clawed my way up to my knees and peered over the hood of the limo. The ghoul driver was slumped forward with his head on the steering wheel causing the horn to blare right in my left ear. Between that and the hood ornament lodged halfway up my rectum, I was pretty damn pissed.

"Amy?" I asked into the comm.

"Yeah, Bubba?"

"You got eyes on the funeral director?"

"Yeah, but the truck slammed forward when you hit it and the radiator must have blown. I can't get a good shot through the steam."

I was about to tell her that I didn't care if she could shoot him, I just needed her to tell me where he was when I learned his location the hard way — by him finding me. A pair of hands wrapped around my throat from behind, and I felt myself lifted from the ground. The undertaker spun me around and, just like his wrestling namesake, chokeslammed me onto the hood of the car. I felt things pop loose in my ribcage that I was pretty sure were supposed to stay unpopped, and whole new dimensions of pain sprang into being all over my body. The only benefit to having a super-ghoul slam me almost through the engine block of a Lincoln was that he dislodged the hood ornament from my ass.

I lay there thinking of new curse words and mostly just groaning when I felt sharp teeth dig into my left thigh. I looked down at the lewdly placed ghoul and did the only thing that came to mind — I punched him in the side of the head. He popped loose with a slurping sound and looked up at me, grinning.

"You taste good, fat boy. I'll enjoy this," the ghoul said, then bent his head back to my leg, teeth bared.

I caught him in the temple with my right knee, and we rolled off the hood of the car onto the street with me atop the scrawny ghoul. I wedged an arm under his throat to keep him off me and said, "Amy, a little help anytime!"

"Got my own problems, Bubba," was her only reply. I chanced a look back to the roof of the church and saw Amy standing on the ridgeline of the building with a man in a dark suit. *Shit, there are more of them,* I thought.

My attention snapped back to the problem at hand when he tossed me a good six feet off him. I clicked my comm. "Skeeter, why didn't you tell me ghouls had super-strength?"

"Bubba, can we just assume that everything in the magical world is super-strong? Except for faeries, everything you've ever fought can whoop your ass in a fair fight. That's why —"

"Yeah, we don't fight fair. I know the drill. Got it." I got to my feet just about a half-second before the undertaker got to me, so I was in the perfect position to catch him with a shoulder in the gut and pick him up. I spun to my left and charged, slamming the ghoul spine-first into a parked Escalade. Metal screeched, glass shattered and pieces of overpriced plastic exploded all over the sidewalk, but the bastard kept scrabbling for my throat and flinging ghoul-spit all over the place. I've fought some nasty monsters in my time, but there's a special kind of gross when you know the thing slobbering all over your face ate part of a running back for breakfast.

I managed to wriggle one arm free and start punching the ghoul in the side of the head. He started to slow down with the biting after the fourth good shot to the temple, and after six, his eyes rolled back and he sagged in my grip. I stepped back, and he slumped to the ground, all rag-doll limp. I looked up at the church and saw that Amy was getting the worst of it with her ghoul, so I sprinted in her direction. Good thing for everybody involved the sprint was less than fifty yards, or I would have been even slower getting there than I was. I got to the low point in the roof where Amy climbed up, then realized that a downspout that held Amy's weight with no trouble was not going to be a very good idea as an access point for me.

I heard a shouted "Shit!" from above me, and looked up to see Amy clinging to the edge of the roof by her fingertips.

"Drop, I'll catch you!" I yelled.

"You'll miss!"

"I'll catch you, I swear! I've got great hands for a d-lineman! All my coaches said so. Now jump!"

Amy looked down at me, looked up at the ghoul reaching for her wrist, swung her legs to get a little more momentum, then dropped.

She flew backwards about a foot off the three-story roof of the church, flattening out and spreading her arms to give me as big a target as possible. I stepped up, looked up, stepped about a foot to one side, and braced myself to catch my falling girlfriend.

I missed. She landed flat on her back in the holly bushes that ringed the church, crashing through the prickly bushes with a scream of pain and fury the likes of which I haven't heard since that unfortunate spring break incident with the harpy and the wet t-shirt contest.

"Bubba!" she shrieked. I grabbed her outstretched arm and pulled her out of the bushes, adding to her truly impressive collection of scratches and rips in her clothing. I didn't mind the torn clothing so much, but I did feel bad about the bleeding. I set her down in the grass, and she immediately started beating the hell out of me.

"I told you you were gonna miss! I knew you couldn't catch me and you were just gonna let me fall to my death!"

"Ow! Quit it! I knew you weren't gonna die, so I didn't have to catch you. But I do have to do something about him."

"Him who?"

"Him him." I pointed behind her, then shoved her to one side and launched myself at the onrushing ghoul. Amy landed in the bushes again, getting me another solid cussing, and I speared the ghoul like he was an ACC quarterback. He folded up like an origami swan, and I ran full-tilt into a two-foot diameter oak tree. It was nice hearing bones crunch that didn't belong to me for a change, and when I backed up, the ghoul fell to one side, dead. I stomped its head flat just to be sure, then went to pull Amy out of the bushes again.

"Don't touch me," came a small voice from the greenery. I'd heard that tone before, and I decided it would be a good time to check up on the sheriff. And to make sure that Amy didn't have a sniper rifle when she was able to stand up again. I picked up the Remington from where it lay in the grass and walked back around to the front of the church.

"Skeeter, let me know when she decides not to kill me. And maybe remind her that I'm really nice to her most days and hardly ever dump her in thorn bushes," I said.

"You know I'm still on comm, right?" Amy's voice cut through, and the temperature dropped about eighteen degrees.

"I know, I just figured you weren't speaking to me until the bleeding stopped, so I — oh shitballs."

"What?" Amy and Skeeter asked simultaneously. Then Skeeter dialed in the video feed he had linked to my belt buckle, and I heard him say, "Oh shit is right."

The funeral director ghoul wasn't quite as dead as I thought he was, and he apparently recovered quicker than I expected, or he'd been playing possum, or something. He was standing over the eviscerated body of the Presbyterian preacher and holding the semi-catatonic mother by her hair. His whole face was stained red, and he broke into a huge grin when he saw me. His grin faded as I raised the Remington to my shoulder, centered his face in the scope, and squeezed the trigger.

Click. There is no sound more mournful in the world than that of an empty firearm. Not even the crumple of the last can in a twelve-pack can match that of a hammer clicking on an empty chamber when you really, really need to shoot something. Nothing that deep went through my head at that moment. I just muttered "shitballs" under my breath and threw the gun aside. I started running across the church lawn, marking the third time in twenty-four hours that I'd run after something that had neither boobs nor beer. I think that was some kind of really depressing record for me.

The undertaker saw me running at him and grinned again. He came at me like a really angry gazelle, all long legs and arms, with a side order of really pointy teeth. We crashed together amidst the headstones and manicured grass, and he went high as I went low. That never goes well for the skinny guy going high, ask any wide receiver. I caught him around the knees and drove my shoulder into the ground. I heard a loud *pop* beside my ear as his knee dislocated, then felt an explosion of pain in my shoulder as he bit into my trapezius. Hot blood poured down my shoulder and my right arm started to go numb. I stood up and slammed the ghoul spine-first into a headstone.

His head flopped back and cracked into the polished granite with a sound like a wet cantaloupe falling from a great height. His grip loosened on my neck and head, and I was able to get a little separation. I stepped back as he got to his feet, his head lolling on his neck and his eyes rolling in opposite directions.

"Ready to quit?" I asked. "Promise to leave town and never eat living people again and I won't kill you."

"Screw you, human. The Messiah has come, and he promises that our time is coming. Soon we won't have to live in the shadows any longer. Soon we will be the hunters, and you humans will be what you always should have been — the prey."

My blood ran cold at the mention of The Messiah, an evangelical leader of monsters that was planning some kind of beastie revolution. He also happened to be my kid brother-turned-werewolf, Jason. I looked in the ghoul's eyes and saw the hunger there. This guy was never going back into the closet. Between Jason's proselytizing and the taste of fresh meat, he was well and truly off the deep end.

"Fine, then. Let's end this shit." I took one step forward, then dropped to one knee as three shots rang out in quick succession. The ghoul dropped face-first into the grass, and I looked up to see Sheriff McGraw standing over him, Glock in hand.

I walked over to the sheriff and put a hand on his gun, slowly lowering his frozen arm. "That was good shooting, Sheriff. Might have saved my life."

"I never killed nobody before. Never even had to draw my weapon in fifteen years of law enforcement." His eyes were a little wild, and I led him over to a headstone and helped him sit down. I stepped around and grabbed his chin, making him look me in the eye.

"You've still never killed anybody, Sheriff. You shot a monster. That was not a person, no matter what he looked like most days. He was a bloodthirsty monster who's been digging up dead people and eating their bodies. He was trying to kill me, and you put him down just like you would a rabid dog." I kept my voice low and even, and held his eyes with mine to whole time so he could hear the truth in my words.

"That's good, Bubba, keep him focused on the fact that these things weren't people," Amy said over the comm. The sheriff made no sign of hearing her, so I figured he lost his earpiece in the fight.

"He buried my daddy and my uncle Joseph. I shook his hand at every funeral in Telford for nigh on ten years." His voice started to get that far-away sound again, so I grabbed his chin again.

"He was a monster, and he was going to kill a lot of people. If a bear goes bad and comes down the mountain into town, what do you do?" When he didn't answer, I repeated the question. "What. Do. You. Do?"

"I shoot it. I put it down to protect the town," he said, and I thought I saw a little bit of life come back into his eyes.

"That's what you did today. You put down a wild creature that threatened your town. You protected, and you served. You did your job, and these people will see tomorrow because of it."

He started to nod, then froze. His face crumpled up and I thought he might puke on me for a minute. "Do you think he ate my daddy? Do you think he ate my Uncle Joe?"

"Do not tell him the truth," Amy said in my ear. There was no way in hell I was gonna tell this man on the edge of a breakdown that yeah, it was pretty likely that the ghouls ate part of his father. That was a little much for anybody to take.

"No. I'm sure he didn't. Ghouls usually like living flesh and only resort to eating the dead as a last result." It was a complete lie — ghouls would rather eat a dead thing than a live thing any day, but I was kinda counting on the sheriff not having much of an occult library in the mountains of Tennessee. And I figured there were some questions he didn't want to dig too deep for the answers to anyway.

I walked the sheriff back to his car, and Amy met me there. He looked at the two of us, then around at the carnage in the cemetery. There were half a dozen dead ghouls in various states of disassembly, at least ten dead funeral-goers, including both of the guest of honor's parents and the Presbyterian preacher. Folding chairs were scattered everywhere, the casket was lying open on its side, and the limo was crashed into a couple of mourners' cars. It looked like either a monster attack or a frat party.

"How the hell am I gonna explain this?" the sheriff asked.

"Gas leak," Amy and I said in unison.

"What?"

"There was a gas leak at the funeral home, and it mixed with the embalming chemicals to induce a psychotic fugue state on anyone in the vicinity. The entire staff was affected, but the explosion at the funeral home purged any remaining dangerous chemicals from the area," Amy said without missing a beat.

I stared at her, my mouth hanging open. "What?" she said. "This isn't my first ghoul attack. And we have protocols for dealing with this kind of thing."

"But there hasn't been any explosion at the funeral home," the sheriff said.

"Yeah," Amy said, "about that..." A fireball erupted from over the trees a couple of blocks behind the church, and we all turned just in time to see a black helicopter rise up past the smoke.

Amy turned and looked up at me, all tattered clothes and bloody pinpricks from being dropped in a holly bush not once, but twice, by her adoring boyfriend. "So, Bubba . . . Can I get a ride home?"

"Have you forgiven me for dropping you in the bushes?"

"I'll forgive you almost as soon as you take me back to that hotel and let me get a shower."

"Deal." I turned to the sheriff. "Sheriff McGraw." I stuck out my hand.

The giant stood up and shook my hand, then shook Amy's. "I'm sorry I doubted y'all. I reckon there are stranger things on heaven and earth and all that."

"I hope you never have to find out about any more of them, Sheriff," I said.

"I do, too. But if you ever need backup, son, you don't hesitate to call. I'd be honored to stand beside y'all again."

I thought about Jason and the hell he was trying his damndest to raise, and I shook the sheriff's hand again. "Sheriff, if I ever need a good man in a fight, I know who to call." Then I helped Amy into the truck and we rolled out of Tennessee.

9

STONE COLD CRAZY

The phone rang. I ignored it. It rang again, and I pushed the button to send Uncle Father Joe to voicemail. It rang again, and I pushed the button again. I stared at the phone where it lay on the railing to my back deck and said, "I can play this game all night."

It rang again. Apparently I was weaker than I thought, because this time I answered. "Sure, come on over, Joe. I've got another steak I can throw on the grill."

"Bubba, it's February. I know we live in the South, but it still gets cold," Joe replied.

"It's over thirty. That's grillin' weather. Besides, if you stand close enough to the Weber you stay warm," I said.

"Tell him he's an idiot!" My girlfriend, the thin-blooded Agent Amy Hall, shouted from the other side of the sliding glass door. She loved a good steak as much as anybody and approved the idea of me grillin' as long as it didn't involve her being anywhere cooler than sixty degrees. So she was making a salad. I didn't know what that was for—as far as I knew, Skeeter wasn't coming over.

"She says you're an idiot, Padre. What did you do?" I said.

"I think she means you're an idiot for grilling outdoors when it's forty degrees outside," Joe replied with a chuckle. I knew Amy would never call Joe an idiot. For one thing, he was a smart dude with the pieces of paper to prove it. For another, she had a lot of respect for men of the cloth and wouldn't insult one unless he really deserved it.

"You could be right, Joe. Now since I reckon you didn't call to talk about my IQ, or my steaks, what's up?"

"You've got a case."

"Not today. Today I've got a pair of New York strips been mari-natin' for about thirty-six hours in my special bourbon sauce, and in about ten minutes they're gonna be on a plate next to a baked tater the size of my fist covered in enough butter to stop a lesser man's heart just from looking at it. And after I eat my steak and my tater, and drink about fourteen beers along with it, I'm gonna put a scary movie on the TV, settle down on the couch with my girlfriend, and reap all the benefits of the parts that make her jump and snuggle up on me. I can have a case tomorrow." I could almost see my night swirling around the drain even as I described it to Joe. When the supernatural nasties come out of the shadows, I usually don't get to decide when I kick their asses.

But this time Joe caught me off guard. "That's fine. You can't really do anything about this until tomorrow anyway."

"Huh?" I was so surprised I almost dropped my beer. But I am a professional, so I set it on the porch rail.

"The monster isn't killing anyone, and it'll take you several hours to get there anyway, so you may as well start out in the morning. Enjoy your night. I'll email all the files in a few minutes." Joe clicked off, and I stared at the phone until I remembered it was time to flip the steaks again.

Ten minutes later, I carried two of the finest pieces of dead cow flesh I'd ever prepared into the dining room, only to find Amy sitting at my computer. "You've got mail," she said, moving my mouse.

"I don't want mail. I want taters." I plopped one steak down on her plate and the other on mine. I went over to the stove and reached inside, grabbing a couple of tinfoil-wrapped tubers and juggling them over to the table.

"I'll be there in a second," Amy said. "This is pretty interesting."

"Don't care," I said. "Joe said nobody's dead, so I ain't in a hurry to do anything but eat and spend some time with my woman." I grunted a little as I said it, trying to make light of my own caveman tendencies.

"Fine, but you're eating some of my salad," she said as she got up and came over to the table. She slid in beside me and I just stared at her for a minute. She was a dead knockout, tall, blonde, blue eyes and the kind of smile that looked like it belonged on a spokesmodel. Not a tiny woman at five-ten and maybe one-eighty, but she had curves in all the right places and legs that looked good running or standing still. She moved through my house with an easy grace, like she'd been there forever instead of less than a year. She still had her place in D.C. but stayed with me a fair amount on weekends and whenever she could get away. She was heading back to the city in the morning for some kind of necromancer's trial, so I wouldn't see her for a week or two until that mess wrapped up. I thought for a few seconds about how different my life was since she stepped into it, then shook my head and picked up my fork.

"Uh-uh, pal. You know the deal." She wagged a finger at me and I put my utensil down. I bowed my head while she spoke. "Our father, thank you for this meal you have put before us, and thank you for this time we have had together. Please look after us as we go out into the world tomorrow to do our jobs, and keep us safe until we can be together again. Amen."

"Amen," I echoed. I wasn't much into prayer before I met Amy, the product of seeing too many things that prayer didn't have a good answer for. Even working for the Catholic Church, I wasn't exactly one of their most devout followers. But that was another thing Amy had brought back into my life—a belief that there might be something out there that was good, instead of just all the bad things we fought all the time. And if I could ask a higher power to keep her safe until I could get back to looking out for her, I didn't have a problem with that.

"So what did Joe send me?" I asked after the first few bites of steak had soaked into my system. The meat was pretty close to perfect, with a smoky flavor of my bourbon sauce brought out by some mesquite I laid under the grates of the grill.

"What makes you think I read the file?"

"'Cause you spent too much time looking at my email. Either you're suddenly interested in penis enlargement surgery or you were reading the case file. And let's be honest, out of those two, the case file is the only one I've got any use for."

Amy laughed and blushed a little bit. I loved that blush. This was a woman who had faced down vampires, elves, weres and God only knows what else, but one dick joke and she blushed to the roots. I almost got up right then and kissed her.

"The case is odd," she said. "You're right that no one has been killed, but there's definitely something nasty running around in Memphis."

"More than one something nasty," I agreed. "There's a transplanted selkie on the docks with a serious attitude and a rigged underground casino, there are a couple of major voodoo practitioners and at least one wizard that I know has a thing for young boys. But they all typically understand the rules and don't shit in the local water supply."

"I'm not going to ask what those rules are, but this thing is attacking children."

I was almost out of my chair when I felt her hand on my arm. I settled down and motioned for her to go on. "We don't have much, just a little bit of grainy ATM camera footage from across the street, but it looks like an elemental attacked a group of high school kids, then attacked the school itself a few days later."

"A fire elemental?" That's what people usually summon when they want to cause as much destruction as possible. An eight-foot tall fire-dude with a bad attitude usually gets your point across.

"That's another odd thing—it seems to be an earth elemental, particularly a stone elemental."

"I've never even seen one of those," I said. I hate fighting things I've never seen. I never know where the next punch is coming from.

"Well, we've got some crappy video from the attack on the kids and some crappy video from the attack on the school."

"And this is what Joe sent me tonight?"

"Yup. Wanna watch?"

"Not in a million years. Tonight we have a double feature—*Cabin in the Woods* and *Hostel*," I said in my best innocent voice.

Amy laughed and finished her glass of wine. "Well, let's get started on that first one. If you're lucky, I'll be so scared at the end of it that I'll need to spend the whole next movie in your arms for protection."

I said a silent prayer to Joss Whedon, God of the Nerds, asking him to look out for me in my hour of need.

The next morning I fired up the laptop and opened my email as Amy was gearing up to head back to the nation's capitol for another rough week of dealing with bureaucrats and politicians. If I ever had to choose between facing down soulless monsters from the lower reaches of hell or dealing with Capitol Hill, well, I think it's kinda the same thing. Amy was looking fine in a pantsuit with a jacket custom-cut to hide her shoulder holster. I was still in cutoff sweats and a sleeveless Def Leppard t-shirt because I like to look *good* for when my woman wakes up. I had at least tied my hair back and run a comb through my beard, so I wasn't in full Hillbilly Jim mode.

"So what's the video look like?" Amy asked, grabbing a bagel off the counter. That was a new thing since she started spending time at my place—actual food in the house. Before, I kept beer, pretzels, tequila and microwave popcorn. Now there were green things in my fridge that were supposed to be green, not green because the pizza was three weeks old.

"Looks like crap, but as far as I can tell, you're right. It's either a rock elemental or Ben Grimm on a bad day." I clicked the button to send the video to the big TV across the room, and we watched as a trio of teenagers did skateboard and bike stunts for a couple of minutes in the school playground. Nothing exceptional, just some kick-flips, some jumps and wheelies, the kind of crap kids do when they're bored, but not really dedicated to trick riding or skating. Then a ten-foot pile of rocks lumbered into the frame and casually back-handed one of the kids off his bike. Then the elemental, or whatever it was, picked up the bike and hurled it into the path of the other kid on his bike. He went headfirst over the handlebars, landing in an awkward roll on his helmeted head and shoulders.

The kid with the skateboard helped his buddies to their feet and the first bike kid and the skateboard kid half-carried the second bike kid out of our line of sight. The rock monster stomped over to the abandoned bikes and proceeded to crush them into little balls of aluminum and rubber. I recognized the names on the tubes—Cannondale and Giant—not cheap bikes by any stretch. His vendetta against thousand-dollar bicycles complete, the big guy stomped off screen and the video went to black.

"We don't have anything any better from the thing attacking the school the next day," I said, clicking a couple of buttons and closing the laptop lid. "I'm gonna ride out there today and stake out the school tonight. Then tomorrow I'll start interviewing people at the school about the damage."

"What was done to the school?" Amy asked.

"The trophy case at the school was thrashed, one of the science rooms was wrecked, a bunch of equipment and chemicals strewn all over the place, the floor of the gym took a beating just from the thing walking on it, the boys' locker room was torn up, some other random damage," I said.

"But nothing to the administrative offices? Nobody pooped on the principal's desk or destroyed the teachers' lounge or trashed the library? Those all seem like relatively standard targets in school vandalisms."

"Maybe so, but you're thinking like a human. Who knows what an elemental likes or doesn't like about high school? Maybe he took exception to the trophies being brass instead of bronze, what do we know?"

"We know that elementals are usually directed and don't just randomly attack buildings."

Skeeter's face popped up on the TV. "She's right, Bubba."

I jumped at the sight of my best friend's face in 60" high definition. "That is not something I need to see before I'm done with breakfast, Skeeter!"

"That's what she said," he shot back, and we both giggled. Amy didn't look amused. For some reason, that joke always falls a little flat around women. Course, so do most of my jokes, so it's not like it was a surprise.

"How the hell are you on my TV?" I asked my technical expert, best friend, sidekick and sometimes backup.

"When you got the new TV, I put it on your network. Then I linked it to your Skype account. Then I linked your Skype to our Bluetooth connection, then I installed the webcam on top of the TV so I can see you, and *voila*! You've got Skeeter TV."

"If my cable bill goes up because of anything you just said, I'm gonna hit you so hard I have to apologize to your mama."

"This doesn't—never mind," Skeeter said. "This doesn't sound like a rogue elemental, so I think Amy's right. Something or someone is controlling this thing, so you need to find out who and stop them."

"The finding out shouldn't be too hard. I just go to the kids who got their bikes crunched and ask who hates their guts," I said.

"Not too hard, he says," Skeeter mocked. "This from the guy who everybody loved in high school. From the guy who was part of the Homecoming Court for three years in a row!"

"I didn't win," I protested. "I hated school as much as the next guy, and my big mouth got me in plenty of trouble, too."

"Yeah, that your football juice got you out of just as fast." Skeeter kept needling.

"Whatever," I grumbled. "I'll go take a look around, see what I can come up with."

"Take some real artillery—Bertha is only so much use against a creature made of stone," Amy said. I stood up and walked her to the door. I heard the familiar sound of a black helicopter setting down in my driveway, so it was time for her to go. I stopped her with the screen door still closed.

"Be careful," I whispered to her.

"You too," she whispered back, then threw her arms around my neck. I kissed her, eliciting a low whistle from Skeeter's image on the TV screen, but when he started into "Bubba and Amy, sittin' in a tree," I pointed my Judge revolver at the screen. Skeeter shut up for once, and I had a very nice goodbye kiss with my girlfriend. That was a weird word for me—girlfriend. The last one of those I had my brother killed in front of my face. Sometimes when I dreamed about her, she had Amy's face. Those were the nights I woke up sweating, with Bertha already in my hand. It was pure luck I hadn't shot holes in my ceiling yet.

It was the middle of the afternoon when I rolled into Memphis, so I went straight to the school. Amy had hooked me up with more different badges than I used to have fake IDs, but they all involved me looking more like a cop and less like a biker, so I took a few minutes in the parking lot to smooth my hair down, tie it back into a ponytail and put on a sport coat. I got out of the truck and looked at myself in the side mirror. *No, I don't look like gorilla got into the Brylcreem, not at all.* I slipped the appropriate badge into my pocket and walked up the steps of the high school.

The bell rang just as I reached for the door, and a couple thousand balls of teenage hormones came surging out at me in a wave. I turned sideways and grabbed onto the center post of the doors to keep from being carried away like a jon boat in a hurricane and pulled myself against the tide of almost-humanity into the hall. I followed the signs to the Main Office and walked in behind what was either an overdeveloped high school junior or a tragically underdressed high school teacher, I couldn't tell which. The little girl in front of me smacked her gum all the way to the front desk, so I figured "student." *Good. I don't want to think about most of my old high school teachers wearing tank tops. But there was that one drama teacher...*

The authoritative throat clearing of the school secretary interrupted my trip down memory lane. I swear, it's like they take a class in that or something. The woman who sat behind the main desk at my high school could, honest-to-god, stop traffic six blocks away by clearing her throat and looking over the top of her glasses at you.

"Can I help you?" she asked in a tone of voice that made it very clear she had no interest in helping me whatsoever and was having trouble believing that I had the sheer audacity to disturb her with my nonsense.

Suddenly thirteen again, I fumbled for my badge holder, flipped it open, realized I had it upside-down, corrected that, dropped the badge holder onto the desk, picked it up, then finally just handed it to her and grunted, "Principal."

"Mr. Massey has bus duty until 3:45. Do you have an appointment?" She shifted from evil dominatrix to sweetness and light in about half a second, and I couldn't keep up with her.

"Uhhh...no?" I stammered. I took a deep breath, stomped on my own big toe to help me focus, and then tried again. I picked up my badge and said, "I'm Agent Brabham from the Department of Homeland Security. I understand that there was an act of serious vandalism here the other night?"

People have one of two reactions when I mention "Homeland Security." If they're god-fearing, right wing, gun-toting Fox-News watching people who love their country, they snap to attention. If they're NPR listeners, they get a suspicious look in their eyes. I took a chance with my secretary by the flag pin on her lapel and the "USMC MOM" sweatshirt she was wearing that she wasn't going to screw around with national security, even if my story had more holes in it than a truckload of Swiss cheese. I was right, she snapped to.

"Well, agent, it wasn't much, not enough to attract the attention of Homeland Security. I'm sure y'all have much more important things to be worrying about, don't you?" She seemed awful flattered that I was there, even if she sounded like she was trying to run me off.

"Ma'am, we take attacks on our education system very seriously. And vandalism is a gateway crime. Hardened terrorists often get their start dropping cherry bombs down toilets in locker rooms." *If there's a word of truth to that, then it's a wonder I'm not friggin' Osama bin Laden.* I might have blown up the plumbing system in my school a time or three.

"Now, I understand Mr. Massey has bus duty, but is there any way that I could speak with him? I do have limited time to dedicate to this case, so I need to get right to work if I'm going to catch these terrorists."

She sat up in her chair ramrod-straight and picked up a walkie-talkie from her desk. "Mr. Massey, please return to the main office." She spoke into the walkie as she clicked the button on the side.

A tinny voice came back at her. "I'm sorry, Mrs. Ramsey, I still have six buses that I need to get loaded."

"There's a man from the government here about the attack the other night?" Mrs. Ramsey spoke softly into the walkie, as if it weren't going to go loud and clear to every walkie-talkie in a couple miles.

"I'll be right there." Mr. Massey didn't sound too happy to see me. I reckon not everybody can be the kind of blindly loyal patriot Mrs. Ramsey was.

I wandered around the office looking at the various plaques and things displayed on the wall. After about five minutes, a slight African-American man in his fifties came in, walkie-talkie in one hand a cane in the other. He marched right up to me and held out his hand.

"Dub Massey, principal."

"Robert Brabham, Homeland Security."

"What brings you to Memphis, Mr. Brabham?" Massey moved around the desk and sat down.

"Well, we're investigating a series of linked attacks in the region and we feel that the vandalism at your school may be connected somehow."

He laughed, not a fake laugh of somebody who's hiding something, but the honest laugh of a man who has nothing to hide. "Well, Mr. Brabham, I hate that you've wasted a trip, but I assure you that whoever wrecked our trophy case is not a threat to national security. Unless you're worried about Olympic Village, which you shouldn't be. I'm pretty sure we don't have any future Olympians here, either."

"Be that as it may, Mr. Massey, we take these types of potential threats very seriously. Could you take me to the crime scene?" I felt ridiculous even saying most of the things that were coming out of my mouth, and Massey clearly felt the same way.

"If you mean the lunchroom, then certainly. Or would you rather check out the science lab that was wrecked?"

"Let's start with the trophy cases. That seems more personal somehow than a science classroom." I said.

"Fair enough. Please follow me." He stood up and grabbed a cane leaning behind his desk. He walked briskly, with just a little limp. I looked at the cane, then back at Massey. He looked to be about fifty.

"Gulf War I?" I asked.

He looked down at the cane. "Yup. I went over for Desert Storm and left a little piece of me in the sandbox." He thumped his leg with the cane. It gave a hollow metallic *ring*. "Nowadays whenever somebody's holding up the line at the airport, it's probably me."

"Thanks for serving," I said.

"It was a long time ago, and it paid for college and grad school with no student loans, so I guess it was a fair trade." I looked at him, but he didn't seem at all bitter. It wasn't a trade I'd have made, but it wasn't like I chose a career with a great retirement plan, either, so I kinda understood. We walked down one short hall, then turned right into a deserted cafeteria.

Massey pointed to one wall of the lunchroom. "There you go, Agent Brabham. One pair of destroyed trophy cases." We walked over to the smashed cases. All the glass was gone, and the pieces of the shattered trophies, medals and memorabilia had all been swept up, leaving just a wooden shell with a cracked mirrored back. I looked around inside, but all I saw was me in a cheap suit looking back.

"I thought you said they wrecked all your trophies?" I pointed to one smaller case standing intact beside the two destroyed ones.

"It's interesting. They didn't touch that case at all. That one houses our academic trophies and awards. These held all our athletic achievements. We had the State Championship baseball team for the last three years, and our softball team won the Regional Championship last year."

I looked at the intact case. It was mostly small gold-colored plastic statues and medals. There was a second place Academic Bowl trophy and a third place Math Team competition plaque, but mostly just certificates and a couple of framed photos. I opened the case and took out a photo labeled "Academic Bowl 2014."

"Can I get a copy of this photo?" I asked.

"Of course, anything you need. But why would you need a copy of that picture?"

Skeeter's voice buzzed into my ear and said, "Yeah, what are you going to tell him about why you need that picture, Bubba?"

"We feel there might be a correlation between students that are exceptionally invested in after-school activities and targets for Al Queda recruitment," I said. "With the decrease in their recruitment among the disaffected youth, they're moving toward more Cleaver-esque recruits. Since many of the athletes are prime targets, I want to cross-reference your academic stars against athletes and see where the overlap is. Then we can begin to vet potential subjects."

Massey's face said that he clearly had no idea what I was talking about, which was good, since I didn't either. I'd just strung a lot of words together that I heard on Fox News and counted on the mention of Al Qaeda to distract the nice man long enough for me to leave with the picture. It worked, and I took a photo of the picture with my phone and put the framed photo back in the case.

"Can I get a copy of the academic files for each of the students on the Academic Bowl team?"

"Is there more you may need to know? I can help you with insights into my students."

"I'm sure you can, but I find it's better to absorb the information at my own pace. I may be back tomorrow with more questions." We went back to the office and I spread the files out on a conference table in the teacher's lounge.

"What am I looking for, Skeeter?"

"Probably the smartest kid in school," my own personal black gay Jiminy Cricket replied.

"The principal has no idea that this was all about class warfare, does he?"

"Nope, he's got no clue that he's living *Revenge of the Nerd*. Check that one." Skeeter drew my attention back to a file I'd just passed over.

"Stephen Bentley? Nah, not him." I glanced at his photo—good-looking, smiling kid.

"Why not? He looks smart."

I looked at his picture again. "Yeah, but he's too good-looking. We're looking for somebody seriously ostracized. Besides, this kid also plays JV baseball, and you heard the principal talk about the baseball team."

"You sure this is gonna be a geek going after the popular kids story?" Skeeter asked.

"Wrecked two athletic trophy cases but not a scratch on the academic one? Oh yeah. And did you see the pictures of the kids that got their asses stomped the other night? They made Carlton from *Fresh Prince* look black, they were so white."

"Carlton was black, Bubba."

"Carlton was a total Oreo, Skeeter, and you know it."

Skeeter at least snorted a little on that one. "Black on the outside, white on the inside, I get it. So what's the play?"

"I think I'm going to take this footage of the off-campus attack over to the guidance counselor and see if she can identify any of our victims. Then I'll go talk to one of the kids who got his ass handed to him by a pile of rocks."

I cleaned up the files and turned to leave, almost running over a small blonde woman on my way out. I reached out with one hand and caught her just above the left elbow and kept her from falling, but I couldn't keep her armload of books from tumbling to the floor.

"I am so sorry," she exclaimed, kneeling down to pick up all her scattered papers and stuff.

I got down on one knee to help her, apologizing myself. "No, it was totally my fault. I wasn't looking where I was going, and to be honest, you're so small, I just missed you." She was a tiny thing, maybe a hundred ten pounds in combat boots and five foot even on her best day. She smiled at me, a radiant grin that bounced off her platinum hair.

"Well, I guess it's easy to overlook us mere mortals from way up there." She held out her hand. "Terri Drummond."

"Robert Brabham. Agent Robert Brabham." I noticed her smile tense up at the corners the way normal people do when I add the "agent" part to my name. At least I didn't tell her what agency really paid my bills these days. People get nervous enough around Homeland Security. You start mentioning the Department of ExtraDimensional, Mystical and Occult Nuisances, DEMON for short, and they look around for the nearest emergency exit, or the men in white coats. I stood up and held out my hand to help the pretty little teacher to her feet.

"What do you teach here?" I asked.

"Honors English," she replied, smiling again now that we were on safer footing. *Bingo!* If there was anywhere I could find the smartest kids in school, it would be under the wing of the hot Honors English teacher.

I gave her my most disarming smile, which usually wavers between "psychotic hillbilly" and "murderous biker" but I'd combed my hair back tight before coming into the school, and an application of expensive beard oil that Agent Amy gave me for Christmas had me looking almost respectable. Or at least respectable enough for Memphis. "Do you think you have time to help me with my investigation? It'll only take a few minutes, and I promise I won't ask you to violate any student's privacy. But there have been a couple of attacks that we think may be related to the vandalism here at the school, and we want to stop it before anyone gets hurt." I thought that playing to her nurturing side might help. I mean, I don't have a nurturing side myself, but I've heard of it, and figured if anyone would have one, it would be a teacher. Nurturing is kinda their thing, unless it's my twelfth-grade English teacher. Torture was her thing.

Ms. Drummond looked up at me for a few long seconds, then finally nodded. "I heard about those boys getting beaten last night. We need to make sure whoever is responsible is caught, and quickly. Our students deserve everything we can give them."

"My sentiments exactly." I didn't mention that I might be giving one of her deserving students a size-sixteen foot in the ass, but I figured that would probably offend that whole nurturing side. I held the door open and ushered the little teacher into the lounge.

I pulled my tablet out of my bag and called up the video. "Can you identify any of the students in this video, Miss Drummond?" I asked.

"Mrs. Drummond," she corrected me.

"Sorry. Mrs. Drummond." *Good for me,* I thought. *The last thing I need to do is fall in lust with a high school teacher, no matter how cute she is.*

"No problem," she replied, watching the video. "Yes, I know all these boys. Mark Jackson, Steve Tolbert...I believe that's Nathan Carpenter, but I can't be sure. He's running away too fast. That one on the ground is Eric Wilkinson, he's the starting pitcher for the baseball team—ouch, I guess he *was* the starting pitcher."

"The doctors say he should recover fully, but it will take up to six months. He'll miss all of this season."

"That's terrible! This is his senior year, he was playing for scholarships. UT, Memphis, Vanderbilt—they all came to see Eric play as a junior and told him he could expect a lot of scholarship offers this year. Oh, that's just awful for him."

"Do you know of anyone that would have a problem with these particular students, Mrs. Drummond?"

"What do you mean, a problem?" She gave me a look that said she knew I was asking more than I was saying, so I had to step lightly. Not much was getting past this one, blonde jokes be damned.

"We think this attack might be a type of retaliation. Not saying these boys deserved to be beaten like this, but maybe somebody holds a grudge...?"

"There was an incident last year...I don't know if I should even bring it up..."

"Anything you can share would be helpful. Please?" I pushed gently.

"There was a student in my CP English Four class, that's College Preparatory English," she explained at the confused look on my face. "Steve Tolbert and Mark Jackson were also in that class...so was Nathan, now that I think about it. There was a...I guess you could call it a teasing incident, I thought it was more than that, but the administration disagreed." By the look on her face, she'd been pretty pissed at the "administration" at the time, and the memory was bringing the fire back.

"What happened?" I asked.

"We were studying *The Diary of a Young Girl,* by Anne Frank, and talking about Judaism, and one day as we were watching part of the film, Steve Tolbert puts a yarmulke on another student's head and yells out 'I found the Jew! Call the SS!'"

"That sounds pretty stupid, but not terrible," I said.

"It would have just been stupid, except the student was the one Jewish boy in the class, and they put the yarmulke on with Super-Glue. He had to shave his head to remove it, and he still got chemical burns on his scalp."

I let out a low whistle. "That's a little much," I agreed.

"I pushed for a lengthy suspension, but it was baseball season, so Steve got a warning. The other students, the ones who brought the yarmulke and glue, didn't even get that."

"Let me guess—Mark and Nathan."

"Exactly."

"Who was the victim?"

She hesitated. "Mrs. Drummond, I need to know anyone who might have reason to hurt these boys. And if anyone had stuck something to my head with crazy glue, I'd want some revenge."

"His name is Jacob Lloyd. He's one of the brightest boys in school. He wouldn't hurt anyone, I'm sure of it."

"Unless he was pushed far enough," I said. "You said Eric Wilkinson wasn't in that class?"

"No, Eric barely makes good enough grades in regular English to keep his eligibility, he would never cut it in my Honors class."

"So it was something else that made the monster go after him," I mused. "Do you know where Eric is today, Mrs. Drummond?"

"I know he's not in school. I assume he's still in the hospital," she said.

My mind starting running over and over different permutations, but none of them came out good. Boy is in hospital, can't move one shoulder at all and looks like one big bruise from head to toe. His best buds, who got the beatings of their lives, would be on the way to visit him as soon as school let out—*oh crap.*

"What time does school—" An ear-splitting electronic tone cut off my question. Mrs. Drummond pointed to the speaker on the wall and smiled as a voice broke in for afternoon announcements. The hall-ways outside the teachers' lounge went from grave-silent to the din of a thousand or more teenagers all bolting for freedom at the same time.

"Crap," I muttered. "I'm sorry, Mrs. Drummond, I've got to run. Thanks for your help." I shoved all my gear back into my soft-sided briefcase and hauled ass out the front door. I navigated the sea of small people fairly simply, only to find that when I'd parked my truck in the visitor's space in front of the school that I'd also parked it right in the middle of the student pickup lane, where hundreds of heli-copter parents sat in their cars waiting to pick up little Jimmy or Suzy and haul them away to soccer, or flute practice, or whatever other damn thing they did.

I got in the truck, started her up, and sat there. I've been to a lot of sporting events and concerts, and usually somebody will ascribe to the dude code and let you out into traffic. Not so much at schools. Those crazy carpool ladies will stop their minivan in the middle of a row of traffic because one little ankle biter left his lunchbox, but they aren't letting anybody in line for nothing.

So I sat there. I sat in the parking lot in front of the school for a good twenty minutes before a dad in a pickup paused long enough to let me back out of my parking space and peel out of the lot, headed for the hospital and hoping I got there before any more kids needed to be admitted.

I peeled into the hospital parking lot and slammed on the brakes. "Skeeter, we got a problem."

"I see it, Bubba." The cameras Skeeter planted all over my truck, my belt buckle, my favorite Bass Pro Shops ball cap and my bullet-proof vest were a little invasive sometimes, but they did shortcut a lot of description. Like now, I didn't have to tell Skeeter that there was a ten-foot pile of boulders stomping towards the front of the hospital; he could see it himself. I also didn't have to mention the two teenagers hiding behind a bench beside the door, or the rent-a-cop trying hard to take aim at the elemental while simultaneously holding his bladder and sphincter closed tight.

"What's the opposite of earth, Skeeter?"

"Interestingly enough, fire. Earth and water are considered female elements, while fire and air are considered male elements. So fire is an opposition element to earth."

"Fire, I got." I hopped out of the truck and opened the back door. The back seat flipped up to reveal a two-drawer sliding gun locker. I slid out the bottom drawer and grabbed an M4 with underslung Colt M203 grenade launcher. I popped a 40mm white phosphorous flare into the breach of the grenade launcher, slipped two more plus a couple of M1060 concussion grenades into the pockets of my jacket, and stepped out to wreck an elemental's day.

"Hey, Stoney!" I yelled, but the moving rock pile ignored me. I sighted on the elemental and pulled the trigger. The grenade launcher made a soft *whump* sound, and I watched the projectile streak toward the monster, bursting into white-hot flame as it did. The signal flare hit the thing square between the shoulders, and fire bathed the creature for a few seconds before winking out.

"Skeeter, fire might not be the answer," I said as I chambered a second round and brought the rifle up to my shoulder. I put another round solidly on target, with even less effect. The elemental slowed but only paused for a second before going back after the cowering teenagers. I dropped a high-explosive round in the launcher and brought it to bear on the thing.

Just before I pulled the trigger to blow that rock pile back to gravel, Skeeter came over the headset. "Stop! That won't do anything!"

I lowered my rifle and said, "What?"

"I don't think it's an elemental. If it was, your fire should have had more effect. You're gonna have to try something different." Something different looked like it had only about ten seconds to get between the monster and kids, so I jumped back in the truck and jammed her down into gear. I was in second and accelerating fast when I turned left to face the creature. I snapped my seatbelt into place and stomped the gas pedal to the floorboard. The truck leapt into motion, and two seconds later I crashed into a ten-foot pile of rocks with a couple tons of Detroit steel wrapped around my body.

Rocks, safety glass and the front left quarter panel of my truck exploded across the parking lot, and the elemental, or whatever it was, collapsed back into just a heap of inanimate rock. I got out of the truck and checked myself for injuries. Other than a small cut under my eye and a bruise from the seatbelt that was going to be really impressive, I seemed okay. I took a couple deep breaths, decided my ribs weren't broken, and walked over to the bench.

"Y'all okay?" I asked the boys.

"Yeah. What was that thing?" the shorter of the pair asked. "It looks like the thing that almost killed Eric last night."

"I'm pretty sure if something that big wants you dead, you're going to die," I said, picking more glass out of my beard. "You got any ideas who wants to beat y'all's asses?"

"You mean besides every 4-A school in the state?" the taller one said, getting up from where he'd been trying to bury himself under an azalea. Pink flowers and dirt decorated his face. "We're the champs, dude, all the ladies want to be with us, and all the men want to be us."

I stood up and turned on the cocky little snot. "Your buddy is in a hospital bed not fifty yards from where we're standing. If I hadn't been willing to put my ass and my truck on the line for you, your dumb ass would be laid up in there right next to him. So you want to shelve the Ric Flair impersonation and answer my damn questions?" I hate teenagers. They know everything right up until the point where they need to know something important, then they don't know shit.

Tall kid, I think he was the one Mrs. Drummond pointed out as Steve in the picture, sat down on the bench and put his hands in his lap. "Sorry, man. I was scared. Sometimes I say stupid shit when I'm scared."

"It's okay," I said. "I understand being scared. I just drove my truck into a walking boulder, remember? I got scared covered. But right now we need information before this thing comes back and really hurts one of you guys. Now think about it, is there anybody you might give a hard time to at school? Somebody on the Academic Bowl team that you guys tease and might have taken it wrong?"

Skeeter's voice came in over my headset. "Or somebody that you bullied until he was scared to go to school? Somebody that's so filled with self-loathing that he can't stand to look in the mirror?"

I reached up and turned off the earpiece. I knew Skeeter was right, but this was quickly turning into high school politics, which was never Skeeter's strong suit. I reached down and helped the other kid, Mark, onto the bench. "Well?" I asked.

The boys looked at each other, then shook their heads.

"You can't think of anyone you've made fun of that might have taken it harder than you intended?" I'm sure they intended it to be as hard as it was, but I was equally sure they wouldn't own up to it.

"Jacob Lloyd," Mark said, half under his breath.

"Who?" I asked, more because I didn't hear him than because I didn't understand him. Being in huge car crashes sometimes does bad things to my hearing. And my equilibrium, and my temper, and my back.

"Oh, come on, Marky Mark, the King of Kike wouldn't have the stones to do anything as stupid as messing with us, man! He's the biggest chickenshit in school!" Steve hopped up, standing on the bench and waving his hands around like a stupid rich white kid parodying a rapper. I reached one arm out and pushed him backwards off the bench back into the flowerbed.

"Shut up, dickwit," I said. "Who's Jacob Lloyd, Mark?"

"He's this kid—"

"He's a lo-ser!" Steve cut in again. He even put the little pause in loser to accent the two syllables. I was thinking more and more that I should have just let the rock monster break him a little bit.

"Mark?" I sat down on the bench next to the kid, giving me the additional benefit of keeping Steve in arm's reach. I've seen kids that were in more need of slapping, but not often.

"Why do you think it's one of the Nerd Bowl kids?" He didn't look up, just sat staring at his hands.

"Because the monster wrecked all the athletic trophies but not the academic ones. Kinda makes sense, doesn't it?"

"Yeah."

"So what about Jacob Lloyd?"

"We tease him a bit."

"A bit?"

He sat there for a long moment, then said, "A lot. We pretty much wrecked his life last year."

"Oh bullshit!" Steve popped back up out of the bushes. "All we did was fuck with the little pussy a little bit. We didn't do nothing to him we didn't do to anybody else. And if you push me down again old man, I'm gonna fuck you up." That last bit was directed at me.

I didn't bother to get up, I just flicked out a punch that caught Steve right in his sack of precious little Steve-jewels. He crumpled to his knees, and I grabbed his hair. "You might want to pick your battles, Steve-o. This is not the dog you want to try and run with." Then I slapped him across the face, hard. I didn't punch him, just laid him out with an open-handed slap that spun him around back into the azaleas.

"What did you do to Jacob, Mark?" I kept my voice even as I watched his face. He genuinely looked like he might have some remorse for ruining the kid's high school life, and I thought this one might be worth saving.

"We videotaped him in the showers after gym class and then Eric cut it into one of the sex ed videos they showed to all the health classes. It was pretty embarrassing, I guess, I mean…you could see his dick and everything."

"And I'm guessing Jacob isn't exactly a big buff guy that walks around showing off his body?" I asked.

"Yeah, not so much, man. Jake's a skinny little dude. He ran out of health class listening to everybody laugh at him. He hasn't been back for a week. I heard…"

"You heard what?" I knew what he was going to say, but I wanted him to say the words.

"I heard he tried to kill himself. Like, took a bunch of pills or something." A single tear rolled down the side of Mark's face. "I felt bad, you know? Like, Jake was my friend when we were little. He helped me with algebra last year and wouldn't even let my mom pay him for it. He said it's what friends do, like we were still buds."

"And then you shit on him in front of the whole school?" I didn't raise my voice, just laid it out there.

"Yeah. I did." He still didn't look at me, but I could tell from the way he held his shoulders that he was just barely keeping it together.

"That little pussy couldn't take it, so he oughta kill himself." Steve stood up. "I'm fucking tired of hearing about how we gotta be cool to all the nerds and retards at that stupid school, man. This is *our* time! We're the fucking kings of that place and we oughta be able to do whatever we want!"

This time I stood up, and I did punch him. I caught the smart-assed little kid with an uppercut that picked him up and dropped him on his ass a good three feet away. Then I stepped over the bench and went after him. He scrambled back on his ass and hands, looking around for help, but there was no help in sight.

"Get up," I said, my voice barely over a growl.

"Dude, I'm sorry, I was just messing with you!" Steve was frantic now, backed up against the outside wall of the hospital with nowhere to go.

"Get up, or I'll pick you up. Then I'll put you on your ass again. I'm gonna repeat the process until you know what it feels like to be help-less, to have somebody stronger than you make your life a living hell. Then I'm gonna strip you butt naked and make you run home to your mama and daddy and let them see what a little bitch you are. I'm going to make you feel the pain you've given to other people all this time, and I'm going to make sure you remember it until the day you die."

"Stop it, Bubba." Skeeter's voice came through my earpiece.

"I turned that off for a reason," I growled.

"And I turned it back on so I could talk to you. You know I've got the override to all your tech. Now back off the little shit, he's not worth it."

"He's worth it. He drove a classmate to try and kill himself; he deserves everything I could do to him."

"Yeah, but you don't deserve what will happen to you." Skeeter's voice was calm, and it was taking the edge off my fury.

"What are you talking about? I beat people up all the time."

"Adult people and monsters. This kid is *sixteen*, Bubba. He's stupid, but he's young. You can't just beat him until he breaks. It's against the law and against what we do."

"He's a monster. He's vicious and stupid and bloodthirsty and deserves to be beaten to a pulp."

"No, he's not. He's ignorant, blind and foolish, and deserves a chance to change. He's you, Bubba, and he deserves the same chance you got."

I took an involuntary step back as the memories hit me—jamming Jerry Dallesandro into a locker in the girl's locker room wearing nothing but his jockstrap; leaving love notes from the head cheerleader in the locker of the captain of the math team, then watching as he brought a dozen roses to her lunch table on Valentine's Day; TP'ing Renee Wallace's house every Friday night for a month and writing lies about her sexual habits in her driveway with spray paint. Skeeter was right, I'd done every bit as bad and more before I met him and decided to be a different person.

"Fuck me," I murmured.

"No thanks, I don't go for white dudes," Skeeter said in my earpiece. "He's an asshole, yeah. But maybe he can see the asshole he's been and change. You did."

Skeeter was telling the truth. I did change, the day I walked up to the front entrance of the school and three of my football buddies were trying to figure out how to run Skeeter's underwear up the flagpole with him still wearing them. I told them to stop, that Skeeter was helping me with math, but they wouldn't stop. A couple of black eyes and one dislocated jaw later, they stopped. Skeeter asked me why I helped him, but I never told him the truth. The fact of it was, when I saw Skeeter fighting back against three guys twice his size, I admired him. Those three football players were gonna kick his ass and do whatever they wanted to do to him, but Skeeter was never gonna lay down and give in. I saw that fire in him, and it made me want to be like that. I didn't save Skeeter to help him; I saved Skeeter that day to help me.

"Boy, let me tell you one thing." I looked Steve in the eye. "The shit you do in high school follows you the rest of your life. You can choose right now to be the kind of person who makes people want to kill themselves, or you can be the kind of person who makes people's lives better. You gotta make that choice, but I promise you one thing—you choose wrong, and I'll be back."

I turned away, stepped out of the flowerbed and walked back to my truck. It wasn't going anywhere with a smashed fender, quarter panel, cracked axle and more other damage than I could guess at. I saw a puddle under what used to be the radiator and let out a sigh.

"Mark, where's your car?" I asked the kid.

"Don't sweat it, Bubba. Your ride's almost there," Skeeter said in my ear. I looked around and saw a black Suburban pulling into the hospital parking lot, followed by a wrecker and a step-side cargo van. All black, of course, even the rollback. They pulled up in front of the hospital, and an agent in tactical gear got out of the Suburban.

He stepped forward and held out his hand. "Agent Smith, sir. I'll be your driver. Do you need anything out of your truck?"

"Yeah," I said, and walked around to the passenger side. I skinned off my jacket, tie and dress shirt, throwing on a shoulder holster with Bertha in it over my t-shirt. I grabbed my Carhartt jacket, slipped my caeastus in the pockets in case I had to go toe to toe with a rock monster, and tossed a few tools in the back before I got in the Suburban. I paused for a second, then stuck my head out the window.

"Mark, get in here," I yelled.

He looked at me, then pointed at himself.

"Yeah, you, jackass. This is partly your mess, come help me clean it up."

He nodded, stood and half-jogged to the back of the Suburban. "Do I get a gun?" he asked as he closed the door. *Kids.*

"Why do I have to come?" Mark asked from the back seat. "I mean, I know what I did was wrong and all, but he sent that thing to kill us!"

"Did you see what my grenade did to that rock monster?" I asked.

"Yeah, nothing."

"Do you think for a second that you could stop that thing from killing you?"

"No." His voice shook enough to put an extra syllable in there.

"So if whoever sent that thing after you wanted to kill you, don't you think you'd be dead?"

Mark sat there thinking as the suburbs of Memphis rolled by. After a couple of stoplights and a right turn into a neighborhood of modest ranch houses and manicured lawns, he said, "Yeah, I guess so. So what did he want? He put Eric in the hospital. The doctor says he might never be able to play ball again. He's probably gonna lose his scholarship, maybe not even be able to go to college. Is that what Jake wants?"

"To ruin your life? Maybe make you feel some of what he feels every day? Probably. There's a lot of shit in this world that it's worse to live with than it is to die from. Maybe he's decided he wants to live, but he wants y'all to be miserable with him."

"So why am I here again?"

"So that if he does want to kill you, I can get it over with quick and be home for supper." I kept it deadpan and watched the kid's face in the mirror built into my sun visor. I saw Agent Smith snicker in my peripheral vision, but he pulled it in quick.

"What!" Mark started reaching for the door handle and looking around for some other way to get out when he found it locked.

"Calm down, kid. I'm not going to let him kill you. I didn't ruin a perfectly good truck just to let you die an hour later. You said y'all used to be friends, right?"

Mark calmed down a little, but his eyes kept darting from side to side like he really wanted an exit. He should have thought of that before he got in a black SUV with a couple of mysterious government agents, even if one of them looked more like an extra from *Sons of Anarchy* than a fed. "Yeah, we were buds back in middle school. I was even on the quiz team with him before I got tall and made the baseball team."

"And got cool and forgot about all your friends."

"Yeah, that too."

"Then maybe you can apologize and he'll believe it. Something tells me your friend Steve back there might have a credibility problem."

He thought about that for a second, then chuckled. "Yeah, nobody will ever believe that Steve's changed. He's a douche to the bone."

"Then why do you hang out with him?" I asked. That's never made sense to me, why kids follow these assholes.

"He hits a mile, is a wicked centerfielder, and has a brother old enough to buy us beer. He's a dick, but he's useful."

I let out a sigh of the ex-athlete and said, "Some things just never change, do they?"

"We're here, sir," Smith said, pulling up to the sidewalk in front of a two-story white colonial with a small front porch. There was a Volvo station wagon in the driveway, parked right up against the garage door. It looked like the picture of middle-class suburbia, with a gabled roof, a couple of white columns holding up the porch roof, and a red bike chained to a post by the front door.

Except for the fifteen-foot animated pile of rocks standing in front of the attic window, it could have been a picture off *Leave It to Beaver*. The monster at the hospital had been almost identical to the one in the video—eight or nine feet tall with a boulder for a head and nothing holding it together but magic. This one was a lot more cohesive, and a lot bigger. Its head, made of what looked like a huge chunk of asphalt, was level with the attic window, and there was concrete or some kind of filler holding its joints together.

"Yeah, I think this is the place," I said, opening the door and sliding out. I walked around to the back of the SUV and opened the tailgate. I pulled out the twenty-pound sledgehammer I'd brought from my truck and started toward the monster.

"What should I do?" Mark asked.

"Try to talk to Jake, and try not to get stomped. I think this thing's sex organs are in its feet."

"Huh?" the teenager asked.

"He steps on you, you're fucked," I said.

I got to the center of the lawn and yelled out, "JACOB!"

The attic window slid open and a skinny kid with curly brown hair stepped out and sat on the monster's shoulder. "What do you want?"

"I want you to stop calling up rock monsters and beating up people." I figured, since he asked, maybe I could just ask nicely.

"It's a golem, you moron. I'm Jewish."

"I don't know what those things have to do with each other," I said honestly. The longer I kept him talking, the less likely he was to sic his monster on me, so I wanted the full-on bad guy soliloquy.

"Golems are magical constructs that we Jews create to do things for us, to protect us, to work for us—"

"To beat up children?" I cut in.

"They aren't children!" Jacob yelled down at me. "They're assholes and they made it so I can't ever go back to that school. Everybody there saw that video! They all saw me…" I saw his face go hard. *Uh-oh.* "Destroy him!" Jacob shouted and pointed at me. He hopped off the thing's shoulder and back in his window, and I hefted the sledge, looking for a weak point in the two-story tower of rock.

"Skeeter, please tell me you got something useful out of that," I said as the golem started my way.

"Well, I haven't got a whole lot of experience with Jewish mythology, but it looks like there should be a stone with a Hebrew symbol carved into it."

"That's great, Skeet. This thing's bigger than a city bus and has about a gajillion rocks in it. How am I supposed to find the right one?"

"It should be close to the head," Skeeter offered.

"Great. Too bad I'm uncomfortably close to its feet." *And fists,* I thought as one basketball-sized hand came crashing to the ground where I had stood only seconds before. I swung the sledge at the thing's wrist and shattered a few stones, but more simply flowed up from the ground to fill in.

"Skeeter, this thing regenerates," I said, dancing back from another ground-shaking blow.

"Yeah, that's a problem. Try to stay out of its way until I think of something."

"Does 'knocking the kid unconscious' count as thinking of something?"

"Yeah, but I don't know if that'll work."

"It's all I got," I said and ran between the golem's legs for the front door. I resisted the urge for a nutshot as I passed through, figuring that it wouldn't have much impact on the magically constructed rock monster. But old habits die hard. I hit the front door at a dead run, leading with the sledge. It splintered into a shower of wood and glass, and I was inside the kid's house. I looked back out the front door and saw the golem flatten the Suburban with two mighty stomps. Mark and Agent Smith bolted in opposite directions, Smith emptying his Glock into the golem to draw its attention, and Mark hauling ass for the front door.

I waved him in like a third base coach telling him to go for home, and he jumped through the broken frame of the door a few seconds before the golem stopped right outside the house.

"Are we safe here?" Mark asked.

"I don't know. It depends on how many of those things your friend has made, and if any of them are small enough to be inside. I don't know if I could handle one my size or not."

"Well here's your chance to find out." Jacob's voice came from the stairs, but the *whoosh* of air I felt came from behind me, so I just dropped to one knee. A fist passed over my head and I spun around to see a much smaller golem in the living room.

"How many of these things do you have?" I said, launching myself to spear the construct in what would have been its gut, if it hadn't been a pile of rocks instead. I hit it solid, but instead of it folding over my tackle and going down, it stood perfectly still and I heard a *crack* as my right clavicle snapped like a twig. I dropped face-first onto the carpet, holding my shoulder as I swore creatively.

I rolled over a couple of times to get out of stomping range and pulled myself to my feet. I put myself in between the golem and Mark, who was on his knees starting to cry. "Back off him, Rocky, and nobody gets hurt."

"Nobody I care about has gotten hurt yet, jackass," Jacob said from the foot of the stairs. I hefted the sledge one-handed and hurled it at the golem, but instead of throwing it at the head, like I would normally do, I aimed at the right leg, hitting it square in the knee-stone. It wobbled and had to take a few seconds to reassemble itself, and that's all the time I needed. I drew Bertha in a backwards left-handed draw because my right arm was completely useless, but after a few seconds, I had her in my left hand, safety off, and leveled at the golem's head. It took two steps forward, and Bertha barked in my hand. I put a fifty-caliber pistol round straight through the strangely inscribed rock in the center of the golem's forehead, and it immediately collapsed back into a ton or so of patio pavers and gravel.

"How did you do that?" Jacob cried.

I grinned. "I'm a good shot, kid. Agent Smith out there is an even better one. Right now he's loading up a Remington 700 with high-explosive rounds, and as soon as he finds the right stone in your big golem out there, he's going to blow it up and you're out of the monster business."

"I'll just make more. I can make as many as I want. I'm a wizard!"

"Yeah, but will it get you anything?" I asked.

"What?" He kept his eyes on the gun in my hand, so I tried to holster it. I couldn't manage to get it back in the shoulder rig with my busted shoulder, so I clicked the safety on and shoved it into the waistband of my pants. It was a lot more uncomfortable than they make it look on TV. For one thing, I've got a gut, so the hammer was mashing into my belly the whole time. For another, the Desert Eagle is a *big* gun, so the barrel was a lot closer to my prized possession than I really liked, safety or not. But I stopped thinking about guns and my penis for a few minutes and turned my attention back to Jacob.

"What good will it do you to beat these guys up?" I asked. "Will it make them like you? Will it make you cool? Will it get you laid? Or will you just have company being miserable?"

"What do you care? What does anybody care?" Jacob started waving his hands around, and they started to glow a little.

"Can we just talk for a minute before you try to reanimate this heap behind me and I have to break your jaw for you?" I asked.

Jacob put his hands down and walked over to the pile of rocks that I'd de-animated. He sat on the rocks and motioned to the couch. I took the seat with a sigh and a wince, then pulled the pistol out of my pants and laid it on the side table.

We sat there staring at each other for a minute before he broke the silence. "All right, talk. You wanted to talk, say something. What kind of adult wisdom do you have that will make me change my mind and want to hug it out with these assholes who have made my life a living hell for the past three years?"

"Nothing. I've got nothing. If you want something to make you feel better, you're looking in the wrong place, kid. I'm not the talker. I'm the punch shit 'til it falls down guy. My partner, he's the talker. But he ain't here. So all you got is me. And all I got is I'm sorry. I'm sorry these guys are assholes. I'm sorry they fucked with you and made you miserable. I'm sorry you had to go through that. But you don't get to kill 'em for it."

"So it's okay for them to drive me to suicide, but I can't return the favor?"

"No, it's not okay. What they did to you ain't okay, and it's gonna haunt you for a long time, but eventually—"

"If you tell me it gets better like some fucking YouTube video, I'm going to animate this golem and rip you to pieces."

"But it does get better, Jacob." Skeeter's voice came from my right, from the TV over the fireplace. I turned and saw my best friend's face on the screen.

"Skeeter? What the hell are you doing here?"

"Saving your ass, as usual," he replied. "Jacob, I'm Billy. Billy Jones.

I'd shake your hand, but it was hard enough to hack your home network and get video. I haven't quite managed teleportation yet."

"You hacked my network? Nobody can hack my network." Jake didn't look nearly as freaked out by the intrusion into our conversation as by the idea of someone breaking his network security. I'll never understand geeks. I'll understand elves before I understand geeks, and elves are some inscrutable bastards.

"You're good, kid. But I'm better, and I've got the whole NSA working with me. It took me ten minutes, that's pretty good. The DOD only took me five. But I'm here now, and I promise, it gets better. High school is the worst, man. Especially for people like us."

"Skeeter, I'm pretty sure there ain't but one person ever been like you," I said.

Skeeter laughed. "He's got a point. I hit almost every check mark on the ostracism list. I'm black, I'm gay, I'm adopted, and I'm smarter than almost everybody. *And* I'm not quite smart enough to keep my damn mouth shut. That didn't make for a good time in high school."

"Yeah?" Jacob's mouth curled up in a sneer. "You had it so tough, how many times did you try to kill yourself?"

"Three." Skeeter's gaze held steady into the camera. My mouth dropped open. This was news to me, and he'd been my best friend for almost twenty years. "I took a fistful of sleeping pills when I was in eighth grade, I ran my car off the road into a tree when I was in high school, and I cut my wrists in tenth grade." He held up an arm to the camera. "It's been a long time, but if you look close you can still see the marks."

He was right, I could. There were very faint white lines on the light brown skin of his wrists. But that wasn't what bothered me the most. Skeeter and I weren't all that tight in middle school, but by the time he learned to drive, I thought of him as my best friend. Hell, I *taught* him to drive. I remembered that wreck, when he ran off the road and hit a tree. He told me he spilled animal crackers in the floorboard and was reaching for them and lost control of the car.

"Skeeter..." I started, but didn't know what say.

"Shut up, Bubba. This one's mine." I snapped my mouth shut and let him roll.

"You see, Jacob, I figure high school is like this torture for every shitty thing we did in a past life, all jammed into four years. But there's one good thing about high school."

"What's that, smart guy?"

"It ends. It ends, and you get to leave, and if you don't ever want to see these assholes again, you don't have to. You can block them on Facebook, ignore their suckass LinkedIn requests looking for a job, and move far enough away that you don't ever have to see them again. And you can find people who see how awesome you are and appreciate you for that, and that turns out to be the best revenge."

"I'm partial to putting them in the hospital and making sure they don't ever play baseball again," Jacob said. I kept my mouth shut tight, especially since my agreeing with him was probably counterproductive. Frankly, I didn't mind a little ass-whooping in the name of justice; I just couldn't let him kill anybody.

"They showed the world my dick!" Jacob shouted. "They uploaded that video to the internet and it went viral. They posted pictures of it all over the school website. They did other stupid shit, too. They egged my house, wrecked the paint on my mom's car. They painted swastikas on my garage door. My dad's an atheist, for fuck's sake, but did they care? No! They just wanted a reason, so they picked on the Jew-boy."

"Yeah, that sucks. It's probably a lot like having people throw fried chicken at you in the cafeteria when you're the only black kid in school. Or cutting out pictures of penises and covering your locker with them because you're the only gay kid. Or burning a cross in your front yard for Halloween. Oh wait, that wasn't Halloween, and those white robes weren't ghost costumes."

"That shit doesn't happen anymore," Jacob sneered.

"Yeah, and people don't call you a Jesus-killer, do they? 'Cause people don't do that anymore? Nobody mutters 'nigger' under their breath if you cut them off in line at the grocery store, and God forbid I walk into a convenience store wearing a fucking hoodie. No, that shit doesn't happen anymore. Ask Trayvon Martin. You've had it bad, kid. There's no question. You didn't deserve it. Still no question. But you're too fucking smart for this. You keep down this road, and it's not gonna be me doing the talking. It's gonna be him," he pointed to me. "And he ain't much for conversation."

"You can still turn this around, Jacob," I said. "You haven't killed anybody. You hurt Eric pretty bad, but we've got a few resources up our sleeve that can get him back to normal better and faster than anybody expects. So if you'll agree to stop raising golems and wrecking schools—"

"And students," Skeeter chimed in.

"And students," I agreed, "we can make this go away."

Jacob sat there on his couch looking between me and Skeeter for at least a minute, then he turned his gaze on Mark. "Just what are you doing here, anyway?"

"I'm here to apologize," Mark said. He reached up and wiped a tear from his eyes. "I never knew it was so bad for you. I didn't know about the swastika shit, man. You gotta believe that. My granddad fought the Nazis in World War II. I grew up hearing his stories. I would never do that."

"But you did the rest of it."

"Yeah, I did."

"Why?" I watched Jacob's face change, and he wasn't a psycho monster-summoner bent on destruction. He was just a hurt little kid whose friend shit on him, and he wanted to know why.

"Man, I wish I had a good answer. But it's all chickenshit stuff. I fucked with you so they wouldn't fuck with me. I wanted to be cool. I was on the team, but I wasn't cool. I wasn't one of them, you know. No matter how I played, it was always something. But when they started picking on you, and I helped, then I was cool. Then I belonged, you know?"

"By making me miserable?"

"I'm sorry. I know that ain't enough, and I know you don't believe it, but I am sorry."

"What about you?" Jacob turned his gaze to me.

"What about me? I hit things. He's the smart one." I jerked a thumb at Skeeter's huge head on the screen.

"Yeah, but have you ever apologized to him? For the shit you did before y'all were friends?"

"Huh?" I was honestly confused. I couldn't think of anything I'd done to Skeeter. As far as I could remember, we'd always been friends, ever since that day at the flagpole. "I didn't ever do anything to him."

"Oh bullshit," Jacob said. "You were the jock, right? You're telling me you never screwed with the gay kid?"

"No, not that I remember. Did I, Skeet?" I looked to the screen, and his face told me everything. "Shit. What did I do?"

"There was the time you put the 'faggot' sign on my back and I walked around most of the school day without knowing it. Three teachers even saw it and did nothing. Then there was the time you and your buddies thought it would be funny to cut out pictures of me and the kicker for the football team and tape them together like we were kissing, then photocopy them and post them all over school."

"Okay, I gotta admit, I remember that one, but it was more on Dennis than on you." I even smiled a little at the memory.

"Yeah, well do you remember that Dennis transferred after that year?"

"Yeah, but his dad got a job somewhere out of state."

"His dad got that job and left town because Dennis came out to him when that picture went up, and he couldn't face being seen by his bowling team and hunting buddies with his fag son. He moved out of state and stuck Dennis in a private school that 'reprograms' gay youth. Dennis hung himself in his room second semester."

I collapsed back into the couch, my mouth hanging open. I had no idea. I assumed Dennis was straight because he always had a date to the dances after football games. I mean, he was on the football team, even if he was the kicker. "Are you sure?" I asked, my voice real quiet.

Skeeter reached down and held up a piece of paper to the camera. It was a string of photo booth pictures, like from old carnivals. It was Dennis and Skeeter. In the first picture they were smiling at the camera, then in the second they looked at each other, and in the third they were kissing. "This is what we really looked like kissing, Bubba. Not like the half-done Photoshop job y'all did with scissors and tape."

"Oh my God, Skeet. I never knew. I am so sorry. I didn't know. I thought it was just some fun, you know. Just…"

"Just messing with the gay kid, fucking with Dennis because being a kicker is the gay thing to do on the football team, because you can't be gay and cool, because—you know, I don't know why, I can't imagine why somebody who's fundamentally decent would do that shit. So tell me, Bubba, why did you do it?"

"I don't know, Skeet. I don't even remember where the idea came from anymore. All I can say is I'm sorry." My guts felt like I'd been punched by a Sasquatch. I just sat there in silence, all the little slights from all those years ago coming back to haunt me in the living room of a kid I'd come to stop or save, and still unsure of which one it was going to be.

"You've made up for it since then, Bubba. You didn't even know you were doing it, but you have. But back then, for just a minute when you had that idea that you thought was funny, you changed a bunch of lives." He turned his attention to Jacob. "And that's what you're doing right here, Jacob. You've got a power to change a lot of lives. You can do things that only a few people can do. You've got the magic, now it's all about how you use it. Are you going to destroy people, or are you going to take all that pain, all that hurt, and turn it into something good?"

Jacob sat there on the couch, just staring back and forth between Skeeter and me. "Is all that true?" he finally asked.

"You can Google Dennis Farner in Georgia if you want to confirm it," Skeeter said.

"What do I do now?" Jacob asked.

"Well, that depends on you," I said. "If you want to throw down, put your mojo into that pile of rocks beside you and we'll probably tear up your parents' house. And frankly, as bad as my arm hurts, I'm past the point of screwing around, so I'll probably just shoot you. If you think you might be willing to try to forgive these assholes and stop tearing up the whole town, then you and Mark move all these rocks out of your living room, you deactivate the walking mountain in the front yard, and we leave. The government sends your school a check for the trophy cases, we send a healer to Eric's hospital room, and somebody finds a way to sew Steve's lips together. Because if I ever hear another word outta that kid, I'm gonna come back here and kill him myself."

Jacob looked from me to Skeeter, then to Mark, then back to Skeeter. "Thanks. I hate you had to go through all that shit, and I'm sorry your friend died."

"Me too," Skeeter said, looking down at the strip of photos. "He was pretty awesome. But he's part of the reason why I do this. I feel like if I can help somebody else, it keeps him alive somehow."

Jacob turned to Mark and stood up. He held out a hand and said, "You wanna help me move all these rocks?"

"You gonna use any of them to kill me?" Mark asked, a little half-grin on his face.

"Not until we get the vacuuming done, at least," Jacob said. Mark took his hand, and the boys started cleaning up the mess, hauling the rocks out to the back yard and tossing them into a creek.

I went out the front door and motioned Agent Smith over. "You got another Suburban?" I asked, pointing at the mass of twisted metal and shattered glass.

He nodded and pulled a radio off his belt. "Clear, come on around," he said into the walkie. A black Suburban came around the corner, followed by the black rollback wrecker I'd seen earlier. Or an identical wrecker, I didn't know how many DEMON had in Memphis. The Suburban pulled up to the sidewalk and a pudgy red-haired agent with a goatee got out.

"I'm Agent Smith. I'll be your driver for the trip back home," he said.

I looked from Agent Smith to Agent Smith. One red-haired, one blonde, one clean-shaven, one with a goatee. "Y'all ain't kin, are you?"

"Agent Amy explained to us that you wouldn't be paying much attention to our names, so we might as well all be Agent Smith. We just wanted to see if you'd notice," Agent Smith #2 said. "My name's actually—"

"Amy's right, Smith is fine." I waved him off and got in the truck. I strapped on my seatbelt and pushed the button on my earpiece.

"You there, Skeet?" I asked.

"Yeah," he answered.

"You okay?"

"I don't know, Bubba. Are you?"

"I didn't know a lot of that stuff, Skeeter."

"I didn't want you to know a lot of that stuff, Bubba."

"You know you're my best friend, right?"

"Yeah, and you're mine."

"Even though I probably killed your first boyfriend?"

"You didn't kill Dennis. Dennis killed Dennis. And what you did sure didn't help, but it wasn't the cause, either. He had a darkness inside him, Bubba. I tried to help him fight it, I swear to God I did. But sometimes…"

"Sometimes the darkness wins," I said.

"Yeah, sometimes it does."

"But not today."

"No, Bubba. Not today."

"Skeet?" I said after a pause.

"Bubba, if you say you love me, I am going to sign you up for every gay dating site in the state of Georgia. You'll have bears hunting you down from miles away."

"Then I'll just say I'll see you in a couple hours."

"Take a Vicodin for that collarbone. It's gonna need to be set when you get home."

I did just that, chased it with three beers, and passed out before we got half an hour outside of Memphis.

HIGH ON THAT MOUNTAIN

I was sitting on my back deck, looking out over the purple and red sunset across the Georgia mountains, enjoying the company of one gorgeous federal agent and the taste of a beer that has been sitting in a mountain creek long enough to be almost too cold but not quite. It was a Saturday afternoon in August, which meant that it was hot everywhere but on top of my mountain and that I was off the clock. Without SEC football to occupy my afternoon, Agent Amy and I were kinda at loose ends as to how to best occupy our time. I had a few suggestions, but those were currently being put off until an undetermined "later." At least she was smiling when she shot me down.

Then it happened. It happens almost every time I get a little peace and quiet, and every time Amy and I get any hint of alone time. My cell phone rang. I didn't even look at the display—it was Skeeter. It was always Skeeter, and no matter how much I liked my best friend and technical guru, there were a certain number of special moments I didn't want to share with him. I didn't let it spoil my mood; I just reached into my pocket, pulled out my phone, and flung it off into the woods. The satisfying crash and tinkle of electronic pieces through the trees told me I had scored a direct hit on one of the loblolly pines that surrounded the house.

It took Skeeter all of half a minute to call the house phone, but that didn't do him any good. I ripped the last house phone out of the wall months ago and never bothered to replace it. The only time I need a landline is winter, and that's only for the one or two times a year that I get snowed in. And I don't really care about it then, but sometimes Skeeter worries if he can't get ahold of me, and I feel bad when he gets all bundled up like Ralphie from *A Christmas Story* and drives over in his VW Beetle to check on me. I do think he's got the only four-wheel drive Beetle in existence, though. So calling the landline didn't do him no good, either, on account of there not being anything to receive the call.

Then Amy's phone rang. She pulled it out and turned it so that I could see "Skeeter" on the display. I reached under my chair and drew the Colt 1911 pistol I kept hidden in a holster on the bottom of the chair.

"You have a forty-five hidden on your back deck?" Amy asked.

"You don't?" I replied. "Pull!"

She stared at me for a second, then understanding spread across her face and she flung her phone into the air in a graceful arc. RuPaul's "You Better Work" blared out across the mountains from the tiny speaker as the phone whirled from her hand. I tracked it with my pistol for a second or two, waiting until it hit the top of its curve and started to descend. Then I squeezed the trigger on my Colt twice, hitting with the first and blowing the phone to bits. RuPaul cut off in mid-sashay and scattered circuits and microchips all over the forest. I felt bad about that for a few seconds, then blamed it on Skeeter in my mind, so I felt better.

"You know those are expensive, right?" Amy asked, wiping tears of laughter from the corners of her eyes.

"Yours belonged to the government, right? They can afford another one."

"Yours didn't," she pointed out.

"Mine belonged to the Holy Roman Catholic Church, maybe the only organization better equipped to spend money than the U.S. Government." I propped my feet up on the rail and leaned back. "You might as well sit back down. It'll take him ten or fifteen minutes to get here from his place."

It was only about five minutes later when I heard a motorcycle rolling up the drive. "Shit," I said, getting to my feet and sweeping most of the beer bottles into the recycling bin. Since Amy started coming around, I found out all sorts of stuff I never knew about living in the new world. Like that red plastic tub the trash men left by the curb one day? That's for recyclable stuff, not just to separate the porn from the rest of the trash. My trash collectors have all seemed real disappointed since I figured that out.

"What's wrong? That sounds like Joe's bike," Amy asked.

"It is Joe's bike, which means Skeeter called Joe when he couldn't get ahold of me. Which means it's something important, not just some new tech thing Skeeter wanted to mess with." I opened the sliding glass door and went into the house. I grabbed my shoulder rig off the back of a dining room chair and strapped it on. I checked Bertha and saw she was loaded with regular ammo, with one in the pipe. My spare magazines were loaded with silver and cold iron. I used to carry some phosphorous rounds, but an unfortunate incident with a road-side fireworks stand forced my move into less incendiary rounds. I walked through the den, gearing up as I went. My Buck hunting knife went on my right hip. My Judge revolver loader with four-ten shotgun shells full of blessed silver and Holy Water-imbued rock salt went into a pancake holster at the small of my back.

"You expecting trouble?" Amy asked from where she stood by the sliding glass door. She looked like something out of a movie—a good movie, not the stupid action flicks I usually watch. The orange sunset made her hair look like something on fire, and the silhouette of her in the doorway made me want to pick her up and carry her away to somewhere people still believed monsters were just stories and that humans were the worst monsters out there.

"Nah, I thought I'd roll kinda light on this one." I wasn't kidding. Just two guns and one knife was pretty light for me.

Joe didn't bother knocking, and the look on his face made me rethink my position on heavy artillery. He ran up onto my front porch, flung open the door, and paused when he saw me standing in the den.

"What are you doing here?" he asked.

"I live here, Joe. What are you doing here?" I couldn't resist.

"You didn't answer your phone."

"I didn't feel like killing anything today, so I shot the phone."

"You should have answered the phone," Joe said, and the look in is eyes told me it was serious.

"Well, you're here now, so why don't you just tell me what's up?"

"It's Aunt Marion," Joe said. Aunt Marion was actually my great-aunt, who lived up on the hill.

"What about her?"

"She called 911 a little while ago and said that a pack of wild dogs was surrounding her house and tearing up her vegetable garden. Sheriff Alston was gonna send a couple guys up there, but I convinced him to let us handle it."

"How'd you hear about it? Alston got you on speed dial all of a sudden?"

"No, Miss Marion called Skeeter when you wouldn't answer the phone, then Skeeter called me, and I called the Sheriff to keep him from having to replace deputies."

Shit. Now I really felt like an asshole. If anything happened to that old lady because I was screwing around, I'd never forgive myself. Or more like I'd never forgive Jason because there was no question in my mind who was responsible for the "pack of dogs" surrounding my aunt's house.

I was out the door and halfway down the steps when I realized that I'd left my keys on the counter. I gave a little shrug and hopped onto Joe's motorcycle. His helmet was sitting on the seat, but I tossed it into a flowerbed and kicked gravel up in an arc as I cranked the cycle to life and sped off down the driveway to Aunt Marion's house.

A unt Marion lived almost at the top of the mountain, way back at the last pole in the power and phone line. She didn't even have a phone until the 1980s when the county rolled out 911 service, and she told them folks in no uncertain terms that she was an old lady that had been paying taxes in this county for all her adult life and there was no way in hell that she wasn't going to get the same level of emergency, fire, and medical care as them newcomers down in the valley. There was a crew on the mountain running wire the next week.

Other than the telephone/power pole off to the side of the house and the wires running into the building, the place was unchanged from when Great-Grandpappy Beauregard and Aunt Octavia lived there back at the turn of the century. The twentieth century, that is. The house was your basic one-story log and mud construction with a big porch running all across the front and down one side. An old Chevy C-100 pickup circa 1955 sat in the front yard with a three-legged cat sitting on the roof of the cab and a greying basset hound asleep on the ground under the back wheels. I slid the bike a little sideways parking next to the truck, and the cat hissed at me and jumped down into the truck bed to get away from the dust I kicked up. I ignored it. I've always hated that cat.

I drew Bertha and slammed home a magazine of silver bullets as I hopped off the bike and started off to the right-hand side of the porch, keeping the gun down low and ducking a little to keep my head below the line of the windows. "It's me, Aunt Marion, don't shoot!" I hollered.

"You wouldn't answer your phone, Robbie!" she yelled back from a window by the front door. Unless Aunt Marion had renovated recently, which I found highly unlikely, that window was in the front room right by a coat rack. I bet she was tracking my every move with Uncle Billy's old twelve-gauge.

"I'm sorry about that, Aunt Marion. Now put the shotgun down, I'm coming up on the porch."

"Any dogs out there?"

I looked around. The only things in the yard were me and that damn cat. "Nope, no dogs out here. I reckon you ran 'em off."

"I reckon I sure as hell did. I put a load of silver birdshot in one o' them bitches and you shoulda heard the yellin'. You'da thought I was killing her."

"Probably felt like it. Birdshot ain't no joke, Aunt Marion." I opened the door and stepped inside. I pulled the door closed behind me and shot the deadbolt home. It probably wouldn't stop a werewolf, but it did go three inches into a metal frame, so it wasn't bad as far as doors go.

"Birdshot hell, Robbie. You and I both know it was the silver that furry bitch couldn't stand." Aunt Marion stood up and shuffled over to give me a hug. She was a wizened little woman, less than five and a half feet tall in her prime. I'd be surprised if she topped five feet now. Her face had that run of lines that looked like some kind of woodcarving, and her hair flew around her head in an unruly laven-der-tinged halo. I hugged her gently, feeling the shoulder blades sticking out from her back under my hands. Marion Octavia McFadden was pushing ninety, and I was always scared hugging her, ever since middle school when I broke a dude's hand giving him a high-five.

She shuffled into the living room and sat down in her old wooden rocker. She leaned the shotgun against a heavy oak end table with cigarette burns in the finish and picked up a cup of tea. "I was having my evening tea when those damn mutts started sniffing around. I bet it's done gone cold." She took a sip. "I was right. Here, Robbie, go heat this in microwave for me."

I never even argued, just stood up and walked to the kitchen, put the teacup in the microwave for ten seconds, then brought it back. I sat in an overstuffed armchair that looked like it had lost one too many fights with Marion's crazy cat. Marion sipped her tea for a long minute until I cleared my throat.

"What do you want, Robbie? Do you want some tea of your own? I'm sorry, you'll have to fix it yourself. I wasn't expecting company, so I only made the one cup. Besides, I'm almost out of whiskey, and I don't feel like sharing." I probably forgot to mention that Aunt Marion only ever drinks coffee or tea with a solid slug of whiskey in it.

"No ma'am, I was just hoping you could tell me more about the dogs that attacked you this afternoon?"

"Don't you mean werewolves, Robbie?"

I didn't respond, just sat there gaping at her. In all my life, Aunt Marion had never given much indication that she knew what was going on when the menfolk of the family went out hunting for days at a time. I know I never said anything to her, and Pop didn't, and Grandpappy sure as hell didn't. He was so closemouthed he once went a month without speaking a complete sentence.

"Close your mouth, Robbie. I've always known our big family 'secret.' Good lord, son, look at who my mother was! She was with Beauregard when he first started out hunting, so there was no keeping anything from her, and I was an inquisitive child, so there no keeping anything from me. She decided to be totally honest with me as soon as she found me sharpening my own stakes at the age of seven. I even used to ride with Daddy and your grandfather when we were children. Sometimes Octavia would come along with us, although she was already an old woman in those days. Not old like I am now, but old enough."

"So you know," I said. "Then you know who's behind it." Jason, my younger brother, was building an army of supernatural creatures to forcibly pull the rest of the things that go bump in the night out into the light. I don't know why he couldn't see that the fight was unwinnable for him. Human beings breed at the drop of a hat. Weres and other supernatural creatures mate for life and breed once if they're extremely lucky. The sheer numbers of it doesn't work for the boy, but math was never his strong suit.

"Yes, I know it's your jackass little brother. But what did he want from me? Why is he harassing an old woman? Shouldn't he be down the mountain beating your ass again?" Aunt Marion reminded me oh-so-gently of the last time Jason and I tangled, when he took my own sword and stabbed me right through my sizable gut with it.

"I don't know, Aunt Marion. Did he say anything?"

"I don't think he was here. It looked like another wolf was in charge. It was a big mottled grey thing. Looked mean as hell."

"And they came as wolves? They didn't travel as people and shift when you wouldn't give them what they wanted?"

"No, you dumbass, ain't you been listening? They never told me nothing about what they wanted, just showed up on all fours and started scratching at the doors." Aunt Marion's tea wasn't working fast enough to calm her nerves.

I stood up and headed for the door.

"Where you going?" Marion asked from her chair. I heard just the slightest tinkle of rattling china and knew that no matter how tough she was, the old bird was scared now that the adrenaline was wearing off.

"I'm gonna go see if they left a clue, or a message, or anything that would tell us why they were after you. Don't worry, Aunt Marion. I won't let anything come after you again." I looked at her, this tough mountain woman now a shrunken husk, sitting in her rocking chair with a quilt on her legs because the circulation in her feet was gone, a teacup half full of whiskey rattling on the saucer, and I hoped I was telling the truth.

I walked out on the porch and flicked on my Bluetooth earpiece. "You there, Skeet?" I said to the air.

"Yeah, we're here," Skeeter's reply came in my ear.

"We?" I asked.

"Joe and I are here with Skeeter." Amy's voice came across like she was sitting right next to me. Which I wished she was, of course, but it was a lot safer for her and Uncle Father Joe to be holed up in Skeeter's Fortress of Nerditude. Jason hadn't managed to get in there after him last time, and we'd beefed up security since then.

"Good, that means y'all are safe. What do we know, Skeeter?" I slipped on a pair of specially rigged shooting glasses with a tiny camera and transmitter in the frame, so everybody could see what I was seeing. Which right now was a whole bunch of nothing.

"We don't know shit, Bubba. We got no video of them coming up the road, no sensors in the woods have been tripped, we've heard nothing unusual out of any of our contacts in the supernatural world. Nothing."

"They didn't come up the road," I said. "Aunt Marion says they were full-on wolf the whole time they were here. So they came through the woods. But nobody gave us a heads up?"

"No, and none of my tech shows anything, either."

"That means—"

"Either that somebody found our moles and killed them and found our tech and disabled it, or they got exceptionally lucky." Skeeter cut me off.

"Nobody's that lucky," Amy said, and I could see her chewing on a thumbnail, her brow furrowed in a way that's almost cute, or it would be except for the fact that when she comes out of her pensive pose, it's usually guns blazing.

"I found something," I said, more to direct their attention to the screen than because I thought they'd miss it. I hopped off the porch over to the right side of the house and stepped over a low picket fence that was smashed flat to the grass. This patch of ground had been surrounded by that two-foot white picket fence my whole life, and to see those white stakes muddy and scattered pissed me off as much as Jason running three feet of steel through my gut. I mean, I was still pretty pissed about the stabbing, but wrecking Aunt Marion's fence and defacing the family plot was something else entirely.

"What is that, Bubba? It looks like . . ." Amy's voice trailed off.

"We're up in the mountains, darlin', it's exactly what you think it is —a graveyard. This is where a couple generations of my family are buried. Back when it was too hard to come off the mountain in winter, or when we were on the outs with one church or another, this is the family burial plot." It was maybe thirty yards on a side, not a very big plot, but Marion kept it real nice. She mowed and either used a weed eater or, more likely, got down on her hands and knees and pulled the weeds around the headstones.

I saw Great-Grandpappy Beauregard's stone, with his wife Vera next to him and their oldest son Richard. Grandpappy was buried down in the Baptist cemetery, like most of our people had been for the last fifty years or so, but there were a few graves in this little patch stretching back to Great-Great-Uncle Dargin, who fought for the Yankees in the War of Northern Aggression, what a fair number of people on this mountain still call the Civil War. I was a little surprised when I found his stone there, but Pop explained it best. He looked at Uncle Dargin's stone, shook his head and said, "You can't choose your family, son."

There were a dozen graves, and eleven of them were undisturbed except for a few dog turds on Great-Grandpappy's patch of grass. He was the first Monster Hunter in the family, so I reckoned somebody decided to show his opinion of the family business right there. I scooped it up in a napkin out of the truck and threw it off into the woods, promising to figure out who'd crapped on Great-Grandpappy's grave and explain to him the error of his ways.

But one grave, on the far right side in the front row, was halfway dug up. The grass was torn and a huge hole had been started. It looked like whatever had been digging there got interrupted, and by the few drops of blood on the grass, I figured I knew what the interruption was. I looked at the headstone—Octavia Brabham McFadden, beloved wife and mother. Great-Aunt Tavvy, Aunt Marion's mama and Great-Grandpappy Beauregard's sister. According to all the stories, she went monster hunting with her brother and provided the brains to his brawn. She was kinda like his Skeeter, except a chick, and a white chick, and having to break a lot shit to figure stuff out. Okay, maybe that last part was pretty much like me and Skeeter.

"Skeet, you got any idea why these furballs would want to dig up Aunt Tavvy's grave?"

"No, Bubba, I got no clue. I'll call into the house to Miss Marion and let you know."

"Nah, I'll go talk to her. Maybe she'll make some lemonade and come sit on the porch."

"You just want her to trot out the Jack Daniels and make you some Lynchburg Lemonade," Skeeter said.

"I don't give a shit about the triple sec, I'm good with just a healthy slug of JD in my lemonade," I replied, stepping back over the broken fence and silently planning to come over the next free weekend I had to fix it. I stopped just outside the fence and knelt down.

"Y'all see this?" I asked. I reached down and picked up the shiny thing that had caught my eye. It was a dog tag. Not the military kind, but the kind that went around a real dog's neck. I picked it up and turned it over in my hands. There was no owner's name on it, just "Tommy" and a number.

"You got that, Skeeter?" I asked.

"Yeah, I got it. I don't know if I know what to do with it, but I got it. I'll run the number against local veterinarians to see if the dog got micro-chipped there or something, then figure out who owns it from that."

"But why would anybody let their normal dog run with a pack of werewolves?" Amy asked.

"The better question is why would a pack of werewolves put up with a normal dog in their midst?" I mused. "Something's goofy here, and I bet we'll find out exactly what that is when we find little Tommy here." I slipped the tag into my pocket and stood up, my knees going off like rifle shots.

I made my way back across the yard, looking over the remnants of four or five generations of Brabhams scattered across the mountaintop. Over yonder was the truck Great-Grandpappy took to Atlanta when he came back with the sword that Jason stuck in my guts and stole from me more than a hundred years later. It was little more than a lump for kudzu to grow on these days, but if you looked close, you could still see the shape of the flatbed. In the side yard by the house was a huge old oak tree with branches the size of my thighs hanging over the house. A knotted hemp rope hung from one of those limbs with an old tractor tire swinging from the end of it. I remembered pushing Jason on that tire swing when we'd come up here visiting every Sunday afternoon. He was a carefree little shit back then, always yelling for me to push him higher and higher, then laughing like crazy when he jumped off at the highest point and tumbled halfway to the porch before he stopped rolling.

Aunt Marion came out on the porch with two tall Tupperware

cups and sat in one of the rocking chairs. I sat in the one beside her and took my drink from her hand. "That Skeeter boy said you wanted some lemonade. I didn't have none made up, so I just poured you a Jack and Coke instead."

"That's my favorite flavor of lemonade, Aunt Marion."

"You find anything out in the yard?"

"Just a bunch of big damn tracks and this. Looks like some kinda dog tag." I reached into my pocket and handed her the aluminum heart-shaped tag.

"Tommy, huh?" She turned it over and over in her hands, then I watched realization dawn across her face. Her eyes went wide, then flashed cold and chips of ice. "That little son of a bitch. I know who was with your brother's bitch and the rest of them dogs."

"Who was it?"

"It was my good-for-nothing cousin Gerald. He ain't been worth a damn his whole life, but I never thought he'd turn against his own blood."

"Maybe he thought Jason was his blood, too," I said.

Marion turned to me, whip-quick, but her jaw relaxed when she caught the look on my face. "I reckon he is, at that. No matter how much you'd like to, you can't pick your family."

"And you can't wipe them on the back of the couch, neither," I said, finishing the old joke. "But what's the deal with Gerald? And why were the wolves digging around Aunt Tavvy's grave?"

"They wanted this," Marion said, pulling an old pocket watch out of a pocket of the Carhartt work shirt she wore as a jacket. It was a battered gold watch, obviously older than she was. Any design that had ever been on the outside of it was worn away long ago from handling, time, and lots of hands that had polished it smooth as glass.

"What's so special about an old watch? I mean, I appreciate that it's an antique and all, but is that worth digging up a grave for?" I asked.

"This was your Uncle Billy's pocket watch. He and your Aunt Tavvy found it when they were trapped in a caved-in coal mine a couple hills over. It was his uncle David's. He got caught in a cave-in and died some years before your Great-Grandpappy Beauregard and my Gran, or Aunt Tavvy, went up to the mine to investigate some tommyknockers. They found more than tommyknockers—there was a whole passel of ghosts in that mine, not to mention a sumbitch mine boss trying to get everything shut down so he could take the claim and the gold behind the coal for himself. But Gran and Beauregard and Grandpa Billy came out of that hole in the ground with this watch, and they told the rest of their lives how that old watch let them talk to the ghosts and got them out of the mine safe."

"So now Gerald wants it because why?" I asked.

"Gerald's just a little pissant, been jealous his whole life that Grandpa Billy passed the watch down to his children and grandchildren instead of to Gerald's people. He always said we was more Brabham than McFadden, and the magic oughta go where the blood is truest, not just to the namesakes."

"That sounds stupid. Sorry to say, but it does."

"That's 'cause Gerald's a dumbass, Robbie. He don't know his ass from a hole in the ground 'til he steps in one. He's been bitter as a pill his whole damn life because Grandpa left this house to my daddy instead of his daddy."

"What does he want with this watch?" I asked. "I mean, being able to talk to ghosts is fine and all, but it ain't like they're great in a fight, and Jason would still have to get them on his side. I can't see a bunch of dead dudes giving much of a shit about a fight between a werewolf and his big brother."

"I can't either, but didn't I hear about Jason trying to set himself up as this big-deal monster messiah or something?"

"Yeah, that's his whole deal. He's gonna bring monsters out of the shadows and knock humans a couple rungs down on the food chain." I shook my head at the idea. It was stupid, but Jason had always been a go big or go home kinda guy.

"That's why he wants the watch." Aunt Marion folded her arms over her skinny chest.

"I don't get it," I admitted.

"It don't just let you talk to ghosts, Robert. It lets you *control* ghosts. And all kinds of other dead and undead things."

"Shit," I murmured, then looked at Aunt Marion. "Sorry about the language."

"I think 'shit' just about covers it, son." We sat there for a minute sipping our drinks, which were appropriately a lot more Jack than Coke, when I had an idea.

"I got it. Or at least I got something," I said, standing up and pressing the button for my headset. "Skeeter, send Joe up here with the truck and a spare helmet. I need to get Aunt Marion into the bunker with you before it gets dark."

Skeeter's voice came through my headset. "What are you gonna do, Bubba?"

"I'm gonna use her watch to get advice from my Great-Grandpappy."

A couple hours later, I found myself once again on the inside of that broken-down little picket fence, this time sitting on a bucket I had carried up the hill just for that purpose. You see, once a body gets north of the three hundred pound mark, getting all that mass up off the ground gets harder and harder. But a five-gallon bucket, usually used for large quantities of paint or motor oil, when turned upside down, makes a perfect seat, no matter how big the posterior that's to be perched upon it. Besides, I used the bucket to haul a case of beer and ice up the hill. After I mostly filled in Aunt Tavvy's grave, I put the beer in the depression that was left, 'cause there always seems to be either too much or not enough dirt left when you try to fill a hole back in, never just the right amount. Then I poured the ice over the beer and sat waiting for dark.

I didn't have too much experience dealing with ghosts, most of my experience coming from supernatural creatures of a more tactile nature, but I figured if I sat on Great-Grandpappy Beauregard's grave and called to him while holding the watch, he'd probably show up sooner or later. If nothing else, just to find out what jackass was making all that noise. So I sat on my bucket, drinking beer out of a

JOHN G. HARTNESS

shallow grave, and watching the first lightning bugs blink their little butts on and off down the hill near where the honeysuckle grew. Uncle Father Joe was with me, making sure, as he put it, that I didn't offend any dead people or get the world invaded by pissed off poltergeists.

I finished off my third beer and tossed the empty can off into the woods.

"I don't think that's exactly biodegradable, Bubba," Joe said from where he sat on the ground under a spreading live oak tree. Joe was closer to two hundred pounds than three, so I wasn't worried too much about his knees. He'd also never spent any time on the defensive line of an SEC football team, so his joints hadn't endured quite the level of punishment in his twenties that mine had. Neither had his liver, on account of him going to seminary and me going to the University of Georgia. One of those institutions involves sipping sacramental wine, the other involves beer bongs and keg stands. You figure out which one I went to.

Joe was sitting in the graveyard with me watching for ghosts because my efforts to send Aunt Marion back to the bunker with him where it would be safe met with limited success, to say the least. To say more would involved a five foot tall old woman threatening to beat my ass if I didn't shut up about locking her up in some hole in ground and leaving her out of her own fight. I'm not the sharpest knife in the drawer, but I know when to pick my battles. And I knew enough to not cross any of Great-Aunt Tavvy's line.

"I don't think I exactly give a shit about littering, Joe. It's my mountain, or at least my family's mountain, so I reckon I can toss a few beer cans on the ground, long as I do it where Aunt Marion can't ever find them."

"That's a good idea, son, because if she sees so much as a pop top where it ain't supposed to be, she'll whoop your ass like you was still a little feller trying to play giddy-up on the sow." I knew that voice, but it wasn't quite right. I turned around on my bucket and felt my mouth fall open a little bit. Standing on his own grave was my Great-Grand-pappy Beauregard, the original Monster Hunter. He looked a lot like

278

Grandaddy, and little bit like me, but nothing at all like Pop. Great-Grandpappy Beauregard was a barrel-chested man well over six feet tall, a giant back in the day when he was alive. He had the long beard that mountain men favored at the start of the twentieth century, but his hair was cropped short. He wore coveralls, a plaid flannel shirt, and weathered brown work boots. He held a double-barrel shotgun in one hand, and I could see the hilt of my sword sticking up over one shoulder.

Joe jerked up to one knee and his hand went to his hip where he had a Colt 1911 holstered. I chuckled a little and wasn't all that surprised to see the ghost do the same. Joe realized what he was about to draw down on and let his hand drop by his side. He did stand all the way up, though. I did the same, showing respect to my elders, I reckoned.

"I reckon you're my Great-Grandpappy Beauregard," I said giving the ghost a little wave.

"And I reckon you're Robbie, my great-grandson. That would make you Leila and Eugene's oldest boy, right?" The ghost flickered a little when he took time to think about what he was going to say, but otherwise he looked almost solid. Just not quite. He didn't glow blue, like Obi-Wan Kenobi or nothing like that, he just was a little *less here* than real people.

"Yes, sir."

"How are they doing?" It was odd, standing in a cemetery making conversation with a ghost, but I reckon that's the story of my life—odd.

"Pop's dead. He died last year. I don't know about Mama. She left a long time ago."

"Ran out on y'all?" the ghost asked.

I nodded. I didn't like talking about my mama, even to family. Even to dead family.

"I ain't surprised. She wasn't mountain people, so I figured she might not stay. And she wasn't monster-hunting people neither, and you need to be one or the other to put up with the life we lead. I'm sorry about your daddy, though. What happened?"

I took a minute to decide whether or not I was going to lie to the ghost, then I figured I had nothing to hide, so I told him the truth. "I killed him," I said. "He went bad, turned werewolf and followed a bad pack leader, so I killed him." It made short telling of a long story, but I figured Pop's wasn't going to be the only blood on my hands before everything with Jason was all said and done.

"Huh," the ghost said and pulled a pipe out of his pocket.

"I don't think you can smoke," I said.

"I can't," he agreed, putting the pipe between his teeth. "But it helps me think. Now what can I do you for?"

"It's my brother," I said.

"What about him?"

"He's the bad pack leader that Pop went off and followed. He's trying to raise an army of monsters to take over the South. Then eventually he'll go bigger."

"What do you intend to do about it?"

"Well, today he's trying to get his hands on Great-Aunt Octavia's pocket watch, thinking it can control ghosts. Aunt Marion thinks Gerald McFadden is behind that, so I reckon I'm gonna go hurt Gerald's feelings on the matter of a pocket watch."

"I reckon that's a pretty good idea. It don't let you control spirits, there ain't much outside some really vicious magic that lets you do that. But that watch will call up every spirit within a couple miles if you ain't careful, and most ghosts are either crazy or just plain mean, so they'd be likely to help your brother anyhow. All right, so you keep Gerald from getting the watch. Then what?"

"Then I reckon I have to deal with Jason."

"And exactly how do you plan to deal with him?"

I didn't meet the dead man's eyes. I knew what I'd see there—a reflection of my own guilt and disappointment in not being able to save Jason from himself. Finally I spoke. "Well, I reckon I'm gonna kill him."

Great-Grandpappy Beauregard stood there silent for a long moment, leaning up against the trunk of that old oak and chewing on the stem of his pipe. When he finally spoke, his eyes had no more of the cheer that was there previously. "Boy, I'm only gonna say this one time. And I'm only saying it because I think it's important, so listen up. We hunt monsters. It's what we do. It's part of who we are, and it's the thing that makes us different from normal people. You ain't never gonna get up in the morning and go to work in some factory or sawmill. We live in the dark places, and we do the dark work so the day people ain't got to. Now if your brother has looked too far into the heart of that darkness, it might have overtook him. And if that's the case, well, it's just like a dog that's got the rabies—you can't do nothing but put it down. But if there's a sliver of doubt, just that littlest bit of hope in the bottom of Pandora's box? Well, then, he's still family, no matter what he's done, and you got to save him if you can."

"That ain't gonna be easy, Great-Granddaddy," I said.

"Shit, son, if it was easy wouldn't nobody need us!" He took the pipe out of his mouth and pointed the stem at me. I could see the flint glimmering in his ghostly eyes as he said, "Boy, you can't save them all. But you got to save the ones you can. Now get on across the holler and whoop Gerald McFadden's ass and tell him to leave your Aunt Marion alone. She's a good woman—keeps the weeds off my head-stone. Ain't many like her left, you take care of her."

"I will, Great-Granddaddy," I said, turning to go.

"Joseph?" Great-Granddaddy's ghost called out to Uncle Father Joe.

"Yes, sir?"

"Stay here a minute, boy. I got a message or two for you."

I stopped right outside the fence and looked back at where Joe stood with Great-Grandpappy until he motioned for me to go ahead. I walked the hundred yards back up to the house and stepped inside, hollerin' for Aunt Marion not to shoot me as I ducked through the door.

"What's the plan from the dead man?" Marion asked.

"I go beat Gerald's ass and hurt his feelings about this watch. He can't have it."

"I told you that, boy. Are you sure you're kin to me? You don't seem smart enough." The old woman laughed as she turned to go into the house. A few minutes later, she came out of the back of the house with her boots on. I gaped at her as she marched right past me and started out the door.

"Where the hell do you think you're going?" I asked as I grabbed her arm gently and spun her around back into the room.

"I'm going with you, where do you think I'm going?"

"I don't think you're going anywhere. I still want you to go to Skeeter's with Joe and wait for word that those werewolves won't be bothering you again."

"I thought we'd done settled this. If you think I ain't going with you on this scrap, then you got another think coming, boy. What, you think just because I'm old I can't put a load of silver shot in some mutt's hind end? Shit, boy, I was shooting big nasties before you were born, and I learned to fight dirty from your Great-Grandpappy himself. So let's go."

"I can't take you with me, Aunt Marion. It's gonna be dangerous, and I can't split my attention between the monsters and making sure you don't get hurt." I was standing in the doorway now, blocking the spry old woman's exit.

"Do you think I can't take care of myself?" she asked me, her jaw set at a belligerent angle.

"I'm sure you can handle yourself fine most days, but this ain't most days. These are real werewolves, and once they know we have the watch, they'll do anything they can to get it."

"Then you need all the help you can get," Marion said. She glared up at me for a minute, then her chin started to quiver. "Please, Robbie. Let me go with you. I know I'm an old woman, and I know I can't shoot as straight as I used to, or move as quiet, or even make it through a fight by myself. But this is my damn watch and my damn house those dogs tried to come into. So I deserve a little respect in this matter. Let me help you catch them." Aunt Marion stood there looking up at me, then went on.

"Those young bastards *ignored* me, Robbie! I shot at 'em, and they ignored me like I was just so much background noise. I can't stand that, and that's what my life's about now—being ignored. Let me matter, son. Just one more time."

I looked down in her eyes, and that's when I saw it. Behind the crows' feet, behind the lines on her face cut so deep you could lose a finger in there, I saw an echo of the woman she'd been thirty or forty years before. Slight but tough, she wore her auburn hair short to keep it out of the way of her shooting. She was a spitfire, a legit Monster Hunter, but those days were long gone. Now she was an old woman fighting Father Time and asking me to give her one last chance to die gloriously. I closed my eyes and offered up a quick prayer to whoever protects fools and sinners. "Fine, you can come with me. But you do what I say, the instant I say it, understand?"

"Done. Now let's go whoop some ass!" She let out a holler and ducked under my arm and out the door. I shook my head and followed her, adding "World's Oldest Sidekick" to my list of strange adventures.

It was the darkest part of the night when we rolled up on the McFadden place. It was laid out a lot like our old home place, but everything looked just a little bit different, just a tiny bit cleaner and newer. The McFaddens had always had a little bit of money, while my folks were usually one step away from dirt farming. Hunting down monsters was spiritually satisfying but didn't pay for shit, and it wasn't until Joe and I came to an agreement that any of us managed to live in anything resembling comfort.

I pulled the truck right up to the front porch and got out, slamming my door and not giving a shit about noise. Anything with even human hearing knew Joe's motorcycle was coming half a mile away, so there was no point in trying to be subtle. Besides, I suck at subtle.

There was a pack of wolves lounging around the porch in a mix of human and lupine shapes and mix of levels of dress. I've learned through the years that when you grow a coat of fur at will, you don't care a whole lot about clothes, but judging from the gasp when she stepped off the running board of the truck, Aunt Marion hadn't been around a whole bunch of naked werewolves before. I gave about half a second's thought to her purer instincts, then decided it was her idea to come along, so the sight of a random pecker or two wouldn't kill her.

Sitting in a rocking chair on the porch was what I assumed to be Jason's latest bitch, a tall good-looking were with long black hair hanging loose down over one breast. She wore a pair of cutoff jean shorts, cut almost high enough to see her grooming habits, a scowl, and nothing else. She stood up as I approached the porch, moving in that liquid way that wolves have, like there's an extra joint to their hips or something. She flowed down the steps and stood in front of the house, arms crossed over her chest.

"Good, you brought our talisman. Now we don't have to go digging up the old woman's bone garden anymore."

"You set foot or paw on my property again, I'll blow it off," Marion said from where she stopped next to me. She aimed the shotgun at the wolf and I pushed the barrel down with one hand.

"I'm here to give y'all a chance to go home alive. You leave now and tell my idiot brother to stop all this nonsense and nobody has to die tonight." I drew Bertha from my shoulder holster and pulled the hammer back. I always rolled with one in the pipe, so once I flicked the safety off, it was party time.

"What if we want somebody to die tonight? Somebody else, that is." A burly he-wolf stepped down off the porch and gestured to a pile of clothes and bloody meat lying in the dirt next to the steps. If I squinted just right, I could almost make it out as human remains. *I reckon that's Gerald McFadden. Oh well, you lie down with dogs, sometimes you don't get up with fleas. Sometimes you don't get up at all.*

"What if we want a couple of somebodies to die tonight? What then, big man? What you gonna do then?" The wolf continued playing the Alpha and stepped up into my personal space. I pegged him as a middle of the pack runner trying to make some bones with the boss's old lady, maybe even make a play for her while Jason wasn't around. He didn't really worry me much, but the growls starting to percolate from the other six or seven wolves around the house were a little bit of a concern.

"You care about this asshole?" I asked the woman.

"You care what I care about?" she asked me.

"I figure if you ain't Jason's bitch, you're at least the Alpha female, and that's some status. So if you like him, he gets one pass for getting this close."

"And if I don't?"

"Give the word."

The wolf who stepped up on me, who I named Dipshit in my head, picked that time to make a grievous tactical error—he got his masculinity hurt. In a wolf pack, there's an Alpha, then there's his bitch. Wolves usually mate for life, and I'd killed Jason's bitch some months back, so I didn't know if this woman was really his mate or just filling the role of his Alpha female. Either way, she had a lot more status in the pack than some random male, no matter how big or brave or stupid he was. Well, this particular male was big and brave *and* stupid, which is a dangerous combination. He decided to open his mouth at just the wrong time.

"You talk to me, boy. I don't need no bitch to fight my battles for me. I'm a man. Better than that, I'm a goddamn *were*, and you got something to say about me, you say it *to me*, not to some bitch who just happens to be warming the bed of my Alpha."

I looked past him to the woman, who turned her back on him and walked back up the steps and sat back in the wooden rocking chair. *That answers that.*

"You want me to talk to you?" I looked down into Dipshit's eyes. They were brown, shot through with the normal were-yellow, but also tinged with red. He was drunk or high, or both. Didn't matter, weres metabolized so fast he'd be stone sober in another five minutes. I planned on him being dead by then.

"You got something to say, say it right here, you chickenshit human piece of—"

I never did find out what I was a piece of, since that's the moment I pressed Bertha's barrel to his forehead and pulled the trigger. A silver hollow point with a wax tip over a holy water reservoir spat out of the barrel of the big fifty-caliber pistol and turned his head into a grotesque soup bowl in half a second. His eyes never even registered that he was dead; he just dropped to the dirt with that same stupid look on his face. *One down, seven to go.*

I stepped across Dipshit's dead body and raised my fist to the heavens. "This is Bertha. She is a Desert Eagle fifty-caliber pistol loaded with silver bullets. If you think for a second that I won't put one of these bullets in each and every one of your dumb asses, then I direct your attention to Dipshit here, who also thought he was invincible." I waved with my free hand at the corpse lying in the dirt emitting all sorts of foul smells and sounds as its muscles went through the final relaxation.

"Now I know my brother sent you here looking for something, and I have it." I held Uncle Billy's watch high so the gold glinted in the little slivers of cold moonlight that made it through the trees. "If you want it, you're gonna have to kill an old woman, a priest, and the meanest son of a bitch you've ever met. If any of y'all wants to run now, I'd suggest it. I won't even shoot you in the back. But if you're still here when I count three, I'm gonna start killing things. And when I start, I ain't gonna stop until there ain't nothing alive in this yard but that mangy blue tick hound dog and my people. Do I make myself clear?"

"Crystal," the wolf-woman said, standing up and dropping her shorts to the porch. Magic flowed over her and she shifted into a half-human, half-wolf transitional beast with muscles to make Arnold jealous in his prime and claws that looked designed by God himself to rip the guts out of a man and scatter them across a mountaintop.

"One," I counted. I held Bertha high, ignoring the half-transformed werewolf ten feet in front of me. Nothing moved on the mountain. Even the cicadas were still, like that second before the first big lightning bolt strikes the ground and half an inch of rain comes down in ten minutes.

"Two." One young wolf near the end of the porch hopped up and ran for the woods. She looked like she'd just had a litter, so I didn't blame her. *Six to go.*

"Three." I didn't let the echo of the word fade, just brought Bertha down and put two in the chest of a charging were. *Five.* I heard Aunt Marion's twelve-gauge bark beside me and saw a fully transformed wolf go down sideways off to my right. *Four.* Uncle Father Joe jumped into the bed of the truck with a bolt-action Winchester 700 and put a .308 round through the eye of a half-shifted were coming at him over on my left side. *Three.*

That was all the easy ones, though. I didn't have any time to spare for Joe or Marion because the Alpha bitch was on me, and in her transitional state, she was seven feet of muscle, claws, and fangs. She dropped a shoulder as she came at me, and Bertha flew out of my hand while my breath flew out of my lungs. I sprawled backward across the front yard, little bits of gravel digging into my ass as the bitch and I scrabbled backwards and rolled over a couple of times trying to find an advantage. The smell of her fur filled my nose, and I got one elbow under myself and flipped us over, shoving one knee into her gut and getting a little separation. I came up to my knees and one hand as she spun around to face me.

Claws filled my vision as I jerked my head back, barely saving my eyesight. A line of pain flashed across my face, and I felt blood bloom from the bridge of my nose where she tagged me. Another paw came down at my face, but I made sure my face was somewhere else. I reached behind me to the waistband of my jeans and pulled my Judge revolver. I brought the pistol to bear on her chest, but she lashed out with a foot and kicked me in the chest before I could squeeze the trigger. I heard a *BOOM* from behind my head and felt the warm spray of blood splash across the back of my neck. I spared a glance behind me and saw the were that was going after Marion fall to the dust, half his face turned to hamburger by the shotgun blast. *I guess that leaves two.*

I turned my attention back to the were-bitch that was trying to rip my face off, but she was gone. I spun around, the Judge out in front of me tracking my every move. Joe was tussling in the back of the truck with a were in human form, and he seemed to be doing okay. Just to be sure, I spun the barrel in the Judge, selected a forty-five long pistol round, and put a silver bullet between the were's shoulder blades. He staggered, dropped to his knees, and toppled out of the truck. Joe gave me a shaky nod, then I saw his eyes go wide as they looked past my left shoulder. *Oh shit, Aunt Marion.*

I spun around, only to have my worst instincts confirmed. The Alpha had Aunt Marion's neck in one hand and her shotgun in the other. She tossed the shotgun to the ground and held Marion up, her feet barely touching the ground, as she shifted back into human form. Her human form would have been a lot more pleasant to look at if she weren't spattered with blood and dirt and scratches from rolling around in the yard with me, but it was still kinda distracting having a naked woman hold your great-aunt by the neck and threaten her.

"Give me the watch or I'll snap her neck like a twig," the wolf-woman said.

"Don't give the bitch the time of day, Robbie," Aunt Marion said, thrashing in the were's grip.

"Hold still, old woman, or I'll kill you and take the watch myself," the were said. She gave Aunt Marion a shake, and I saw the pain in the old woman's eyes. She was tough old bird, but she was north of eighty, and even mountain people only have so much steel in their spine. Another rough shake and a whimper escaped Aunt Marion's lips.

"Hold on, now!" I shouted. "Gimme a second to think."

"There's nothing to think about, and no time to give, meatball," the Alpha said. "You give me that watch right now, or I break your Aunt Marion into a couple of different pieces."

I stood there, trying to figure out if she was bluffing, but everything in me said she wasn't. I pulled the golden pocket watch out of my jeans and held it up by the chain. "Fine, fine. Here you go. Take the damn thing, just stop hurting her."

"Throw it here," she said, a smile spreading across her cold features. Her green eyes sparkled with glee and she held out her free hand. I tossed the watch across the yard and she caught it one-handed. She held it up to catch what little light there was and let go of Aunt Marion's neck. The old woman sagged to her feet, then stood up ramrod straight to her full five foot three inches as she slapped the were right full in the face.

The Alpha's eyes went wide, then narrowed in fury as she half-transformed her right hand into a set of razor-sharp claws, which she then used to rip Aunt Marion's throat out and toss it into the dust. The old woman sagged to the dust and gravel of the front yard, her lifeblood spilling out faster than I thought a person could bleed. I ran to her, but the light was already fading from her eyes.

"She hit me," the were said, her eyes registering shock at her instinctive actions.

"Not like I'm going to," I said, standing up and getting nose to nose with her.

"I don't think so, human," she said, then shoved me backward. I fell onto my butt, and by the time I scrambled to my feet, she had transformed into a wolf and dashed off into the woods, the pocket watch in her teeth.

I turned to Aunt Marion, lying in the yard in a puddle of her own blood. I knelt by her head and picked up her body. There was a wry smile on her face, and I knew that fiery old woman had gone out on her own terms. I held it close to my chest as the last of her life spilled out onto the ground, and when I looked up, Joe was standing there over the both of us.

"You want me to say anything over her?" Joe asked.

"You don't need to," I replied. "She was a godly woman. Kept to the Bible and lived a good life. If her ticket ain't already punched to Heaven, then ain't nobody going Upstairs." I laid her body back down and pulled off the tatters of my t-shirt to cover her face.

"We might need some of Amy's government connections to keep there from being an autopsy, though," I said after I pressed the Bluetooth headset transmitter in my ear.

"I'll take care of it, Bubba," Amy's voice came through the headset. "And Bubba?" she said.

"Yeah?"

"I'm sorry."

"Me too," I said. "One more thing Jason has to answer for."

"And now he's got your Great-Grandpappy's watch, and he can control the dead," Amy said.

"Well, funny thing about that," I said, reaching into my pocket and pulling out a much older, much more battered pocket watch. "They took the watch Pop gave me when I graduated high school. I kept the one Great-Aunt Octavia walked out of that coalmine with. It won't let me control dead people any more than it would let Jason, but it does make the veil a lot thinner, so I can talk to people a lot easier."

"So now what?" Joe asked.

"Now we find my brother. He's got his army assembled, and whatever he's been planning, he's ready to pull the trigger. He never would have come after family if there was another way, so we're coming up on the endgame."

"Why wouldn't he mess with family early?" Amy asked. "You know, get the opposition out of the way."

"Because he knows that family's my only religion, and once he crosses that line again, it's for the last time. No, whatever he's been planning, it's almost time. We just gotta figure out what and where."

"And how to stop him," Joe said.

"Yeah, how to stop him and his army of weres, vampires, sasquatch, and other baddies," Skeeter's voice came into my ear.

"We're gonna be outnumbered, underpowered, and have no real idea what we're up against until we get right into the middle of the shit," I said. "This would be a good time to remember vacation plans in Guam."

"Outnumber, outgunned, and no time for prep?" Amy said through the Bluetooth. "Must be Tuesday. Let's do this."

I called in the cleaners from DEMON to come deal with the mess and the paperwork, then climbed into the truck and started down the mountain after Joe's motorcycle. Just before the house fell out of sight in my rearview, I turned around and saw the phantom image of Aunt Marion beating the hell out of a ghostly Gerald McFadden all the way across the driveway.

BAD MOON RISING

"Where is he? Where is the little sonofabitch?" I snarled as I paced my back deck.

"We don't know, Bubba." Agent Amy Hall, my girlfriend and field agent for DEMON, the Department of Extra-Dimensional, Mystical and Occult Nuisances said as she sat on the railing with a Blue Moon beer bottle next to her.

"Well, why the hell don't you know? You're the damn government, y'all are the kings of sticking your noses in where they don't belong, why can't you find one damn werewolf in the middle of the Georgia mountains?" I drained the last of my Bud and flung the bottle off the deck. It never hit the ground, I drew Bertha and exploded the bottle with extreme prejudice, just like what I wanted to do to my asshole little brother.

"Just calm down, Bubba, we'll find him." Amy said as she went into the house to recycle her bottle and bring us another round. She came back with a Blue Moon apiece for her and Skeeter, a Bud for me and a can of Coke for Uncle Father Joe.

I cocked an eyebrow at the priest, and he shrugged. "I'm driving, Bubba, and these mountain roads can get real windy after a couple drinks."

"Fair enough," I said. "The last damn thing I want to do is pick pieces of motorcycle and Catholic priest out of the trees."

"We're doing all we can to find Jason, Bubba. But the sad fact is that since he killed your Aunt Marion back in May, he's been lying pretty low," Amy said.

"That just means he's planning something," I grumbled.

"You're probably right, God help me for saying so," Skeeter said. "And I reckon it's gonna be big. It's been almost a year since y'all fought last time, and he's been building an army ever since."

"I know," I replied. "I know he's got a bunch of wolves, and a bunch of Sasquatch."

"And there's been an increase in vampire activity throughout the area lately, not to mention some of the less savory of the Fae." Amy said.

"I hate vampires. And I ain't all that keen on the Fae, either. They creep me out."

"Yeah, all that ethereal beauty really gets to a guy," Skeeter snorted a little through his beer.

"You just like it 'cause all the fairy guys are homos." I grumbled.

"I do like to refer to Faerie as a 'target-rich' environment, but they're not all gay, Bubba." Skeeter corrected me.

"They ain't?"

"No, they're just what you would call 'heteroflexible.'"

"I don't know that I'd ever use that word, Skeeter, but whatever."

"They're not human, so they aren't as hung up on certain things as we are."

"How in the hell did we get from my pain in the ass little brother to the mating habits of the Fae? Dammit, Skeeter, you need to get laid. All you ever talk about is sex."

"You ain't lying. But back to your asshole brother, a topic guaranteed to cool my libido. I've spent a little time lately on the Darknet, those places on the internet that Google pretends don't exist? Well it sounds like something big is coming up, and it sounds like it's going down somewhere near here. Well, Georgia at least."

"Any idea what it is?" I asked.

"Not yet. Nobody seems to know. But there are a lot of vampires, weres of all flavor and dark magicians converging on Georgia Labor Day Weekend." Skeeter said.

"Yeah, no shit, Skeeter. We call that DragonCon, and it happens in Atlanta every year." I tipped back my beer and glared at my best friend and tech expert. "If you ain't got nothing better than a metric shitload of weirdos landing in Georgia for Labor Day, then I reckon it's time to replace you with a toaster."

"Well that might be, smartass, but this convergence of weirdos looks like it's happening in Athens, not Atlanta. And last time I checked, they hadn't moved DragonCon."

"Waitagoddamminit," I said, barreling into the house and through the kitchen. I found what I was looking for stuck to the fridge with boob-shaped refrigerator magnets and grabbed it. I carried it back outside, flipping pages as I went.

"Fuck," I said as I held out the fridge calendar to Amy.

She looked down at the date where my thumb rested. "Fuck," she agreed.

"What is it?" Skeeter asked. I held out the calendar. He looked at the circled date and sat back down. "Fuck," he exhaled as he went down.

"I suppose this is the point at which you tell me the significance of the date, perhaps without the profanity?" Joe asked.

"Sorry, Father," I said. "I know what Jason's going after, and why he's been bringing in baddies from all over the South to help him. He's planning to hit me where it really hurts."

"He's attacking Wrestlemania? Wasn't that in the spring?" Joe asked.

"That's a good guess, but this is way worse. He's going after my heart, Joe. He's attacking the Dawgs." I saw the confused look of Joe's face and explained. "My brother is bringing an army of supernatural nastiness down on the University of Georgia football home opener. He's going after my Bulldogs."

~

We got to Athens on Thursday afternoon for the Saturday afternoon game, and the city was already jammed with people. There were pregame festivities starting as early as Wednesday, but most of those were at frat houses, or small alumni get-togethers for just a couple hundred people. I didn't figure Jason was gonna mess with anything less than the main event, so we took an extra day to prep weapons and make a supply run to Atlanta for some of the more specific things Joe needed.

Even among the crowds in all kinds of wild variations on Bulldog-themed vehicles, we made a little bit on a splash as we came rolling up. My new F-250 was black, with chrome everywhere and a custom grill with a skull right in the middle behind the cowcatcher. I had a little bit of a lift kit put on her, and a custom muffler that didn't muffle much of anything. In other words, everybody heard me coming. The rack of KC lights on the roof of the truck concealed a 30mm machine gun mount that I really hoped I wouldn't need this weekend, but I had it if I needed it. Joe's Harley Softail was blue with a ton of polished chrome and brought plenty of thunder of its own. Tucked in his saddlebags were flasks of holy water, magazines of blessed bullets, and a fistful of ash wood stakes that might have once upon a time been baseball bats.

Skeeter brought up the rear in his mama's minivan. When she passed, Skeeter spent all of one summer turning that van into a mobile command center, with all the tech of his home setup in a Chevy Astro conversion van with pictures of cats airbrushed on the sides. Skeeter's mama was a wonderful woman, but as she got on in years, she went a little strange with her love for her pets. Skeeter had only ever taken Rolling Thunder, as he called the van, out one time before he realized that he put in a lot of tech, but zero armor plating or weapon systems, so he was kind of a sitting duck in it. He only brought it out this time because he'd replaced all the glass with bullet-proof plexi, and equipped the grocery-getter with a set of run-flat tires.

We pulled up in front a small house a mile or so from campus, and before I even got out of the car the front door flew open and a couple of little tow-headed girls dashed out, waving their arms and screaming like there was no tomorrow. Of course, I reckon when you're seven, there is no tomorrow. There's probably a lesson to learn in there somewhere, but I ain't a smart enough man to teach it!

"Uncle Bubba! Uncle Bubba!" The girls squealed as the barreled into me, knocking me into the side of my truck and pulling me down to my knees for hugs and kisses. I complied with a grin, then looked up at Amy standing over us, one eyebrow crawling way north into her hairline.

"Uncle Bubba?"

"Yeah," I said, ducking my head a little to try and hide the blush. "My old buddy—"

Just then said old buddy made his appearance, wheeling out the front door and down the ramp to meet us. Hank Russell was a hearty-looking Asian man in his early thirties, with a thin goatee and the barrel chest that comes from piloting a wheelchair for years. A grin split his freckled face, and he looked good, even if there were a few more grey hairs on his chin since the last time I saw him. I went over to him, a little girl hanging off each leg, and slapped hands and gave him a hug. "How you doing, brother?"

"I'm gonna have to add a motor to this thing to keep up with those two if they don't stop growing," he said, pointing at his twin daughters.

"I'd put in at least a six-cylinder, bro. You ain't keeping up with them on some four-banger."

"True enough, Bubba. True enough. Now why don't you introduce me to your friends. Girls, go inside and make some lemonade for Uncle Bubba and his friends, okay?" The girls squealed and ran inside, slamming the screen door behind them.

"Damn, Hank, they're getting big," I said. Hank rolled up the ramp onto his porch and we followed. I leaned against the rail at the side of the house, keeping a clear line of sight to the driveway. Joe grabbed a chair and turned it so his back was to the house and took a seat on the other side of Joe. Amy sat next to him, and Skeeter set a small black box with a screen on it down on the patio table and sat across from Hank.

"I'm the only one who will ever sit with my back to an entrance or driveway," Skeeter said. "Everybody else is paranoid."

"It ain't paranoid if they really are out to get you," I said.

"Bubba?" Amy Hall has an uncanny ability to put a whole paragraph into one word and a look. For example, in just saying my name in that tone she asked me if Hank was all right to know what we were about, and how freely we could talk in front of him.

"Hank's good, babe. Hank Russell, meet Agent Amy Hall from DEMON, Father Joseph MacIntyre, and Skeeter Jones. Y'all, this is Hank Russell. We were roommates for a couple semesters in college before my life got weird. But he knows all about weird, don't you, Hank?"

"Weird is kinda my thing. I'm a professor of Religion and Philosophy at the University, with a focus on Far Eastern Mysticism and Occult Studies."

"So that means you believe in things that go bump in the night?" Amy asked.

"Agent, it means that I am one of the things that goes bump in the night." He reached down and took off the blanket that covered his legs, showing that he didn't actually *have* legs. Hank's lower half was the body of snake, resplendent in green and gold scales. He slid forward out of the chair and held out his right hand to Amy, who was staring at where she expected to see legs and instead saw a thick serpent's body.

"What the holy hell *are* you?" She asked, backing up. "We don't have any record of anything like you in our database."

"Neither do I, and my database is way better," Skeeter said.

Amy turned to Skeeter. "Why is your database better?" She asked.

"Because your database is made up of everything the United States government knows about supernatural creatures and phenomena."

"Right, so why is yours better?"

"Because my database is made up of everything *everyone in the world* knows about supernatural creatures and phenomena."

"Point taken." Amy crossed her arms over her chest and looked grumpy. She's adorable when she's grumpy. She's frankly adorable no matter what.

"I'm a naga," Hank said. "I'm part man, part snake, all adorable."

"Until he molts on your rug," I chimed in.

"That happened one time, and I was really drunk," Hank protested. "Besides, I bought a new rug."

"How have you managed to function in human society?" Amy asked. "I mean, I understand the wheelchair grants a certain level of invisibility, but this," she gestured to his lower half. "Is something else entirely."

"I have a couple of ways of getting around that," Hank said. "First, and simplest, is I'm kinda made of magic, so I can cast illusions that I have legs. The illusions are enough to fool most humans, even if they bump into me. And for limited periods of time I can actually manifest legs, although it's painful and time-consuming and involves much molting. I'll do it to walk my girls down the aisle, but that's about all."

"Yeah, about the girls..." Joe said.

"They're human. My wife and I adopted them as infants." Hank's face got sober and I watched the emotion flicker across his eyes. "When she was killed in a car accident, the girls were five. I explained to them that Daddy was different from most people, that he had snake legs, and it was his secret identity, like Spider-Man, and they needed to help me keep my secret. So far, so good."

"Hank and I have been through a lot, and he's volunteered to keep his ear to the ground in the supernatural world of Athens for me, trying to figure out what Jason has planned," I said.

"But so far I've been useless. None of my local contacts have heard from Jason, and none of my regional contacts from the Dark Fae or nastier creatures are saying anything. Whatever he's doing, we're going to have to figure it out on our own."

"Hank has also volunteered his house as our base of operations as he takes the girls somewhere far from here for the next few days. That gives us a place close to campus to work, and gets him and the girls out of harm's way." I said. "So let's start unloading our stuff while Hank gets his stuff loaded into his van.

"Yeah, about that..." Hank said.

"What about that?" I asked.

"I'm not going."

"What do you mean you're not going?" I cocked my head to one side, looking at Hank like a Labrador trying to figure out a combination lock.

"I mean, Sandy's sister Patricia is coming to get the girls, and I'm staying here to help you fight."

"No, you're not."

"Yes, I am."

"Not."

"Am."

"Not."

"Am."

"Boys!" Amy stepped between us before I decked my half-snake buddy in the wheelchair, which probably would send me to some special section of seating in Hell. "Cut that shit out. Bubba, Hank is a grown man. Or Snake-man, or whatever. You don't get to make decisions for him." Hank nodded, a smug grin on his face. I almost warned him what was coming, but decided he deserved it. So when Amy whirled on him, I plastered my own smug grin in place.

"And you, Hank, are an inconsiderate jackass! You adopt a pair of twin girls, they lose their mother, and then you risk your life in a fight that's not your own? Parent of the Year, you are not! But we need the firepower, so you get to stay."

"Like you were going to stop me?" Hank asked.

"Don't underestimate the resources of the United States government, pal. I have toys even Skeeter can't pronounce. So get your daughters to safety, because we need to head into town tonight and see what we can find out about Jason's plans."

"Fine," Hank said. "Patricia will be here in a few minutes to get the girls, then I'll go molt myself a pair of legs and we can go see what we can find out about your asshole brother's plans. Make yourselves at home while I take of some business."

We did just that, with me planting myself in Hank's recliner and drinking his beer until a couple hours later he walked out of his bedroom pulling at the crotch of his jeans.

"What in the hell is wrong with you?" I asked. "You got jock itch or something?"

"Think about it for a minute, Bubba. My anatomy is usually a little different. I'm just trying to get everything arranged right. It's been a long time since I grew legs, after all."

"Oh, 'cause snakes don't have balls. I get it. We gotta get you some of those Duluth Trading Company jeans, man. They're like a nice hotel - plenty of ballroom." I laughed at my own joke, but as usual, I was the only one in the room with any damn sense of humor.

"One - snakes have balls. We just don't typically keep them dangling outside our bodies for the entire world to take a shot at. Or laugh at, as the case may be. Two - how about we just save the world, and I won't have to worry about growing legs again to save it?" Jake growled, tugging at his newly-discovered nuts.

"Sounds like a plan. Let's go downtown and see what kind of trouble we can get into." I headed toward the truck.

"I'm going to let you guys handle the roughhousing tonight," Amy said. "I'll stay here and help Skeeter get the command center set up while you go shake down the seedy underbelly of Athens."

"I suppose that means that I'm the one drafted to be the moral compass of the group," Joe said, opening his Harley's saddlebags and slipping a Ruger LC9 in a paddle holster at the small of his back, then throwing on a loud blue Hawaiian shirt to cover the gun.

"You're the one that signed up for the collar, Padre," I said. I checked Bertha in her holster, made sure I had two more magazines for the Desert Eagle under my other arm, and put on a long-sleeve black dress shirt open over my Cactus Jack T-shirt.

"Did I miss a memo? Should we stop to buy me a gun before we head into town?" Hank asked.

"Can you still military press a ton and a half? Are you still functionally bulletproof? Can you still spit venom that eats right through a man's face?" I asked. Hank nodded at all three. "Then I think you're okay without a gun. But if you want a knife or two, there's some in the glove box."

~

Downtown Athens on a Thursday night is just like every other college town getting ready for the weekend. Except busier. And louder. And more crowded. And with better music. And prettier college girls. Walking down Broad and Pulaski, checking out the coeds in their short-shorts and tank tops made me long for the days when I was young and able to chase girls, not things that wanted to rip girls limb from limb. I let out a sigh.

"Penny for 'em, Bubba," Joe said.

"I was just wondering what life woulda been like if I hadn't blown out my knee. If I'd finished school, settled down with some normal girl, lived a normal life in the suburbs, that kinda melancholy crap you always think about right before a big fight where you know there's a not-insignificant chance that you might die."

"Boring," Hank said.

"What?" I asked.

"It's boring, bro. I live that life. I carpool, I live in the 'burbs, I have a minivan for Christ's sake! But what did I do the second after you called? I made arrangements to get the kids out of town and jumped at the chance for a little excitement. Come on, Bubba! You do something important. You're like an entire infantry division, or a whole Supernatural Sheriff's Department, man! How many people are alive because of you?"

"Yeah, and how many people are dead because of me, Hank? And how many more people are gonna die? Maybe not directly because of me, but at least partway. I killed my father, dude. I killed him with my bare hands and left him facedown in a creek. I'm walking around downtown Athens trying to figure out how I'm gonna kill my kid brother before he kills me. That's my life. Everybody around me dies, most of the time because of something I do, or don't do. So I'd take a little boring, if anybody'd ever make the offer."

A voice crackled to life in my ear, and my heart bounced a little just hearing her. "I tell you what, redneck. You get through this in one piece, and I'll take you back up to that cabin on the mountain and bore you so hard you won't be able to walk for a week. How does that sound?" Amy asked through our comms.

"Sounds great, baby. I reckon this means you've got the command center up and running?"

"Mostly," Skeeter's voice joined Amy's. "We don't have video yet, but I've got some intermittent surveillance by linking all the traffic cams and ATM cameras, so as long as you're near a corner or a bank, we can see you. I should have the feed from your shoulder cams up in a few minutes." Skeeter had rigged these tiny cameras to each of our shirts so he could see everything that was going on. They didn't even look too weird, long as nobody looked too close. Just looked like an extra button high at the neck of the shirt.

"Good," I said. "At least we're halfway there. Got any ideas on where we should hit next?" I asked Hank.

"We should try Betty's Place. You haven't killed too many vampires lately, have you?"

"Not since I offed that touring ballet troupe last year in Charlotte," I replied.

"They weren't local, so nobody will care. Let's go," Hank turned down a narrow alley to his right that I would have sworn wasn't there ten seconds before, and disappeared.

I shrugged at Joe and turned into the alley, the priest right behind me. "Why did you ask about vamps?" I asked.

"Because Betty takes exception to people who kill too many vampires." Hank knocked on a door and a small window opened, speakeasy-style. "It's Hank, the naga that lives outside of town. I bring friends who come in peace and will abide by the rules of sanctuary. They are under my protection and their behavior is bound by my word of honor."

A voice on the other side of the door mirrored Hank's formal tone and said "Come and be welcome, naga and guests. Understand that the rules of sanctuary are in effect and all who cross this threshold must abide."

Hank turned back and looked up at me. "Bubba, I don't know how to say this except bluntly. Do not start any shit in here. You are a tough son of a bitch, but there is old magic within these walls, and if you cross any lines or violate their hospitality in any way, it will be very bad for all of us."

"I promise not to start nothing," I said. *I never said I wouldn't finish nothing, though.*

The door opened and we followed Hank into a low-ceilinged room dimly lit with honest-to-God candles and torches mounted into the walls. Of course, it being the twenty-first century, the candles and torches were all LED bulbs, but they flickered like the real thing and were dimmer than shit, just like the real thing. The bar was a long, skinny rectangle of a room with a few tables on one side and a bar on the other. There were no video games, no dartboards, no window back into a kitchen. Just a pair of pool tables and a lot of dedicated drinking space. This was a *bar*. A place people came to drink, and shoot the shit, and maybe get laid.

There was a jukebox playing Journey's "Open Arms" and a wall of mirrors behind the bar reflecting the bottles of top shelf liquor and the flicker of the fake candles, as well as about two-thirds of the images of the patrons sitting at the bar. Hank heard me draw in a sharp breath and spun around. He latched onto my right hand before I could reach Bertha, and he was a lot stronger than I remembered from college. Maybe he had a lot more motivation.

"Don't do it." He said, his voice low and his eyes hard. "I told you not to start any shit here."

"That was before you failed to mention that it was a vampire bar," I hissed. I heard Joe gasp behind me and now we all knew the score.

"This place is a sanctuary for all supernaturals and humans alike. Nobody starts trouble here, or bad things happen."

"But let your friend draw his weapon, Henry. He can find out for himself." The voice came from the vicinity of my left elbow, so I looked down to see a pixieish woman with close-cropped black hair standing beside me. She hadn't been there five seconds before. I was willing to bet she hadn't been in the room five seconds before.

I looked down at her and caught her eyes full on. I felt the weight of the ages behind her gaze, and knew that I was looking at the oldest damn vampire I'd ever seen or heard of. "Ma'am," I said, lowering my right hand to my side. "I apologia for my behavior. I wasn't completely briefed on the clientele of your establishment before we arrived."

"Welcome, Bubba the Monster Hunter, to what I suppose you would call a Monster Bar," the little woman reached up and threaded her arm through mine and led me over to the bar. She spun around and hopped up onto a stool, patting the one beside her. I sat. I looked back at Hank and Joe, but they were already heading to a table in a corner.

"They'll stay out of our way for a little while. We need to talk, you and I."

"I'm fine with talking. But first, with whom am I talking?" I asked.

"Such grammar," she said with a grin. "And here I have all these reports of a giant idiot with a gun to match his girth and the vocabulary of a particularly profane gorilla."

"Well, I don't speak gorilla, but I do have a big gun. And I'm afraid I still haven't caught your name."

"I'm Elizabeth, but you can call me Betty."

"And Betty when you call, you can call me Al." I did my best Paul Simon impersonation, but she just looked at me with wide, blank eyes. "Never mind," I said. "I'm Bubba." I stuck out my hand.

She put her tiny hand in my giant paw and we shook. "I know who you are. You've made quite the impression in our community over the past few years. You are a very different man than your father and grandfather."

"Exactly what community is that?" I asked.

"Monsters, of course," she replied, sipping red liquid from a glass the bartender placed in her outstretched hand. I was pretty sure it wasn't wine, but I left my Bela Lugosi jokes on the shelf.

"Is that what you call yourselves?"

"It's how you see us, so it's easy enough. And we don't really care too much about labels. When you live as long as we do, they matter less and less."

"So I've made an impression."

"Not necessarily a good one after your run-in last year with a certain ballet master."

"He certainly didn't make a good impression on me, but he made a pretty good one on the hood of that city bus." I chuckled a little. I tried to be polite, but it's just not in my nature. "Sorry."

"Don't be. He was a pretentious ass. I hated him and hated his dances. But you killing him did cause a bit of an uproar. There was talk of a move against your family."

My voice went flat. "That would have been a bad decision."

"I agree. That is why I counseled against it. But now you are here, in my bar, and you are going to ask me to choose sides in your little family feud."

"No, I'm not. I don't care if you like me or my brother. I just want information."

"And by giving you that information, I lend you my tacit support. You must understand why that is a bad decision for me. There are many in my community, some in this very room, who would take what I have spent so long building. I have a good life here. There is good music, plentiful feeding, and the nearest Monster Hunter leaves me alone."

"Hell, until ten minutes ago I didn't even know you existed," I said.

"Your handler knew. He has known of our existence since he moved into his role within the Church." I looked over at Joe and shot him a *You knew about this shit?* look. He shrugged as if to say "what can I do?"

"Okay, so Joe knew about you and I didn't. Makes no difference to me as long as you aren't killing people or screwing around too much with the local human population. From what I can see, you don't overstep. So now what's the plan? You gonna help me find out what my idiot kid brother is up to, or is fur gonna be thicker than beer and you gonna stick with the monsters?"

"I don't know yet. What I do know is that there are people here who are allied with your brother, and there are people who would see him fail. I will allow you to speak with whomever you would like, as long as they are willing to speak with you. Whatever you can glean, all the better for you. Come see me before you leave and I will have made a decision."

"Nah lady, that ain't how this works. This isn't some role-playing video game, where you get to send me on quests to see if I'm worthy of your help. This is the real world, with real people, humans and not, and real consequences to our actions. Now my brother's been running all over the South for a year or more talking shit about some kind of supernatural uprising, forgetting that there's a hundred humans for every one vampire, were, witch, Fae or other beastie out there. Y'all can unionize, y'all can listen to motivational speakers, y'all can hold a pep rally the night of the full moon if you want, it ain't gonna change the fact that if you try to attack humanity head-on, you're all gonna die." My voice had gotten loud by now, and the nobody in the bar was pretending to ignore me anymore. For my part, I wasn't pretending to speak only to Betty."

"Some of y'all might have met me. Some of y'all might have heard of me. And some of what you heard might have been good, and a lot of it was probably pretty bad. I doubt I'm particularly well-liked in bars like this. Honestly, I'm a little disappointed there ain't a picture of me on the dart board."

"We took it down when we heard you was in town," yelled a were from over by one of the pool tables. He was tall and skinny, probably a were-deer or something like that.

"I appreciate that," I replied. "But it don't matter what you've heard. All you need to know is that if my little brother is batshit crazy and don't care who gets hurt in his little vendetta, as long as the list starts with me. And he might take me out. But it won't matter. I ain't the only monster hunter out there. Hell, the government's got a whole department dedicated to studying y'all, and you can believe they ain't doing all that research to help you get a better refund on your income taxes. They're studying you so they know how to kill you. I've killed a bunch of y'all, it's true. I've killed trolls, and vampires, and faeries and cupids and succubi and a few things I can't even pronounce. But I ain't never killed nothing that wasn't gonna do the same or worse to me, and that's more than I can say for Jason. I ain't gonna stand here and be stupid enough to ask you to stand next to me when the shit hits the fan in the next day or two, but I will ask you to stay home. Leave this fight to me and my brother. Don't buy his line of bullshit, and don't make me kill you by throwing your lot in with the wrong crowd.

"Because that's what will happen if you raise hand, fang or claw against a human being on my watch. I will kill you, and I will make sure you are for-real dead. Now y'all have a good night." I nodded to Betty and turned to walk out the door.

A big vampire stepped into my path before I could get there. He must have been pretty old, because the power rolled off him like smoke off a fourth of July grill. "That was a nice speech, Hunter."

"Thanks." I looked just a little above his eyeliner. It's always a good idea to avoid looking in a vampire's eyes if you can get away with it. They know the drill, so most of the time they don't even get offended.

"I am Starnes. I lead the coven here in Athens." I saw a little bit of fang poke out from between his lips as he spoke to me.

"Good to meet ya." I shook his hand, then shifted my gaze to lock eyes with him. His went wide for just a second, then he caught himself. He behaved, he didn't try to compel me or whammy me or whatever you want to call it.

"We will not aid you in your battle with the self-proclaimed Messiah of the Otherworlders."

"Is that what the little jackass is calling himself these days?" I tried not to laugh and almost managed. It's hard to deal with that level of pretentious from somebody you remember getting his first zit.

Starnes smiled up at me, a genuine smile that made him look almost human. "It is indeed. As I said, we will not aid you in your coming conflict," he raised his voice so the entire bar could hear him. "But neither will we aid your brother. The Vampire Coven of Athens will not participate in this battle. So I have spoken, so shall it be."

It was damn creepy to hear every vampire in the bar repeat "so shall it be," but at least one nest of bloodsuckers was out of the fight. I nodded at Starnes and pushed open the door onto the street.

I walked the length of the alley and turned back out onto Polaski before I stopped. Then I leaned against the wall of a bar called Pat O's and let out a sigh of relief. I had just stared down a bar full of things that usually I hunt for money or sport, and not a drop of blood was shed. That was either a sign of maturity or fear, both of which could get a hunter killed.

"Nice work in there," Amy said into my earpiece.

"You think?"

"I do. You got everybody out of there without anybody or anything dying, and you got the local vampires to swear to stay out of the fight. That's two major victories in one night."

"I'm with Amy," Joe said. "That was more than I hoped for when I suggested we visit Betty."

"Yeah, one of these days we're gonna have to have a chat about Betty and what other kind of places you know about that you've never mentioned," I said.

Joe looked down at his toes and generally stumbled around for a few seconds before he finally said, "There's a lot of things I know that might only get in your way, Bubba. That's kinda what a handler does - I handle you. If that offends you, I'm sorry, but it's kept us both alive this long, so it's on the list of things you're just going to have to deal with." He was looking me almost in the eye by the end of his little speech, and I was reminded that Joe was no small man himself.

"Well, Joe, if it gets me killed, I'm gonna be pissed."

"Me too," he replied.

"All right then," I let out a big breath and looked at Joe and Hank. "What's next?"

"I think I'm next," came Skeeter's voice over the comm.

"What's up, Skeet?" I asked.

"You know how I mentioned that I have a list of names and keywords that I run a constant search on, and whenever one of them gets a hit, I investigate?"

"Yeah, like the Patriot Act, only hunting monsters instead of terrorists."

"Exactly. You *were* listening!"

"It happens. What's up?"

"I just got a hit on one of the names. I'll be honest, Bubba, I forgot I put the name on the list. It's never gotten a hit before, not from Google, not from a local newspaper, nothing. But a few minutes ago, it came across on a missing persons report from Louisiana."

I had a bad feeling in the pit of my stomach. "I think it's going to be good that there's a bar right behind me, isn't it?"

"Yeah, probably," Skeeter replied.

"What's the name?" I asked.

"Remember, I put this name in when I first started the system, right after we started working with Joe. I just haven't gone back through to take it off the list. I didn't mean anything—"

"The name, Billy." I hadn't called Skeeter by his given name since his mother died. It seemed apropos, given the name I was pretty sure was about to come across his lips.

"Leila Templeton," he said.

"Are you sure it's her? Not just somebody who has the same name?" I asked. I was still leaning back against the wall of the bar, bricks pressing into my shoulder blades. I let my head fall back against the solid wall with a *thunk*, the solidity reassuring as my feet were convinced the world was swirling out of control underneath me.

"That's what took me the last twenty minutes to check out. I hacked the police database. They had a picture from… from her…"

"Say it."

"Her family. Her family provided the police with a recent picture for the search. It's her, Bubba. It's almost twenty years later, but it's her."

"Guys, help me out here," Amy cut in. "I'm sorry, but who is Leila Templeton and why is she going missing suddenly more important than the war Jason is trying to start?"

"Because she's the reason for everything," I replied. "It all makes sense now. Turning Pop, making me kill him, Brittany, kidnapping you, even having his bitch threaten Joe earlier this year. It all goes back to her. Shit, this is all her fault."

"You can't do that, Bubba." Joe said. He reached out and put a hand on my shoulder. "No one is responsible for Jason's action but Jason."

"I know, but I can't help thinking if she'd stayed, how different everything would have been."

I heard Amy's whispered "Oh no" over the comm and nodded, even though she couldn't see me.

"Yeah, babe. Templeton is her maiden name. Legally, I reckon she's still Leila Brabham, and technically, even though she walked out on us almost twenty years ago, she's still my mother."

The next thing I remember I was sitting in the cab of the truck talking to Amy over the video comm Skeeter had installed in the dash. "I was sixteen and a truckload of trouble when she walked out. Pop was hunting on a contract for the government, and the last thing he told me before he got in his pickup truck and rolled down the mountain to find and dispatch a pack of were-gators that were making life difficult down in some nameless Alabama swamp was that I was "the man of the house" while he was gone. I think what he wanted was for me to make sure the firewood was split and that there was gas in my car before I parked it at night. What I thought that meant was that I didn't have to listen to nothing Mama said, because I was too big and too full of myself for anybody to talk to. I was the star offensive and defensive lineman for my high school football team, and I had worked all summer saving up for a '65 mustang in jet black. I was hot shit on a stick and nobody could tell me any different, including my mother.

I never knew how my parents met, it must have been somewhere out when Pop was hunting, because Mama wasn't mountain people by any stretch. She was a lot more town than she was country, and I woulda swore she'd never eaten a tomato off the vine before coming to marry my Pop and live in his house. She tried her best to put some kind of culture into me and Jason, and for a while it worked. On Jason, at least. I was always too wild, too big, too hairy, too crazy to be tamed.

It all came to a head while Pop was out of town. Jason came home from school, grabbed his .22 and went out looking for some squirrel. I liked that idea, since we hadn't had a good squirrel stew in months. Mama objected, on account of Jason not having done his homework yet, and he told her that since he was going into the family business, the only thing he needed to study was what to kill with silver and what to kill with cold iron. Then he flung the screen door open and stomped down off the porch into the yard. She looked at me like she wanted my help, and all I did was shrug and tell her he was right.

When he came back, she was gone. I sat on the steps with a six-pack of Bud waiting on him, and that was the first time me and Jason drank beer together. I told him how she cried because he didn't respect her, then she yelled at me and cried because I didn't respect her, then she hollered about Pop and how she didn't respect herself. I thought then that she was gonna be all right, because usually when somebody gets a good gut-aching cry on, they don't feel up to much driving, but she proved me wrong. She packed most of her clothes in a suitcase, threw it in the back seat of an old Chevy Caprice Classic we had, and drove off down the mountain.

I sat on the porch and held my little brother while he cried for his mama, and I held him every night for a week when the dreams came and he ran screaming into my room in the middle of the night. Eventually Pop came home, and by that time me and Jason had figured out the beginning of how to live without her, and Pop had pretty much been living without her ever since he went back out hunting, so it was the three of us until I went off to school. I pretty much got over her leaving by screwing my way through a couple of sororities my freshman year of college, but that kind of therapy just wasn't in Jason. I reckon he never did get over her leaving, and now he's brought her here to show her what he's made of himself."

"There's no way this ends well, Bubba," Amy said.

"We knew that going in," I replied.

"But this is so much worse. It's so much more personal…maybe you oughta just leave it alone. Let my team handle it. They've trained for something like this, and they can—"

"They can what, Amy?" I cut her off. "They can nuke Athens back to the stone age? Because that's what it's gonna take to beat Jason and an army of monsters. This only goes down one of two ways. Either we take care of business from thirty thousand feet with a couple of smart bombs, or we get up close and personal and end this, once and for all. I know which way my vote's going. What about yours?"

"I'm with you, babe. Whatever you decide, I'm with you. You know the players, and you've been in the game a lot longer, so whatever play you call, I'll run it. I just wanted you to know there was another option."

"I appreciate it. I can't tell you how much," I said.

Just then there was a knock at the window. It was Hank, holding a flyer on neon green paper. I rolled down the window and he stuck it in my hand. "I think this is where it's all going down," he said, a little out of breath.

"You okay there, buddy?" I asked.

"I just walked six blocks in Athens in August. I haven't walked anywhere in probably six years, Bubba. So yeah, I'm a little bit the worse for wear. But I got us this." He handed me the flyer. "BON-FIRE" was acrosss the top, right above the words "In the Magic Courtyard (parking lot C)" with directions and some squiggles about the Dawgs and their opponent, but the important that hit me was the picture. It was a huge bonfire, with wolves and humans dancing around it, and being burned at the stake was a woman, just into her late fifties, with long dark hair and frightened eyes. Jason must have drafted some hellacious artists into his little army, because there was no mistaking my mother's face. Even after all these years, I recognized her instantly. The first woman I ever loved, the first woman ever to break my heart, and the root of all this pain and suffering.

I read the flyer, then crumpled it up and threw it into the floorboards of the truck. "Tomorrow at midnight. That's when it goes down." I said for the benefit of Amy and Skeeter listening in on their electronics.

"So what do we do until then? Try to hunt Jason down and his band of monsters before they can start their party?" Skeeter asked.

"No," I said. "I'm gonna engage in a time-honored University of

Georgia tradition. It's something we Bulldogs do the nights before the home opener every year. It's a ritual passed down from seniors to underclassmen for generations, and I'm gonna do my part to uphold it."

"What are you going to do?" Amy's voice had a worried tone to it, like she knew she wasn't going to like the answer. She probably wasn't.

"I'm going back to the bars downtown and I'm getting stupid drunk. I've gotta fight and maybe kill my little brother tomorrow night, but there's nothing anywhere that says I have to be sober tonight."

"Be careful," Amy said. "Remember, you're not as young as you used to be."

"What's the worst that could happen?" I asked. "After all, I'm with a priest and a soccer dad. How much trouble could we get into?"

～

"When you asked me how much trouble you could get into," Amy said with a sigh as the guard took the handcuffs off and handed me and envelope containing my personal effects. "I thought you meant it as a rhetorical device, not a personal challenge."

"I might have been working through some issues last night," I grumbled.

"And what, if anything, do the two of you have to say for yourselves?" She turned on Father Joe and Hank, who looked pretty good for guys who had just spent the night in a drunk tank, probably for the first time in their lives. Hank had hardly any blood left on his face from his broken nose, and Joe looked just like normal, only a little more wrinkled and with bloody knuckles. I probably looked like I'd taken a header through a plate-glass window onto a sidewalk, but that's because I had.

"We plead the Fifth," Joe said. Amy opened her mouth to light into him, but he waved her off. "I am bound not only by the laws of the confessional but also by the Guy Code to never speak to any female of what took place last night, particularly not the wife, ex-wife, girl-friend or mother of any of the participants."

"The sanctity of the confessional does not extend to bar fights," Amy protested.

"Well it damn well should, as many Irish Catholics as I've ministered to," Joe rebutted.

"What am I going to do with you?" Amy asked.

"Pick up my impounded truck, drive us home, let us sleep for six hours, and then help us start an interspecies war that may destroy the very fabric of humanity. That's my suggestion, anyway," I said.

"But can we stop at Denny's on the way? I could totally go for a Grand Slam right now," Hank chimed in. I high-fived him, and Amy gave me one of those looks that said "Men" like it was a curse word.

An hour later we walked back into Hank's house with our bellies full and our hangovers pushed to the side. "What's it look like, Skeet?" I asked as I sat down behind Skeeter and the wall of computer monitors he had set up on the dining room table.

He clicked his mouse a few times and opened up a satellite view of the bonfire site. It was a parking lot just east of the stadium, and an empty area had been cordoned off in the center. I saw a pile of wood with a 4 x 4 post sticking out of the center, and a few people milling around the site. No hint of Jason in the satellite image, and everything looked basically normal, just a big bonfire setup for the opening game of the season.

"What's our approach look like?" I asked.

"We've got plenty of clear entrances, but the sightlines suck for us. It's basically a clear field of view for fifty yards in every direction. There are sniper positions available at the top of the stadium, but I get a feeling Jason wants this to be a little more up close and personal."

"Yeah, that's my guess, too. I can't imagine he would go to all this trouble to get me up there just to put a bullet in my head from half a mile away. He could have done that a hundred times in the past year. He wants to look me in the eye when we finish this."

"And so do you," Skeeter said. I looked at my best friend. His brows were knit, and his allergies must have been acting up, because there was a lot of moisture in his eyes. He just looked at me for a long moment, then cleared his throat. "We're really going to finish this, right?"

"One way or another, Skeet. This ends tonight. All the running around, all the bullshit—it's over after tonight."

"And we might be, too."

"Could happen," I nodded. "If we knew the outcome, wouldn't be no point in playing the game, would there?" I gave him my best lopsided grin and stood up from the table.

"Don't get dead, Bubba. I need somebody to look after."

"I ain't ready to die yet, Skeeter. I don't think Heaven's ready for me, and I'm pretty sure Hell's scared I'd take over." I bumped fists with my best friend and went into the spare bedroom where I got horizontal for a few hours.

It was full dark by the time I woke up and I could feel somebody else in the room with me. I didn't move for a second, just lay still facedown on the mattress enjoying the feel of Amy lightly rubbing her hand across my back.

"I know you're awake," she said. "Your breathing changed a minute ago and you went all tense for a second. Then you figured out it was me and relaxed again."

"And I want to stay relaxed, so I figured I'd just pretend to be asleep a little longer."

"So we don't have to talk about it?" Amy asked.

"Talk about what?"

"Talk about what's coming. Talk about what might happen. Talk about the fact that your psychotic brother has kidnapped your long-lost mother and plans to kill her and you tonight in some crazed plan to take over all the supernatural beings in the Southeastern United States."

"Yeah, I'm good not talking about that," I mumbled, face still down in the pillow.

"I'm not." There was a finality to her voice that I couldn't avoid.

I rolled over and sat up, leaning against the wall in Hank's spare bedroom. The wood paneling pressed into my bare back, and I adjusted the pillow behind me. "Okay, let's talk," I said. "My brother wants to kill me. That's pretty screwed up. He's also a werewolf, which makes it a lot easier for him to succeed with the whole killing me thing, but I'm no slouch in the killing department myself, so I put our chances there at about fifty-fifty. I don't know how much backup he's bringing, or what kind of critters he's using, so that probably puts us at sixty-forty. So there's a decent chance I won't get out of this whole, or at all. I don't want that to be the deal, but it is. I hope I don't leave you alone after tonight, but this is on the list of things I've got to do."

"I know, and I'm fine with all that. But the elephant in the room isn't Jason, it's your mother. What are you going to do about her?"

"I'll be honest with you, I don't know. There's a bunch of feelings all tied up in that, and I can't really deal with most of them right now. So I'm just pretending that she's nobody I know, just an innocent bystander that I need to get out of trouble before the bad things get her. Anything else will have to wait until morning to deal with."

"If there's a morning," Amy said.

"Well, if I ain't around to see it, we're gonna need your men in black helicopters to come in guns blazing. Because no matter what happens, we can't have Jason and his bunch of monsters running loose all over Georgia. So whatever calls you need to make—"

"Already done," she said.

"Fair enough. We got anything else we need to talk about?" I asked. I sat up and pulled on a black t-shirt.

"I've just got one more thing to say…"

I put a finger on her lips like I saw some skinny kid do in a chick flick on HBO. "Don't bother. I love you, too." Then I leaned in and kissed her like it was the last chance I'd ever get. Because for all I knew, it was.

~

Half an hour later we were loaded in my truck and headed to the stadium. Joe was in the passenger seat, with Hank in the back seat. They were both packing twelve-gauge Benelli shotguns, with Colt 1911 pistols on their hips. I had Bertha in my shoulder rig, with my Saiga semi-auto shotgun in the back seat by Hank. I had a pair of kukri strapped to my back and the custom-made caestus Amy gave me for Christmas hanging from my belt. Traffic was surprisingly light until we got just outside the stadium gates, then it started to back up. Apparently Jason had passed out a lot more flyers than just the one Hank found, because there were a lot of cars pulling into the lot and dumping Bulldogs fans out to get drunk and rowdy before the big game.

I pulled the truck into an empty spot a little further away from the festivities than most people chose to park, and opened the back door. Hank slid out and handed me a long black leather duster. I slid it on, effectively hiding my knives and Bertha, and clipped the Saiga to my belt so it hung out of sight as well. The three of us looked like rejects from *Tombstone* or a Motley Crüe video walking through the parking lot in the August swelter wearing head to toe black leather and flack jackets, but I wasn't going into this fight without every advantage I could muster.

I pressed my earpiece. "Skeeter, you got us?"

"I got you five by five, audio and video. I've hacked the security cameras in the parking lot so I can see everything that's going on. Looks like Jason is waiting on you. So far it's been all about crushing Georgia Southern and standard football bullshit."

"Then let's get this party started. Amy, you ready?"

"I'm in position," she came in loud and clear. "I hope this works."

"That makes two of us," I said.

The crowd parted like the Red Sea as we approached, leaving a ten-foot alley that led up to the pile of wood. Standing on a platform tied to the pole was a woman I never thought I'd see again, my mother. Her dark hair hung limp across her face, plastered across her cheeks with sweat. Her skin was pale, with beads of sweat dampening

316

her forehead, and her eyes were out of focus. I couldn't tell from the distance whether she was drugged or if Jason had beaten her senseless. It didn't matter. I had a war to stop, and the opposing general was standing next to the bonfire with a Zippo in his hand.

"Bubba," Jason said to me as I approached. "That was a nice trick last week, switching pocket watches on me. I'll have to give you credit for that one, that was pretty smart. Don't matter though. I've got plenty of friends even without ruling the dead." He paused for a second and something changed in his eyes. It was almost like he was my little brother again. "You know it don't have to go down like this."

"I know," I replied. "So why don't you put that lighter in your pocket, untie that woman and go home. Disband your little freak parade, tell everybody the party's over, and we'll call it square."

Jason's eyes bulged out, and the psycho was back. "Square? We'll never be square, Bubba. You killed my mate. You murdered Megan in cold blood, you son of a bitch!"

"My memory of it is a little different, bro. My recollection involves her tying to rip my throat out. And besides, who sent her into a fight she couldn't win, Jason? Who threw her in the deep end when she wasn't ready? You want to look at who killed your bitch, little brother, you better look in the mirror."

He lunged at me, but got control of himself. He looked around the assembled crowd, probably a third non-human, and grinned. "How are you gonna fight me, Bubba? I've got an army here! I've got vampires, ghouls, weres, witches and warlocks, sasquatch and humans. And they're all gunning for you. What have you got? You've got a priest and a snake-man? All the bullets in the world aren't gonna be enough to save you, unless you brought an army I don't see."

"That's your cue," I said into my earpiece, and the night erupted in thunder. Forty motorcycles roared to life on the edge of the parking lot and rolled toward us, complete with a West Virginia biker on each and every one. Overhead, a sound like thunder came from every direction and spotlights illuminated the field from a squadron of blacked-out helicopters. Ropes dropped from the choppers and a dozen black-clad body-armored agents of DEMON fast-roped to the ground to stand behind me. Agent Amy Hall dropped her rappelling helmet to the asphalt with a clatter and shook her blonde ponytail free as she loosened her MP5 in its sling and stood next to me. Two dozen black forms flowed over the top of the bleachers and sprinted for where we stood, the clan of Florida vampires I'd met a couple years ago standing side by side with Charleston, West Virginia's dirtiest biker gang to form a perimeter between Jason's supernatural allies and the drunken civilians littering the parking lot.

Just when all the noise had died down and the helicopters peeled off back to base, a battered red Pinto sped into the parking lot with a horde of zombies staggering along in its wake. The scrawny necromancer behind the wheel pulled to a tire-screeching stop behind me and got out, waving a six-pack of Bud over his head and shouting orders to his zombies. The passenger door to his car opened up and Elvis Presley stepped out in all his white jumpsuit glory, a Glock 19 on his hip and a shotgun in his hands. Wayne McCalla, the doppelganger I saved from prison in Atlanta a while back, stepped up onto the roof of the Pinto and shouted out "Elvis has NOT left the building!"

"Here's my army, little bro. It's every civilian and monster I've helped out in the past two years. I've got half of Brar'kin's sasquatch clan, a rakshasa with an unfortunate LSU fetish, a doppelganger, more bikers and vampires than you can shake a stick at, a snake-man, a preacher, and an entire damn government agency backing me up. Now do you still want to throw down, or do you and your people want to turn around and go the hell home?"

He stared at me for a second, and I swear I almost saw him froth at the mouth. I'd never seen Jason so pissed, not even when I pantsed him in the middle of the gym at his Junior Prom. His head whipped from side to side, little drops of sweat flying from his hair as he looked to his band of monsters. They all looked a lot less interested in this fight now that it wasn't just three of us standing between them and a human tapas bar.

"Attack!" Jason screamed, and he drew Great-Grandpappy's sword as he came at me. He shifted into his half-wolf form, which put him over seven feet tall and three hundred pounds of nothing but muscle. The Zippo lighter flew out of his hands toward the pyre, but a shot rang out over the parking lot and it exploded harmlessly several feet away.

"I'm in position on top of the press box," Skeeter said in my ear.

"Nice shot," I replied.

"I've been practicing. Now kick his ass, Bubba. I've got your six." Skeeter clicked off and I drew my kukris just as Jason slammed into me and hell erupted all across the Sanford Stadium parking lot. I heard Amy's MP5 chatter out three-round bursts, and Joe and Hank's shotguns spat fire into the night, then I was neck-deep in my own battle and knew nothing but hair and muscle and blood.

Jason was big, bigger than me, and stronger. I knew it, too, so for once I concentrated on being faster and more fluid. I've always been the straight-on bruiser, so when I went backwards onto my butt and back as Jason hit me, it caught him flat-footed. I planted one of my own feet right into his gut, and shoved off as I rolled backward. But my brother was ridiculously agile in his half-wolf form, so he just flipped onto his feet while I was sprawled on my back like a tattooed turtle. I rolled over and jumped to my feet, but Jason was already on me, slashing at my middle with the sword. I blocked his strike with my kukri, bending his wrists and strike down toward the ground with the curved blade. He spun around and came at my neck in a nasty overhead strike that probably would have cut me in half if it had landed, but I crossed my blades under his, pushed up to open his arms in front of his body, and kicked him in the balls with my steel-toed Wolverines.

Let's face it, if you're gonna fight naked, eventually somebody's going to hit you in the junk. It wasn't fair, it wasn't pretty, and it certainly wasn't sporting. I also didn't give a single shit about any of that. Jason's eyes went wide and he sucked in a breath as his testicles bounced off his liver, and I twisted around with his sword still trapped in my kukri blades. He couldn't hold his sword and grip his swollen nuts at the same time, so as I spun around, the sword, and my kukri, clattered to the pavement.

I reached down to my belt and slid my hands into my caestus, custom-built silver-lined and -spiked armored gloves that Amy gave me for Christmas. I flexed my fingers a couple of times to get the fit just right, then waded in to scrap with Jason. My first punch landed on the side of his elongated snout, opening a deep red furrow and making him howl with the pain. He lashed out at my midsection with his claws, but the ceramic plates in my body armor held up. After a couple of worthless swipes like that while I jabbed at his tender nose, he changed tactics and punched me in the chest, swinging from the hips in a solid uppercut. I heard the armor plate shatter, but I was too busy gasping for air to think about what that meant. Jason followed up with a double axe-handle shot to my head, but I rolled out of the way and caught it on a shoulder instead. My left arm went instantly numb and I heard the *crack* that mean I'd broken my clavicle. Again.

I dropped to one knee and looked up at my brother's smiling half-wolf face. "You thought you could beat me, Bubba? You can't even stand toe-to-toe with my for five minutes."

"I don't have to," I said, and punched him in the side of his knee. The silver one-inch spikes tore through ligament and flesh, and Jason went down. We knelt on the asphalt, gasping in the August heat.

Jason abandoned all subtlety at that point, he just dove at me and started trying to choke me with this hands. We rolled over and over across the lot, neither one above to get a good position on the other. At some point I noticed that there were a lot of bodies piling up all over the place, then I got a claw raked across my cheek and I focused my attention back on Jason. He got into position on top of me, ready to choke the life out of me, and I slammed my head upward into his snout. I heard a *crunch* from his nose, and he reared his head back in pain. That gave me all the room I need to bring both silver-clad fists up under his jaw and knock him momentarily senseless. I shoved Jason off me and rolled to my feet, feeling something hard under my hand and coming up with it. I looked down at my right hand, and Great-Grandpappy's sword was there.

I heard Great-Grandpappy Beauregard's voice ringing in my ears, and the last thing I thought before Jason came at me again were his words. "We hunt monsters. It's what we do. It's part of who we are, and it's the thing that makes us different from normal people. You ain't never gonna get up in the morning and go to work in some factory or sawmill. We live in the dark places, and we do the dark work so the day people ain't got to. Now if your brother has looked too far into the heart of that darkness, it might have overtook him. And if that's the case, well, it's just like a dog that's got the rabies—you can't do nothing but put it down. But if there's a sliver of doubt, just that littlest bit of hope in the bottom of Pandora's box? Well, then, he's still family, no matter what he's done, and you got to save him if you can."

I looked into my brother's eyes as he came at me again, and there was nothing human left in there. The little brother I taught to shoot, and fish, and swim, and ride a bike—he was gone. The only thing left was pain and rage. I set my feet, squared my shoulders, and as he charged me, I lifted the tip of my sword, leaned forward just a hair, and impaled him on the length of my blade. The shining metal came out of his back in a spray of crimson, and he sagged against me, all momentum shattered. I put a shoulder into his chest and pushed him back, pulling on the sword as I did. It came free with a grinding of steel on bone, and my insides quivered as I remembered the feeling from a year ago. I raised the blade, looked into my brother's eyes one last time, and took his head off with the family sword.

A fountain of blood shot several feet into the air and splattered everything within ten feet, including me and my mother, who was still tied to the pole awaiting her fate. Jason's body dropped to the ground, and a sudden silence descended on the battle. Everyone froze, as if every nasty there could feel its connection to Jason suddenly snap. Almost as one, the evil sasquatch, bad vampires, werewolves and zombies all ran or shambled off from wherever they came.

Within minutes, the only monsters left in the parking lot were the good guys, the dead guys, and Jason's pack. A naked and very curvy female werewolf came up to me in her human form and knelt in front of me. "What should we do, Alpha?" she asked.

"I'm not your Alpha. I'm not even a wolf," I replied.

"You have slain our Alpha, now you are our Alpha. And we can make you a wolf, that's easy." I thought I saw a little bit of a grin on her downcast face but I couldn't be sure.

"Get out," I said. "I abdicate, or surrender, or whatever. I quit as your Alpha. I'm not part of your pack. Now get out of here and do what you wish." I motioned, and she stood up, blurring into wolf shape as she did. The remaining weres followed, and I was alone with my crew. The bikers and vamps just gave me a nod and a wave as they vanished into the night. Elvis and the idiot necromancer rolled out in their Pinto, the few surviving zombies trailing along behind. A helicopter landed in the parking lot to pick up the wounded and healthy DEMON agents, and I kissed Amy good night as she hopped in the chopper and flew off to make all this officially disappear. That left one thing to deal with.

"Y'all wait for me by the truck," I said to Hank and Joe. Then I took my earpiece out and took the three steps over to the bonfire, where my mother was still tied up. She was struggling against her bonds now, apparently whatever Jason gave her had worn off. She smiled as I walked up.

"Robbie, thank God—"

I held up a hand to cut her off. "I've got a couple of things to say to you, and then I'm going to turn and walk away. I don't ever want to see you again, and I don't ever want to hear from you again. As far as I'm concerned, you died the day you walked out our front door. But I want you to know that you did this. You broke something inside my little brother, and that caused a lot of people to get hurt here tonight. So you need to know that, and you need to own that."

I looked at my mother, standing there with Jason's blood spattered across her face and a look of horror in her eyes. My brother's body lay at my feet, his blood soaking the wood and the stench of gasoline and coppery blood filling my nostrils. I reached behind her, cut the ropes holding her to the pole, and said, "Go."

She opened her mouth, but I just shook my head. I reached out with one finger and ran it down the side of her face. I held it up to her gaze. "You see that? That's your son's blood. All over your face. And whether you believe it or not, it's all over your hands, too." With that, I turned and walked down the pile of wood and to my truck. I slid in behind the wheel, looked over at Skeeter in the passenger seat, and drove off into the night.

THE END - FOR NOW

ACKNOWLEDGMENTS

Thanks as always to Melissa Gilbert for all her help, and for trying in vain to teach me where the commas go.

Thanks to Melissa as well for her amazing cover, and of course to all of you for reading!

The following people help me bring this work to you by their Patreon-age. You can join them at Patreon.com/johnhartness.

Sean Fitzpatrick
Sarah J. Ashburn
Noah Sturdevant
Mark Ferber
Andy Bartalone
Nick Esslinger
Sharon Moore
Wendy Taylor
Sheelagh Semper
Charlotte Henley Babb
Andreas Brücher
Sheryl R. Hayes
Amaranth Dawe

Butch Howard
Andrew Bolyard
Lawrence Nash
Delia Houghland
Douglas Park Jr.
Travis & Casey Schilling
Michelle E. Botwinick
Carol Baker
Leonard Rosenthol
Lisa Hodges
Patrick Dugan
Aloof Fox
Arthur Reisfeld
Darrell Grizzle
Kristie McKinely
Melissa Cole
Leia Powell
Noella Handley
Bob Dobkin
Jeremy Snyder
Candice Carpenter
Theresa Glover
Salem Macknee
Jared Pierce
Don Lynch
Jeremy Wilhoit
D.R. Perry
Andrea Judy
Anthony D. Hudson
John A. McColley
Mark Wilson
Dennis Bolton
Shiloh Walker/J.C. Daniels
Andrew Torn
Sue Lambert

Emilia Agrafojo
Tracy Syrstad
Samantha Dunaway Bryant
Steven R. Yanacsek
Scott Furman
Rebecca Ledford
Ray Spitz
Lars Klander

ABOUT THE AUTHOR

John G. Hartness is a teller of tales, a righter of wrong, defender of ladies' virtues, and some people call him Maurice, for he speaks of the pompatus of love. He is also the best-selling author of EPIC-Award-winning series *The Black Knight Chronicles* from Bell Bridge Books, a comedic urban fantasy series that answers the eternal question "Why aren't there more fat vampires?" In July of 2016. John was honored with the Manly Wade Wellman Award by the NC Speculative Fiction Foundation for Best Novel by a North Carolina writer in 2015 for the first Quincy Harker novella, *Raising Hell.*

In 2016, John teamed up with a pair of other publishing industry ne'er-do-wells and founded Falstaff Books, a publishing company dedicated to pushing the boundaries of literature and entertainment.

In his copious free time John enjoys long walks on the beach, rescuing kittens from trees and getting caught in the rain. An avid *Magic: the Gathering* player, John is strong in his nerd-fu and has sometimes been referred to as "the Kevin Smith of Charlotte, NC." And not just for his girth.

Find out more about John online
www.johnhartness.com

FALSTAFF BOOKS

**Want to know what's new
And coming soon from
Falstaff Books?**

Try This Free Ebook Sampler

https://www.instafreebie.com/free/bsZnl

**Follow the link.
Download the file.
Transfer to your e-reader, phone, tablet, watch, computer,
whatever.
Enjoy.**

Made in the USA
Columbia, SC
12 July 2024